Behii

Smile

Mary Grand

First published in the United Kingdom 2018

ISBN   9781980419488

Dedication

For Susan,
who shares my love for Mottistone Down
and muddy dog walks.

March 2016

He found her early that morning on Mottistone Down. From a distance she looked dramatic, beautiful even, draped across the smaller Longstone, the mellow, yellow-red morning light softening the image. However, closer to, he saw her face, traces of tears on her cheeks. For the first time, he saw the woman behind the smile.

Chapter One

September 2015

Lowri's stilettos clicked on the marble floor of Orly airport. She tipped up her chin, pushed her shoulders back, put on her calm, in control smile. Ignoring the luxury shops, she walked quickly, guilt making her petrified she would meet someone she knew. Finally she arrived at the agreed café, and paused. The front of the café opened on to the concourse. Peering inside, she saw a sea of people. Her eyes darted around: where was he? The thin veneer of confidence started to crack and she panicked. Maybe he hadn't come? Then, breaking through the din, she heard,
    'Lowri, over here.'
    Twisting round, she saw him sitting across the café at a small red table by the counter, partially hidden behind the queue. She had been imagining this moment for weeks; pictured him wearing casual clothes but, of course, he'd come from the hospital. He was wearing his neat grey suit which matched the flecks of grey in his hair; he grinned over at her.

1

Blinking away tears of relief, she pushed her way apologetically past the occupied seats and clambered over bags strewn over the floor. He calmly folded his newspaper, stood up, leant forward and took her case.

'It's chaos here today,' he said. Taking her arm, he gently pulled her towards him and kissed her on the cheek. Simon was short like her. He didn't have to bend down awkwardly and try to aim a kiss at her, like throwing a dart at a board. Instead their faces touched and lingered.

'You made it.' He held her close. The relief in his voice surprised Lowri. For once, she realised, he hadn't been sure of her. Simon usually wore an air of someone who expected life to go his way.

'It's been a long six weeks,' he said, tracing her face with his fingers as if reminding himself of every detail. The lightness of his fingers made her shiver.

As she looked deep into his eyes she felt a wave of relief. She had allowed a nightmare scenario to build up in her mind: him being furious when she told him, but it seemed silly now.

'I'll get us a drink. Glass of red?'

'No. Um, no thanks.'

'Are you sure?'

'Really, just water.'

'Something to eat?'

'Nothing, thanks.'

He frowned. 'You OK?'

Lowri gave a ghost of a nod. He responded with a reassuring smile and left her while she sat down on the edge of the hard plastic chair opposite his.

Simon's voice was loud and carried so that she could hear when he placed his order. Lowri loved languages. Although she knew Simon was using the right vocabulary, his accent was dreadful, and she cringed. Like a musician with perfect pitch, for her, hearing the discordant words grated. They hurt her ears.

She sat with her fingers neatly clasped together, resting on the table. As she tilted her right hand, she saw her mother's 'don't make my mistake' wedding ring. She covered it with her left hand, where her bare finger still showed the indentations left by the rings she had removed that morning. In her mind she went over the things she wanted to discuss with Simon before they left the airport. They were difficult, but she wanted to start their holiday with no underlying tensions from things left unsaid, so that nothing would ruin their perfect week.

Eventually Simon returned with a tray, sat down, and handed her the bottle of water and plastic cup. With some difficulty she twisted the cap on her bottle. Despite the cold weather, her hands were sweating and shook a little as she poured the water into the cup.

'How was your flight?' As he asked, he took a large bite from his baguette. Lowri smiled. She guessed they would have to go through a few pleasantries.

'OK. Heathrow was crazy. I had to walk miles, but the flight was quick. I got a window seat. You know, I may be thirty-five, but that is the first time I have ever flown on my own.'

'That's not so unusual. I hadn't flown alone until I started to work over here a few years ago, so I must have been, what, mid forties, then. I enjoy it now. I tell you, it's a lot more civilised than the ferry.'

'Oh dear. How did it go?'

'Nightmare. There were loads of kids running around, and it took so long. I wish now I'd hired a car for the week.'

Despite the racket in the café there was an awkward silence between them. She watched him, waited, and

3

sipped her water. Enough chatting: he knew what she was waiting for him to tell her.

However he missed his cue, saying, 'Work here has been fantastic – Pierre had a lot to show me.'

Lowri clenched her teeth in frustration as he started to go into detail about a complicated orthopaedic procedure he'd been observing. She sat back and crossed her arms, biding her time, giving the occasional serious nod and a fair impression of being interested.

Finally Simon took another bite of his baguette and Lowri grabbed the opportunity. 'So, how did it go? You know, telling your kids about me?'

He picked up his teaspoon and stirred his coffee, staring at the swirling liquid. 'We visited them both, as you know, but I'm afraid Rosemary wasn't well. She was in a bad way.'

'But you did tell them about us, didn't you?'

'It wasn't the right time.'

'Oh, Simon.' She clenched her fists, desperately disappointed. She really needed him to have done this. Trying to calm her voice, she said, 'You've done the difficult part. You've told Rosemary about us. I wish you'd told your children.'

'Rosemary needed more time than I realised to get used to the idea. She wasn't ready for us to go telling the kids.'

'They're both in their twenties. You said they already guessed things weren't going well.'

'I know, but it's a huge thing for Rosemary. It's the end of nearly thirty years of marriage. I can't rush her: it wouldn't be right.' He was using his rational, sensible voice that made any objection sound childish and unreasonable.

'And the flat? Have you found somewhere, moved out?'

'Not yet.'

She stared down at the table: he had done nothing. How was she meant to tell him now?

'Don't do that,' he said.

'What?' She looked up.

'Don't shut me out. Listen – I promise when I get back I will tell the kids and I will sort out the house. You have my word.'

Lowri forced her lips back into a smile that pushed her cheeks up and stopped the tears that burned behind her glasses.

'Have you heard from Jack?' he asked.

The mention of her husband grounded her. 'Not really, just the odd text.'

'He's enjoying Florence?'

'His lectures are being well attended,' she said, quoting one of Jack's horribly formal texts.

'He must miss you translating for him.'

'His Italian is very good. Of course he didn't mention missing me.' It hurt speaking the words. She took a deep breath; she couldn't put it off any longer. 'Listen, Simon, there is something I need to tell you. It's really important.'

Simon raised a finger to her lips. 'Shh. No more heavy talk, not here.'

Lowri moved her head back and gritted her teeth. She glanced around the café. Somewhere she had read that people used background tracks of 'ambient' café sounds to study or go to sleep to: the recordings had obviously not been made in here. There were large families, groups of students with rucksacks, all looking excited and stressed. The layers of sound were increasing; a baby had started screaming, and some children had turned up the volume of the noisy game they were playing on an iPad. Maybe this wasn't the place to tell him: it wasn't the kind of news to shout over a table.

Simon seemed to sense her unease, and asked, 'Did you look at the pictures of the gite I sent you?'

Of course she had: she had absorbed every detail of the photos: the tiny terraced house, the wooden floors and the country-style bedroom with flowered bedspread and curtains; the possible setting of her future. 'It's really lovely, perfect.'

'Wait until you're actually there, listening in the evenings to the crickets, drinking rosé. It's heavenly, and Auvers-sur-Oise has some great restaurants now. I think Van Gogh had something to do with the place.'

'He died there, eighteen-ninety. His grave is there, next to his brother's.' Remembering facts always made Lowri feel better. She took a sip of water.

Simon smiled. He liked the fact that she knew stuff like this. He said it was one of the reasons she was more his type than Rosemary. He looked at his watch.

Lowri noticed that he had finished his baguette, and quickly drank the remainder of her water. 'I looked up the gite. It's only about an hour's drive outside Paris, isn't it?'

'Ah...um...–' he squirmed.

'What?' She screwed up her eyes, peered at him: what now?

He sat forward and held her hands. 'I have a chance to watch a new procedure this afternoon–'

'You want to go back to work?'

'Just for a few hours. I promise, after that, the rest of the week is just for you. You don't mind, do you?'

This wasn't fair, but she gave in. 'What shall I do while you're at work?'

'I've organised everything. Marie, one of the doctors, has to visit her mother in Auvers-sur-Oise this afternoon. She's going as soon as she finishes her morning list. She can give you a lift to the gite, then go back to her mother's. I'll drive down this evening. I thought you could settle in. There's a small shop by the gite; it has everything we need. With your French, you'll have no problem shopping.'

'Have you got a key for me then?'

Simon put his hand in his pocket and took out a bunch of keys. Lowri frowned at the key fob, a black and white photograph of Rosemary's Maine Coon cat, and pushed the keys into her bag.

Simon shifted uneasily on his seat. 'One more thing: I haven't said that much to Marie about who you are. She's guessed, I think. She's very discreet.'

'Oh–' The word 'discreet' seemed dirty: she had instantly become Simon's 'other woman'.

He grimaced. 'Sorry.'

A man behind her stood up, jamming his seat hard into the back of Lowri's. She frowned at him, expecting an apology, but he didn't say anything, and left.

Simon patted her hand. 'You are glad you came, aren't you?'

'Of course.'

'Sure?'

'It's not quite how I imagined, that's all.'

'Once we get there it will be wonderful. No snatched meetings, just me and you with all the time in the world.' His face was very close to hers now, his eyes full of longing. 'God, the past few weeks have been hell. Every time I saw something special, I wanted you to be there, to share it with you. And in the evenings I wanted you–' He laid his hand gently on her cheek. Lowri reached up and laid her hand on top of his, wanting to stay trapped in this moment when nothing apart from them mattered.

His eyes narrowed. 'Damn work,' he said, the passion tight between them.

Simon's phone sounded. He took his hand away and read the text. 'Ah, Marie is just leaving the hospital. We ought to make a move.'

'OK. I just need to go to the ladies. 'Lowri stood up. She was aware of Simon watching her walk away. Self-consciously she clung to her shoulder bag and smiled at the floor.

The ladies' room was crowded. Despite the cold weather, Lowri felt flushed and longed to run her hands under cold water. She walked to a basin. Being only five foot two, she always felt the need for heels. Despite that she still had to stand on tip toe to avoid ending up with water splashes on her new camel coat. She tried to steady her hand as she reapplied her bright cherry lipstick and smoky eye makeup, then looked at it critically. Before Simon she would have called her make-up understated; her friends called it boring interview make-up. Well, they would have approved of this new look, although Lowri found her lips felt stiff and stuck together and her eyelashes brushed annoyingly against her glasses. She had managed to ignore Simon's suggestions of freeing her brown hair. It was in its normal tight 'updo', or a bun as her mother would have called it. That at least felt like her.

When she returned to the café Simon's seat was empty. Lowri looked around and saw that he was buying a book. The thought flashed through her mind that maybe out here, away from the secret meals and snatched coffees, he might already be finding her boring. Simon loved adrenalin rushes, excitement: what if he was dissatisfied with what was left when that was taken away? She walked over to the shop, glancing at the newspaper headlines. One said Prime Minister David Cameron wanted to provide for the resettlement of Syrian refugees, and another 'How to breathe yourself slim'. Lowri was ashamed at which one she knew she would like to read.

Simon walked over to her. 'Come on, I managed to park out there. I told Marie we would meet her outside one of the hotels to save her driving in here.'

They left the airport buildings and walked over to Simon's BMW. As Lowri climbed in she smelt the clean leather seats; everything inside was immaculate. The late September sun was low in the sky. She pulled down the visor, but was too short for it to make a difference. Simon drove confidently away, but she sat slightly forward, her hands clasped together. She had forgotten how nerve-wracking it was being a passenger in a British car over in France.

Soon they were pulling off the main road into a large but fairly empty car park in front of a smart chain hotel. Simon parked near the entrance, got out and looked around, then got back into the car.

'She's not here yet.'

'Right.'

'You'll like her. She can't speak much English, but she's very friendly.'

Simon was tapping his fingers impatiently on the steering wheel.

They sat in awkward silence. It reminded Lowri of years ago when her mother would see her off at Merthyr station to go back to university. They would stand waiting for the train, not knowing what to say: everything seeming too trivial or else too important to talk about.

Lowri undid her seat belt and looked around. The edge of the car park was lined with enormous horse chestnut

9

trees; the sun bounced off the yellowing leaves; shiny brown conkers peeped out from their protective cases. For the first time, Lowri noticed it was a beautiful autumn day.

'Look at the conkers lying on the ground,' she said. 'I don't suppose they'll be picked up by any children. It seems such a waste.'

Simon looked at her and grinned. 'My kids loved conker fights when they were little. Tim and I would have battles in the garden.'

'It sounds fun.'

'It was. Seems a lifetime ago now. Still, it's easy to remember the highlights and forget things like the sleepless nights. And I don't just mean when they were babies: those teenage years aged me.'

'But you'd like to do it all again, wouldn't you?'

'Of course. I told you that, but there's no rush.'

Before she had time to respond, a small blue Renault screeched into the car park and pulled up next to them. A tall, efficient-looking woman with short brown hair jumped out.

Simon opened his door and embraced the woman, who was talking in rapid French. Lowri saw Simon nod seriously and speak calmly, but it had little effect. He grabbed Lowri's bags, put them in the back of Marie's car, and gave her a quick peck on the cheek.

'She's a bit upset about her mother. I'll be down about five I guess. See you later.'

Simon was back in his car and driving away before Lowri had done up her seat belt.

'Bonjour. Simon tells me you speak French?' said Marie.

'Oui.'

'Dieu merci,' Marie said, and started to drive away, continuing to speak in French. 'My mother is very ill. It's her heart. She should be in hospital. Her doctor's an idiot, and now I find out that my father has gone out for the day leaving her alone. Mum could hardly talk on the phone the other day. I rang for an ambulance, had it sent to the house. You know what she did?'

Disconcertingly, Marie looked at Lowri for a response. Lowri shrugged and looked pointedly through the windscreen.

Fortunately, Marie refocused, but she didn't stop talking. 'My mother, she sent the ambulance away. Can you believe it? Today, I will go and sort this out.' She drove fast down main roads. They were relatively quiet, but her driving was erratic and Lowri found herself staring fixedly ahead. Marie carried on talking in the same fast, agitated manner. There were no more pauses for Lowri to respond, but she found the way Marie flung her hands around terrifying: this woman needed to calm down.

It must have been about three quarters of an hour later that they came off the main road and started down the smaller country roads to the gite. Marie, however, did not seem to have adjusted her speed. They came to a narrow bend and screeched around it. Lowri grabbed the side of her seat: it was like being in a real version of one of those awful 3D experience rides. She was staring at the road ahead. What could she do? She could hardly demand to be allowed to get out here in the middle of nowhere. Sitting back, she tried to relax: there was nothing she could do. Marie obviously knew the roads well. Lowri would have to trust her.

The road started to twist and turn. There was a very tight bend coming. Lowri held her breath and felt the car start to tip.

'Mon Deiu!' screamed Marie.

Lowri opened her mouth to scream, but couldn't. Everything happened so quickly. The car skidded off the road. Lowri held her breath, pushed her body back in the seat, and gripped the seat even harder. The trunk of a tree appeared to be hurtling towards them. She put up her hands, but heard a thundering bang. Then everything went black.

Chapter Two

Lowri awoke. She could hear a siren screaming. As she tried to make sense of the people in uniform she started to remember where she was. Suddenly the pain gripped her and she groaned.

A paramedic said something about an accident, a hospital. Gathering her thoughts was like trying to fit together tiny pieces of a jigsaw.

'Marie wasn't injured badly. She told us about you. We've contacted Simon.'

Lowri tried to think: siren, ambulance? Hospital? Marie? She was in so much pain. What had happened to her? She watched as the paramedic filled a syringe, and panicked. 'No, stop. I'm pregnant.'

'Are you sure?' Lowri saw the concern in the paramedic's eyes.

'Yes.' She tried to instinctively put her hand on her stomach, but couldn't move either of her arms.

The paramedic talked quietly to his colleague, and returned.

'It's alright. We'll be careful,' he said, as he gave her the injection. The world drifted away.

The next thing Lowri was aware of was a hand resting on hers. The voice was muffled as if her head was under water. 'Lowri. Lowri, it's Simon.'

She opened her eyes and looked up at a white ceiling, then tried to turn towards the voice, but the pain in her neck frightened her.

'You're in hospital. I'm here. Don't worry. Try not to move.'

Her lips felt cracked and dry. She heard the scraping of a chair, then saw Simon's face looking over her, his eyes creased with worry. He squeezed her hand. 'You were in an accident. You were hurt, but you are not to worry.'

She saw him try to smile. Exhausted, she closed her eyes.

Some time later, Lowri awoke and murmured. Immediately Simon was back looking over her.

'An accident?' Her voice sounded gravelly, slurred as if she had been to the dentist.

'You were in a car. Marie was driving. The car swerved and hit a tree.'

The words slowly sank in: a car accident, of course.

'Marie?'

'She rang me at the hospital, and I came straight here. She wasn't hurt. She feels terrible. She was distracted by worry over her mother.'

'Where is she?'

'They're doing some observations. They said she can go home when they've finished. She's very worried about you, feels dreadful. She'll come and see you as soon as she can.'

'What's wrong with me?'

'They haven't done all the tests yet. There was chest trauma resulting in fractured ribs, lacerations to your left arm. The worst damage they think is to the left side of your face, from the broken windscreen.'

Lowri found that her left hand would not move, so lifted up her right and touched her face. She could feel bandages.

'They're going to transfer you to another hospital later today. You'll have more tests. They'll assess your face, and then they'll operate.'

He was talking slowly, choosing his words carefully.

'An operation?'

'That's right; it's a good hospital.'

She put her right hand on her stomach.

'They told me you're pregnant.' He looked very serious.

'You are pleased, aren't you?'

Lowri scanned his face. In films a man would often panic on hearing the news he was to be a father but then his face would be flooded with joy and pride. She saw the look of panic, but it wasn't going anywhere.

'It can't be mine,' he said hoarsely.

'You want more children.'

'One day, maybe, but not now. Not like this.'

The harsh words felt like plasters being torn off a gaping wound.

'We don't know the baby will have survived, do we?' he asked.

A warm tear trickled down her face. It wasn't meant to be like this.

'I want the baby. I want it to be well,' she said, with only enough energy to speak the truth.

'Of course, yes. I suppose you do.'

She watched as he ran his fingers through his fringe, and then automatically neatened it.

'There must be a chance that the baby is Jack's, surely?'

'No, I don't think so. It was August when I slept with you. Then I missed my period. I did a test. It was positive. I hadn't seen Jack for a while.'

'Did the test say how many weeks pregnant you were?'

'No.'

'Well, then, it could have been any time before me. We only had sex once.'

If she'd had the energy she would have made a sarcastic remark about that, but instead she closed her eyes. Why was Simon being like this? She had really thought he would be pleased. They talked about having children, a new life together, buying somewhere in France. He'd work in the hospital, and she'd carry on with her online translation work. Their children would run among sun soaked fields of sunflowers; it would be perfect.

She felt Simon rub her hand.

'Lowri, wake up.'

She opened her eyes.

'They've been trying to contact Jack in Florence. He's coming here.'

The pictures of sunflowers and children vanished.

'No. He doesn't even know I'm in France.'

'They had to contact him as your next of kin. His number was on your phone. They managed to speak to him.'

'No. He can't come here.'

'Yes. He's travelling now.'

'I don't want to see him.'

'You have to. He is still your husband.'

'He left me.'

'They don't know that.'

'You should have told them.'

'I couldn't. The thing is, I needed to know there was someone here looking after you.'

'What do you mean? You're here. I don't need Jack.'

'The thing is, I can't stay. I'm sorry. I'm going to have to go.'

'No.' She moved her hand on top of his, holding it as hard as she could.

'I have to. I heard from Rosemary. She needs me.'

She tried to sit up, but couldn't. 'No. You have to tell her about the baby.'

'It's not that simple.'

'She'll understand. I know it's difficult–' Lowri sank her head into the pillow and closed her eyes. She was so tired. Her face hurt. She wondered when her next dose of painkillers was due. Why was Simon making everything so complicated?

'The thing is, Lowri, I haven't told Rosemary about us yet.'

His voice was quiet. She wondered if he hoped she was asleep. She wished she was dreaming, but she knew that she wasn't.

Opening her eyes, she looked at him. 'What?' She let go of his hand.

'She doesn't know anything about you. I haven't told her yet.'

Lowri couldn't believe it. All this time Rosemary hadn't even known Simon was seeing someone else, seeing her.

'You promised.'

'Life is so complicated, Lowri. You have to understand.'

'Do you even love me?' The tears blurred her eyes. She could hardly see him.

'You know I do. I have to take things in stages with Rosemary. First, when she is ready, I will tell her about us, and then, at the right time, about the baby.'

'What about me?' The words were a desperate cry for help as she felt herself falling into an abyss.

'I'm sorry, but the right thing now is for me to go.'

'You can't leave me.'

'I have to. Jack will be here soon.'

'But I need you. I'm having your baby.'

'You don't know that. Listen. Maybe you need to see if you and Jack can sort things out. You said he wanted children.'

'But this baby isn't his–'

'Think about it. He doesn't know about me, does he?'

'No.'

'Then it might be much better not to tell him. This baby: it could mend your marriage.'

'You're leaving me for good? This is the end?'

Lowri lay very still. Simon had come into her life when she'd been so unhappy. He had been there for her the day after that terrible row with Jack, and he'd offered her a future ... a perfect life. But now he was snatching it away, shredding it into tiny pieces. As if to confirm this, he said, 'I've taken the keys to the gite out of your bag.'

He moved closer to her. 'It doesn't have to be the end,' he said in that same steady, logical voice. 'We can talk when you get better, and I know you will. I've had a good look at your notes. You're not to worry. It's just your face–'

'What about it?'

'It will take time to heal. You'll need operations–'

For the first time it dawned on her how much people had been going on about her face. 'Is it that bad?'

'Don't panic.' She could see that he was now smiling. How he could do that? 'You are not to worry about anything. I do hope the baby will be well. They will check everything in the next hospital.'

'Next hospital?'

'I told you. They're going to move you there. It's better equipped.'

'Equipped for what?'

'To look after you. Now, listen. I shall leave now. I am sure Jack will be with you soon.'

Lowri was trying to think straight. Simon really was leaving her.

'I have put your case down by the bed. It got a bit battered, but the clothes are OK. I was able to find your health card. You're not to worry about money. If you need any work, or anything that's not covered, I will pay.'

'Work?'

'Try not to worry. I shall ring the hospital. I know enough people there to be kept informed of your progress.'

She looked deep into eyes. He brought his face close to hers.

'You are so special. I never deserved you,' he said.

He kissed her cheek, but she was thinking of that word 'deserved': past tense. She, Lowri, was now in the past.

The doctor came in and leant over the bed. He spoke in French. 'We have tracked down your husband. He is going to come to you soon.'

Lowri looked at Simon, and translated, 'Jack is coming.'

He stood up. 'That's good. Goodbye, Lowri. You are in safe hands. Take care.' She heard him walk across the room, open the door, and leave.

Never in her life had Lowri felt so lost. For the first time there was no plan. She thought of her baby: what was she going to do?

A nurse came in. 'We are going to move you now.'

'Do you know how my baby is?'

'Try not to worry. They will do tests. You must rest now.'

Porters pushed her along corridors. It felt cold and very strange to be rushed past people in everyday clothes, visitors as well as nurses and doctors. People glanced over and quickly averted their eyes. She was taken to an ambulance. She lay back, and closed her eyes.

The journey felt a long one but they arrived and she was again lifted on to a trolley. Kindly doctors spoke but she felt miles away from them, and eventually she drifted into a deep sleep.

Lowri woke up in a different bed. It was much quieter, darker. She was aware of someone moving at the side of her bed. Slowly she tried to open her eyes. She felt she was only seeing through one. She tried closing it and everything went dark. Maybe only one was working? She couldn't be sure.

The person moving didn't speak, but then the door opened and someone came over to her.

'Good morning, Lowri. I am Doctor Moreau.' The woman spoke in English.

Although Lowri was fluent in French, it was comforting.

'I would just like to do a few checks.' The doctor shone a bright light into her eye. 'Your operation went well. You have been very lucky.'

Lucky? Lucky to be alive? They said that to people when awful things had happened. Was she paralysed? Panicking, Lowri tried to move her legs. To her relief she could feel them. Then she tried to lift her arms. Her right was stiff, but could bend. It had the drip attached. The left felt very heavy, and bandaged.

'I can't see through my left eye.'

'There is a bandage. We think the eye will be OK. Though, of course, we are concerned about your facial wounds.'

The words hit home: facial wounds. Why did they keep talking about her face?

'What's the matter with my face?'

'The left side was badly cut by the glass. As I say, you've been lucky. The surgeon is very good.'

'So, will it get better?'

'We will see about that. You need to rest.'

'I'm pregnant–'

The doctor nodded. 'I was told–'

'Is it still? Am I still–'

'We don't know.'

'How soon will I know about the baby?'

'I am going to arrange an ultrasound to see how things are. Do you know the date of conception?'

She nodded. 'I'm not sure: six or ten weeks.'

'OK. Well, the ultrasound should tell us a few things. We shall be able to see if there is a heart beat.'

'When will I have it?'

'When your husband comes. We will do it as soon as we can.'

'Please, I would like to do it before.'

'Without your husband?'

'Yes.'

'You are sure you feel up to it?'

'Yes. He doesn't know yet, you see, that I am pregnant. I don't want to build up his hopes.'

'We can arrange it for this afternoon then. It would help us to know.'

She smiled at the doctor. 'Thank you.'

The doctor left and Lowri lay in a daze. Her life had been turned inside out. A nurse came and propped her up with pillows. She closed her eyes but was woken by a quiet knock on the door. Lowri looked, somehow expecting Jack to come in. However, it was not Jack, but Marie. She had a few light cuts. She looked very pale and her eyes were red. On seeing Lowri she burst into tears and spoke in frantic French.

21

'Oh God, I am so sorry, so very sorry. I had to leave the hospital, and then they moved you–'

Lowri couldn't stop the feeling of anger welling up. How dare she come in here looking so miserable? She was the one who had been driving so badly, yet she had hardly a mark on her.

Marie came over to Lowri. 'This is all my fault. I was in such a hurry, and then the sun was in my eyes. I couldn't see. Lowri, your poor face. I am so sorry. Everything, everything is such a nightmare.' She collapsed on the chair next to the bed.

'You were driving like a maniac,' said Lowri.

'I know. It was so wrong. I don't know what got into me.'

'You don't look very hurt.'

'I'm not. I wish it was me lying in the bed.'

'But it's not.'

'No. I know. If only it was different.'

Lowri started to weaken. Marie looked wretched.

'How is your mother? Have you been to see her yet?'

Marie started to cry again. 'My mother, my lovely mother, she died. They discharged me late last night. I spoke to my father. He said she was getting better. Then early this morning she died. If I had been there maybe she would still be alive–'

Lowri was stunned. 'I am so sorry.'

'I shall never forgive myself. I was angry with everyone: the doctors, my father. It screwed my brain and, because of me, this has happened to you.'

'It's alright, Marie.'

'No. No, it isn't. This is my entire fault.'

Marie paused.

'Here, we have the best plastic surgeons.'

'Plastic surgery?'

22

'Oh, maybe not. Never mind. But if you ever want it, you contact me through Simon. Please, I need to do something.'

'How are your family?'

'They are bereft, but I am so angry with my father. He should have taken her to the hospital, but he hates to make a fuss. It is madness.' Marie started to cry again.

'I'm sorry.' Despite the fact this woman had caused her so much pain Lowri desperately wanted to comfort her.

'No, it is I who am sorry. Where is Simon?'

'He has gone. Um, my husband Jack will be here very soon.'

'I see. If he needs to talk to me, of course I will not mention Simon. I do understand.'

A nurse came in, took Lowri's temperature, and started to write on a chart. She then took her blood pressure, and checked the drip.

Marie talked to the nurse and then to Lowri. 'Things are settling well. That's good.'

'You don't need to stay; your family must need you.'

'You're right. My sister is distraught. Even my father, now he feels guilty. He will miss her. I know that. She was just lovely.'

Marie started to cry again. She folded her arms around herself as if she was keeping the pieces together. 'This is the blackest day.'

'You go: look after your family.' Lowri managed the faintest of smiles.

'Thank you. Yes, I will, but Lowri you must take care. You will need courage. I am so very sorry.'

'You are not to worry about me,' said Lowri forcing a smile and not meaning a word of it. 'I will be fine.'

Marie left. Lowri lay back, exhausted from the tsunami of grief, and allowed the smile to melt away. It wasn't so long since she'd lost her own mother. She knew the journey ahead of Marie: it was hard and lonely. She didn't know if she could be angry with her any more. But she longed to shout at someone. None of this was meant to have happened. There was no-one here. She was alone.

The world couldn't see her like this: in pain, scarred, single, frightened and alone. Somehow, from somewhere, she had to get back the Lowri that always had a smile, the Lowri who always coped, but right now she had no idea how she was going to do it.

Chapter Three

Lowri was taken for her ultrasound. The nurse spoke in French. Once again, Lowri was grateful she spoke the language. The nurse moved the screen so that Lowri could see it. She lay very still as the nurse spread the cold gel on her stomach and she held her breath, waiting.

Her glance darted between the screen and the nurse. The room was womb-like quiet, nothing outside mattered. The nurse broke the silence. Her voice startled Lowri.

'Ah, that is good.'

'What?'

'I can detect a heartbeat.'

Lowri exhaled deeply, releasing so many emotions. 'You can hear my baby's heart?'

'I can.'

'My baby is alive?'

'Yes. That is very good,' repeated the nurse. 'Now, you see that tiny bean? That is your baby. I am going to measure the head and rump ends of the embryo, find out the size of it."

For a moment she was caught in the wonder of it: that tiny shape was a baby. One day it would be a child, a teenager, an adult. It was incredible. She felt like she was the first person who had ever achieved this miracle, that this was unique, the most special baby ever to have been conceived.

'And how old is my baby?'

'I would say six weeks.'

'It couldn't be more like ten weeks, could it?' Lowri wasn't sure what she wanted the answer to be.

'Oh no, definitely not, but when you go back to England I'm sure they'll do another ultrasound, give you more exact dates.'

The baby was Simon's. Deep down she had known. Lowri looked back at the screen and talked quietly to her baby. 'I'm sorry; it's all a bit of a mess out here.

Remember this, though: you are not a mistake. I want you. You were meant to be and I love you.'

Lowri was back in her bed being fed a drink through a straw when Jack arrived. She had given up trying to work out what she would say to him. She had sketched out a story. He stood at the door nervously scratching his stubbly chin. He hated hospitals.

'Entrer,' the nurse said.

Lowri noticed the flirtatious glance from the nurse. Despite wearing an old blue shirt and jeans, and his dishevelled blonde hair, he was attractive. It was three months since she had last seen him. Lowri felt shy, as if she was on a first date.

'I'm sorry they called you.'

'It's OK.' He edged closer to the bed. 'You look awful.'

'Thanks.'

'Sorry. I just didn't expect it to be so bad, that's all.'

The nurse quietly left the room. Jack sat on the edge of the seat next to the bed. Lowri could turn her head now, and she looked at him.

'Sorry you had to leave your work.'

'It's OK. I was coming home at the end of the week. I'm on holiday now.'

'It must be beautiful there at the moment.'

'It is. Anyway, tell me what happened. What on earth are you doing over here?'

'I came to have a holiday. I was doing airbnb and a woman called Marie was giving me a lift to the gite. She was very upset. Her mother was very ill. She was driving too fast. It all happened so fast. One minute I was looking at the autumn trees, the next there was a loud smashing sound, everything went black.' Lowri stopped. Her head was thumping. She felt very sick.

'My God, that's horrific,' said Jack.

'I woke up in hospital. Apparently we swerved off the road and hit a tree.'

'And how is this Marie?'

'She's OK. I got the worst of it.'

'Where is she?'

'She was sent home'

'She left you?'

'It's really sad. Her mother died this morning.'

'I'm sorry, but you still need to sort things out; insurance and things.'

She watched him anxiously trying to get his head around the practical implications of the accident. He was hopeless at this side of things.

'I'm covered by my health card. Marie only really speaks French. There's no point in you talking to her.'

'But–'

'Please Jack. She's in an awful state over her mother.'

'I should do something.'

'Please. Leave it. I'll contact her later if I need to. I can't take the stress of it at the moment.'

'There is something else,' she said quietly.

Jack frowned. 'What is it? What's the matter?'

She tried to inhale courage, but her ribs hurt too much. 'I've been told that–' The words were hard to say. 'I'm pregnant.'

She watched his face, eyes wide, and mouth open in disbelief.

'My God, Lowri.'

The room seemed very quiet.

'You're sure?' he asked eventually.

'Yes.'

'Everything, you know, is alright, after the accident?'

'They said the baby is OK.'

'Wow, that's good then. We're going to have a baby.'

'No–' The word rushed out.

Jack rested his hand on hers.

'I can understand you not wanting anything to do with me, but I will help you in anyway I can with the baby.'

The guilt tugged at her. 'Stop.'

He looked up.

'This is not your baby.'

'It has to be.'

'No. I'm so sorry. After you left me, I met someone else. I was lonely. I thought you'd left me for good, Jack. The reason I am in France was that I came to meet him. He is the father of my baby,' she paused, 'but he doesn't want to know. He's left me.'

The words came tumbling out: huge, cold, rough boulders of truth.

'You're having a baby with someone else?'

It was all Jack could focus on. Lowri understood why: you focus on the part that hurts the most. When they first got married they had both known they wanted to start a family, but it hadn't happened. The frustration and heartache was made worse by watching other couples conceiving, planning their second and third child; the agony of buying toys and clothes for other people's babies. Before things had started to go wrong between them, Lowri had been undergoing tests to see if they could find out why they had not been able to have a baby, but the doctors had found no reason.

'I only slept with him once,' Lowri said, and saw Jack cringe: maybe it made it even worse after the years they had been trying. 'I'm sorry.'

'Who is it?' he asked, unable to look at her.

'I met him in a restaurant.'

'A stranger?'

She paused. 'Well, no-one you know.'

'What does he do?'

'He's a doctor. Listen, there's no point in talking about him. He's left me.'

'But the baby?'

'He doesn't want it. The thing is–' She closed her eyes. 'He's married.'

'Lowri. God, this isn't you.'

'He said he was leaving his wife. He lied.'

Jack sat back. Lowri couldn't see him. She heard his chair scrape on the floor. 'I'm sorry, I need to get some fresh air. I'll be back.'

It was so sudden. He just got up and left. Lowri almost felt relieved. As she had started to tell Jack what had happened, even she had been horrified at how seedy it all sounded. She could hear her mother telling her not to make the mistakes she had made. It looked like she had in some ways, but one thing she was determined was that her baby would never feel she, or he, was a mistake.

A nurse came in carrying a tray and dressings. The nurse pointed to the bandage on Lowri's left eye and smiled. 'It's coming off.' The nurse carefully started to remove the dressing. Lowri waited for the light, but it didn't come.

'I can't see,' she cried.

'Je vais chercher le médecin,' replied the nurse.

Lowri spoke firmly. She didn't want the doctor. She wanted a mirror. She needed to know. 'Un miroir, s'il vous plaît.'

She saw the panic in the nurse's face as she repeated that she would get the doctor, and left.

After a few minutes Dr Moreau appeared holding a mirror, accompanied by the nurse. 'Lowri, you are worried about your eye?'

'I can't see,' she said, close to hysteria. The doctor came closer and examined her eye.

'The eye is very bruised. It is hardly open. We will know more soon.'

'I need to see what I look like.'

'Would you like to wait for your husband?'

'No. Please, I would like to do it with you.'

'You need to be prepared, that is all, but believe me, there are people here with a lot worse injuries than you.'

'Can I look now?'

'OK.'

Lowri took a deep breath. The nurse helped her sit upright and then held the mirror for her. She touched it with her hand. Was that her? Shocked, she put down the mirror. The doctor spoke gently. 'The bruising will die down. Eventually the scarring will become less red.'

Lowri picked up the mirror again. Her greasy lank hair stuck to her head. She was very pale. There were yellow bruises around her right eye, but she most of the damage was on the left side of her face. Her left eye was very swollen. She could hardly see the eye itself, but a deep, red and raised stitched gash ran from her scalp tracing an ugly path past the outside corner of her left eye, across her cheek, past the edge of her nose and then down to her lip, which was dragged down. It was as if she had two faces: the right side remarkably clear apart from the bruising; the left, swollen, shattered. It wasn't someone she recognised. It was like she was wearing some awful mask on one side of her face. The two sides were like a 'before and after' photo. Who was she now?

'You have been very lucky,' said the doctor, looking in the mirror with her. Lowri glared at her, thinking that she would have been lucky if she had not had her face smashed up in an accident, but said nothing.

'Your cheek bones are intact. Your nose: it will stay slightly askew, but it will heal on its own.'

'The scars?'

'The aim is for you to go back to the UK in about a week. The team there will remove the stitches. You will be given gels and continue on antibiotics–'

'And the scars?' Lowri repeated.

'Your scars will take nine to twelve months to settle down. They go through various stages. They are red, hard and raised now. Obviously, there are stitches at the moment, but the scars will become lighter in colour and soften with time.'

'But they will never go?'

'No. There will always be some scarring. They are very deep.'

'My mouth and my eye are slightly dragged down.'

'They will stay like that. One day, of course, you can think about more surgery. It could have been a lot worse. You had a brilliant surgeon.'

Lowri stared in horror. She tried to move her mouth but only the right side went properly into the shape of a smile. The other side of her mouth lagged behind.

Lowri felt the doctor was waiting for her to make an effusive speech of thanks, but what on earth was there to be thankful for? All the time she'd been lying here, the words facial wounds had floated around, but she had never pictured anything like this. How was she meant to leave here and live a life out there, looking like this? No wonder Simon and Jack had left her. Who would want to stay with a freak?

She watched tears weave their way along the scar, silently falling, making her nightie wet.

The doctor was still there.

'What about surgery? You know, plastic surgery?' she asked.

'There will be many options available, but you must first give time for healing.'

'How long?'

'My advice would be to wait a year. And, of course, you are pregnant.'

'A year?'

'Yes, you have been in a major accident, undergone a lot of trauma. You are lucky to have survived. I would strongly suggest a long period of recovery, of rest, trauma therapy if you need it. Let nature play its part. In time you may be ready to consider treatment. But remember this: things will never go back as they were.'

'You mean I am scarred for life?' said Lowri quietly.

'It is not the end of the world, you know.'

Lowri glared at her, thinking it was very easy to say these words. 'It will take courage but I am sure your husband and family will support you.'

Lowri flinched at the words family, support, and courage. She didn't have any of them. She wanted to take this blanket and put it over her head and never ever come out.

The doctor stood up. 'I will prescribe something to make you comfortable. You must rest. The more you fight this the longer it will take.'

After the doctor left the room Lowri lay in shock, her eyes closed. Nothing had prepared her for the state of her face. How was she meant to carry on with those scars? She had mental pictures of herself sitting alone at toddler groups, or back in the house, frightened to meet up with her friends in Southampton. Her poor baby would have to live with a single mother, looking like this. How was she going to carry on?

Chapter Four

Lowri was lying with her eyes closed when she heard him.

'Lowri.'

He moved into view.

'I saw my face.' She could hardly bear to look at him.

'I'm so sorry.'

'It is so much worse than I thought it would be.'

'It does look painful.'

Lowri sighed. She longed for a cotton wool lie, 'no-one will notice,' 'it will go back to how it was in weeks,' but Jack wouldn't be able to hide his feelings over this. He loved beauty and perfection; he must find it appalling.

'I will never look the same again. I will never go back to normal.' Lowri said the words to herself as much as to Jack.

They sat quietly, and then Jack spoke.

'Are you certain about this man not wanting to stick by you?' Despite it all, she tried to smile; only Jack would use such a quaint term as 'stick by you'. His public school 'doing the right thing' mentality never left him.

'He said he'd give me money, but he doesn't want anyone to know he's the father.'

'Would you want him if he eventually left his wife?'

The thought hadn't crossed her mind. 'My head says no, but I don't know. I'm so tired, Jack.'

'What are you going to do when you leave here?' Jack always looked to her for plans.

'I'll go back to the house I guess. We will have to sort out the money sometime. I'll need to buy my own place for the baby.'

'Lowri, we don't have to get divorced.'

Lowri opened her eyes wide, shocked by the unaccustomed firmness in Jack's voice.

'Of course we do.'

'No. I've been thinking: I could look after you.'

She saw his gentle smile: it was the Jack she had fallen in love with, the Jack she had married. 'No, you can't; you love someone else.'

'Things haven't worked out with the other person: I tried, but I think it's too late.'

For the first time she looked at him properly: under the natural tiredness, his eyes were red-rimmed.

'But you said they were the love of your life.' She couldn't help throwing it back, but then she saw Jack flinch.

'They were; they are; but since leaving you, I tried to talk to them. It made me realise there's no hope.' He stared at her with eyes so full of hurt that she started to relent. 'I got it all wrong, and I dragged you down as well.'

Lowri's mind went back to that night with Jack, just months before. It was, a hot sticky evening in June. She was sitting in the garden in the shade, the smell of other people's barbeques filled the air and she could hear other people's TVs. Everyone had windows and doors open. The house was in a smart quadrangle of new houses and maisonettes, all very close to each other. In the mornings sometimes she would open her curtains at the same time as the neighbours and they would all try and pretend not to have seen the other in their nightclothes. Well most did that: her neighbour Zoe would do her 'greet the dawn' yoga stance in full view and greet her neighbours at the same time.

That evening she was sitting with a large glass of water with ice cubes and lime. From the open window upstairs she could hear Jack talking on his phone. At first it was a quiet Mumble, but then his voice seemed to be getting louder, more agitated. Only a few months ago she would have gone to find out who he was talking to, what the matter was, but things had become formal and strained between them over the past few months. They didn't argue: if anything he was nicer and more polite to her, particularly when he was finding yet another way of getting out of going out with her. It had taken quite a while for her to realise that they had not eaten a meal, gone out to the cinema, or slept together for weeks. In fact only the previous night she had hinted at it to him. He'd been hugely apologetic without giving a reason, had opened wine, slept with her, but he was like a stranger acting a part he had never really wanted.

Lowri had heard Jack's voice louder, more upset, and then the words, 'You don't understand. Lowri was a mistake.'

The world came crashing down: 'mistake.' She thought she could have borne any other word, but not mistake. That word was too loaded. She had ran inside and up the stairs, and thrown open the bedroom door. Jack looked at her wide eyes, 'I've got to go,' he said, and ended the call.

'Who was that?' she screamed.

They were both shaking: Lowri never shouted. However, even before Jack spoke, she saw him pressing his phone.

'No-one,' he said idiotically.

She grabbed his phone and, her vision blurred by tears, she read, 'All calls deleted'.

'Why did you say I was a mistake?' she screamed. Jack went pale; he had no idea why that word of all words should be tearing her apart.

Jack slumped down on the bed, and put his head in his hands. 'I'm sorry. I didn't mean it.'

She sat down, calmer but feeling very sick. 'Who was it?'

He didn't look at her. 'I can't tell you.'

'There is someone else then?'

He nodded. 'I'm sorry. You don't deserve this.'

Lowri started to cry. She had suspected it for weeks, but she didn't want to hear it. 'Is it serious?' It was a stupid question: of course he wasn't going to say 'no', but there was a tiny bit of her that held on.

'I am starting to wonder if this person,' said Jack quietly, 'is the love of my life.'

She gasped as if she had been struck.

'I thought I was.'

'I'm sorry. I do love you, Lowri, but I'm so confused.'

'Who is it?' she asked again.

'I can't say,' he repeated.

'Why?'

'There is no point in telling you–'

She turned on Jack. 'No point? Is she married as well?'

'Look, Lowri. I'm sorry.' He put his head in his hands. 'I'm so tired, exhausted.'

Lowri sat down. 'And what about me? You get to waltz off into the sunset with your one-time love and leave me in tatters.'

'The last thing I want is to hurt you.'

'Well, you failed.' Lowri burst into tears.

'Can you give me time?'

'What do you mean?'

'I'm not saying I want a divorce, not at the moment, but maybe we could have some time apart. I was thinking of going to Florence on my own.'

Lowri clenched her fists; how many more times would he hurt her? They'd been married five years and always went to Florence for August and September. Jack lectured at a summer school at the university over there on renaissance art before returning to his university work here. His Italian was not quite perfect, but very good. Lowri could sometimes translate for him, but most of the time it was a holiday for her.

She leant over, pulled out a handful of tissues, and wiped her face. 'Is that what you want?'

'The problem is, I don't know what I want.' He stood up. 'I think I'll go over to the island and stay there before I go to Florence. Is that OK?'

What was she meant to say?

Jack owned another house over on the Isle of Wight. His parents had bought it for him and his first wife Holly. Lowri had never been there. She always stayed in Southampton, took care of the pets and worked while he went over to walk and paint. He had never asked her to go over and she had never particularly wanted to go. Her life, her friends were in Southampton. Occasionally, she had suggested they sell the island house. It seemed very extravagant to own two houses, but there was no mortgage on the island house and he seemed to like having somewhere to escape to.

Jack had left her that evening. They had communicated by the odd text, but that was all.

It seemed extraordinary to be sitting here now in the hospital with him.

'I am sorry you've been hurt,' she said.

He smiled. 'You are so lovely. Only you would lie in a hospital bed saying that.'

'I've got in a mess as well.'

'It's my fault; I should have handled things better.' He took a deep breath. 'I've been thinking, about me and you.'

Lowri frowned. 'What about us? Jack, I'm not in the mood to discuss divorce today.'

'No. Quite the opposite.'

She wanted to sit up, look deep into his eyes, try to judge what he was really thinking, but of course she couldn't. 'We can't get back together as if nothing has happened. You've just told me you still love someone else. In any case, I'm going to have a baby. I'm not the Lowri you left.'

'But you are going to need someone to look after you, and I hate being on my own.'

'You don't love me: I was a mistake. Remember?'

'Look, Lowri. I shouldn't have said that. I'm not sorry I met you. You are one of the kindest, brightest women I have ever known. I have never met anyone with whom I have so much in common. We click, don't we? We like our indie films, eating out, going to exhibitions–'

'We did, Jack, when we first met, but we haven't done those things for a long time.'

'We could do them again. We could be friends. Let's face it, we get on better than lots of married couples we know.'

'I don't understand–'

'What I'm suggesting is that we live together again, we could bring up the baby.'

'Be a couple like before?'

'Not quite. Tell me, do you still love me, you know like you did when we got married?'

She had to think, did she? 'I don't think so.'

'That's good. This will only work if we both feel the same. I love you, but I'm not in love with you, I'm not attracted to you.'

'Gosh, thanks.'

He smiled. 'I'm sorry. That was very blunt, but we have to be clear. If you feel any more than that for me this won't work. I don't want to hurt you again. I'm not saying we go back to sleeping together or anything like that: it would be platonic. We could be friends, nice to each other, not hurt each other.'

'That's madness.'

'Think about it, Lowri. You don't want to go on living in that house in Southampton on your own do you? Listen, I've thought of something much better.'

'What's that?'

'Why don't we move over to the Isle of Wight, live in my house there?'

Lowri felt her stomach clench in panic. 'I can't go there. I can't go to the island.'

'Why not? It would be a fresh start for you. I could commute to the university. And there's something really exciting, I've been commissioned to paint a fresco in one of the rooms at Elmstone Manor. They've asked that I use the materials and techniques of Michelangelo. Can you imagine that? It's my dream.'

'But I can't go to Elmstone.' Lowri felt desperate.

'Why ever not? We can take the animals,. We could live in the village like a proper family. You'll love it there: beaches and hills to walk on with Cassie, a lovely little school for our child to go to. It's the life my parents always wanted for me.'

'But they wanted you to have that life with Holly. Maybe it's why I never went there. I thought of it as Holly's house.'

'It's a long time since she's been there. Anyway, it's my house. It should have a family living there. My Mum would be so thrilled if she knew I was there and she had a grandchild. You'll enjoy the village; they are so friendly, and you can get involved in things, go for long walks over the downs–'

40

Lowri cringed. How could she explain? 'But Holly's family live there.'

'Just her sister Heather, who runs a café. She gets on with everyone. She'll help you get to know people.'

'She won't want me coming and living in the house where her sister lived with you'

'Honestly, she won't mind. Heather was actually quite hurt. It wasn't just me who was confused by the way she suddenly just left. She never talked to Heather and has never been back to the Island since .Neither Heather nor Holly's other sister Rosemary who lives on the mainland have seen anything of her.'

Lowri took a sharp intake of breath at the name. 'Does Rosemary go there a lot?'

Jack shrugged. 'Don't think so. I haven't seen her when ever I've been there. Her husband is always working, a doctor I think. Heather says they're always busy. Think about it, Lowri. This could work.'

She lay staring at the ceiling. Maybe she could go? Rosemary wouldn't be there. Heather wouldn't even know about her. It sounded wonderful: idyllic even. Then she remembered her scars.

'Will people mind, you know, I'll look different?'

'Of course not. They will look after you.'

'And what about the baby, us; will we tell people?'

'Why should we? That's our business, isn't it?'

'I suppose it is... I'd have to give up my Polish group.'

'But you won't be doing that for a while anyway. All your translation work is done from home. It would be perfect.'

'I suppose so—'

'What do you say then?' Jack was sitting forward, his eyes wide with excitement.

'I suppose Cassie and Fizzy would love it—'

'Exactly.'

Lowri took a deep breath which actually hurt her ribs. However, despite that, she said, 'OK then, yes. We'll try.'

'Great. Now, I'm going to ring Mum. You know she's been so unwell. This could be just the thing to cheer her up: a baby. At last, a grandchild: it will give her something to live for.'

'You'll tell her the baby is yours?'

'Of course. Why not?'

The clock ticked quietly. Lowri saw nurses in the corridor, the night shift coming on.

'OK. You go back to your hotel,' she said, granting him release. 'I need to sleep now.'

'I'll come back tomorrow.'

'Good. See you then.'

Jack grinned. 'Gosh, this is so exciting. We can have a nursery. There are some wonderful schools there and we can take our baby down to the beach, have picnics on the downs.'

She laid back, closed her eyes, and pictured the perfect life he was painting. Why shouldn't it be hers?

Chapter Five

In her café on the Isle of Wight, Heather set out the freshly baked fruit scones on a china plate, and glanced out of the window. The sun was breaking through the foggy morning. She could see the downs in the distance. Whatever was happening in her life they were the constant.

Her parents had previously owned this café in the village of Elmstone. She had grown up here with her sisters, Rosemary and Holly, but she had been the only one who had wanted to take over the café. As she looked around it, wooden tables scrubbed, wood burner lit, stone floor swept, she felt nothing but pride.

This morning she was slightly distracted. She was thinking over the phone call from the night before. It had been from Jack, Holly's ex, asking her to tell the people at the manor that there would be a delay in his return to work. Apparently Jack's wife, Lowri, who he was separated from, had been in a serious car accident while on holiday in France and he felt he ought to go to her.

As she set up the café she was thinking about this girl Lowri. Heather had only heard about her from Jack, but it was sad that things hadn't worked out with them. Jack didn't seem to have much luck.

At that moment Heather's 'resident potter' Dave arrived for work.

When Dave had first turned up for his interview she had been very unsure. He wasn't particularly tall, but was broad, had tattoos on his arms, very short hair, and his cockney accent contrasted sharply with the soft burr of Island voices. He was definitely not the kind of person who she usually had working there. She had only gone ahead with the interview because of the references and the pictures of his work. In fact, before meeting him, her only reservations had been why someone with this level of experience and reputation should want to come and work in a small pottery on the Isle of Wight.

The interview, to her surprise, had gone much better than she expected. Dave was on an extended 'creative retreat' from the business he co-owned with someone in London. His partner was happy to continue to run the gallery in London while he sought fresh inspiration here. Heather had quickly explained the other duties that came with the pottery, including taking small groups and classes of children from local schools and had been relieved to find that he had done some of this kind of thing before. He didn't find it easy, but was willing to take the classes. Dave had been with them now for six months and, apart from his appalling organisational skills, all had gone well.

'Morning all,' he said, his voice bouncing off the stone walls.

'Hi Dave. OK?'

'Bloody freezing innit, and so dark.'

'The clocks will go back soon. It will help the mornings. You look tired: were you working late?'

'Yeah. God knows what time I finished, but it's great working here on me own at night. A fox walking past the window: never get used to that!'

'What were you working on?'

'Been walking down Compton really early and sketching the waves, the movement of them. It's really stormy, and now I want to capture it on the new pots I'm doing. I'm trying out new glazes. It's dead exciting.'

Heather smiled. She loved the passion Dave had for his work.

'One of those posh bowls you made sold the other day. I was surprised. We've only sold mugs and things like that before.'

Dave grinned. 'I'm really pleased. I know I send most of my individual pieces to London, but I thought there would be people down here willing to pay more. The ones that know their stuff realise they're paying a fraction of what they'd be paying in London.'

Heather laughed. 'Well, they live in a different world to someone like me whose last dinner set came from Argos.'

'These are not the sort of thing you eat your Frosties from. Now, in London I did make a dinner service to order for a new restaurant.' She saw him look around. 'One day, you know, I could do it for you.'

'When I win the lottery. Anyway, don't stop the mugs with the fish on: the tourists like them.'

'Don't worry. I'll keep churning them out for you. Just don't tell anyone in London. They'll think I've completely sold out.'

'I don't see why. I like your mugs. Anyway, speaking of more mundane things, you've remembered you have a class coming in today?'

'Shit, no.'

'Dave, I told you, and I wrote it on your calendar.'

'It fell off. I think it's behind the table.'

'For goodness' sake, Dave. You have enough stuff in for them, do you?'

'Yeah, I've bags of their clay. Don't give them my porcelain.'

'I saw some of what the last group made; they were good.'

'It's only pinch pots, but if you give them a few ideas they can do decent work. So, any coffee on the go?'

'Have you had any breakfast?'

'A Mars bar.'

'I'll get you a scone.'

Heather started pouring the coffee. 'I had a phone call from Jack last night.'

'Jack? The painter?'

'That's him.'

'I like him; he's alright, into renaissance stuff. We had a really interesting chat one day. You know he is doing that fresco in the manor, we were talking about the clays and earths he is using for it.'

'He rang me because his wife, Lowri, has had a bad accident.'

'Didn't you say they were separated?'

'Yes, but he's gone to see her.'

'Didn't Jack used to be married to your sister Holly?'

'He was. It was a messy divorce as they say.'

She handed him the coffee, two scones and butter. 'Go on: help you face the kids.'

'Thanks. Hope they're better than the lot on Saturday. They got through so much clay.'

'You need to be stricter.'

'Nah, don't like to be. I want them to have a go and be a bit creative.'

'This class will have a teacher and assistant coming with them, so they'll keep things under control for you.'

Noises of dishes in the kitchen caught Dave's attention. The kitchen led off from the café through a large open archway. 'Carina in?'

'Of course.'

'Up or down today?' Dave asked.

'Good mood so far. Mind you, I haven't told her that Gill's not coming in yet.'

'I saw her outside The Six Elms last night, smoking, cadging drinks off friends.'

'Her mother would have a fit. She's so unreliable. I wish I'd never agreed to take her on.'

'Kids will be kids.'

Carina came out of the kitchen carrying a tray of pastries. Heather glanced over. How did she manage to look like that this early on a wet miserable morning? Like Heather, she was wearing the café tabard (many sizes smaller than Heather's: who would have thought they even made them in a size six?). Carina was staggeringly good looking, tall, slim, with milk-rose skin and large blue eyes and, added to this, she was very blonde. If Carina was out serving in the café most people seemed flattered to be served by her. Men of all ages flirted. Even women became giggly, played with their hair, and fluttered eyelashes. Heather had read in a magazine left by a customer that people like Carina enjoy what they called the 'halo effect'. That meant that because she had one very strong positive attribute, in Carina's case beauty, people assumed she also had lots of others like honesty, kindness, intelligence. Heather did allow herself to occasionally feel resentful but on the whole she accepted that that was the way life worked and let Carina enjoy the limelight.

One of the few people who didn't seem to stand in awe of Carina was Dave, and Heather loved watching them together. Carina really didn't know how to handle him; he was like an alien to her.

'Watcha,' Dave said.

Carina did not respond.

'They look good,' said Heather. 'What are they?'

Carina held the plate up, ignoring Dave. 'For you, I have made the *cornetti*.'

'Just one cornetto,' sang Dave, laughing.

Carina gave him a glassy stare.

'Look like croissants to me,' said Dave. 'Italians pinched them from the French, then?'

Carina flushed. 'Actually, croissants were first made in Austria. I have made some cornetto alla crema, they are the ones filled with custard, and cornetto alla marmellata, are filled with jam.'

'They look marvellous,' said Heather in a conciliatory manner.

Carina smiled. 'My Nonna made these every Saturday for my Papa.'

'My Dad would be looking for his kippers,' said Dave. 'Every morning except Sunday he had kippers with bread and butter. Right, I'd better be off, see ya.'

'I'll come and lend a hand if it goes quiet,' shouted Heather at his back, 'and don't forget to put your calendar back up.'

Carina shuddered. 'I don't know how you can have him here.'

'He's very gifted. Anyway, he's friendly enough. The kids like him.'

'He is too rough. Not like my Ken. He is a gentleman. He is my Romeo.'

Heather rolled her eyes: love must be blind. A director might cast Carina as Juliet but he would definitely not cast Ken as Romeo.

Heather remembered the day when widower Ken returned from his holiday in Italy. It had been his first holiday since losing his wife. To the astonishment of the entire village, he came back having met and married a young, beautiful Italian, Carina, twenty five years younger than himself. She became the new, very glamorous, lady of the manor. There was gossip, of course, that she was just after his money, but Carina had declared her love for Ken to such an extent that she had silenced most tongues in the village. It had initially surprised Heather when Carina approached her asking for work in the café, Ken was extremely wealthy: his wife certainly didn't need to work.

'I am so lonely,' Carina had said. 'Ken, he wants to spend all his time with his horses. Me, I have my dreams for the manor, but I need other things to do. I shall bake for you and people will be amazed.'

Heather thought she understood: already she could see that Carina needed an audience. But then Heather needed help in the café: the arrangement suited them both. Granted her mood swings were difficult to cope with at times, but then, as Heather told herself, no-one is perfect.

Carina glanced out of the window in disgust. 'Look at this terrible weather. How can you English people survive?'

'We're used to it; we like the seasons to change. You've been here ten years now. I'd have thought you'd have got used to it.'

'Never,' said Carina, shaking her head. 'I say to Ken, if it wasn't for you and this manor, I would go back to the sunshine. But as it is, Ken is my love, my world. I shall never leave him.'

Heather smiled. 'I am sure Ken appreciates how lucky he was to meet you.'

'Ken è la mia vita. Without him, I am nothing.'

Then Carina came over, and put her arm around Heather. 'You and your sisters are my family now. I am so lucky to have you in my life. I rang Rosemary last night, by the way. She is worried about her husband Simon.'

'I know. I do hope things between them are all right.'

'She said he kept texting someone on his work phone when they were away. I said to her she should take his phone, see what he was doing, but she wouldn't. Do you think he has taken another woman?'

'Oh no. I am sure it was work. He's obsessed with it, you know.'

'I think their visit to Italy may help their marriage. I'm jealous. I wish I was going.'

Heather was surprised. 'When is she going there? She never said anything to me.'

'They haven't fixed a date yet. I thought she told you everything?'

'So did I.'

'Of course, Rosemary and Simon can afford to travel as much as they want. Maybe that's why she never said anything: you know, because of the money.'

'What about money?'

'Nothing…it is no matter.'

'Tell me, what?'

'She told me she thinks maybe you are jealous of her and Simon. She is married to a consultant and, of course, your Lee, he just works in the hotel.'

'He is a very gifted chef.'

'Of course, he is an excellent cook, his Bruttiboni is nearly as good as mine, but Rosemary does not think like us. She can be, as you say, a bit of a snob.'

'She's never told me she has an issue with Lee.'

'You must not worry about it. I don't think there is anything wrong with you having a younger husband: lucky you, that's what I say.'

Heather gritted her teeth. Although there had been some comments in the village about her marrying a younger man, Rosemary had always been supportive and said she really liked Lee. Why was she saying these things behind her back when they'd always been so close? Carina, unaware of having put her foot in it, said, 'Now, I made some cupcakes as well. I go and get them.'

Carina returned with a tray of panettone and decorated cupcakes.

'I meant to tell you, Carina. Jack might be delayed in coming to work in the manor with you. He rang me last night, asked me to pass on the message.'

The smile on Carina's face melted away. She pursed her mouth and her eyebrows dipped. 'But I need him to finish the fresco.'

'Unfortunately his wife, Lowri, has been in a nasty accident in France.'

'But they are separated now. Jack is in Florence.'

'The hospital contacted him; he is on his way to see her. Anyway, the accident sounds pretty awful.'

'I hope he doesn't end up having to look after her. He is right in the middle of the fresco; the scaffolding is up and the walls are prepared. There is a lot for Jack to do. I want it finished for the spring.'

'He is a very talented painter.'

'He is the only person who shares my passion for the Renaissance. Together we will transform the manor.'

'But Ken doesn't share that dream, does he?' Heather said. 'These dreams cost money.'

Carina gave an indulgent laugh. 'I know, and it is taking longer as Ken thinks only of his horses, but one day the manor will be magnificent.'

'You love it, don't you?'

I do. Still, after ten years of living there, every morning I wake up and think, I am the mistress of a Tudor manor. My brothers, they may be clever, but they all have boring jobs. None of them live in a manor, like me.'

Heather grinned. 'I think you were always destined to marry a rich man and live somewhere grand, Carina.'

'That is what my papa always said, he would be so proud of me now.'

'Your mother has never been over has she?'

'No, she will never leave the village, my papa would have come, it is sad he died. My mamma she likes only to see the pictures of Lizzy.'

Heather smiled. 'That is the way with grandmothers I think. So, how is Lizzy?'

'My daughter is obsessed with horses. She is like Ken.' said Carina. 'He has bought her a new pony for her tenth birthday, says it's perfect for her. I don't know about these things, of course, but he says she is very good at jumping. Me, I do not see why a girl needs to ride horses, out in all that wind and sun. It is not good for her skin, but she does not listen.'

'They get on well. It's lovely for Ken, I am sure he thought he'd never have children.'

Carina looked around. 'I see Gill's not here yet?'

'She's not coming in. It's just me and you, I'm afraid.'

'Again? You must find someone else. We have Christmas soon and you're going to need more help.'

'I know. It's not easy finding people who will come out here to work. They need a car or someone to give them a lift now the buses have stopped running this route.'

'You and Lee work all hours. Poppy should help more. It is right for the daughter to help her mother.'

'Poppy comes in when she can but she has a lot on with work and the wedding and everything.'

'That's not until May.'

'I know, but she feels under a lot of pressure to get things just right. With her fiancé Alistair's family being so well off, and his sister Georgia feeding her all the latest trends, it's a lot of stress.'

Carina put her arm around Heather. 'You are the ones who will have to pay the money, not Georgia. I worry about you.'

Heather appreciated the hug. 'Thanks. You mustn't. I'll cope.'

Carina went over to the pantry and took out some more cakes to put on the counter.

'You know Ken and I shall give you the manor for the wedding. I told you I think of you as family.'

'I know, and I'm really grateful.'

'You should consider changing the day, though. In Italy, Sunday is the luckiest day to get married.'

'I'm afraid Poppy has chosen the Saturday, but the manor will be the most wonderful place for the reception. Poppy went for her second appointment with the designer in Knightsbridge the other day. She was showing me the drawings of her dress. It's going to be incredible. And she has four bridesmaids now.'

'I hope Alistair or his family are helping out with all this. I saw the quote for the caterers, and it was very expensive.'

'How did you see that?'

'You left your laptop open. It's alright. I shall not tell anyone.'

'The caterers are some contacts of Alistair's sister Georgia's. Apparently, they wouldn't come to the island for anyone else, but she gets them a lot of business. As it is, they've had to turn down much bigger events than ours. It's like the photographer, another friend of Georgia's. Although he's very expensive, he said it's hardly worth him coming. Honestly, you'd think they had to travel to Russia or somewhere, not the Isle of Wight.'

'I think Rosemary would have liked to be asked to do the photographs.'

'I know. I was surprised. I thought she'd like to relax and enjoy the day. I tried to explain how things were: this is what Poppy wants.'

'His family should help out, shouldn't they? Even in Italy now the groom's family sometimes pay half.'

'They haven't offered, and I'm not asking. I only have one daughter, and she will have the best day of her life, the perfect wedding.'

'You have too generous a heart, Heather. You look after everyone, don't you?'

'I try. Now, back to today. We have this group of school children in later. I thought we'd cordon off the end there for them.'

'Will they need lunch?'

'No. They'll be bringing packed lunches. I expect the teachers will buy coffees and things.'

'OK. We have a coach trip, don't we?'

'That's right. They'll come about twelve; at least we've been warned.'

A bell sounded customers arriving. Heather took their order and glanced out of the window. The café garden looked inviting. The sun was breaking through the clouds. In the centre, a small stone fountain trickled water and a blackbird was drinking. However, the wood burner bore witness to the early morning chill.

'I guess you'll be inside. You go and sit down. I'll bring your drinks over.'

Heather quickly put on her manager's face, friendly without being familiar, competent without being officious. She had perfected it over the years. The look that said she was in control, no worries. If only they all knew.

Chapter Six

It was the end of the day and Heather was bagging up the remaining scones when her phone rang. She saw it was Jack ringing and quickly picked up.

'Jack, how are things?'

'She's in a bad way. It was a nasty accident.'

Heather could hear the emotion in Jack's voice.

'How bad?'

'Internally, I think it's just bruising, broken ribs.'

'But that's good, isn't it?'

'Of course. Her face is going to be scarred, though.'

'Oh dear.'

'It's one side of her face; there are a lot of stitches. The scars are going to be very deep down the left side of her face.'

'I am sure it will start looking better soon.'

'No. She will always be scarred, but the doctor said she was very lucky: she can still see and everything.'

'It sounds like there's a lot to be grateful for then.'

'But she will never look the same. She's very upset.'

'What happened in the accident?'

He told her that Lowri had been with a friend, Marie, and they had crashed.

'And how is she in herself?'

'Feeling pretty rough, as you can imagine. Anyway, I have some other news.'

'What's that?'

'Lowri and I are getting back together.'

'Really? That's wonderful.'

'It is, isn't it? She's going to come over to live in the Old School House; we're going to live on the island together.'

'She's coming here?'

'Yes. It will be a new start for us.'

'That's great. I'm looking forward to meeting her.'

'Thanks Heather. Right, I'd better go. Tell Carina it will be a week or two.'

Heather put down her phone. Carina appeared from the kitchen undoing her tabard.

'I've finished in the kitchen. Heard you on the phone— was it Jack?'

'Yes. He was saying the accident was pretty bad.'

'Did he say when he'd be back?'

'A few weeks, he thinks. Maybe less. Apparently she has a lot of stitches in her face. She will be scarred for life, though.'

Carina gasped. 'But that is a tragedy. How will she cope? I would want to die if that happened to me.'

'It is awful, but things like her sight are not affected–'

'But she will never look the same.'

'I suppose not. One good thing to come out of this is that Jack and she are back together, and the plan is to bring her here to live.'

Carina thumped her tabard down on the counter. 'This is ridiculous. Jack can't get back with her just because he feels sorry for her.'

'He loves her Carina; they were never divorced.'

Carina flapped her hand dismissively. 'It was just a matter of time. He was pleased to be free of her. Why does she want to come here anyway? She has no friends here. How will she earn a living? Or does she expect Jack to provide for her?'

'She does all her work online so that isn't a problem.'

'It's a big mistake. I hope she changes her mind.' Carina picked up her bags. 'I'm off now. OK?'

'Of course. I'll see you tomorrow; we need to talk about this party on the 17th, our pre-Halloween and bonfire party. I need to get the food order in. I hope the village support us.'

'I'll come in early; we can talk then.'

Heather smiled. 'Thank you, Carina. I don't know what I'd do without you.'

Carina gave her genuinely grateful smile. 'Do you fancy coming to watch a film this evening? Ken and Lizzy are both out.'

'No, sorry. I have writing to do at home.'

Carina's face hardened. 'Writing? You are always writing! What is it about then? You never tell me.'

'I can't talk about it.'

'I don't see why not.'

'It's my own world.'

'I do not understand. Right, I will go. See you tomorrow.'

Heather put the bags of scones in a basket. They only sold freshly baked scones in the café, but some customers were happy to buy them a day old to take home.

Dave appeared, looking worn out.

'It all went OK?'

'The kids were good. The teachers had the measure of them. I enjoy it when the kids get on like that.'

'Good, see you tomorrow.'

When he had gone the café seemed ghostly quiet. In the evenings like this Heather often felt her mother's ghost watching her. It was comforting rather than scary and she liked to catch up and talk to her. On the wall she had a photograph of her mother with the three girls: Heather, Holly and Rosemary, all in their teens. Twenty five years since her Mum had died; time was a strange thing. It felt forever and at the same time only yesterday since she had been with her. She could hear her voice, feel her soft arms. Every day she missed her. A piece of Heather had been taken away when she lost her, never to be replaced. Around the edge of the photo, her mother had added pressed flowers of the girl's names; the glass had preserved them well. Her mother was wearing a white apron on which she'd embroidered tiny roses. She was plump and motherly. Heather realised her appearance was becoming more like her mother's. Heather's friends had all loved her Mum and would tell her their troubles. Heather, the eldest of the three girls, stood next to her in the photo, her arm threaded through her mother's. Rosemary was the other side, her wild curly hair blowing around. Holly stood, just to the left of Rosemary, slightly apart.

This evening, as she often did, Heather talked to her mother. 'We had some bad news. It was about Jack's new wife. Funny to think you never even met Jack, never went to his and Holly's wedding. Time passes silently, doesn't it? I wish you'd been here when Holly and he were going through all their troubles. Maybe Holly would have told you what she was so upset about. You understood her. She was so different to me and Rosemary. Sorry, she still is, and I didn't mean to talk about her as if she was dead. I'm glad you at least knew she'd got into university. You'd have loved her graduation. The only one of us to do it.' Heather looked away from the photo, cleaned the coffee machine and then went back to her mother. 'Anyway, I was going to tell you Jack's new wife Lowri has been in an accident. She's going to come over and live with Jack in the Old School House. Sad to think it was where he and Holly had started out. They seemed so happy. I'd love to have had her living here—'

Heather looked out of the window. She could see only a few stars in the blackness. She looked back towards the photo. 'Rosemary is still having problems with Simon. You know she said a few things to Carina on the phone about me and Lee. It's not like her, Mum. I guess she's stressed. Mum, there's more I should tell you, but I can't bear to. It's me, you know, good old dependable Heather. I've got in such a mess, Mum. I can't tell you, can't tell anyone, but maybe I can sort it out on my own. I have to, don't I? I have no option. Goodnight, Mum.' She walked away from the photograph.

On the work top she kept her laptop. She opened it, turned away the screen so that her mother couldn't see, and logged on.

Chapter Seven

It was raining when Lowri and Jack left the hospital. She was wearing the one pair of trainers and jeans she had packed. They had arranged to make the journey as easy as possible. Zoe was happy to hold on to Cassie and Fizzy a bit longer, and because Jack's car was over on the Island, they didn't have to go on the car ferry. He told her they could go on the Red Jet, which was apparently a bit like a hovercraft, and a lot quicker than the car ferry. On the way to the Red Jet they would call at the house and pick up some clothes for Lowri. Going out into the noise and every day business of the streets was a shock; suddenly she wanted to run back to the safety of her hospital bed. Jack helped her into a taxi which was going to take them to the airport.

As she sat in the back of the taxi Lowri saw the driver glance at her in the mirror. Their eyes met and he looked away. Looking down, she twisted her mother's wedding ring, which she'd replaced on her finger.

Jack rested his hands on hers. 'OK?'

She nodded then said 'Oh, Marie came in again, poor thing. She left her insurance details–'

'Good, I know a solicitor on the island. Don't worry, we can leave everything with him.'

'Thanks.'

As they approached the airport Lowri saw the hotel car park where she'd got into Marie's car. If only Simon had taken her – life sometimes seemed full of 'if onlys'.

When they arrived, Jack stayed close to her. She heard the click click of stilettos on the marble floor, and turned to see a smart woman, smiling confidently. Only days ago, she thought, that was me.

'I need to go to the ladies,' she said, and left Jack. The lights seemed brighter today. She brushed her hair. She hadn't tied it back, and she pulled it as much as she could over her face. The bruising and scars shouted through her makeup. Then, in the mirror, she saw a little girl standing next to her, staring up. The child's mother came out of a cubicle and the child said in a loud whisper, 'Mum, what's the matter with that lady's face? The woman grimaced as she looked over at her. Seeing her expression in the mirror Lowri smiled . This was normally reciprocated, but today the woman continued to stare. Shocked, Lowri looked back at her own reflection and realised that only one side of her face formed her 'greeting smile.' Without speaking woman took her daughter's hand and quickly led her out of the room. Mortified, Lowri pushed her brush back into her bag and rushed out. She hurried over to Jack.

'What's the matter?' he asked.

Lowri told him what had happened. 'Do I really look so awful? Have I become some sort of monster?'

'Try not to let it get to you,'

'But it was so rude. It was like I was a dummy in a shop. They just stared. It was so intrusive.'

'Come on. It was probably a one-off.'

On the plane, she took Jack's seat with her left cheek to the window. She didn't turn when they were offered drinks. She would rather appear rude than have another person stare at her.

At Southampton Airport they took a taxi to their house to pick up more things for Lowri. Jack would return later to collect the pets from the neighbours. Lowri glanced over at Zoe's: she was desperate to see her Fizzy and Cassie, but was worried about upsetting them by leaving them again so soon. It seemed better to leave them be.

The house felt cold and uninviting. Jack followed her upstairs into what she now thought of as her room.

'I'll go and pick up a few things as well,' said Jack, reaching on top of the wardrobe for an old brown case bought in a garage sale. 'You'd better use this: the other one is all battered now.'

Lowri put the case she'd brought from the hospital on the bed and opened it. She stood staring at it. She had bought it especially for her holiday with Simon: cream leather. The last time she had left this house it had been to go to France: a new start she had thought. Her case had been smart, packed with sexy underwear, beautiful clothes, and her best cosmetics. She remembered the nerves, excitement, and the anticipation of telling Simon about the baby. How had she got all that so wrong? She opened the other case: large and practical. This case was who she was now. This was Lowri making a very different kind of fresh start.

'I'll go and have a look in my old study, see if there are any of my art materials left there. I'll be coming back, so don't worry about forgetting things.' Jack left the room.

Lowri imagined him rummaging through her stuff; and as soon as he had left the bedroom she quickly shut the door and went over to her bedside table. Digging to the bottom of a drawer, she took out a large white envelope. Inside there were cards, used tickets and a menu, mementos of her times with Simon. Carefully, she concealed the envelope in a bundle of socks and underwear, and placed it in the bottom of her case, promising herself that soon she would throw it away.

Lowri breathed in deeply. That was when she detected it: her home's distinctive smell, the one people only notice when they've stayed away, the one that made a house their own. She tried to picture Jack's house on the island, but she had never even seen a photograph of it. Like Holly, it was an unspoken part of their lives. The house in her mind belonged to Jack and Holly. Maybe she could take things that would force the house to acknowledge her, and forget Holly?

Lowri's gaze strayed to a small watercolour of the Brecon Beacons: that part of her that she took everywhere, a glint of happiness from her childhood when they would go for a trip from her town of Merthyr Tydfil with the chapel. She took it down. Returning to her bedside table, she picked up a framed photograph. It had been taken sometime in the 1970s, before Lowri was born. It was her mother standing formally in the back garden. The reason Lowri liked it was that her mother looked so happy: she had long curly black hair that shone. She even had lipstick on. It was very hard to imagine that pretty young girl was the mother she had known: few smiles and dowdy clothes, but maybe that was that how all children felt looking at old pictures of their parents, not really being able to imagine them young and in a life without them. With this, she put another photograph that went everywhere with her; a photograph with the words 'My Dad' written at the bottom of the frame. It was not a very good photograph, difficult to make out the features of the large man in a hat, but she always took the photo with her. Finally, she picked up the only other photo she wanted, from years ago in Poland on her year abroad while at university. She looked naive and excited, standing by one of the Great Malsurian Lakes. Such a beautiful country, one day she would love to go back.

Lowri went over to the dressing table. From her drawer she found her engagement and wedding rings, carefully placed in a small jewellery box. Taking them out, she tried to put them back on to her finger, but they seemed smaller and it was an effort. She picked up her makeup and filled several cosmetic bags. Then she caught sight of a small bottle of perfume. Spraying a small amount on her wrist, she breathed in the memory of the perfumery in Florence. They had gone there the first year of their marriage, an ancient building with high ceilings that had been a chapel. She had chosen a perfume that had been the favourite of a Tudor queen. Lowri placed it carefully in her case. There were also some small pieces of blue and white Polish pottery, which she wrapped up carefully. The only other things she added from her dressing table were her hairbrush and hairdryer; she needed them to style her hair, to form the veil.

She opened her large wardrobe, one end full of skinny jeans, and tight jumpers she'd worn with Jack, the other smarter tailored trousers and blouses she wore with Simon. She left the tailored clothes, and packed jeans and tops. She looked down at her stomach: of course soon she would need to think about maternity clothes, but not yet. She also grabbed a handful of old underwear and pushed it in the case. In the bottom of her wardrobe was an array of shoes, all with heels. She left most of them. She picked out a few pieces of jewellery, scarves, shoes and accessories, filled her wash bag and then zipped up her case.

Jack called up the stairs, telling her that a taxi had arrived. Lowri went downstairs. The taxi drove down into the town.

'Oh, look. There's that French place. We loved it there, didn't we?' said Jack.

She looked over. She could hardly remember going there with Jack: to Lowri it would be 'their place': her and Simon's. This was the restaurant where she had first met him.. When Jack had left she decided that it would be good for her to go there without him, to prove that she could carry on her life. She decided to go down an hour before her Polish group meeting on the Monday. Glancing in, she had seen that it was very quiet and, armed with her Kindle, she went in. The waiter recognised her. She could see him looking over her shoulder for Jack.

'It is just me. I'm on my own now.' He looked searchingly and nodded her to a table. She was relieved to be taken to a decent table, one by the window looking over the Solent. A complementary glass of red wine was brought to her. It felt odd sitting on her own. She quickly turned on her Kindle and read while she waited for her food and then while eating. A couple were sitting close by. She realised the one thing she didn't want was pity. As she left she gave them a huge grin to prove how happy she was to have been eating alone.

The following week she had gone in more confidently, chatted to the waiter and actually looked around as she ate.

The Monday when she had met Simon for the first time had not started so well. She had had a bad day and was distracted. As she sat with her glass of red wine and looked at the menu her mind was churning over the day. Jack had come unexpectedly to collect some things. As soon as she had seen him she had realised that all she had been doing was burying the hurt: it was still there as raw and painful as the evening he walked out. Cassie, her cocker spaniel, had nuzzled up to her, each comforting the other. She didn't know what she had done all day, but had somehow got to the restaurant.

Suddenly the waiter coughed and, startled, she dropped the menu, smashing her glass and sending the wine everywhere.

'Oh no,' she said, close to tears.

'Ce n'est pas grave, Lowri,' said the waiter, trying to comfort her.

65

She had looked around, very embarrassed, and caught the eye of the man on the next table. He grinned reassuringly, as she stood up to stop the wine dripping on to her jeans.

'Don't worry. It's only wine,' the man said.

'I feel so stupid.'

'Look, would you like to come and sit here?'

'Oh, no. I couldn't do that.'

'You could while they clear up your table.'

'You sure?'

'Of course.'

'Well, thank you,' she said, and sat opposite him. She noticed that he was drinking water, but she ordered another glass of red wine for herself.

'I'm Simon.'

'Lowri.'

He grinned. 'That's a Welsh name. Is that where you're from?'

'Originally, yes.'

'I spotted the accent as well.'

'Did you? I try to hide it, but it tends to come out when I'm in a flap.'

'I like it.' He looked around the room. 'You eat early.'

'I haven't seen you in here before.'

'No. It's my first time in here. I've often walked past, though. Wondered what it was like. My wife works up in London on Mondays, so I thought I'd treat myself. I've just come back from the Isle of Wight.'

'Oh. My, um, my husband owns a house over there.'

'Really? It's a lovely place. Where is his house?'

'Let me think, something to do with trees. Yes, Elmstone.'

'Good grief. That's where my sister-in-law lives.'

'I suppose the island's not that big, is it?'

'I suppose not. Still, it's quite a coincidence.'

Lowri found this reassuring somehow: it gave them a common bond. She began to relax and when she saw her table still wasn't ready she made no attempt to move to an empty one. Instead, she asked, 'What do you do over on the Isle of Wight?'

'I work at the hospital every Monday. I operate there.'

'What kind of doctor are you?

'An orthopaedic surgeon.'

'Wow, very clever.'

'What about you?'

'I do online translation, Polish mainly. The work is sent to me by an agency, and I translate. Either way actually. Sometimes Polish stuff into English, sometimes the other way round. Tonight I go and do voluntary work with a large Polish group, conversational English.'

'That's very good of you.'

'Oh no, I love it. It's good for my Polish as well. There is such a large Polish community here in Southampton. It's good to get to know people, build bridges. The fact I lived in Poland for a year and loved it so much means a lot.'

The waiter came over. 'La table est prête, Lowri.'

'Oh, Merci.' She started to get up.

'Look, why don't you eat with me?'

'Don't feel obliged–'

'Really, it would be good to have someone to talk to.'

She gestured to the waiter, and sat down again. Louis gave her an annoyingly knowing look and handed them menus.

'Je vais avoir la salade de tomates et fromage s'il vous plait, Louis.'

Simon raised his eyebrows. 'I heard you speaking French earlier. You are very good... the Sole Meuniere, please,' adding, 'Let me order you another glass.'

'So, as you have family over there, do you go over to the Isle of Wight much?' she asked.

'No, not really. My wife, Rosemary, works on weekends. Her sister runs a café there, so it's difficult to find a time when we are all free.'

'A café? I'm sure my husband Jack said his ex grew up above a café there.'

'What's her name?'

'Holly.'

'Goodness. Holly is one of my wife's sisters. There are three of them: my wife Rosemary, Heather in the café, and Holly, your husband's ex. They grew up together at the café at Elmstone. I think their mother was into flowers, going by their names.'

'Gosh. It's a small world.'

'So Holly was married to your husband Jack? I was actually related to him by marriage.'

'So, did you know him well? I don't recall him talking about you; strange with you living in Southampton.'

'I don't think things were easy when he broke up with Holly, but even before then we didn't see much of him. I never even got to his and Holly's wedding as I was working. Rosemary was always much closer to Heather. I only met him and Holly when we went over to the island to visit Heather, which wasn't that often. Jack paints doesn't he?'

'That's right. He loves going over there, says it's inspiring.'

'It's a lovely island. I'm surprised you don't fancy moving over there as he's kept the house.'

'I'm better off here.' She looked away. Why she didn't just say that she was separated from Jack? There was nothing to be ashamed of. But part of her didn't want to admit to failure, and in any case maybe it was better for a

68

stranger to think she was with a husband. 'I have work and pets to look after here.'

We have cats. Maine Coon, like mini lions. Very big and hairy. What do you have?'

'A cocker spaniel, Cassie, and a cat, Fizzy. So, do you enjoy your work? Long hours in the hospital?'

'My wife and I are both workaholics. I work in the week generally, unless I'm on call. Rosemary works a lot at weekends.'

'Busy people.'

'Yes. We don't have a lot of holiday time. We do have a small gite in France, went when the children were younger, but hardly go now.'

'What does your wife do?'

'She's a photographer. She's very good, does a lot of weddings, but other things as well. When we do go away she spends all her time taking photos. So, Jack lectures in history or something doesn't he?'

'History of art. Mainly renaissance art.'

Simon nodded. 'Ah, Leonardo, Raphael, Michelangelo–'

'That's it. Jack is particularly interested in Michelangelo and Botticelli.'

'Madonna of the Magnificat, um, and Birth of Venus?'

'You know your renaissance. I can't escape it, living with Jack. The lectures I've heard on The Birth of Venus, the perfect woman. Funny, I always imagined that the perfect Italian Renaissance woman would have jet black hair, but apparently it was all about blonde women. That's why the Venus is blonde. Woman used to spend all this money to dye their hair with all kinds of dangerous chemicals.'

'We think this obsession with looks is a modern thing, but it's not, is it?'

'Not at all, and I tell you these artists are the worst. Jack is always waxing lyrical about the perfect form, male and female, symmetry of faces and the like.'

'So, do you and Jack have children?'

She blushed. 'No. Um, actually, I should have said. We're separated now.'

'I'm sorry.'

'It's only happened recently.'

He looked down at his food. 'This really is good. I shall come here again.'

'Yes, it always is. So, do you enjoy your work?'

'Yes. I'm doing some research with a surgeon in France. I go over to Paris sometimes. I have to say, I love it there. I keep telling my daughter to get her French up to speed and go over there.'

'Your daughter is a doctor as well?'

'Training, and my son is at university. Maths. You say you translate Polish, but you spoke French very well.'

'That's right. Languages are my thing.'

'I'm impressed. I struggled with languages, I guess science is my thing.'

'I love learning them, speaking them: each has their own beauty.'

'When I go to Paris I'm always amazed at how well so many of the staff speak English. It puts my French to shame. I work with a brilliant orthopaedic surgeon, Pierre. He has very good English. The trouble is, sometimes, like today, he emails me stuff in French. My French is pretty good, but I get stuck on some of the technical stuff.'

Lowri put down her knife and fork. 'Do you have it on you?'

'Of course.'

'Well, I could have a look for you.'

'Oh really? You don't mind?'

'Not at all. It would be interesting.'

'What languages do you speak?'

'Polish is my main language, and then French, Italian. I'm trying to teach myself Mandarin at the moment.'

'Why did you choose Polish?'

'In Merthyr Tydfil, where I come from, there's a large Polish community, so that's where my interest started.'

He leant down, took a few sheets of paper out of his briefcase and handed them to her. She skimmed them and then proceeded to translate them. Occasionally, Simon stopped her for clarification. He listened intently, obviously fascinated by the work. When she had finished he sat back.

'That's fantastic. Thank you. Your French is really very good.'

She looked down.

He smiled. 'I have to say, it has been an absolute pleasure to share this meal with you. Shall we order dessert?'

'I think I'm rather full.' Lowri looked at her watch. 'Gosh, time has gone. It's been lovely to meet you, Simon, but it's time I left.'

They stood up, split the bill, left the restaurant together and said goodbye.

The following Monday Lowri went to the restaurant and felt a shiver of disappointment that Simon wasn't there. Of course, if he had been it might have been kind of creepy. The waiter brought over her usual glass of red wine and she sipped it. Suddenly she saw the door open and realised it was Simon. He walked in confidently.

'Hi, Lowri. Look, I'm not stalking you or anything, and if you would rather I went, that is absolutely fine. It's just I really enjoyed chatting last week.'

She smiled. 'So did I.'

'Would you like to eat together again?'

She put her head to on side. 'Um, your wife wouldn't mind?'

Simon sat down. 'It's fine. I'm not trying to start anything here, but it's great to be able to chat. Is that OK?'

She smiled. 'Yes, OK. It would be nice, thanks.'

He sat down; they ordered the same food as the week before, chatted about their weeks. The following Monday they did the same. Slowly, they created a routine. They swapped phone numbers, just in case one of them couldn't make it. It never seemed dramatic or even very exciting, far more comfortable than that. It was as far from an affair, in Lowri's mind, as could be imagined.

Chapter Eight

Simon frequently sent Lowri texts. They chatted about all kinds of things. They made each other smile. She found herself thinking increasingly about Simon. One week he mentioned how smart one of the women in the restaurant looked and for the first time she had felt self-conscious about her jeans. She had gone out and bought some linen trousers, a silk blouse and a pair of slightly higher heels than she normally wore. When she had arrived that week he had been enormously complimentary about her appearance. The following week she had dressed in the same way, wearing more makeup and again she had been complimented. It was wonderful to be noticed. Jack had seldom commented on her appearance.

Slowly, Lowri put together a hazy picture of Simon's home life. She realised he and his wife were well off, but Rosemary remained a rather distant figure. When Simon mentioned her it was as if the joy was drained from him. The words 'complicated' and 'difficult' were mentioned but not much else. Lowri felt there was something wrong but he never even hinted about leaving Rosemary. It didn't matter, Lowri decided, they were just friends. There was nothing physical: they had never kissed or even held hands.

Then, one Monday it dawned on Lowri that things were changing. She knew that the Polish group would not be meeting that evening. She had been about to text Simon, to explain that she wouldn't be at the restaurant when she realised that she had been looking forward to meeting him all weekend. She had bought a new pink blouse and she knew he would like it. Also, like a child collecting pebbles and shells, she had been collecting stories and thoughts all week to share with him. For the first time, she allowed the niggling guilt to surface. Simon was married and, however

73

much he might grumble about his wife, there was no talk of a separation. On the edge of cancelling, she decided to go and talk to him face to face: this must end.

She was sipping wine when Simon arrived. They ordered their food. As always, only she had wine. Simon never drank. All the time they chatted she knew she must say something but, aware this would be their last meeting, she put off the moment. As she ordered another coffee at the end of the meal, Simon noticed time was passing.

'You're going to be late.'

She stroked the rim of her glass. 'Actually, I don't have the group tonight.'

'But you still came.'

She looked over at him and they both knew.

'I don't think I can see you anymore,' Lowri said quietly.

'Why?'

'You know why: this has changed, and you are married.'

Simon put down his glass of water. 'Rosemary has problems. I can't tell you what, but it means I stay with her. I don't want to. I would like to have left years ago, but I can't. Meeting you is the best thing in my life. I understand if you don't want to see me any more, but I would miss it more than you can imagine. Maybe we are both a bit lonely: is it something we both need?'

Lowri looked at him. He looked close to tears. 'I love coming here. It's your wife that worries me.'

'She has no idea. Me and you, it is platonic, isn't it? We're good friends; that's all.'

She smiled. 'OK. I see that.'

'Good. So you don't have a class. What will you do now?'

'I'll just go back to the house. What about you?'

'Rosemary is away.'

'Oh, right.'

'Actually, I was thinking of going to the cinema.'

'The Odeon?'

'No. They're showing Amélie in a small cinema very close to where I live. I love it there.'

'I used to go to indie films with Jack. It was how we met.'

'You could come now if you would like. We could drive there.'

'Where exactly in Southampton do you live?'

He told her and she grinned

'Gosh. You are slumming it mixing with the likes of me. It's a gated community, isn't it?'

'Oh yes. No riff raff.' He looked embarrassed. 'I don't like it much, to be honest, but Rosemary says she feels safe when I'm working nights. Anyway, how about going to see a film?'

'I don't know.'

'Please, it would be so lovely to go to see it with someone, not just sit there on my own again.'

'Of course I'll come,' she decided.

For the first time they didn't say their goodbyes at the entrance to the restaurant. It seemed very odd not to wave goodbye and go their separate ways. They didn't hold hands. She looked around, felt guilty about people seeing them out together. They arrived at Simon's car and he opened the passenger door. It was very tidy. Jack's was always a mess, with papers, books and various items of his art paraphernalia strewn around.

'Gosh, you're tidy.'

He laughed. 'I can't stand messes.'

Lowri got in, but the smell of the clean leather seats and the quiet purr of an expensive car made her feel nervous, like she was doing something really wrong. What was she doing? Then the CD player sprang to life. To her amazement it was a woman speaking. 'Pouvez-vous me dire où sont les toilettes?' And then, repeated in accented English, 'Can you tell me where the toilet is?'

Lowri burst out laughing. 'What on earth?'

'I want to improve my French.'

She felt irrationally flattered. They both relaxed. They parked outside a small independent cinema on the corner of an area of large Victorian houses. Inside was comfy, with sofas in the foyer and a bar selling organic snacks, tapas and a good selection of wines.

'Shall we get a bottle? You said you lived close by. I could get a taxi.'

'Oh no. I don't drink.'

'Never?'

'No. But come on, let's get you a decent glass.'

Simon bought them drinks and they sat on the sofa.

'Do you come here a lot?'

'Not as often as I'd like.'

They were sat very close, Simon reached up and touched her hair, she shivered, and he kissed her. Despite all they had said, in that moment, any pretence of 'friendship' melted away. They held hands as they went into the cinema and were both aware of each other's every breath as they watched the film.

Afterwards, Simon put his arm around her. 'Coffee?'

She frowned. 'Here?'

'No, my house.'

She panicked. 'I don't think so.'

'It's very close by.'

'I can't. I'm sorry–'

Simon pulled her closer. 'Please, Lowri. I need you. You have no idea how much–'

She shook her head; tears stinging her eyes. 'Simon. We can't. If we sleep together, that's it. This way I can at least pretend–'

He pursed his mouth and exhaled deeply. 'I'll call a taxi.'

Lowri couldn't judge his expression, was he sad or angry. She tried to guess the coldness in his eyes. It was like when he talked about his wife: his face was blank, closed. She got into the taxi. He silently walked away. She knew this was it: this was the end and it hurt far more than she had expected.

Lowri woke the next morning at five. Cassie was sleeping on the end of her bed. She felt so empty. Simon had gone from her life. She went into the bathroom, and looked at herself

'Good grief, what do you look like?' she asked herself. She had broken her cardinal rule of removing her make-up before going to sleep. 'Good job Simon didn't see you looking like this: at least he will remember you looking good.'

Her phone rang and she went to read the text. 'I'm so sorry. I shouldn't have treated you like that. Please don't let it spoil our friendship. It means more to me than you could possibly know. S x'

She sat down on the bed, and clasped the phone to her chest. Thank God. 'I'm sorry. I panicked,' She texted back.

'See you Monday?'

'Of course.' She wrote the message and then added xxx.

A reply came 'xxxxx.'

She grinned; it seemed so childish, like teenagers sending kisses.

Nervously, she went to the restaurant the following Monday. He wasn't there. Her heart sank: she should have realised he wouldn't come. She sat down, sipped her glass of wine, ordered her food. Suddenly, Simon came running in, panic on his face. 'I'm sorry. I missed my red jet, had to get the next one. I should have sent you a text, but my battery had run down.'

Under the safety of the dimmed lights they were allowed to touch fingers, hands. Leaving Simon to go to her teaching was hard. She found herself counting the days, hours until she would see him again.

'I am going to talk to Rosemary soon. I have to be with you all the time, and I can't bear being apart from you.'

'You said she was vulnerable.'

'She can be, but she has family, friends. They can support her. Honestly, she doesn't love me. She just likes me to be there to pick up the pieces. I stayed for the children but they are grown up, away from home now.'

Simon had to go to Paris for a few weeks at the end of July. It seemed an eternity. She met up with him again on a swelteringly hot August evening. The restaurant had some tables outside and they were looking for shade even at six in the evening. Simon was carrying his suit jacket. Lowri was in a sleeveless summer dress. She had tied her hair up in a ponytail.

'Hi, beautiful,' he said. The wave of relief and joy at seeing her was palpable. I love your hair like that. Don't ever cut it short, will you?'

'How was Paris?'

'Hot.'

They ordered. She had salad. He had the fish. They ordered a bottle of water.

'I missed you so much,' Simon said.

'And me. It felt forever.'

He touched her hand. 'What's the matter? You look upset?'

'I didn't expect it to be so hard.'

'I'll order wine.' Simon ordered her a bottle of cabernet sauvignon.

She drank the first glass quickly. Simon stayed with water.

He leant forward and held her hand. 'I'm so sorry. I am going to have to go away again.'

'To Paris?'

'No. I have to go with Rosemary to stay with the children–' He paused. The words shot home: going away with Rosemary.

Then he looked directly at her. Lowri saw him take a deep breath. She knew instantly that he had something big to tell her. He's going to finish it, she thought. Her heart was beating hard. It hurt, and she was biting her lip, trying to stop herself from crying.

'We are going to tell them that we are separating.'

Lowri gasped. She couldn't believe it. 'You've talked to Rosemary?'

He kept a steady gaze. 'Yes. I've told her I have met someone else.'

'How was she?'

'Better than I expected. It's done.'

'I can't believe it.' Lowri wanted to laugh hysterically, but Simon looked very serious.

'We are going to tell the children together. We'll visit them both in their homes. Rosemary can by hysterical. It's why I insisted we talk to them together.'

'That will be difficult.'

'The children are expecting it. It's Rosemary that will need handling. Anyway, after that I have some courses to go on. I'm so sorry.'

'How long will it be until I see you again?'

'Six weeks. And at the end of that I go to Paris for a few days.'

'It's a long time.'

'Listen, I've had an idea.'

She stopped as Louis brought their food. Suddenly she didn't feel hungry. She sipped her wine instead: she mustn't cry. It would look so....needy, but to suddenly know that soon she and Simon would be together was wonderful.

'I have an idea,' said Simon. He leant forward, grabbed her hand. 'Is there any way you could come over, and meet me?'

'Come to Paris?'

'Yes. What about it, Lowri? We could stay at the gite. It would be wonderful.'

'I don't know–'

'Could you get the time off?'

'I can do my work anywhere, so of course, I can rearrange things. I'd need to organise someone to have Cassie and Fizzy. Zoe is always offering.'

'Well, then?'

Lowri sat back, and took a long drink. 'It sounds lovely.'

'So you'll come? Please, it will be perfect. You know, I was thinking we could think about moving there. I could work in the hospital. You could teach, or carry on your translation work.'

'Are you serious?'

'Of course.'

She fiddled with her food with her fork. 'The thing is, Simon, I do want to have children. Soon. Time is passing for me, you know. Would you want to have another family?'

He grinned. 'Of course. I can't think of anything I'd love more than to have a family with you.'

She looked up. He looked so happy: it was infectious.

'I'll come.'

'That's great. I'll text you details, but you can fly to Orly from Heathrow.'

'With you?'

'I think I'll be going over on my own for a few days, get some work done. I'll meet you at Orly airport, then I'll sweep you away. The gite is only an hour away from Paris, but it's like you have travelled a hundred miles.'

'Um, the gite. Will Rosemary mind you taking me there?'

'She's not going to want the gite. I'll sort it. She never liked it there.'

They ate their meal in a dream, kept smiling. Lowri had drunk most of the bottle by the time they left.

She swayed slightly as she stood up. Simon put his arm around her. He whispered in her ear, 'Rosemary is away.'

She swallowed. 'Tonight?'

'Please, Lowri.' He kissed her, his lips hot.

She didn't answer, but went with him to his car. They drove to his house in silence, went through the gates. It was very quiet; nobody was about. They went quickly inside.

Lowri tried not to look at the family photos on the walls in the hallway. Everything here: the wallpaper, that hideous lamp, the spare shoes on the rack; it was all about Rosemary. An anonymous budget hotel would have been better than this. She regretted coming. As if sensing her panic, Simon held her hand tightly. 'Come on.' She followed him up the stairs.

He pulled the curtains. They quickly undressed, and he kissed her. There was passion and need there that Lowri hardly remembered with Jack. This was so different: he kissed her eyes, her cheeks. She felt her face relax and looked deep into his eyes. Their love making was soon over. Simon lay back panting, and grinned. 'Gosh sorry, bit quick.' Then Lowri's eyes caught sight of a framed photograph on the wall. It was black and white; a young girl and boy. His children, children who didn't know about her. She felt the photograph looking down at her and saw Simon follow her gaze. She sat up quickly, and put on her clothes.

'Are you alright?' he asked.

'Of course.' She painted on the smile. 'It was wonderful.'

He looked up at the photos as well. 'Sorry. When we are in France, I promise you it will be perfect.'

She looked back at him. Every part of her wanted to believe him.

Chapter Nine

'Out you get then.' Lowri blinked, brought abruptly back to the present. Jack was waiting for her to get out of the taxi.

At the Red Jet terminal they joined a long snake of people. Lowri knew people were looking at her, avoiding her, looking at Jack. She noticed he always stood on her right side, her 'normal' side. What were people thinking? Did they think she had some terrible illness, had been abused? She had no idea.

Lowri watched a group of girls, all taking selfies, all doing the same pouty poses. She saw them deleting most of the pictures, saying things like, 'God, I look awful'; 'my eyebrows are hideous'; 'my eyes look tiny'; and so it went on. It seemed so sad that they hated their looks so much.

Lowri had never been on the Red Jet before. It reminded her of going on the hovercraft to France, just much smaller. She sat in an airline-style seat, read the safety leaflet and watched the safety video avidly. She tried to imagine how to put on a lifejacket. However, the main message she remembered was to keep smiling like the woman in the blue suit, and remove stilettos. After this, she put in her earphones, turned up her iPod and shrank down into her coat.

To her surprise, the steward came round offering drinks. She couldn't imagine having time to finish one. She was fortunate that the day was cold but calm; the journey quite steady.

They were met in Cowes by another taxi. The driver seemed preoccupied with his satnav and talking to someone on a hands-free phone. She listened to the taxi driver. He had a soft burr of accent which reminded her of the West Country. The roads seemed quieter than the mainland. She could always see hills in the distance.

'That's the prison,' said Jack, pointing out sprawling buildings.

'Funny, you don't think of somewhere so picturesque having a prison. It's big, isn't it?'

'They've combined three together now.'

'It's weird: a whole community in there completely separate from the rest of the world.'

'A lot of people work there. It's important for the island. That opposite, it's the only hospital, St Mary's.'

Lowri's heart jumped. It's where Simon worked every Monday. She tried to imagine Simon walking through the corridors. He would be someone important, respected in there: a bit like the prison it was its own world and community.

'That's the Koan,' said Jack pointing to a huge inverted multicoloured cone in the hospital grounds. 'I think that was meant to go round. It just sort of stands there now. We go right here at the roundabout. You know this is the only bit of dual carriageway on the island. We call it the motorway!'

'It's like going back in time.'

'That's what people say, but it's not really, People here face the same problems as everyone else. Oh, now the forest there, Parkhurst, that has red squirrels. You know it's a crime to bring over a grey. I've only seen one or two of the reds: they're very shy.'

Lowri looked at Jack. 'You seem more at home here than I expected.'

'It's a great place.'

'I'm surprised Holly never comes back.'

Jack looked out of the window.

'You don't talk about her much.'

'It was her choice to cut herself off.'

They travelled through countryside in silence. The autumn leaves on the trees were the sunshine on a misty damp day. She noticed boxes outside some of the houses with home-made signs saying the price of the cooking apples or bunches of chrysanthemums.

They drove through small villages: Carisbrooke with the castle up on the hill, through the pretty village of Shorwell, then Brighstone. Here she saw a large church, café, surprisingly busy shops and a pub.

'There's a lot more here than I realised,' said Lowri. 'Didn't you say Ben from your department and his wife had a holiday place around here somewhere?'

'Yes, at Brook. You can get there if you turn left by the church.'

'I ought to take Cassie to the beach. Are dogs allowed down there?'

'You can. It's a great little beach, round the corner from magnificent Compton Bay.'

'Did Ben keep the holiday cottage after he broke up with his wife?'

'Yes, I think so—'

Jack was interrupted as the taxi driver screeched to a halt. 'Bloody birds.'

Lowri saw a brightly coloured pheasant in the middle of the road. With a loud crackling noise it ran into the hedge.

'They're everywhere at the moment,' explained Jack. 'There are farms that breed them and the shooting season has started.'

Lowri wasn't listening. The screeching brakes had startled her. For a split second she was back at the accident in France; her heart was beating fast; she clenched her fists,

'You alright?'

Lowri nodded, and the taxi driver started again.

They left the village and were back in countryside, until finally they turned off the main road and into a long narrow road. They climbed up the lane, higher and higher. She noticed dried up blackberries in the hedges, and an angry blackbird shouted from the top of the hedge. Beyond them there were sheep and cows in the fields. To the left she saw the entrance to a small car parking area.

'That's one of the paths leading on to the downs and the Longstone. There's another path opposite our village just up here on the right.'

The taxi turned off to the right.

'This is it; this is Elmstone,' said Jack. Lowri could feel his excitement, like a child arriving at their holiday home. The village consisted mainly of old houses named after their original purpose: the dairy, the farmhouse, the vicarage, the bake house. All these places seemed now to be homes. There was a small church, a pub, and a café. Finally they turned into a small close, and there was Jack's house, 'the Old School House'. As Jack paid for the taxi, Lowri looked at a neat stone building which formed a kind of L shape. The stone was grey, the window frames painted white; ivy grew over some of the walls.

'It's beautiful.'

'It was the school and school house which they combined. The school bit is rather dark. I don't think they believed in children getting distracted by looking out of the windows.'

As Lowri got out of the taxi her first inclination was to pull her coat around herself: the wind was fresh and cold. The beech trees had yellow lichen growing on them. Jack pointed to it. 'Good air here.'

Beside the front door she had noticed a sign hanging off a nail attached to the wall. She expected it to say 'The

Old School House' but to her surprise it said 'Holly's House'.

Jack saw her look at it. 'Sorry, I'd stopped noticing that. We'd better get a new one saying 'Lowri's house',' he laughed nervously.

As he pushed opened the door; she saw a pile of post on the mat. The hallway was large and square with rooms off it; the stairs started in the centre and wound round to the landing. At the top of the first flight of stairs there was a large oil painting signed by Jack. A girl wore a simple long white dress, had white alabaster skin, blonde hair in ringlets flying in the wind. Lowri recognised the pose was like that of the woman in 'the birth of Venus'.

'You've signed it.'

Jack blushed. 'I painted it years ago but I am very proud of it.'

'It's very good - the woman?' Lowri walked up the stairs to look at it more closely.

Jack came up and stood besides her. 'It's Carina. As soon as I met her when Ken brought her here I knew she's be the perfect model for this painting, it took me months. She was pregnant but I didn't paint that in. Towards the end of working on it Holly left me, I think painting this kept me sane.'

'So is Carina really this beautiful, is she naturally blonde?'

'Yes she was perfect.'

'Glad she kept her clothes on.'

He laughed.

'Why do you have the painting here? Didn't she want it?'

'She asked me if I would like to keep it, I do love it, and it is a good place to hang it.'

Lowri started to walk back down the stairs. On a small table in the hallway stood a replica of the statue of Michelangelo's David. Lying next to it was a note.

Lowri picked it up and read it out: 'Popped in to put a few things right, Carina x.'

'Carina as in the painting?'

'She keeps an eye on things. An old house like this needs airing and heating.'

'So what does she do? You know, as a job?'

'Runs the manor where she lives with her husband Ken, and helps Heather at the café.'

'Good gracious. A manor? Really?'

'Yes. Elmstone Manor.'

'Where is it?'

'From here, you walk out the village, cross the road and up to the Longstone and then behind that is a path down through some woods. That leads you down to a gate into the manor gardens.'

Lowri went into the kitchen. Jack followed her. Everything was gleaming. Her eyes went to the back door. 'There's a cat flap.'

'I'd forgotten. The owners before us had put it in. We never got round to taking it out.'

'Fizzy will be pleased.'

'Don't let her go bringing mice and rats into the house.'

'We'll have to shut the kitchen door: that way they will be contained.'

'I'd forgotten the joys of having animals in the house.'

In the fridge she found milk and butter, bread in the bread bin, even a casserole (labelled 'pheasant') waiting to be heated up, and a perfect Victoria sandwich in the cake box.

'Carina has thought of everything,' said Jack.

Lowri left the kitchen and went into a bright sunny room at the front of the house. It felt lived in. There were yellow chrysantheMums in a vase, and no dust on the surfaces. On the walls there were a number of good renaissance prints, images of perfect beauty everywhere.

Jack put his hand on the radiator and glanced over at the grate. 'Gosh, she's even set the fire for us.'

'Isn't it a bit odd Carina coming in doing all this?'

'Not really.'

'She has a key then?'

Jack shrugged. 'A few people have.' He looked around the room. 'It's quite cosy, isn't it?'

There was a knock at the front door. Lowri heard it open.

'Ello,' a warm, seductive voice called.

'Ah Carina. Come on in,' shouted Jack unnecessarily as Carina pushed open the living room door. Lowri gasped. She had assumed that the painting had exaggerated the woman's beauty, but it was as if the painting had come to life. Jack said he had painted it when he was with Holly. That must be about ten years ago, yet the woman hadn't aged at all. She was wearing a Barbour, tight black cords, and Hunter wellies. By her side was a black Labrador who followed her and sat obediently at her side.

'Jack,' Carina said. She walked over to Jack, and kissed him on both cheeks. Her voice caressed his name. The Italian accent reminded Lowri of a soft Welsh melodic voice, but Carina played with every sound. She turned to Lowri.

'Ah, Lowri,' said Carina. Her eyes swept over her. 'It is lovely to finally meet you.'

'Nice to meet you too.'

'I am so sorry about your accident.' Carina's glance touched her scars. 'We 'ave all been so worried. We are all so fond of Jack and know how anxious he has been.'

'That's kind of you.'

'We can all get to know you now, yes?'

Her words were warm.

'Of course.'

'You are so brave. I think I would be hiding away.'

Lowri bristled slightly. 'I have no option–'

'Of course not, scusa.'

'Thank you for the casserole,' said Jack.

'My Ken went shooting. I was making a casserole, and it was no trouble to make two. I know how much you like pheasant Jack.' She threw him a glowing smile, then turned to Lowri. 'Many times, he comes for roast dinner after church with me and Ken. Then of course he can continue his painting.' Carina smiled. 'It is a very ambitious project. I am sure he has told you about it.'

'Yes, of course'

'The fresco is in the drawing room. It will be magnificent.'

'It is a mammoth project,' said Jack, smiling. 'I did point out to Carina that Michelangelo had a team of a dozen artist's helping him.'

'But you are only doing one wall; they did all the walls, the ceiling. If you concentrated better you would be further along.'

'I told you the drawings are done. We'll get back to it soon.'

'This must be expensive?' asked Lowri.

'It is, but Ken will be 'appy with whatever I do,' said Carina, tossing her head in the air. She looked at Lowri. 'I am very lucky. I have a wonderful husband. I am afraid,

90

though, for Ken horses will always come first. Now Jack, he understands the need for beauty and culture.'

'I saw the painting Jack did of you–'

Carina put her head to one side. 'He is a magnificent painter. I have never seen any paintings of you. I expect they are all over in your real home.'

'No,' said Lowri. 'Jack has never painted me.'

'I am surprised. Jack, you must do that soon.'

Jack nervously smiled. 'Carina was saying she would help me collect the pets.'

'Oh, thank you.'

'Carina is so good with animals. I mean, look at her dog. Cassie would be jumping up, barking'.

'Cassie is a cocker spaniel. It's the way they are.'

Carina gave a smug smile. 'Of course. Right, well I'll leave you to settle in. I hope you'll feel very welcome here.' Jack followed her to the door.

'Thanks Carina,' Lowri heard Jack say.

Lowri could hear her lower her voice. 'It must very difficult for her. I didn't realise she was so badly scarred.'

Lowri listened to Carina's low, intimate voice. She told herself it was probably how she spoke to all men, particularly attractive men like Jack.

'Shall I take your bag upstairs?' asked Jack after Carina had left. She followed him up.

Jack pushed open an old oak door. Lowri looked into a room with a double bed, and a large window looking out on to the garden. In the distance she could make out a grey strip of sea. The room was bare of personal things, like a comfy guesthouse room.

'I thought you'd like this room,' he said. Lowri saw him go over to check the wardrobe and the drawers, wondering why he was doing it, but all he said was, 'My room is down the hallway. I have an ensuite, so you have the bathroom to yourself. There are four bedrooms altogether.'

Lowri, of course, had known they would have separate rooms, but she couldn't help a pang of sadness. It seemed a rather sad, lonely room.

Later that night when they went to bed and Jack was about to retreat to his room they said their goodnights on the landing like guests in a hotel. Lowri found herself dreading going into her room, alone. Then she reprimanded herself: just because it was strange, different, it didn't mean there was anything wrong with it. It was simply a matter of adjusting, being mature about what they had arranged.

This way there would be no drama, a steady life that people out there understood. She wasn't alone: she had a home and what to so many people must appear a pretty perfect life.

Chapter Ten

Heather woke early the next morning; it was still very dark. She left Lee asleep in bed, went downstairs, made coffee and logged onto her laptop.

An hour later, Lee came down. Despite the hours he worked he always looked bright and together. This morning he was in jeans and T shirt, his long fair hair tied back.

'You're up early,' he said.

'Just writing.'

'Again?'

Quickly, Heather shut down her computer. 'Finished now. I thought I'd pop down to Jack's, take a cake. I don't want to stop, but it seems friendly.'

'Which cake have you made?'

'The chocolate.'

'Good, she'll like that.'

'Why are you up early anyway? You didn't get in until past two.'

'We're a chef down today.'

'What about breakfast?'

'I'll eat there. You got a busy day?'

'Usual.'

'OK. See you later.'

As Heather left the house to go to work the sun, a ball of white, spread across the ice grey sky. Heather loved the fact that every day here nature gave new gifts for her. Today the distant hills were grey green, and a low mist hung over the fields. Enormous spider webs spread across the bushes. Crows competed with the cracking sounds of pheasants. Swallows sat on the telephone wires, practising their flights for the long migration ahead. Whatever the future held she knew that, unlike Holly and Rosemary, she could never leave.

She rang the doorbell, waited. A bleary eyed Jack came to the door. 'Hi Jack, I'm so sorry to come this early.'

'It's good to see you. Come on in.'

'I just brought a cake for Lowri. I'm not staying–'

'You must come in.'

'No, really. I guess she's asleep?'

'No. It'd be good for Lowri to meet some people. I'll be getting her dog Cassie soon, so that might help her get out a bit.'

Feeling kidnapped, Heather followed him, and they started to walk up the stairs together.

'Lee out surfing?'

'Not this morning. He's got an early start at work. He was out yesterday though. Why go out after the summer is beyond me, although he tells me the surf in the winter is much better. He's got all this gear, the right wetsuit, hat and things but I still think he's mad.'

'The waves at Compton are fantastic at the moment. I'd love to get down to paint them but Carina keeps me working at the manor.' Jack stopped and knocked on a door. 'This is Lowri's room.'

Heather vaguely registered the 'Lowri's' rather than 'our' room. Jack opened the bedroom door.

'Lowri, you have a visitor. This is Heather.'

Lowri appeared to have been engrossed in a book but as soon as she saw Heather she lay the book down and smiled at her. Heather, trying to hide her shock as she took in the scars and the lopsided smile, smiled back. She noticed that despite being in bed Lowri had already put on her make up and her hair was drawn forward to mask her cheek, but still the stitches, redness and bruising showed like graffiti across her face. Heather knew Lowri must be in

94

her thirties, but she reminded her of Poppy when she'd been off from school ill and allowed to go to her mother's bed.

'Sorry to bother you. Jack told me to come up–' she said, holding out the cake.

'Thank you. Gosh, that looks lovely,' said Lowri, taking it.

'I'm very sorry about your accident but I'm glad you've come here to stay.' Heather glanced out at the grey cold day. 'Not the best time of year for the island. Everything is packing up for the winter, and I'm afraid we don't often get snow.'

'I can't say I'm too keen on it anyway. We used to get it where I grew up in the valleys.'

'Ah, you're Welsh. Do you have family still there?'

'Just my aunt, my mother's sister. My parents have both died. Her brother, my uncle, lives in the States somewhere. I've never met him.' Lowri pointed to the watercolour she had put up. 'That's Brecon; we used to go there for trips when I was little.'

'Where in Wales are you from?'

'Merthyr Tydfil, a town in the Welsh valleys. So, Jack tells me you run the café?'

Heather sat on the edge of the bed.

'That's right.'

'Carina works with you, doesn't she? She worked hard getting the house ready for us.'

'Did she cook for you?'

'She made us a casserole. It was delicious, and her cake was amazing.'

'She breaks the rule that you can't trust a thin cook. She's brilliant.'

'She's very pretty as well, isn't she?'

'Gosh, yes. Stunning. No-one could believe it when she came back here with Ken, she is so, um exotic for our village.'

'How did Ken meet her?'

Heather smiled 'Carina doesn't talk about home much but I got the full story out of Ken. Her family are not well off. Her father died years ago. Carina was acting as a guide in a kind of Renaissance stately home. They got talking; he showed her pictures of the manor. She was very excited to meet someone who actually lived in such a place. They went out for a drink, fell in love, and now she is here, living her dream.'

'A real-life fairytale.'

'It is.'

'So has the manor been in Ken's family for generations?'

'No. His father was from Ireland, where he made his fortune. He'd come here on holiday, loved it, then he saw the manor. It was in a bad way. He bought it, I think, as an investment. He had some work done on it. Anyway, when he died he left it to Ken. He had come over to sort out selling it. While he was here he met Jane, who was local. I think he'd have loved to sell it and move back to Ireland, but her family were here and so they stayed. When she died and before he could move, he met Carina who loves the manor, so he is still here.'

'Wow. Quite a story, and how exciting for Carina.'

'Some people have it all, don't they? Look at me: I need to lose at least three stone. The doctor said that my blood pressure is too high. I should probably wear some make-up, get a hair cut. I used to go swimming. I was in squads and things as a kid, but I don't have the time now. I'm lucky Lee, my husband, doesn't seem to mind.'

'Good'

'I guess so. I've two sisters. They got the looks. Holly of course you know about.'

'I've only seen a few pictures of Holly. She's dark like you.'

'Yes, prettier though. She was the clever, petite one.'

'And you have another sister?' Heather noticed Lowri's voice was shaking. She wondered if she was feeling unwell.

'That's Rosemary, my other sister. She's over in Southampton. She has really curly hair. She's the arty one, a photographer. Married to Simon. He's a doctor, something to do with bones.'

'Is your sister – um – happy? I mean, it can't be easy being married to such a busy man.'

Heather was slightly taken aback by the odd question. 'They have their ups and downs I guess. He's been working away again recently, France I think. So, no. It's not always easy.'

Lowri seemed flustered. 'It must be even harder for her being ill–'

Heather was confused. 'She's not ill as far as I know.' Then she looked searchingly at Lowri. 'You were in Southampton. Do you know them somehow?'

'Oh, no. Never met them.' Lowri reached out to a glass of water, her hand shaking. She sipped carefully.

Heather looked around the room. 'Didn't Jack say you had a dog?'

Lowri nodded. 'A cocker spaniel, Cassie, and a cat, Fizzy.'

'Both will love it here. There are so many fantastic walks for the dogs. Biddy, my Dalmatian, she lives with my husband's family now. She loves it there on the farm and gets company all day. I still get to see her, but I felt it was selfish to keep her from such a good life.'

97

'Gosh. I can't imagine giving up Cassie, but then I suppose you were trying to do the right thing for Biddy?'

'Exactly. I still go out with the dog walkers when I can. You ought to go. They meet about half seven at the Longstone up on the downs each morning.'

Jack came in. 'I'm going out for a cycle soon. Let yourself out, Heather.' He turned to Lowri. 'Will you be alright? I won't be long.'

'I'll be fine.'

Jack came over to her, glanced at Heather, then to Lowri's surprise, kissed her lightly on the forehead saying, 'See you later.'

As he left, Heather said, 'It's so lovely to see Jack and you together. True love, eh?'

Lowri replied with a smile.

'This house deserves to be a proper family home. I think it's wonderful the way Jack has stuck by you. He'll look after you, I'm sure. So, how are you feeling now?'

'Getting better, thanks. The doctors kept telling me how lucky I am.' Heather took in the fleeting smile but also saw sadness in her eyes.

'You've been through a lot. It'll take time. It must all still hurt.'

'I know I'm lucky to be alive, but you're right. It does all hurt, and I'm so scared of how I'm going to live with the scars. I mean, it's only looks, but all the same, I don't want people to stare at me.'

To Heather's surprise, she saw tears running down Lowri's cheeks.

'It's been such a shock for you.'

'It's a lot to come to terms with.'

'You need time to heal on the inside as well as the outside.'

'I think so.'

There was an awkward silence. Then Heather said in an overly bright voice, 'My daughter Poppy is getting married next year.'

'That's exciting.'

'Yes, she met this boy Alistair when he was over here for Cowes Week. His father owns some kind of yachting business. She was waitressing. She was a student over at the university at the time. Anyway, she left and went to live with Alistair, although she comes home quite a lot. Poppy and Alistair are actually thinking of living over here. His father wants to open some kind of business in Cowes, so I might have Poppy living here.'

'That would be lovely for you.'

'Yes, I'm lucky.'

'Great for you and her Dad.'

'Actually, Lee is her stepdad. I brought her up on my own until she was about twelve, so we're very close.'

'My Mum brought me up. She found it difficult sometimes I think.'

Heather glanced over at the photographs.

'You said your Mum brought you up. Where was your Dad?'

'He died when my mother was pregnant.'

'Oh, how sad. He looks a lovely man. It must have been hard on your mother, losing him. Were they married?'

'Of course.'

Heather smiled. 'More than me then. Poppy's father was a nice enough chap, but very young. I've always gone for younger men! Anyway, it would never have worked.'

'Didn't your parents want you to get married?'

'Not really. Anyway, Rob, that was his name, he'd always wanted to go abroad to live. My dream was to run the café one day. I could never live anywhere other that the island.'

'Was that difficult? You know, here in the village. Did people mind you being a single mother?'

'No, everyone was very supportive.'

'And was Poppy OK?'

'Of course, and anyway, people are so much more accepting of different types of family now, aren't they? Thank God.'

'So you never regretted having Poppy?'

Heather sat back. There was an intensity about Lowri's questions: somewhere along the way the conversation had taken a serious turn.

'No, not for one minute. Funny, it never crossed my mind not to keep her. I know that's not the right thing for everyone, but it was for me.'

'And Lee, how did he find taking on a child?'

'Poppy was twelve years old when we met, so that was fun! Not long before I got together with Lee she'd said to me that if I ever brought home a man she would, quote, 'make his life a living hell'. Some friend in school had been telling her how much she hated her stepfather. So it was a rocky start, but then they found they both loved surfing. They sort of bonded over that. I feel very lucky.'

'It all worked out then?'

'I was lucky. So, the other picture there, is that your Mum?

'Yes. I lost her about three years ago. Seems longer in some ways.'

'It must have been hard. I think you get very close when it's the two of you.'

Lowri shrugged. 'Maybe. So, you've taken on the café. Do you enjoy it?'

'Of course. It belonged to my parents. It's my home, and I love baking.'

'Your life sounds perfect.'

'I wouldn't go that far, but I do love my family.'

Lowri sat forward. 'Can I tell you something? Only a few people know–'

Heather sat closer. 'Of course. What is it?'

'I'm pregnant.'

Heather looked shocked. Her eyes widened.

'Congratulations. Jack must be delighted.'

'He is.'

'When is your baby due?'

'May sometime. We'll get dates when we have the next ultrasound.'

'Right.' Heather mentally worked out the dates. Surely they'd been separated? As if reading her mind, Lowri said, 'Our separation wasn't set in stone.'

Heather laughed. 'Fair enough. So, how are you? Have you been very sick?'

'No, not at all. Breasts hurt, though.'

'God, I had all that with Poppy, but it's worth it in the end. Oh, I'll have to get knitting. I know babies don't wear knitted things now much, but I always make this one pattern. It's like a cardigan with a hood. It can be useful. A spring baby, yes, it could be just right. So, I guess Jack's parents are over the moon? Holly always felt under pressure to have children, but I think she had a few problems; she would never tell me about them. Still, now it's happening; they must be so excited. It's their dream to have a little version of Jack. You have to have a boy, you realise that?'

'I'll try.'

'Doesn't Jack's Mum have bad rheumatism, or is it arthritis?'

'Rheumatoid arthritis. Had it for years. His Dad is very caring to her.'

'Not easy in other ways, though, Holly said.'

'Not always.'

'He writes in some religious paper about family values and things. They were always nagging Jack to start a family. It drove Holly nuts.'

'You know a lot about him. I haven't met them much. Jack prefers to visit them on his own. Obviously, they were at our wedding but his Dad didn't say much. Jack said he didn't really approve of a second marriage. He was very upset that Jack got divorced.'

'I can imagine. We didn't have a very easy introduction. You know, when Jack and Holly got married, Poppy was very young, but she was very excited to be a bridesmaid. Jack asked me to pretend I had a husband tucked away somewhere. I was really upset about it. I was proud of me and Poppy. Anyway, I did it for Jack and Holly.'

Heather sat back. 'You know, we've been planning a party for Halloween. It's a few weeks before. We find we get more people than on the actual night. Kids like to do all that trick or treating and things, don't they? I do hope you and Jack will come. It's actually next Saturday.'

'It's very kind of you to invite us, but I don't think so. To be honest–'

'Why?'

'Nothing.'

'What, Lowri?'

'I just can't face people.'

'That's nonsense.'

'You don't see the way people look.'

'Jack will look after you. Please come. You'll see, people will be much nicer than you think.'

'I don't need nice, but then I don't know what I need. I'm not used to pity.'

Heather smiled gently. 'I expect you're used to people admiring you–'

'Why on earth do you say that?'

'You are so small and petite.'

'People used to tease me about being so short when I was younger. I was also very skinny. You can imagine the names. What with that, and being the class geek– Still, I never let them see I minded, pretended it was funny. Mum said that was the best way to be.'

'Children can be a bit mean. How the kids nowadays manage with all the social media stuff I don't know. It's a lot harder for them. You hear of young teenagers wanting Botox and things. It's terrible.'

'I was watching these girls at the ferry taking selfies. They were so self-conscious. It's really sad, but you don't realise at that age.'

'It's true. How many of us look at pictures of ourselves in our teens and wish we looked like that now?'

'I certainly do now. I do forget, you know, about the scars. Then I look in the mirror. It still shocks me.'

'The one side of your face is hardly marked, actually.'

'I'm like two people, aren't I? Which one am I now?'

'What is it they say? Don't let your scars define you,' said Heather. Even as she said it the words sounded trite.

'You sound like one of those quotes on Twitter.'

'Sorry.' Heather laughed and stood up. 'I have to go off to work. When you feel up to it, try to come dog walking. Everyone will be so busy making a fuss of your dog they won't be looking at you.'

'Jack showed me where the Longstone is. I'll think about it. Thanks for coming. You've cheered me up.'

'Good. Now, remember. I expect to see you at the party.'

Heather went downstairs and met Jack, changed into cycling gear and doing stretches. 'We're doing the usual pre-Halloween party. Make sure you bring Lowri.'

'I don't think she'll want to come.'

'You have to encourage her. She can't hide away.'

'I know, but I can understand her reluctance to go out.'

'You have to help her, Jack.'

'OK, OK. I'll do my best.'

'Look after your wife–'

'Does Lee ever tell you, you can be very bossy?' said Jack, grinning.

'All the time, but I'm right. Look after Lowri. She seems very young.'

'She's thirty five, not a child.'

'But vulnerable. She told me you're expecting a baby.'

Jack looked abashed. 'Yes.'

'Congratulations. It's exciting.'

'Of course. My parents are delighted.' His voice sounded light, but Heather saw the lines of stress on Jack's forehead.

'Are you alright Jack?'

'Of course. Why shouldn't I be? Everything is working out, isn't it?'

'It seems to be.' Heather looked at him, but it was clear he wasn't going to say anymore. 'I'll be off then. Take care.'

As she walked away Heather was thoughtful. Something was wrong. She couldn't work out what, but something back there didn't add up.

Chapter Eleven

The next day as Lowri got dressed she realised her skinny jeans were a bit tight: soon she would have to think of ordering some maternity things. It was a bit of a shock. She knew of some woman who started wearing maternity wear the day they found out they were pregnant. She wasn't so sure. It struck her that nine months was a long time: maybe you'd get fed up with wearing the same things all the time. Of more interest to her was the incredible range of equipment. People had said when she took her pets around that it was like taking things for a baby. Well, they were wrong. It was utterly confusing. So many different kinds of prams, cots, nursery furniture, special baths and car seats. It was endless, but it was fun looking through them all.

Lowri had received two appointments from the hospital: one to remove the final stitches and one for her ultrasound. Jack was excited about the ultrasound.

'It will be good to see the baby,' he said. 'Make it all more real. I'm going over to Southampton tomorrow. I'll bring your car back with me.'

'Thanks.'

'It's too much to be getting taxis all the time.'

Lowri went upstairs, found her laptop, and got on with her work. Later, she received an email from Aneta in her Polish group. She was very sorry Lowri would not be with them. There were some members now though whose English was very good, so she was sure the group would continue. Lowri was pleased, but she realised that maybe now she would miss them more than they missed her. It was all well and good doing all the translation online, but it was the people, the spoken language that she missed.

Her hospital appointment came before the appointment for the ultrasound. Jack said he would take her. As they approached the hospital Lowri realised how nervous she felt. She had not thought about the accident that much but the night before she had had some terrible nightmares. This morning she had been very sick and she didn't think it was the pregnancy. Jack drove her there but didn't go in with her.

'You're better off on your own,' he said although, of course, she wasn't.

She walked through the white corridors. How come all hospitals smell and feel the same? She found herself wondering if Simon was there: it wasn't Monday, but maybe he had come over? This added to her nerves, and at one point she had to rush to a toilet to be sick again. Finally, she got herself to the doctor, went into a polite patient role, and behaved relatively normally.

The doctor removed all the final stitches, and then sat down with her. 'Now,' he said, 'you must wait for your body to heal itself. You of course are also pregnant, and you must take care of yourself. I would like to see you in three months.'

'But how soon can I have work done?'

'I think in France they said to wait some time, didn't they? I agree with that. In any case you will want to wait until the baby is born.'

She fiddled with the hem of her jumper. 'It is awful, looking like this. I feel different. How do I get back to being myself again?"

The doctor looked at her kindly. 'I know it sounds hard, but you can't go back to who you were. You've changed.'

'But I don't want to—'

'I know, but it's happened. Look, I'm not one of these 'every cloud has a silver lining' people. I have seen too much to be like that. I see a lot of people go through what you have gone through; many a lot worse.'

'Don't tell me I've been lucky.'

'No. I won't say that, but the people who cope best are the people who see it as a new start.'

'But I don't think people will let me. They stare, say things.'

'People can be cruel. I think it's fear of the unknown. But you can't hide away for the rest of your life. You, like them, have to find ways to cope.'

'I can't make people not notice.'

'Of course not but, if you can hold yourself with confidence, they will treat you differently. The more confident you are, the more positive they will be back.'

He saw her looking away. 'I don't think you believe me, do you? We have a group here, meets monthly. You could come to that.'

'I don't know–'

'Look. I will give you some leaflets. Go online. There are some great support groups out there. You will cope with this, Lowri. I'm sure of it.'

She stood up, tried to smile, glanced at a mirror. For the first time she saw that only one half of her face seemed to smile, and even that part she knew was fake.

'If you get down,' said the doctor, 'you must talk to your GP. OK?'

'OK.'

'And you are pregnant. Congratulations. It will be good for you, give you something else to concentrate on. Good luck.'

Lowri left the room and walked through the sterile, white corridors, where the pictures and poems that hung on

107

the walls failed in their job of distracting or cheering her up. Outside, she met the usual group of smokers. She felt like she wouldn't mind joining them, but went over to the car where Jack was waiting.

They drove in silence, it was cold out, and people were wrapped up, looking down at the pavements. Lowri was glad when they got back to the village and she could get into the house.

'I'm going to pack,' Jack said.

'What do you mean?'

'I have lectures for the next two days. I'll stay over there. I'm going to get the Red Jet and then drive the animals back in your car.'

'Oh, yes. Thank you.'

'That will be on Friday.'

'I thought Carina was going to help.'

'She's going to go over on the Red Jet and I'll pick her up. We'll travel back together on the car ferry.'

'I'll send texts to Zoe to remind her.'

'Good.'

'Make sure you take some decent bottles of wine for her. She's had them for weeks.'

'Of course,' Jack paused. 'We have the party at Heather's café on Saturday.'

'Oh, I don't think–'

'You have to come. People keep asking me how you are, and it looks like I'm hiding you away.'

Lowri looked over at the paintings, the beautiful faces, smooth and untouched.

'You are going to have to get used to going out, Lowri. Remember, it's not just you that you have to think about now. My Mum has been telling all her friends. See, it's good we are doing this for them, isn't it?'

She smiled back, and went into the study where she now kept her laptop. It was a lovely room and she found it a good place to work. There was an old fashioned leather table in there. Lowri placed her laptop on it and sat down. She looked around the desk, saw Jack's laptop and the printer, but next to it was beautiful embossed printer paper, and a small box of sealing wax and seal. It was so typical of Jack to have such things, his rebellion against technology.

After about an hour Lowri's mind wandered and she thought about what she would do if she was on Facebook. For the past few years, to the frustration of her friends, she had refused to go on, but suddenly it seemed an attractive way to talk to some people without having to leave the house. Setting up the page was straightforward until she came to uploading her profile picture. Obviously, her small group of Southampton friends knew about the accident, but she didn't want to talk about it and she certainly didn't want to put pictures of herself scarred. Then she had an inspired idea. If she was very careful with her privacy settings, she could restrict her audience to more distant friends, people back in Merthyr. None of them knew about the accident. She could live life on Facebook as if the accident had never happened. Excitedly, she scrolled through her phone, found old pictures of when she and Jack had first been married. For her profile picture she found a particularly sentimental picture, and even found a frame of hearts for it.

Then she started to write about her new life on the Isle of Wight with her wonderful husband and their idyllic cottage. She decided to wait to mention the pregnancy. It wasn't difficult to find a few people she knew from Merthyr who responded to her friend requests with surprising speed. She looked at their pictures. Most were living in small new estate houses, or even back with Mam. Some had children and partners. She 'liked' their pictures and was flattered with the enthusiastic welcome she was given.

'Great to hear from you Lowri. Wow! You have the most wonderful home. You look as gorgeous, and other half looks fit.'

Lowri grinned, that was the first time any of them had called her gorgeous. After she had logged off, she looked up some of her childhood photos that she had previously scanned to her computer. One showed her flying a kite, and looking sideways at the camera. Her eyes were anxious: the smile eager to please, pleading with the world to like her. That picture must have been taken over twenty years ago and yet she knew she was still trying to smile out at the world in the same way. Still, that was normal. Everyone wants to be liked, don't they? At least now she had her Facebook page: a place she could always be smiling, a place where life was perfect.

Chapter Twelve

Friday came. Lowri awoke excited. Today, Cassie and Fizzy were coming home.

It felt a long day waiting. She tried to immerse herself in her work, and then went on to Facebook. She was busy writing about her fantastic night out at an intimate restaurant with Jack when she heard barking. Her heart leapt and she ran into the hallway. Carina was standing with Cassie on a lead, Jack carrying a cat carrier from which a loud mewing sound was coming. Cassie pulled towards her and Lowri rushed over to her, took the lead and detached it from her collar. She sat on the floor as Cassie jumped all over her and then sniffed the scars on her face. Lowri turned her face away, Cassie seemed to understand and nuzzled closer to her.

Carina looked down. 'She's pleased to see you again.'

'I've really missed her.'

'I'll just get the rest of their stuff from the car,' said Jack.

Lowri looked deep into Cassie's dark brown eyes, the black nose with flecks of grey. 'Oh, I've missed you so much.' Cassie kept very close to her, tucked her nose under her chin. The small gesture seemed the most loving and accepting thing that had happened since her accident. She wiped away a tear and hugged Cassie close. Then she heard a mewing again from the carrier, got up off the floor and went to release Fizzy. Fizzy crept out and looked suspiciously around at the room and then at Lowri. Lowri picked her up. Fizzy was a thin tortoiseshell cat. In the house she was quiet and very clean. Outside, her aim was to hunt and kill. She had decided early on in their relationship that Cassie was a waste of time and mostly ignored her.

'Hey, it's alright Fizzy. This is your new home. Wait until you see the garden. There are shrew, mice, and rats out there, and there is a cat flap for you.' Fizzy struggled. She was never one for too much fuss, and as Lowri put her down she jumped up on to a chair and looked around.

'Thank you, Carina. It's lovely to have them home.'

'Cassie enjoyed the car ferry. She did bark, though, in the pet's area. There were a lot of dogs in there.'

Lowri laughed. 'I can imagine. She likes to chat.'

'It was very different from having my Rex. He is quiet and well behaved, but Cassie seemed to want to meet everyone.'

'She expects the whole world to love her, and usually they do. Thank you for doing this.'

Carina turned to Jack. 'I hope you will be able to come and work tomorrow. All the materials are there waiting for you. It won't be too long until we open to the public in the spring. There's a lot to do.'

'I know.'

Lowri left them talking and went into the kitchen, followed by Fizzy and Cassie. She put their bowls down and saw that Fizzy looked at her bowl hungrily. Lowri had wondered about keeping Fizzy in for a few days but knew that would drive her mad. Maybe letting her out briefly now while she was hungry would be a good idea: she would want to come back for food..

'Come and see your cat flap,' she said picking Fizzy up and carrying her over to it. She pushed the flap back and forth a few times and suddenly, without warning, Fizzy dived through it. Lowri opened the back door and followed her into the garden, closely followed by Cassie. Fizzy was sitting on top of one of the fences. Cassie soon got her confidence and, nose down, tail up wagging; she was off sniffing and marking around the garden. Fizzy sat and watched her with her usual look of disdain.

After a few minutes Lowri went back inside, closely followed by Cassie. She closed the door and picked up Fizzy's bowl. Feeling rather foolish, she called through the cat flap, tapping the bowl. Luckily, Fizzy came straight away and climbed through.

'Now, remember,' Lowri said to Cassie, 'Fizzy eats first, and don't look at me like that. You know you would eat her food as well given half a chance, so you sit and wait.' She put the food down. Cassie sat waiting and Fizzy, after sniffing it carefully, ate her tea, and lapped neatly from her bowl of water. She then walked over to her bed, where she sat washing herself meticulously.

'It's your turn Cassie, but only a small amount. Your meals are all out. You'll need a walk, and then I'll feed you properly.' She put down some food for Cassie and it was gone quickly, followed by huge gulps of water, which she spilt all over the floor.

'Honestly, Cassie you should learn some table manners from Fizzy.' Lowri stroked her long black ears. Lowri saw that Fizzy was settling down to sleep. She had probably been on edge all journey and was finally settled. Fizzy may not make the fuss of Cassie, but Lowri was sure deep down that the cat had missed her and Fizzy was pleased to be back with her.

'Come on, Cassie. We'll go out in the garden, take a ball.' At the word 'ball' Cassie's tail started wagging furiously. 'You've been curled up asleep in the car, haven't you? Look at you, full of beans now.' This time Lowri put on her coat and smart trainers. It was turning to dusk outside. She could hear crows overhead flying back to their roosts for the night, but it was very quiet. It was a cold crisp evening; most people would be closing the curtains, settling down.

She walked around the garden, enjoying the quiet, and threw the ball for Cassie, which bounced over to a large wooden summerhouse-type building. She saw the lights were on inside, and went over to it. She noticed a patch of earth in the border, slightly raised. There was a cross on it but there was nothing written on it. There were windows, but they had blinds which were shut; the light just peeked through. Lowri made her way around to the door, and found it was locked. She remembered that there were some hooks with keys on just inside the kitchen door and started to make her way back to the house, just as Jack came out.

'I was thinking of going down the manor, I need to get my stuff from my studio.'

'It's locked. I was coming to find the key'

'I have it.'

They started to walk back towards the wooden building. Lowri went to follow Jack inside, but he blocked her way.

'I don't mean to be funny, but I use this as my studio and I like to keep it as my space.'

'Oh,' said Lowri, not really understanding. 'By the way, what is that cross for, did you have a pet that died?'

To her surprise Jack went red 'it's nothing, just leave it.'

Lowri left him and went back to Cassie. She could hear Jack rummaging inside, then the lights went off and he came out. 'See you later then.'

She heard Jack leave, and suddenly she wanted to get out. The house that had felt her refuge now felt like her prison. There wouldn't be many people around. It would be a good time to go. She raced back into the house, put on some more foundation and brushed her hair, checked her

114

parting was on the right side and her hair flopped as much as possible over the left side of her face. She found her red jacket and pulled up the hood, found Cassie's lead and a large torch, and left the house.

Cassie was very excited and pulled hard on the lead. Lowri could feel it hurting across her chest.

'Stop, Cassie. I can't do that.'

Cassie seemed to sense her upset and slowed her pace. She remembered the walk that Heather had told her about, and strode through the village, passing the houses, lights shining through the gaps of the curtains. Houses always look so snug in the evening, the warm lights and TVs flickering. Still, you never really knew, did you, what was going on in there?

The cold white LED street lights lit up the droplets on the pavement and she walked carefully. On the other side of the road she saw another dog walker, a man with a collie, who called out 'evening,' but carried on. She was relieved at the anonymity. The sky was dark indigo blue with tiny pin pricks of stars scattered around. A magnificent moon was glowing white. Jack was right: it would be wonderful down the beach. Once out of the village, she crossed the road. She stood at the gate. Ahead of her lay a mass of dark fields that led up to the ridge of the downs where she guessed the Longstone was. Suddenly, she felt scared and was tempted to go back to the village with its street lights and houses. However, Cassie was pulling and so she pushed open the gate and went through. Tired of being pulled by Cassie, she let her off the lead and immediately regretted it as Cassie disappeared into the darkness. She turned on her torch and was relieved to find that she could locate Cassie by the gentle tinkling sound of her dog tag.

Lowri shone the torch at her feet. The ground was uneven. She realised that the apparently practical trainers she was wearing were no replacement for walking boots. She slipped on damp grass; it was hard walking but she didn't want to go back.

It was very quiet. Even though the sea was some distance away, the wind coming in was cold, and hurt her face but she loved this feeling out here of being alone. It surprised her: she had always thought of herself as a town girl. Maybe it was the accident that made her relish the anonymity, the freedom from prying eyes. She also realised that downland, even at night, had a gentleness to it. It wasn't challenging her like mountains did. Lowri started the steep incline up the side of the downs. She stopped to catch her breath. With her damaged ribs it was a struggle. She would have to take it slowly. Occasionally she heard an owl or a sheep bleating. It was hard to know how far away anything was as the sound seemed to travel. There were a few aircraft passing that she hadn't noticed in the day, and a slight shush of traffic down on the Military Road. There was more light than she expected. With her torch she could see quite clearly where she was going.

Eventually she reached the Longstone and found to her surprise that it was actually two stones, one tall and upright, the other short and flat. The outline the taller one made against the dark sky was slightly threatening, a feeling of being in the presence of something ancient and unknown. Not far from them was an information board and she shone her torch to see what it said. She read that Longstones marked a Neolithic burial ground, that the bodies were left out for the birds and then the bones buried. Lowri looked around and shuddered, thinking of the ghosts that must inhabit the place. She looked back to the board, and continued reading that Saxons may have used this area as a meeting place and that the nearby village of Mottistone may get its name from this. People would meet to announce judgements and host debates. Somehow, standing up here alone with Cassie, the past felt more real than the present.

It was then her phone rang. Surprised that she even had signal, she took the phone out of her pocket, touched the screen, and put it straight to her ear.

'Lowri, it's me.' The sound of his voice hit her like lightning.

'Simon.'

'Can we talk?'

'I don't know.' Lowri looked around, stupidly looking for somewhere to hide.

'Where are you?'

'Walking on the downs. I'm on the Isle of Wight.'

'I heard you were there. Heather told Rosemary. She also told her you were back with Jack. Is that right?

'It is, yes. We are, um, together now.'

'It's a huge change going over there, living with him–'

'I had to do something.'

'How are you? How is the baby?'

She felt herself relent. 'I've had an appointment. They seem pleased with me. The scar is awful but I'll have to wait before having anything done. The baby appears to be developing well.'

'If you need anything, money, you know–'

'No. No, I have Jack now.'

'You said the baby is well. Did you find out who the father is?'

'I had an ultrasound. They were able to give a rough date.' She could hear him holding his breath.

'The baby is yours, Simon. Jack knows that, but he is prepared to be the father.'

'Jack knows I'm the father?' he exclaimed, the horror in his voice palpable.

'No. Just that he is not.'

'And he doesn't mind?'

'No, he's been very good about it all. We can give the baby a good life.'

'So you love Jack?'

He sounded young, like a jilted lover. She almost felt sorry for him.

'Jack has stuck by me.'

'But he loved someone else–'

'That's over. Me and Jack are together now.'

She looked ahead, back towards her home, and saw a tall totem pole-like television mast with three red eyes staring at her. Looking away, she noticed for the first time a solitary house nearby, nestled among the trees. Lights were shining through a kitchen window.

'I'm glad for you,' he said in a way that was looking for sympathy. However, before she could say anything, he said 'Marie has phoned me a few times. Of course, she has been concerned about you.'

'Tell her I am OK.'

'What about the insurance?'

'Jack knows a solicitor who will sort it all out.'

'I know you have Jack, but if you need anything from me, if you want to go privately for anything, I know the doctors at the hospital. I know who you should see.'

She could feel him pulling her back: maybe he did care, and maybe he really did love her? Was she making a mistake? Had he rung because he wanted them to be together?

'How is Rosemary?' she asked, knowing deep down that she was hoping he would say he was finally leaving her.

118

'Still not too good.' Her heart sank, and then he asked again, 'So Jack knows nothing about me?'

'Oh no. Simply that there was another man.'

She heard the sigh of relief. 'Good. It's important you never tell him. Also, I was wondering about Heather.'

'She came round with a cake and has invited me and Jack to some party. Not sure I will go, though. Why?'

'I need you to realise it's vital you don't tell her about us–'

'I wouldn't.'

'Please don't. It's really important.'

'Of course not.'

'Rosemary doesn't need to hear anything about us, not now.'

Lowri gripped her phone tightly. 'So you really phoned to tell me not to tell anyone about us?'

'Not only that. It's wonderful to hear your voice. I do miss you. You do know that?'

'Do you? You seemed pretty glad to get away in France.' Lowri was aware of a hint of hysteria creeping into her voice and it started to echo around the empty dark fields.

'I had to. It was terrible; heart breaking. But it's just not to be, not now. It might be as well if you were to delete my number.'

The final link, broken. 'OK.'

'I'd better go then. Take care. You are so special, and I never deserved you.'

And there it was again: he had neatly put her into the past; this time, she guessed, for good. The line went dead. Lowri looked down at her phone, found her address book; her thumb hovered over the delete key: maybe later.

Oblivious to her trauma Cassie had continued to run around. Lowri collapsed on to the short stone, buried her head in her hands and wept. This really was the end. She hadn't realised until this moment that there had been a thin thread of hope that one day, somehow, despite all he had done, she and Simon would be back together, living their dream in France. She felt sad, bereaved, and alone.

The wind whistled and the dark clouds seemed to be joining up, creating blackness.

'What's up? You OK?' The voice came from nowhere. Lowri wiped her face with her hands and shone her torch ahead. They shone on a pair of enormous brown boots and camouflage trousers. The man who had spoken shone his torch on his own face, and this alarmed her even more. He was thickset, had a shaved head, an earring, and a tattoo on his neck, which she could see because he only appeared to be wearing a round-necked jumper.

Panicking, she stood up and looked around for Cassie. This was madness: what was she doing up here in the dark on her own?

'Are you alright?' The man repeated.

'Fine,' she said, and started to walk away. It wasn't easy. The grass was slippery and Cassie was nowhere to be seen. Then she heard a loud barking, knew it wasn't Cassie, and shone her torch to see a small terrier. Cassie suddenly appeared. The dogs wagged and sniffed, and then started to play noisily.

'Come on, Cassie. It's time to go,' she shouted, but was ignored.

'Your dog's recall is as good as mine's,' said the man, laughing.

'Actually, she's normally very good,' said Lowri, too offended to remember her fear.

'You're lucky.'

The man started to walk away from her. She called Cassie again but she continued to play.

'Can you call your dog?' she asked.

'Why?'

'Because if you have your dog, mine will come to me.'

'Let them play.'

'I want to go.'

'Your dog doesn't.'

Lowri scowled. Why were all men so useless?

'I do.'

Her eyes were starting to acclimatise to the light, and she could make the man and dogs out more easily.

The man gave her a smile and called his dog, which annoyingly came the first time he called her name. Cassie, however, went charging off down the path behind the stones into the woods'

'She's smelt something. Could be a pheasant.' The man said.

'But I want to go home,' Lowri said and, to her embarrassment, burst into tears.

'She'll come back. Don't panic. Where do you live?'

Lowri heard an owl hooting in the trees behind her.

'I have a husband. He'll come and look for me any minute now.'

'Good. You shouldn't be out here on your own.'

Lowri wondered if he was threatening her, but then he said, 'I'm Dave. Work in the pottery here. It's in the cafe.'

Lowri was sceptical. He didn't look like any artist she'd met. 'I know Heather. She never mentioned a pottery.'

He laughed. 'You think I'm making it up? I'm this deluded man who roams the downs thinking he is a potter in a café?'

That was actually exactly what Lowri was thinking, but she said, 'Of course not.'

'Good,' he said, laughing. 'I'm renting that house.' He shone his torch towards the isolated house.

'You live there on your own?' She paused. Why had she asked that?

'I do the mad old hermit with his dog.'

Again she was thrown by him. She wanted to get away, and she looked around for Cassie, but she was nowhere to be seen. Should she go down the path to look for her? But wouldn't that make her more vulnerable to this odd man?

'Are you on holiday in one of Heather's cottages? I know most of the dogs that are walked up here.'

Lowri looked around fretfully, and then heard a noise in the bushes behind the stones. She shone her torch, and was relieved to see Cassie.

'Good, she's back.' Lowri called Cassie, but she skirted around the edge of the bush and, as soon as Lowri approached her, Cassie ran off, just out of reach. She knew there was no point in carrying on this humiliating charade. She had done it too many times when Cassie had a ball. The only way to get Cassie to come was to ignore her. Dave came over.

'She doesn't want to come home with you.'

'Obviously,' she said.

'So, are you on holiday?'

'No. I've come to live in my husband's house.'

'Oh. Are you Lowri, Jack's new wife?'

She bristled at the 'new wife'.

'Weren't you in an accident?'

She pulled her hood closer around her head, raised her hand to her cheek. 'Yes, that's me. The woman in the accident.'

'I'm surprised you are up and about.'

'Just because I look like this doesn't mean I have to stay locked away.'

'I don't know what you mean. I can't see your face properly.'

'Oh, sorry.'

A sharp wind caught her breath, and Cassie came over to her. Quickly she put her back on the lead.

'I think we'd better go,' she said.

'Shall I walk you down?'

She didn't want this weird man knowing where she lived. 'No, thank you.'

'Sure? Watch out for cow pats. The farmer has only just moved the cows.'

Without speaking, Lowri pulled Cassie, who had her nose firmly to the ground and walked as quickly as she could down the hill.

Chapter Thirteen

The next morning, Lowri went downstairs weary after the walk the night before, and from re-running the conversation with Simon over and over in her head. It was wonderful to be greeted by Cassie, who had slept on her own bed in the living room.

'Good girl,' said Lowri. She went into the kitchen and looked out of the window. Fizzy was sitting on her fence again. Seeing Lowri, the cat jumped down and rushed to the cat flap. Lowri looked around the floor. Thankfully there were no dead mice. At which point she heard mewing. Fizzy jumped through the cat flap and rubbed against Lowri's legs.

'Good night out?'

Fizzy ate her breakfast, then started to wash herself on her bed.

'Right, Cassie. I guess you are going to need a walk.'

Lowri ran upstairs, and looked out of the window again. It was cold but dry.

Glancing over at the mirror, she scowled at her face. It looked no better. The scarring was just as red. Funny, when she hadn't looked for a few hours she started to forget: damn mirror. She threw a jumper over it. She thought how she would have sat there for hours putting on make up, checking every bit of her face. Now she couldn't bear to look at it.

She pulled on her jeans, realising she could still do them up: a few more days without having to wear those maternity trousers. She sat on the edge of the bed; she was always tired lately. At least her breasts had stopped being sore; she could lie on her stomach again now. Feeling pretty miserable, she pulled a brush through her hair,

124

brushing it forwards as much as possible, then went downstairs.

'Come on, Cassie,' she said. 'At least you don't give a damn how I look.'

They went out and started to climb up to the downs. In the distance she saw Heather, who waved to her, but she turned and went down another path. When Lowri returned she spent the day working. She liked the feeling of isolation in the study, and immersed herself in her work

That evening it was the Halloween party.

'I can't go,' she said to Jack. 'I'm tired and I look a wreck.'

'You have to. Everyone wants to meet you. Come on. We can show them all that we are really back together.'

'But I don't feel well.'

'Please. We should go together.'

'I haven't anything to wear. It's fancy dress, isn't it?'

'Not too much. Only the children, I think. It's a fireworks party as well, so people will be wearing coats outside. Don't worry about it. Just come.' Lowri went upstairs to the bathroom and Jack called up to her,

'Can you bring me down my phone? It's next to my bed.'

Lowri went into what she now thought of as his room. It was a strange feeling. She felt like she was intruding. The room was very neat and tidy. She picked up the book sitting on the bedside table. She recognised the Man Booker prize winner, Marlon James' book. Jack had already read the shortlist. He was reading this again, determined to look well read in front of the English department at university. She picked it up, flicked through it, then placed it on his pillow. Maybe he would notice it, realise she had done that, and think about her. She picked up his phone and went downstairs.

'We'll need torches. No moon out tonight,' said Jack.

They walked through the village to the café. The air was clear, crisp and cold. Only a few stars twinkled. The café was set back. The holiday cottages were to one side, and the café and studio were in a separate building. Lowri could see smokers outside, and people shouting and laughing. She was desperate to turn and leave. However, Jack grabbed her hand and they made their way in.

It was warm inside. As she went to take her coat off, she realised Jack was helping her. He lay her coat and bag on the chair and put his arm around her shoulders. She looked around nervously, waiting for the stares, but found most people were either too busy talking to friends or were smiling at Jack.

'Hi Jack,' called a few. Lowri realised for the first time how much Jack was a part of this close-knit community. Most of the people here must have known Holly, maybe went to school with her. However, as they glanced from Jack to her the smiles seemed friendly enough. Although she was offered a glass of warm punch, she took orange juice and then Heather came over to them.

'Well done. So pleased you made it.'

Lowri looked down. 'The stone flooring is beautiful. What a lovely place.'

'Thanks. It's not changed that much since my parents owned it. We extended out that way and then added the studio down there where Dave works.'

'Oh, I met him up on the downs. He's a bit, um, strange.'

'I know he seems a bit rough around the edges, but he's a nice chap and really talented.'

'Is he?'

126

'Some of his one-off pieces are over on display.'

Lowri glanced over. She looked at a large bowl. The blues and greens seemed to come alive under the light. It was the kind of thing that seemed to grab you and keep you looking at it.

'He works in porcelain, which apparently is harder to work with, but he says he likes the finish. He also makes his own glazes, gets some startling results,' said Heather. 'He gets his inspiration from the sea. You can see he has carved fish and shells into some of the smaller pots. Very clever.'

Carina came over.

'Hi Lowri. Good to see you again. How are Cassie and Fizzy?'

'Really good. I took Cassie up to the Longstone last night.'

'You are brave to go up at night. The stones, you know, are a place of death.'

Heather interrupted. 'Don't frighten Lowri. It's lovely up there. Now, come on, coats back on. Looks like it's time for the fireworks.'

Lowri picked up her coat and went outside to stand in the cold darkness. She found herself joining in the clapping and cheering as the fireworks shot into the sky. It wasn't a stunning display, but it was homely and quite noisy. Afterwards, everyone went back inside and Lowri put her coat back with her bag. As she was doing this, a woman who must have been in her forties came over. She was the kind of person who had probably dressed in the same conservative style of trousers and tops since her twenties, and would be in them still at fifty.

'I'm Nicola. I know Jack through church. That's Peter over there. He's our vicar. So, how are you settling in?'

'I feel better now I have my dog and cat. Carina kindly went over to help Jack pick them all up. She's good with animals, isn't she?'

'It would appear so,' said Nicola, but there was an edge to her words. Lowri wondered if Nicola was jealous of Carina.

'It's bound to take a bit of time for me to feel at home here,' said Lowri.

'That's true. When I came here I kept finding people were either related or had been to school together. Something like that. It's a closer community than you realise. People have grown up and stayed here, not moved on. It's bound to take time for an overner to fit in.'

'Overner?'

'Someone from the mainland.'

'I say mainland as well. I must have picked it up from Jack.'

'You know my friend's son calls the mainland 'the other island'. Love that.'

'So you are not from here either?'

'No. My family are from Stoke. But I came here once on holiday and always said I'd want to come back. Funny thing living on an island. It doesn't suit everyone. I watch people when they arrive. Some people seem to quietly sink into the island, become part of it; soon they talk about going to the mainland as if it's going to the moon. Others though never settle, miss shopping centres, lots of theatres, seeing friends and family without the need to get on ferries. They don't usually stay long.'

'But you stayed.'

'I did.'

'Do you go out to work?'

'I work in the hospital. I'm a chaplain there. And I teach as well.'

'What does your husband do?'

Nicola laughed. 'Haven't got one. Thank goodness.'

'Oh, sorry. I just assumed–'

'It's alright. No, I live blissfully alone.'

Lowri smiled, but assumed Nicola was putting a brave face on it.

'Yes, you must come with Jack to church sometime. Sorry, I'm not trying to make you religious or anything, but it's a way of getting to know people.'

'I don't know. I've not been to church for years, since I went to chapel as a child.'

'Fair enough. How are you recovering from your accident?'

'I seem to be doing quite well. I'll always have the scars, though, and I find that hard.'

'I can imagine. At work I meet people who have been in accidents and had operations on their faces. It's very difficult for them. Society expects us all to look the same, doesn't it? In fact, we've become obsessed with one version of beauty to which every one aspires. Look at Carina: she has it all. She has, you could say, won the genetic lottery.'

Lowri caught the edge in her voice again. 'You sound as if you don't like her much.'

'I'm not jealous, if that's what you are thinking. Me the old maid? No, honestly I'm not. I have to admit I'm not too sure about her, and with my job I know I'm meant to like everyone, but then I'm only human.' The intensity on her face relaxed into a smile. 'I'm sorry, Lowri. This is no help to you. You have a good listening manner. Did you know that?'

'No-one has ever told me that.'

'Well you have. Look, in case if you ever want to chat, let me give you my phone number.'

Nicola took out a small notebook and pen, and wrote down the number.

'Thanks,' said Lowri, and pushed the note into her pocket.

They heard Heather raise her voice. 'Finally, we have the fancy dress competition. Come on, kids.'

The children, pushed forward by parents, self-consciously stood in a straggly line. Lowri stood watching them. There was a whole range of pirates, fairies and robots. A robot and a Mummy won the competition. Lowri was tired and ready to go. She looked around for Jack. She saw him talking to Nicola, Carina, and a man she didn't know. She guessed it was Ken, as Carina had her arm proprietorially through his. Lowri went over to them.

'Jack.' She touched his arm. He turned around and put his arm around her.

'Ah, Lowri. Meet Ken, Carina's husband.'

Lowri was briefly diverted by the sight of Carina's husband. She had imagined a tall, good looking man, but Ken looked very different. He must have been about Jack's age, but was short, stocky, with sandy hair, wore baggy cords and a jacket. He had a rather wooden smile, but his grey eyes had that remnant of sadness you see in someone who has had a pain so deep it has never left them.

'It's lovely to meet you,' he said. His voice was soft. There was a lilt in it.

'Are you Welsh?'

'No. I have family in Ireland, but we used to go on holidays in Wales. My mother was Welsh. Where are you from?' asked Ken.

'Merthyr Tydfil. Where was your Mum from?'

'Swansea. We used to go to Gower on holiday to stay with friends of my mother's in Caswell Bay.'

'I like the cliff walk round to Langland.'

130

'You must get to know the beaches here. You have a dog, don't you?'

'That's right, Cassie.'

'Get down to Compton with her soon. Dogs aren't allowed in the summer, but it's glorious. I call it our Rhossili.'

'That big?'

'Goes on for miles. I go riding down that way. Can't get down on to Compton, of course, but you can get there from another beach when the tide is out. You'll love it.'

Carina came over with a jug of punch in one hand, and put her spare arm through Ken's. 'Are you chatting up my Ken, Lowri?' She laughed. 'Only joking. Now, when are you two coming over for lunch? I tell you what: how about tomorrow, after church?'

'We have Nicola and Peter coming,' said Ken.

'That's alright. Let's make a party of it.'

'I don't know–' said Lowri.

Carina interrupted her. 'Of course you will.'

'Thank you,' said Lowri, feeling cornered.

'Let me give everyone a refill,' said Carina. Jack, Ken, and Nicola held out their glasses. Lowri held back.

'Go on,' said Carina.

'No thanks, not tonight.'

'Are you on a lot of medication?' asked Carina.

The condescending tone rather than the question annoyed Lowri. 'Actually, no. I'm not drinking because I'm expecting a baby.'

Lowri wasn't sure who looked more shocked. It was Nicola who spoke first.

'You never said, Jack.'

Jack quickly gathered his composure. 'It's early days, but we're both delighted.'

131

Carina looked hard at Jack. 'But you've been separated–'

Jack froze and looked at Lowri in panic. She realised she should never have sprung this on him.

'We didn't stay completely separate,' said Lowri quickly, trying to smile.

Jack quickly put on a put a bashful grin. 'Nothing could really ever keep me and Lowri apart.' He leant down and shot a kiss on her cheek.

'Well done,' said Ken. 'Congratulations to you both.'

Carina was back smiling. 'Of course, it'll be exciting to have a baby in the village.'

'We have the ultrasound coming up. Early May is the due date,' said Jack.

'A spring baby, that's great,' said Ken.

Lowri looked up at Jack. 'You know, I'm very tired. Would you mind if I called it a night?'

'You need to go back?'

'Yes. I'm very tired.'

'Jack, if you want to stay – you've just started that glass of punch. I can walk Lowri home,' said Ken.

'No. Of course I'll walk my wife home,' said Jack.

Suddenly tired of the act, Lowri stepped back. 'I'm fine to walk on my own. It's really not far.'

'Look, I need a sneaky fag,' said Ken. 'I'll support you over the icy pavements.'

'Lowri's a big girl Ken. Leave her be,' said Carina.

'Of course. I'll be fine,' said Lowri.

'No. I insist.'

'Sure?' interrupted Jack.

'Dead sure. I won't be long.'

'Lowri, if you don't mind, I'll pop down and see Ben. He's over here staying. Is that OK?' asked Jack.

She was surprised. 'Of course.'

'We'll see you tomorrow for lunch?' asked Carina.

'Oh, yes.'

'Why don't you give our church a go first, see what you make of us?' suggested Ken.

Lowri smiled. 'Thank you. I will.'

'Come on. We'll have to be careful,' said Ken.

As they were leaving they met Heather.

'Thanks for the evening,' said Lowri.

'Going already?'

'I'm very tired.'

Heather looked up at Ken who said, 'I am her escort: husband's too busy drinking.'

Heather laughed. 'What a hero. Be careful then. See you soon.'

Lowri did up her coat. They both had torches and they started to walk away.

'Damn, I've forgotten my bag,' Lowri said. 'I'll be two minutes.'

She pushed her way through the people, found it on the table, and left again. However, as she was walking through the car park she heard familiar voices.

'Jack, what's going on? I put all the stuff in the studio for you, but that's not the answer,' Nicola was saying.

Lowri couldn't make out Jack's reply, but they were talking so intently they didn't look up. A cold wind was building up. She could see the branches trying to hold on to their autumn leaves. Winter was starting to push autumn away. Ken chatted as they walked, but Lowri wasn't listening. She was busy wondering what Jack and Nicola were talking about.

They walked slowly. When they arrived at the house, Lowri said, 'I'm glad I left the porch and hallway light on. I suppose having always lived in towns and cities I've not experienced the darkness of the countryside that often. Heather told me you were brought up in Ireland?'

'Yes. My father owned a large stables and stud there. I still own a lot of land over there and would love to do the same one day. It's a wonderful life over there, but first Jane, and now Carina keep me here in the manor.'

Lowri smiled. 'There are worse places to live. I never realised what a beautiful place the island is.'

Ken looked at her, his face suddenly serious. 'It is. When I used to ride over the downs with Jane, my first wife, I couldn't think of anywhere I'd rather be.'

'You don't feel like that now?'

'No. You know, a few years back I was complimenting the gardener on how lovely the garden at the manor looked, but he shook his head. He told me that it might all look beautiful, but he was fighting a battle with some new weed that was strangling all the plants in one of the borders and he was worried it was going to spread. So, you see, I had got it all wrong. It's not always a serpent destroying Eden.'

Lowri looked at him mystified, but he just gave a quick, sad smile.

'Thanks for walking me back.'

'Just wanted to see you were safe. Bye then.'

Lowri let herself in but there was something in Ken's words that unsettled her. It was like he was warning her, but why ever would he need to do that?

Chapter Fourteen

Lowri awoke to condensation on the windows and when she looked out the grass was covered in thick white frost, but the sun was filtering through the white clouds. She bent down to pick up her dressing gown from the floor beside her bed, and groaned: her ribs still hurt.

Feeling the need for coffee before she took Cassie out, she wrapped her dressing gown around her and walked past Jack's' bedroom. The door was ajar, so she glanced in. Everything in the room was neat, untouched, the bed not slept in. The book was there on the pillow, exactly as she had left it the day before. Lowri was shocked to realise he hadn't come home the night before.

Just then she heard the front door opening. Going downstairs, she saw Jack coming in wearing the same clothes as the night before. Lowri was struck with how anxious he looked. He seemed to stoop forward as if the worry was weighing him down.

'Are you alright Jack?'

He looked up and flashed on a smile. 'Fine. I went out for a walk. Gorgeous morning. In fact, I'll go back out, take Cassie out for you.'

'You got up early?' She enquired, giving him a chance to explain.

'Oh, yes. Hope I didn't disturb you?'

He was watching her. When they were first married she would have asked him where he had been, but now she wasn't sure of the boundaries.

'No,' she replied. 'You were very quiet. Thanks for taking Cassie out.'

Jack took the lead off the hook. Cassie went running to him. He said, 'I was thinking, you know. Don't get bullied into coming to church. I can come and get you after and take you down to the manor.'

'I said I'd go.'

'They won't mind.'

'I need to make an effort. I'll come.'

'OK. Well, it's an eleven o'clock start.'

Lowri went to the kitchen. Fizzy came mewing through the cat flap. Lowri leant down and stroked the cold fur.

'You been out all night as well?' she said to her, and put the food down.

Lowri made coffee and ate a banana, then went upstairs to dress. As she went to put on her jeans she touched her stomach. It was hard to imagine a new life growing in there, but it was. She reminded herself of the ultrasound. Yes, it was in there, growing. She wondered if it was a boy or a girl. Would it look like Simon? Would Jack find it hard to love if it did? She stroked her stomach. 'I'm sorry, it's a bit of a mess I'm bringing you into, but you'll be so loved. You are loved now. I promise you that you shall come before anything. Whatever happens I'll fight for you, protect you and love you.'

After she dressed, Lowri went downstairs and enjoyed filling in friends on Facebook about her evening. At least she had the basis of something to write for a change. She decided to upgrade the café to a hotel with large grounds. The firework display definitely needed to be grander. She downloaded some photos of a firework display at Leeds Castle. She hadn't mentioned the pregnancy yet. Should she today? She thought about it, and decided to build up to it.

'We have some exciting news. Will tell you all about it tomorrow,' she wrote.

Within seconds the replies came, some adding balloons and stars, the excitement palpable. 'I bet I can guess....congratulations!'

She didn't reply but pressed on with some work. Soon she was engrossed in translation, and was surprised when Jack came in and shouted that it was time to go. They settled Cassie. Fizzy was sound asleep in her basket.

Walking through the village she heard the sound of church bells pealing. They seemed to be the youngest people approaching the church, but it was a beautiful morning with the sun picking out the frost like stars on the pavements. Inside the church is was cold. There were ineffectual heaters. Nobody would have contemplated taking off their coats.

Lowri spotted Nicola, who came over to her. She looked up at Jack. 'Are you doing a reading?'

'Not today.'

Nicola turned to Lowri. 'It's Peter preaching today. He usually has something interesting to say.

The organ became louder. People stood up and the service began. Lowri hadn't been to church much. Occasionally she had been to chapel when she was little, but her mother had stopped going when she was older.

Peter introduced the service. As Lowri watched the thoughtful man, she could imagine him as a serious little boy, blinking, confused by the world. They used an old-fashioned service book, worked their way through the service. Jack pulled out a kneeler for prayers. She noticed that most people did, so she followed him. It was strange to be so close to the cold stone floor, but then that was apparently the idea: not to be comfortable. She quite liked hiding down there. In the pew next to her, a child sat playing on his phone. Another was reading a book. She wondered at what age it became unacceptable to do these things in church.

Peter climbed into the pulpit. He looked over them, smiled nervously.

'I am going to talk today about the legend of the Longstone. As many of you know, it is said that St Catherine and the Devil had a contest to see who should control the Isle of Wight. The taller iron sandstone pillar was supposedly thrown by St Catherine from way over on St Catherine's Down. The Devil threw a smaller stone, but it fell short and he lost the wager. And so we see that our Longstone symbolised the meeting of good and evil, a place where good triumphs.'

Peter looked around thoughtfully. 'It's hard, isn't it, to hold on to that sometimes? The world is a scary place at times. It seems out of control, but we have been given a good, beautiful place to retreat to: our downs. It is a place to go and be you. When the world gets too hard, when you are tired of pretending to your neighbour that everything is fine, or things don't hurt, it is a place you can go. Breathe in the air, the peace. It will restore you; give you the courage to believe that good can indeed triumph over evil.'

After the sermon they sang a hymn, followed by an awkward moment when everyone was meant to shake hands. To the few who came to her, Lowri said hello. She didn't enjoy it at all: it seemed forced, so she sat down. Lowri found this warded off anyone else from trying to shake her hand. She stayed sitting during communion, and the service ended soon after that.

Ken came over. 'You survived our terrible pews?'

She grinned. 'Just about.'

'Carina doesn't do church, but she does do a good lunch. I'll just go and get Nicola and Peter, and we can go and get something to warm us all up.'

Lowri walked out of the church and looked over at the downs. The sun shone down on them, but they were still crisp and white in the shadows. Ken called her and they all drove to the manor. When she had clambered inelegantly out of the car, Lowri was able to look properly at the house.

'Gosh, it's incredible,' she exclaimed.

In front of her stood a beautiful Tudor stone house. To the right were the stables and paddock.

'It's Elizabethan. The oldest parts of the manor, the south-east wing, dates from the fifteenth or early sixteenth century,' said Jack.

At this point, the wooden arched door opened and Carina came out. She was wearing a long red velvet dress; her hair was loose, and next to her stood a slim self-conscious girl with a mass of blonde curls.

'Welcome,' Carina came forward, and kissed Lowri on the cheek, then Jack.

'How lovely to see you.' She turned to her daughter. 'Lizzy, say hello.'

The girl stepped back and blushed.

'Leave her be,' said Ken. He looked at her adoringly as he ruffled the girl's hair. 'Did you muck out Chestnut this morning?'

'Yes. I walked her round. Can we go out later?

'Of course. Good girl.'

Inside, it was darker than Lowri had imagined. On the walls of the entrance hall were some tapestries and large paintings.

'You can see Jack's influence here,' said Carina to Lowri. 'He helped me track these down. Of course, we can't afford original renaissance art, but these are very good reproductions. Come and see where Jack is working.'

Lowri was taken into the drawing room and was immediately taken aback by the size of the project.

'It's a huge undertaking' she said.

The room had been stripped of furniture and there was scaffolding at one end. The end wall had been treated and there were large sheets protecting the floor.

'All it needs is for Jack to get on with it, he has to etch the drawings into fresh plaster, the word fresco comes from the word fresh you see. It is going to be the most wonderful painting of scenes from renaissance Florence.'

'It is very impressive. I've always known Jack was talented, but this is incredible, the best thing I've seen him do.'

'He is very gifted.'

At this moment Ken and Jack came in. 'I never realised how much you were doing over here,' Lowri said to Jack.

'It is ambitious.'

'Mind you,' said Ken, 'we had to get all kinds of permissions to do it, and Carina gets very frustrated with all the red tape.' Carina slid her arm through his and gave him an adoring look.

The next room they went into was large and light, but the carpets were threadbare, the furniture worn. A wonderful smell of roast beef came wafting from the kitchen.

'Shall I pour the drinks?' asked Jack, who proceeded to do so. He looked very much at home. He poured Carina, Ken and himself glasses of whisky. 'It's orange juice for you, Lizzy, and you now, Lowri. What about you, Nicola?'

'What do you think?' Nicola asked, grinning.

'I would guess: gin and tonic today.'

'Exactly.'

Lowri looked out of the large patio doors. Nicola walked over to her. 'It's a wonderful garden. The roses are over now, but things last a long time where it's so sheltered.'

'I'm not much of a gardener, but it looks very impressive,' said Lowri. Peter came over, but he didn't speak. Lowri wondered if he needed the security of the pulpit to talk.

'I think it's time for lunch, do come on through,' said Carina. 'Bring your drinks.'

Lowri saw Ken refill his glass before they all went through into another panelled room. A large oak table was laid up at one end. Lowri sat next to Ken. 'I'm afraid I know nothing about horses,' she said and looked over at a painting of a beautiful black mare. 'Is that one of your horses?'

Ken flinched as if he'd been struck. 'That was Midnight, Holly's horse. She was stabled here. Jack gave her to Holly for her birthday, but she died soon afterwards. I had that painting done for Holly in memory of Midnight but, of course, she'd gone by the time it was finished.'

Jack fiddled with the stem of his glass. 'It was tragic, but these things happen.'

Carina interrupted. 'The vet didn't really have an explanation though, did he?'

'How awful. It's hard enough losing an animal, but not to know why it died would be really hard,' said Lowri.

Ken looked up. 'It was heartbreaking for us all,' he said quietly.

There was an awkward silence. Carina broke it. 'Anyway, you were very lucky recently, weren't you Lizzy? Mummy and Daddy bought you Chestnut.'

Lizzy smiled, but she didn't speak.

'And we also recently started looking after Biscuit,' said Ken. Looking at Lowri, he explained. 'We stable her here for Nicola.'

'You have a horse here?' said Lowri to Nicola.

'Yes. It's very exciting. Ken knows how much I love horses. I would never have got one if he hadn't encouraged me. I could never afford the time and money involved. You know, if you ever want to ride him, Lowri–'

'Oh, I couldn't–'

'I'm sure Ken would show you.'

'Of course,' confirmed Ken.

'Biscuit is a smashing horse for a novice. Very calm, easy.'

'Thank you. I'll think about it. Did you keep horses in Stoke?'

'Goodness, no. We couldn't have afforded it there, and we lived in the city. I never expected to own a horse, but then Ken heard about Biscuit. I must have got him not long before you lost Midnight, didn't I?'

'Yes. I remember he had the only spare stable then. He's been a good horse.'

'I'm lucky I can ride as much as I want to. Lizzy, you look after him for me as well, don't you?'

Lizzy gave a big grin. 'One day I shall be able to ride a horse as big as him.'

'You will, but not yet,' said Ken. He turned to Lowri. 'So, what did you do before coming here?'

'I did translation work. I still do, actually. It's online.'

'What languages do you speak?'

Lowri told him.

'Wow. That is so impressive.'

'Not really,' said Lowri, blushing.

'Of course it is.'

'Carina is bilingual,' said Lowri.

Carina smiled modestly. 'I had no choice. My English is far from perfect, though.'

'Lowri, you must have gone to university,' said Ken.

'Yes. My degree was in Polish.'

'It sounds like you could have taught yourself, saved the money,' said Carina. The laugh was cold.

'Maybe.'

'Nonsense,' said Ken. 'It's very different. So did you spend any time in Poland?'

'A year. It was amazing.'

Carina abruptly stood up. 'Come on, everyone. Help yourselves to more. We can't eat all these leftovers.'

Lowri glanced at Carina's plate. There was a miniscule amount of food, none of which had been touched.

Carina looked over at Peter. 'So, were you preaching this morning?'

Peter looked startled to be spoken to. 'Yes, um, yes.'

The lunch was very good: rib of beef, thick rich gravy, crispy roast potatoes and fluffy Yorkshire puddings. Carina brought out chocolate cake and cream.

'Ah my favourite,' said Jack.

'I made three cakes, two for the café.'

'Do you work down there a lot?' Lowri asked.

'Most days. Heather needs the help.'

'She appreciates all you do,' said Jack.

'So, Lowri,' said Nicola suddenly. 'You think your baby is due in the spring?'

'That's right, in May.'

'So your baby was conceived in August. I thought Jack was in Florence then?' said Carina.

Lowri could feel herself blushing. 'We were together just before he went.'

'But he went on his own, without you? Why did you go to France on your own?'

Carina maintained a fixed smile throughout, but her words were sharp and Lowri could feel herself getting increasingly flustered.

143

'I think that is their business, don't you?' said Ken firmly, and Nicola interrupted quickly.

'Lots of Spring birthdays around. June as well. I think half my class at school seem to have birthdays then,'

'People were talking about all the June babies on Facebook,' said Lowri.

'Oh, you're on Facebook. I was thinking about joining.,' said Carina.

Lowri panicked. 'I don't go on much. Hardly at all.'

'You seem to be on it all the time,' said Jack.

'Not really.'

'I don't see any harm in it,' said Ken. Lowri smiled at him gratefully as he added, 'I'd thought about going on it sometime to chat to family in Ireland. My brother has a stud there, breeds race horses. He has a great life out there.'

'We're not traipsing off to Ireland any time soon,' interrupted Carina.

Ken looked down. Carina raised her voice. 'Why don't Peter and Nicola and I show Lowri the gardens while you, Jack and Lizzy clear up?'

Lowri noticed Carina hadn't touched pudding and wondered if she ever actually ate food.

'OK,' said Ken. 'Careful though on the terraces. It's very slippery out there.'

They walked along a gravelled patio area and then climbed up a steep flight of stone steps into the garden, Nicola pointing things out._ 'That chestnut tree is six hundred and fifty years old. Hard to imagine, isn't it? See the beech trees: the tips are bare now.'

'Nicola, you know the garden better than me. You wouldn't think I was the one who lived here,' said Carina.

'She works out here a lot, don't you Nicola?' said Peter.

144

Carina pursed her lips, then led them down to a large pond behind which was a small summer house. Next to it stood a weeping willow and an old oak. At one side there was an arbour with a wooden seat. Even on a cold day it was picturesque. Lowri recognised the setting of the painting of Carina.

'It's gorgeous here in the summer,' said Nicola. 'The leaves have almost gone now, but it is a heavenly place to sit then.'

'Did you know that the weeping willow is a symbol of death?' said Carina.

Lowri shook her head.

'Jack was telling me once. Remember Ophelia in Hamlet? She broke off willow branches and tossed them into the river where she drowned herself.'

'That's tragic,' said Lowri. She turned away and started walking towards the house. The vestige of sunlight had faded, the sky grey and heavy. Tiny cold spots of rain started to fall.

'Maybe it's best to go in. It's starting to rain,' said Nicola.

'Good idea. They should have finished clearing up by now. Be careful on these steps,' said Carina. Peter, Carina and Nicola went ahead of Lowri. Lowri put her hand out towards the metal railing, but suddenly she felt a terrible pain in her stomach. Leaning forward, she lost her footing on the wet step, and slipped down the cold stone steps.

Chapter Fifteen

Lowri lay on her side on the wet stone path, arms clutching her stomach, legs drawn up. The pain ripped at her inside.

Nicola came rushing down the steps. 'Carina, get Jack. Peter ring for an ambulance.'

Nicola knelt down next to Lowri, took her own coat off, folded it, and tucked it under Lowri's head. 'It's alright,' she said, her voice high and breathless.

Lowri squeezed her eyes together, lost in a world of pain. She heard Carina shouting, and then Jack say her name. She opened her eyes. He patted her arm ineffectually. His eyes were wide and unblinking.

Lowri felt the sharp pins of rain hitting her face.

'Can you move? We should get you inside,' said Nicola.

With their help, Lowri pushed herself up. The pain seemed to be easing. She made it through the patio doors. She was shivering. Nicola grabbed a throw and put it on the antique embroidered chair, then she helped Lowri ease off her wet coat before she sat down.

Carina came in with another blanket and Nicola wrapped it gently around Lowri's shoulders. The pain seemed to be ebbing away.

'I'm feeling better. Cancel the ambulance,' said Lowri.

'No. They need to check you,' replied Nicola.

Lowri sat very still, frightened that one move could set the pain off again. She felt very sick, then, to her embarrassment, she thought she had wet herself. She slipped her hand in between her legs: blood. Oh God, my baby. I can't lose it, I must stay very still, I must hold on to it.

Jack glanced at Lowri's hand. 'I'll go and see if the ambulance is coming' he said, and rushed out of the room.

The cramps in her stomach started again. Lowri hugged her stomach and moaned. Each one got stronger. She was frightened: how much worse could this get?

The ambulance arrived. After a quick assessment the paramedics sat her in a wheelchair. She glanced back at the stained throw on the chair, and winced. Jack was standing behind Nicola. 'Do you want me to come?'

'Of course you need to go Jack,' said Nicola.

Once in the ambulance, Lowri was put on to a bed, covered with a blanket, strapped in. She tried to smile a thank you to the paramedic but her lips refused to move. Lowri briefly worried about the mess she was making of the bed but then the pain took over.

At the hospital she was taken straight into a cubicle in casualty. Jack sat on a chair in a corner, his arms and legs tightly crossed, face blank. A doctor arrived quickly, and ordered for her to be taken for an internal scan. It all happened very fast.

A nurse helped to remove her trousers and lie down, and asked gently, 'How many weeks are you?'

'About ten, I think.'

As she did the scan the nurse was very quiet. She looked around and gestured to Jack to come closer.

'I am sorry. I can't find a heartbeat.'

Lowri peered at the nurse, waiting for her to look again. The nurse said more firmly, 'There is no heartbeat.'

Lowri stared at the nurse, pleading with her to give a hint of doubt, of hope, but the nurse shook her head. 'I am so sorry.'

'My baby?'

'You have had a miscarriage.' The nurse spoke to her as she might to a child.

However, there was nothing childish or innocent about the word. It was a knife, piercing her. Lowri started to cry. 'No. Please, no. I don't want to lose my baby.'

'I'm so sorry,' the nurse repeated. Lowri wanted to shout at her. Why do you keep saying sorry? Stop being sorry, make it better. But she realised the nurse had turned away, and was printing off the picture on the screen. Lowri realised she had finished. There was no hope.

'It was my fault, the fall, I should have been more careful,' Lowri said to Jack, who stood very still, his arms limply by his side.

He didn't speak but the nurse turned back. 'The foetus is very small. I think you lost your baby a week or two ago.'

'All this time I thought my baby was growing, but it wasn't?'

'I'm afraid not.'

'Why? I can't think what I did.'

'Please, it's not your fault. These things happen. Usually we have no explanation. All we know is that the foetus has not developed normally because of chromosomal, genetic or other problems.'

The words seemed reasonable, but cold. Lowri wondered how many other women she had said them to. Then, suddenly, an excruciating pain gripped her, her whole body contorted. The nurse's eyes widened in alarm. she immediately called for the doctor.

He came in and his cool, gentle detachment was reassuring. 'Lowri, we need to do an operation. There is a risk of you haemorrhaging.'

Lowri looked up at Jack. His eyes were red, and the doctor turned to him.

'We can't wait.'

148

Lowri was aware of Jack signing papers. She was put on to a trolley, taken to theatre, and given an anaesthetic.

Lowri awoke in the recovery room. She looked at the white, sterile walls. A nurse came over. 'Lowri?' Lowri tried to speak but vomited. She felt a strange numb calmness: maybe it was the anaesthetic, but she knew the pain had gone. She felt guilty for the feeling of relief. It meant there was nothing left.

'You will need to stay in tonight so we can keep an eye on you,' said the nurse.

Lowri was taken to a ward with three other women. The lights were dimmed. One lady gave her a gentle smile, another was turned away from her, at least pretending to read her kindle. Only one was asleep.

The nurse carried out her checks, and wrote on Lowri's chart.

'Where's Jack?' Lowri whispered.

The nurse came closer. 'Your husband is at home now. He popped back with some things for you. He'll be here tomorrow after lunch to pick you up. Try to rest.'

Lowri was glad to be there. She was still frightened the pain would return. She wanted to be with people who could help her. She sipped water, but was scared about going to the toilet. Would it start everything again? Then she realised there was nothing there: there may be discomfort, but that was all that was left.

She gently laid her hands on her stomach. There would be no visible scars. She didn't want to talk to anyone about it, but she did feel there should be something to bear witness to the trauma, to her baby's existence. She had been watching the scars on her face heal, but the ones inside her, how she would know when or if they would ever heal? These scars were secret, silent, hidden.

It was a long night. Lowri was relieved when the day shift came on and she was sat up looking at the white paper-like toast. She saw people walking in the corridors, laughing, shouting. She felt tears burning her eyes. She didn't know what she was meant to be feeling, but she felt empty, and knew something very precious had been taken from her.

'Would you like a shower?' a nurse asked.

'I'm allowed?'

'Yes. You can't bathe yet. You'll be given a leaflet to explain. Wash yourself gently.'

The woman in the next bed gave her the same look that she had given the night before. That quick look of empathy comforted her. The nurse helped her out of bed, and carried her kit for her as they walked to the shower.

'Pull that red string if you feel giddy or unwell.'

Lowri took off the hospital nightgown and stepped on into the cold shower cubicle. The shower head was very high up and, because she was short the water dribbled down on her. She was able to wash the grime out of her hair and the dried blood from her legs. She moved carefully, slowly, and patted herself so gently afterwards that she wasn't quite dry. She was damp and her nightie clung to her, but at least she was clean.

It was a relief to get back to bed. Lowri had only towel dried her hair but she rested back on the pillow, exhausted.

When she next opened her eyes she found Nicola sitting next to her, wearing a clerical collar. Nicola touched it. 'It's my pass in to see you,' she said with a smile.

'I lost my baby.'

'I know. I'm so sorry.' Nicola reached out and held Lowri's hand; the warmth was like a baby's blanket.

'I miss my baby. I've never held it, smelt it, or touched it, but I miss it so much.' The hot tears soaked her pillow.

150

'I hate saying 'it', but I don't even know if it was a boy or a girl. We hadn't chosen a name. It will never be.'

'You can still choose a name.'

'What, now?'

'Yes.'

'Maybe. It wasn't my fault, you know. They said it wasn't the fall.'

'I'm sure it wasn't.' Nicola squeezed her hand.

Lowri started to sob. She held her stomach with one hand as if holding herself together. 'I don't understand anything. I want my baby back.'

Nicola sat waiting, then said, 'I went to see Jack this morning.'

'How is he?'

'He is bereaved, grieving. He doesn't find it easy to talk. You know Jack.'

'I've failed him and his parents, haven't I?'

'It's not your fault.'

'I'm being selfish aren't I? Thinking about me all the time, but I don't know how to think about my baby. I saw it, you know, in France, on the screen: a tiny little bean. I was going to give it a good life, a perfect life. Now it won't know, will it?'

'Your baby was loved and wanted.'

'I hate calling my baby 'it'. If I gave it a name like you said, it might help.'

'You could talk to Jack about it.'

'There won't be a funeral?'

'No. We do have a book you can write in if you would like.'

'I wouldn't know what to say.'

'We have a service in the spring. You can come. Write something then if you want to.'

'Spring seems a long way away.'

Nicola looked around the ward, then back at Lowri. 'I have a few days off. Would you like me to come and stay with you?'

'Really?'

'Yes.'

'Thank you. I don't think Jack will want to think about it all.'

'I don't want to push him out. He did mention he wanted to go back to work, but you must ask him to stay if that is what you need. Now, I can pray with you if you would like.'

Lowri shook her head. 'Not now. I'm sorry. I don't mean to be rude.'

'That's fine. I have to go and take communion in the chapel.'

'Thank you for coming in.'

Nicola stood up and then put her hand in her pocket. She glanced shyly at Lowri. 'I hope you don't mind, but I found something this morning. I was walking on Compton Bay.'

Lowri frowned. Nicola pulled out a stone and gave it to her. It fitted in the palm of her hand: a coiled, ribbed spiral-form fossil.

'It's an ammonite. Could be over two hundred million years old. I can't get my head round that or really even the idea of fossils, but I do know it means that that little mollusc from all that time ago is still here with us in some form: it's not forgotten.'

Lowri felt the ribbed stone. There was still sand in the grooves. 'Thank you,' she said and folded her fingers around it, burying it safely in the palm of her hand.

Jack came later to collect her. He looked very pale, ghost like. She was given antibiotics to take home and told,

'We'll send your notes on to your GP. If you get a lot of pain or bleeding contact him straight away.'

'Thank you.'

'I've parked the car round the side. Can you walk?'

'Slowly, yes. I'm not bleeding much. I'm lucky.' Lowri's eyes filled with tears. Jack put his arm around her. He was leaning on her as much as supporting her.

She felt like an elderly couple: walking slowly, shuffling. As they walked along the corridor, Lowri looked into the wards. There were mothers with new babies in little cots, pink and blue cards. Balloons shouted, 'It's a girl. It's a boy.'

'I must not hate them,' thought Lowri. She was glad when they arrived at the car. It was like returning to their bubble.

Jack drove carefully. 'I rang Mum,' he said, looking out of the windscreen.

'I'm sorry.'

'She cried. I hate it when she does that. I don't know what to say.'

As they drove and she looked out of the window, Lowri knew that she was a different person from the one who had arrived at the hospital. She would never be the same again. It was strange, as it always is, when something life-changing happens, to watch other people going about normal life. But who really knew what was going on in their lives? We all act a part, sometimes hiding terrible pain from the world.

Lowri was relived to arrive home. Before they got out Jack turned to her.

'Nicola is in the house. Is that alright?'

'She said about coming to stay.'

'I was thinking of going back to work tomorrow?'

'How are you?'

Jack closed his eyes. 'I am so sorry for what you've been through.'

'But what about you? I know it wasn't your baby, but you had been thinking about it, planning with me.'

'I am very sorry we lost this baby, Lowri. It has to be different for you, but I hate to see you so unhappy, you've been through so much.'

She saw his eyes fill up.

'I'm sorry,' he said again. 'Nicola talked to me. She said we could still have a name for the baby.'

'She said that to me as well.'

'What do you think?

'I was thinking of Aniolku, the Polish word for angel. What do you think?'

'That's perfect.'

He took the keys out of the ignition, and turned to her. 'Lowri–'

'What?'

'Do you still want to stay with me?'

All she could think of was curling up in bed, trying to make the world and the pain disappear. Blinking, she looked at Jack. 'I'd like to. Is that alright?'

'Of course. Good.'

They looked at each other, the space between them full of unspoken words that neither knew how to say.

Chapter Sixteen

Poppy was helping out in the café as Carina couldn't go in and Gill, of course, was unavailable. It had been a busy morning, and Heather was putting out extra scones after lunch.

Poppy came over. 'Mum, go and have a sit down now the lunchtime rush is over. You haven't stopped, and it's been such a hectic weekend with the party.'

'It's alright. Thanks so much for coming in.'

'You're going to have replace Gill. She's never here.'

'I know, but it's embarrassing.'

'But you can't carry on like this. You need to employ someone else.'

'It's another person to pay.'

Poppy came closer to her mother. 'Is money that tight?'

'Oh no. Of course not.'

'Then you need to get more help. People will be put off if they have to wait too long or things aren't up to scratch. You know how the business works. You've always had first class service here, Mum. It's part of the reason people drive out here. It's the service, attention to detail. They'll stop if that slides, and then you'll have less income.'

Heather nodded. 'You're right, love. I heard people grumbling the other day. It never used to happen.'

'There you are, then.'

'But Dave needs help as well. I have to go down and sort him out sometimes.'

'You'd be able to if there was a second pair of hands here.'

'It's true, but who to ask?'

'You could put an advert in the County Press, or, I know, why don't you ask that new woman who's moved into the village?'

'You mean Jack's wife. She has work as a translator. Anyway, she's not well now. I don't know how ill she is. I heard she lost the baby.'

'Oh no, Mum. That's awful.'

'I know, poor woman. She's having a terrible time of it. Good job she has Jack to look after her.'

'Of course. Now, the café, Mum. The woman I was thinking of is called Gita, I think. Her husband is a consultant at the hospital. She's very quiet, keeps herself to herself.'

'You think she would want to work here?'

'She might. It's not easy over here. There aren't many people from different backgrounds and she seems quite shy. It would be a way for her to get to know people.'

'I hadn't thought of that.'

'Her children go to the school over at Ryde. Seem very polite.'

'I'm sure they are, but if her husband is a consultant, don't you think she'll think working here is beneath her?'

'Mum, you're always saying things like that. You should be proud of this business.'

'I am.'

'Well, show it.'

Poppy had red hair like her father, freckles on her nose that she tried to cover with make-up. 'I'm going to send out the save the dates this week. I'll need some addresses. I'm going to send one to Aunty Holly.'

'I know. I really hope she comes.'

'She's not married again or anything?'

'No, but you could write plus one if you want.'

'Good idea. I really like her. I hope she comes.'

156

'You remember her?'

'Of course. I must have been about eleven when she left. She took me on outings to Amazon World, Robin Hill, just me and her. I like Aunty Rosemary as well, of course.'

'I heard her and Uncle Simon were going over to Italy soon.'

Poppy frowned. 'She never mentioned it when I rang to get her postcode. It was an excuse to talk to her about the photographer; she was very nice about it.'

'Good.'

'Yes. We had quite a nice chat. She said she was looking forward to catching up with family at the wedding. She asked me where I was going for my honeymoon. I said Italy and she said that she'd like to go one day but her and Uncle Simon were always working.'

'Maybe for some reason she didn't want to say.'

'Why ever not?'

'I don't know. Now, I'll just put some more coffee on.'

At that moment, a young family arrived. They all looked cold and windblown, with sand on their shoes.

'Hi,' said Poppy, 'been down the beach?'

'We found some really good shells,' said the little boy.

Poppy looked at the chipped limpet shells in his hand.

'Gosh. They are a really good find. Did you see any dinosaurs?'

The boy's eyes widened. 'No, but Dad showed us the footprints.'

'Amazing, aren't they?'

'Right, let's order some lunch,' said his mother.

'Can I have a sausage roll, Mum?' asked the little girl.

'I think we will all have the lentil soup and granary rolls,' her mother said.

'Can we have a cake for pudding though?'

'I don't–'

'Oh, go on,' said the father. 'We all deserve a chocolate cake today.'

She gave in, and they sat down while they waited for their food.

The afternoon drew on and, finally, the last customers left at half past four.

'Thank God. I thought they would never finish their tea. They eked it out for an hour,' said Poppy.

'I know. Still, we can hardly chuck them out. I'll be glad to get home tonight.'

'Oh, Mum, I have something to show you.'

Poppy held out her phone.

'What's that?'

'It's the design for the cake decoration. Do you like it?' Each tier tells another part of mine and Alistair's story. He said he'd make another cake for the evening if we wanted.'

'I think one is enough.'

'Alistair's sister was saying that people do almost like another wedding in the evening. You have another cake, change into an evening dress, and of course there is a band to sort out as well. One of my friends here has a band. I really like them, but I'm not sure they are quite the thing for Alistair's family.'

'Good gracious.' Heather frowned and looked at her daughter. She noticed that she had started scratching her neck again.

'Are you alright?'

'The eczema on my back is awful.'

'Feeling stressed?'

'All brides do, don't they?'

'They do, but don't let it ruin your day. It's meant to be a happy day, you know.'

158

'I keep telling myself that but, I feel so much pressure from Alistair's' family. Well, from his sister. She's always emailing me and texting me about things that she has seen or read about.'

'Sounds like she would like a wedding herself.'

'She would, but Alistair said her last boyfriend left her, said she was too high maintenance.'

'Make sure you are doing what you want, that's all.'

'To be honest, Mum, I'm so confused. I'm not sure anymore. I want them to like it, you know.'

'I know, and it matters what they think.'

'They should be impressed by the manor at least.'

'I'm sure they will be.'

'Mind you, Alistair's sister said she is going to one on a beach in Cornwall. She said outside weddings were really in now. Still, I'm sure they'll like the manor.'

'Love, this wedding is meant to be for you and Alistair.'

'I know, but she understands what people are looking for now. She's going to help me sort out the invitations.'

'The dress looks lovely.'

'Yes, it's gorgeous Mum. It's exactly what I wanted. Alistair's sister said I should go for a ball gown type style. It's what she loves, but I wanted a vintage, country type style, you know, like Kate Moss had at her wedding. That was just wonderful. Mind you, I haven't got her figure, so it's not as slinky. But that kind of thing. The bridesmaids will look a bit like hers as well.'

'It's going to be very pretty.'

'I know, I love it, it was so expensive –'

'Well it's all paid for now.'

There are a few more payments due actually. I'll send them all to you. Is that alright?'

'Of course, everything.'

159

'You are sure?'

'Of course. Don't you dare scrimp on anything. If you want to get things for the evening like a dress, make sure you send me all the receipts.'

'I'm not going that far, Mum. One beautiful dress is enough.'

'Whatever you want.'

Heather looked out of the window. 'Is that Alistair outside?'

'Oh, yes. Alright if I go?'

'Of course, and thank you so much for helping, love.'

Heather watched her daughter leave, then let her face relax from the fixed smile. Good God, what was she going to do? This wedding was going to cost so much. She had read that the average wedding cost about twenty thousand pounds, but this was going way, way, beyond that. She daren't tell Lee. There was so much she couldn't tell him at the moment. It was her mess, and she would have to find a way out of it.

As Heather left the café she remembered she needed to talk to Gita and went to her house.

Lowri had stayed in bed since she had come home from the hospital. Nicola sat with her, just reading, and making cups of tea. Her quiet presence was comforting. She also took Cassie out for walks, and fed and made a fuss of Fizzy. Jack went back to work, and stayed over in Southampton. Lowri bled some more but not as heavily. The painkillers numbed the ache in her stomach. She managed to start walking. She was petrified of going to the toilet. She would walk around the landing, but didn't want to go downstairs.

Heather sent round a cake, but Lowri was pleased she didn't come to see her. She didn't feel like visitors yet.

160

However, late one morning, she was sitting up in bed, when she heard Nicola's voice.

'I don't think Lowri is quite up to visitors'

'Don't worry. I won't stay too long, but you must see I feel so guilty–'

'Just a minute then. Come this way. This is Lowri's room.'

The next thing Lowri knew, Carina was in her bedroom. Her immaculate looks made her want to dive under the duvet.

'Lowri, I am sorry. How are you?'

'I should get up soon,' she said, and she pulled her hair forward, aware it hadn't been washed for days.

'I brought you this.' Carina handed her a small gift bag. Inside were beautiful toiletries.

'Thank you. That's so kind.'

'And one more thing. I don't suppose you want to think about it now, but I thought it would be something to look forward to.'

Carina handed her a large gold envelope. Opening it, she found a large printed invitation. In one corner was an embossed gold masquerade mask

Ken and Carina cordially invite
Jack and Lowri
To our
Elmstone Manor New Year's Masquerade Ball

December 31ˢᵗ - 8pm until 3am
Please come in costume with mask
RSVP Elmstone Manor

Lowri read the invitation and looked up at Carina.
'A masquerade ball?'

'Yes. I hold it every year. It is wonderful. Everyone dresses up in beautiful dresses and masks. I like it to be as close to a Viennese masquerade as possible.'

'Not vicars and tarts then?' said Nicola.

Carina looked horrified. 'Of course not. No, this is very sophisticated. People come from the mainland.'

'Of course, thank you. I will talk to Jack about it.' Lowri put it on her bedside table, sure that she and Jack would not be going.

Carina smiled, but Lowri noticed that she was scanning her room.

'This is a lovely room. I stayed in here, you know.'

'Really?'

'When I first came to the Island with Ken, he had to go away. I was scared to stay in the manor on my own. I was sure there would be ghosts. Holly was so kind and asked me here to stay. That was when Jack was doing the painting of me.'

'I didn't realise.'

'Yes, this was my room then. Jack and Holly, of course, they slept together along the landing.'

Lowri could see Carina taking in the single bedside cabinet, the dressing table with only Lowri's things on.

'Jack is sleeping there while I'm unwell.'

'How is Jack? It must be so awful for him. He is so good with babies. I remember when I had Lizzy, I joked that you would have thought he was the father; always holding and cuddling her. It was sad he never had children with Holly. She left him so suddenly, not long after I found I was pregnant.'

Lowri looked up. 'Do you know why Holly left?'

Carina gave an annoying, knowing smile. 'Ah, I think that should remain a secret. That is the past anyway. The

162

main thing is that you and Jack will be playing happy families again, I'm sure.'

Nicola stood up quickly. 'Carina, I think you'd better go. Lowri is really tired.'

'You're quite right Nicola. I'll leave you to your nursing.'

Carina looked over at Lowri and smiled. 'You know, even our Saint Nicola has her secrets.'

To her surprise, Lowri saw Nicola blush. 'I'll show you out.'

Carina patted Lowri's hand. 'Bye, then. You take care.'

Lowri lay back exhausted. Nicola came running back up the stairs.

'Are you alright?'

'I think so. It's not easy to work out what Carina is saying, is it? I mean, she smiles and sounds friendly. I think she's insinuating things, but I'm not sure if I'm imagining it.'

'I think it's called being passive aggressive. Hard to pin down, but if someone says something that hurts, even if they have a smile and a nice warm fuzzy voice, that's usually what it is.'

Lowri watched Nicola walking agitatedly around the room. Then she came and sat on the edge of the bed.

'What she was saying about me not being a saint–'

'You don't need to tell me anything.'

'No, I want to. You've shared so much with me.'

'What is it?'

'One day, I was chatting to Ken in the stables and I mentioned that when I was younger I'd been a bit of a tearaway. He laughed and didn't believe me, so I told him about the time I'd smoked weed, taken some coke and stuff in my teens.'

Lowri stared. 'You did that?'

Nicola gave a half laugh. 'It was just for a short time, at parties and the like. I was lucky; it never got serious.'

'Wow. I can't imagine you doing that.'

'Everyone has a past, like Carina said. No-one is perfect. I've never made a big secret out of it, but it's not the kind of thing I exactly want to broadcast either.'

'So Ken told Carina?'

'No. I didn't realise, but she was outside listening. It was so unnerving. She came in grinning. Since then, sometimes she hints at it when we are with people. Says things just like she did then, and people I'm sure imagine all sorts of things.'

'That's weird.'

'It's nasty, but it's the way she does things.'

Lowri screwed up her eyes. 'You don't like her, do you?'

Nicola shook her head. 'No. I know I should love everyone, but I don't trust her, and I'm sorry that she is married to Ken. He's a decent bloke, but he looks miserable with her.' Nicola stood up. 'You watch her. For some reason, I think she's got it in for you. I can tell. Just watch your back.'

Chapter Seventeen

A few days later, Nicola came in with Lowri's breakfast.

'Fancy getting dressed this morning?'

'I don't know. There doesn't seem much point.'

Nicola sat down. 'I know it's hard. One step at a time, eh? Let's try and get up, get dressed. Is there anywhere you'd like to go?'

Lowri shrugged. 'I don't know. Maybe the beach. I've not been there yet.'

'That's a great idea. We could go to Brook. It's an easy walk down. We could take Cassie.'

'Cassie has never been on a beach.'

'Never?'

'I've never liked the beach. I walked her along the front at Southsea, but we never went on to the beach.

'Come on. Maybe it would be something new. No-one will be there today.'

'I haven't got anything suitable for my feet: only my trainers, and they're not waterproof.'

'What about walking Cassie?'

'We went to the park. I kept mainly to the concrete path.'

Nicola laughed. 'I have my wellies and boots in the car. You can put on lots of pairs of socks. Now, I'll go and feed Fizzy. She's left bits of shrew all over the patio this morning.'

'She always leaves certain bits. It's pretty disgusting.'

Lowri got out of bed, showered and then dressed. She pulled her hair as far forward as she could, sat in front of her dressing table and started to put on her make-up. She applied one layer of foundation over her scar, then another, then stopped. The scar taunted her. It refused to be covered. For the first time in a long time she looked at her face properly. She tried to pull up the drooping side of her mouth to form a 'proper' smile but, of course, it had changed. Putting her hands on her flat stomach, she felt overwhelmed by the sense of loss. She covered the mirror again, hugged herself, and started to cry. The sobs caught in her throat. Nicola came into the bedroom, saw her, and hurried over. She held her, and stroked her hair until the tempest stopped.

Lowri looked up. 'I'm sorry.'

'It's OK. Come on, let's go down.'

'I don't know–'

'Let's try, together.'

They walked down the stairs. Cassie was waiting for them. Lowri looked down at her. 'OK, then. I'll do it for you.'

Just as they were about to drive off, Nicola said, 'Oh, hang on. I've forgotten my phone. I'll only be a minute.' Lowri held out her key.

'It's OK,' said Nicola. 'Jack gave me one ages ago.'

Lowri sat in the car, waiting and looking around. There was colour everywhere; nature's last flourish before the winter. The orange leaves were turning to brown, starting to curl and fall. Red rose hips dotted the bushes, spider webs strung between branches. She saw a pheasant looking bemused in the front garden. Nicola returned. As they started to drive out of the village, Lowri noticed Carina walking up the road towards the café. She waved and walked on. They drove down the lane that was now covered in leaves, and arrived at the car park for the beach. Cassie jumped out of the car, her nose up in the air. Lowri kept her on the lead as they walked down the short path to the beach.

Lowri looked over at some small cottages to their left.

'Good place for a holiday,' said Nicola. 'Jack's friend Ben from university owns one, doesn't he? I see him when I come down here some times.'

'I knew Ben had a holiday home. I didn't know where. Nice spot.'

'Oh, good. The tide is out,' said Nicola. 'I really should have checked.'

The sky was a light crisp blue. It was strange to be the only people there and to be wearing coats and boots. Nicola let Cassie off. She ran around madly, sniffing and digging holes. Then, before Lowri could stop her, she ran into the sea.

'Stop her,' she shouted to Nicola.

'It's alright. She's not going out far.'

'But she could get swept out,' Lowri was shouting. 'I can't lose her. Stop her.'

Cassie, of her own accord, came running back up the beach and shook herself.

'She's fine.' Nicola looked at Lowri, puzzled. 'Why the panic?'

'I don't know. My mother always said the sea was dangerous.'

'But she was only paddling.'

'I suppose she was.'

'Haven't you ever swum in the sea?'

'No, never.'

'Well, sometime you must come down with me.'

'OK. Not today, though. It looks flipping cold.'

Nicola laughed. 'I agree.'

They carried on walking, seagulls swooping and screeching above them.

'So you grew up in Wales. How come you ended up living in Southampton?'

'After university I saw a job advertised working with the Polish community in Southampton. I came down and found a flat. Unfortunately, the job closed through lack of funding after a year, but I was put in touch with an agency for translation work.'

'Is that how you met Jack?'

'No. I went to a film festival. I didn't have that many friends, and my work was all done at home on the computer. The only people I met were when I took Cassie out for walks. She was my lifeline really.'

'Dogs are important like that aren't they? I see people out chatting and realise that, apart from their dogs, they have nothing in common. The dogs kind of bring them together.'

'Exactly. Anyway, Jack came and chatted to me in the interval. He bought me a warm glass of white wine. I remember drinking it even though it didn't taste very good. He told me he was divorced and asked me if I was coming to the next film. I did, and, well, after that it all happened very quickly.'

'He kept coming over here on his own. Didn't you mind?'

'I had Cassie and Fizzy.'

'But you could have brought them.'

Lowri stopped, and stared at Nicola. 'I suppose I could have brought Cassie, and my neighbour would have fed Fizzy. I never thought about it too much, I think deep down I knew that Jack didn't want me to come over. He liked his space, you know, and then, of course, earlier this year we separated.'

Nicola leant down and picked up a handful of sand.

'And things are better now?'

'I think so. Obviously, losing the baby is very difficult for us both–'

They walked on, the air cold against their faces.

'So you are happy with Jack?'

Lowri stopped, and remembered Nicola talking to Jack after she had left the party.

'Why are you asking?'

'I've got to know Jack over the past few years. He talked to me quite a lot when the two of you separated.'

'I know there was someone else, but that's in the past.'

'Is it?'

Lowri frowned. 'Yes, of course.'

'You're sure?'

'What are you trying to say?'

'Nothing.'

'If you know he is seeing someone else you should tell me who it is.' Nicola looked out at the grey sea. 'No, Jack should do that.'

'So, you do know?'

'I do.'

Lowri could feel the anger burning inside her, what right had Nicola to keep this from her?

'Is it someone here on the Island?'

'I can't say anything.'

'That's not fair.'

'I'm sorry. I can't.'

They walked along in silence, Lowri fuming but knowing that Nicola was not going to relent.

'What about you?' asked Nicola

'I'm OK.'

'Please don't be mad with me, Lowri. I want to help you. How are you coping?'

'Jack and I have our problems. Everyone does. But he is kind to me, looks after me. I like having a husband and, let's face it, who is going to want me now?'

Nicola grabbed her arm. 'Don't say that. That's awful. You're lovely.'

'But I'm not. I'm not just talking about my scars. You don't know me.'

Nicola picked up a stick and started to draw sweeping circles on the sand. 'Everyone has things to hide, puts on a face, a mask. Some try to look tough. Others smile. I think a lot of people are frightened others won't like the real them.'

Lowri looked thoughtfully at the circles Nicola was drawing. 'I think you're right. Mum said sometimes it was best just to put on a smile, some things were best not talked about.'

'She said that?'

'Mmm. I was teased at school and she said if I ignored them and kept smiling I'd feel better.'

'Did it work?'

'Not really. Looking back, it was hard work always trying to pretend things, and hide what I felt.'

'I know what you mean, we have to be polite, don't we? Someone says something and instead of hitting them we smile. The number of times I've stood there with this stupid grin on my face as another of my married friends rabbit on about 'ticking clocks' and 'left on the shelf' in a patronising way. Drives me mad.'

'You don't seem the sort to get worked up by that kind of thing.' said Lowri, surprised at Nicola's confession.

'Ah, you've only seen the church me. Wait till you see the real me.' Nicola laughed.

They walked further along. Nicola bent down and picked up a stone and showed it to Lowri. 'A dinosaur tooth.'

'Are you sure?'

170

'Yes. It's amazing down here, especially when the tide has just gone out. I'll keep that.' She put it in her pocket. 'You'll have to go to Compton one day, see the fossilised dinosaur prints.'

'I shall.'

Nicola picked up another stone. 'See, another fossil. Ken knows all about them. He has a fantastic collection. You must get him to show you sometime. Right, it's getting cold. Shall we make our way back? '

Lowri went to turn, she still thinking about what Nicola had said earlier. Who was this person Jack had been with? Why wouldn't Nicola tell her? She glanced at Nicola and was pretty sure Nicola knew what she was thinking. However, Nicola simply said, 'Good job I have an old towel in the car for Cassie.' She was obviously not going to say any more about it.

On their return to the house they saw Jack's car. When Lowri opened the door, he was in the hallway.

'You're back. We've been to the beach,' she said.

'I guessed from the state of Cassie. I'm glad you got out.'

Nicola came in.

'I need to try and get Cassie clean. I'll just go up and change. My trousers are wet,' said Lowri.

Jack took Cassie's lead from her. 'I'll have a go in the garden.'

'And I'll put coffee on,' said Nicola. 'I've got things ready for lunch. Just a bit more chopping to do.'

When Lowri returned, Nicola was in the kitchen. Jack came in from the garden with Cassie.

'It's no good. I can't get the sand off her with the towel.'

'I'd better give her a wash,' said Lowri.

171

Jack brought Cassie and followed Lowri into the utility room.

'I'll lift her into the sink for you.'

He did this and then, pulling the door behind him, went back into the kitchen.

Lowri started to wash a rather miserable looking Cassie, amazed at the amount of sand that came out of her coat. From the kitchen she could hear Jack talking to Nicola.

'How has she been?' asked Jack.

'It's going to take time. She's been through so much.'

'Of course.'

'She needs looking after, Jack.'

'I know.'

'I think you should tell her who you left her for.'

'There's no point.'

'But there is. She thinks it's in the past, that it's over.'

'It might as well be. Just leave it.' Lowri listened more intently: it wasn't like Jack to sound so angry. Shaking, Lowri pushed open the door, which was ajar. Nicola and Jack were standing very close. The door creaked slightly, and they both turned to look at her.

'Lowri,' said Nicola.

Jack came over to her. 'You should sit down. I'll finish off Cassie,' he said, and went into the utility room, slamming the door.

'I heard you talking.'

'It's nothing. Me interfering again.'

'Jack sounded very upset.'

Nicola put down the knife she was holding. 'I think I'd better go now.'

'But why?'

'I need to go and do some work. You have Jack to look after you now.'

172

'Please at least stay to eat.'

'No, I don't think so.'

'Thank you very much for looking after me.'

'That's fine. I enjoyed your company.'

'Come any time.'

Nicola smiled at her. 'Thank you. I enjoy my own space, you know.'

'Bye, then.' She kissed Lowri on the cheek and left.

Lowri waited to talk to Jack.

Chapter Eighteen

Without speaking, Jack served food out, and they sat opposite each other at the kitchen table. He opened a bottle of wine.

'Want some? I mean, you can now–'

Lowri shook her head. 'I still feel a bit sick.'

Jack looked up as he twirled the spaghetti round and round his fork.

'It was kind of Nicola to help,' Lowri said.

'Mm.'

'Shame she didn't stay.'

'She's busy.'

'But she has been so kind. Why were you arguing?'

Jack kept twirling his spaghetti.

Her heart beat harder. 'Jack, the other night, after the party, I know you didn't come home. Who did you stay with?'

His eyes looked around wearily. 'I was talking to someone, that's all.'

'Talking? All night?'

'Yes. I can talk to people, can't I?'

'But who was it?'

'That's private. Look, we have to have our own space in this relationship. I never ask you about the man you went off with, do I?'

Lowri shook her head. She felt consumed with guilt at the thought of it.

Jack leant forward and touched her hand. 'It's alright. I don't need to know. It works better if there are things we just keep off limits.'

Lowri clenched her fist and chewed lightly on the knuckle, trying to think. 'So does that mean you may sleep with other people sometimes without telling me?'

174

'Lowri, I shan't leave you. I told you. I'll look after you. Do you think you'd like to think about having another baby?'

Lowri dropped her knife and fork. 'Not yet.'

'It's just I was talking to Carina—'

'About us?'

'Just about having children. She mentioned that maybe you should have some tests. It might be that you have problems carrying a baby. It might be best to know.'

'The nurse said there was no reason this should happen again and, in any case, there is no rush.'

'I suppose I was thinking of Mum. She's desperate for grandchildren and she is so unwell. Us expecting really gave her something to live for. Dad said he saw a real change in her.'

She stared at him. Angry tears hurt her eyes. 'I am very sorry about your mother, but I need time to recover.'

'Yes. Of course. Um, sorry.' He looked out of the window. 'I need to get down to the manor and get on with painting. It's really starting to come on. Is it OK for me to leave you?'

She shook her head. 'Of course.'

'Also, on Monday I need to stay over in Southampton for a few days.'

'I'll be fine. Now, I think I'll go back to bed. I'm not hungry.'

'Good idea. I'll see you later.'

Lowri went back to bed. Her laptop was on her bedside table. She logged on to Facebook. She found a pile up of messages on her timeline all asking what the surprise was. She had forgotten she had started this. Part of her wondered if she should just play along the line of being pregnant, but she knew that would hurt too much. She might actually send herself completely off the edge. On her phone, she saw pictures of Fizzy. An idea came to her, and she uploaded it.

'The great news is that Fizzy is expecting kittens.'

Lowri knew that this would be a huge anticlimax, but it would have to do. She would need to do a bit of research into cats and pregnancy but she was sure she could play it along. She then started to write about the wonderful walks and friends she was making. Her eyes blurred with tears, but she kept writing faster and faster: if she wrote enough maybe she would believe it herself.

Over the weekend she went out for short walks with Cassie. She started a kind of nature diary of her walks on Facebook. This was the truth: she really did keep a record of the things she saw, and as she did, she learned about the birds and plants that, even in the middle of winter, she could see. One thing she did fabricate was her baking. She went into the local shop and bought a locally made Victoria sponge and a jar of homemade jam, photographed them, and wrote 'Look at me getting all homely, made this jam and then filled my 'perfect' sponge cake with it.' Her friends were all suitably impressed. She particularly liked the comment 'Well done Lowri, everything you do is perfect.' She would like to have printed that off and framed it.

On the Monday Jack left for the university. Lowri realised her work was piling up: she needed to get back to it. She thought about her Polish friends. She missed them, missed speaking Polish. Maybe sometime she would have to at least go over and visit them.

Lowri worked hard all day. It wasn't until early evening when the doorbell disturbed her. It was already dark. When she opened the door she found Heather holding, of course, a cake. On seeing Lowri she put the cake on a small table and enveloped her in a big hug. 'I'm so sorry.'

She was so warm and loving, Lowri found herself choking back tears.

'Thank you. Come in. Have you time for coffee or do you need to get back?'

'I've finished, thank God.'

Cassie came running over to Heather. 'Hello you,' said Heather, stroking her. 'When is your Mum going to bring you out to meet everyone, then?' She looked up at Lowri and followed her into the kitchen. Lowri made the coffee and they sat at the table.

'Tell me how you are.'

'I'm so tired all the time.'

'I was shattered for a few weeks.'

'Oh did you – ?'

'Yes. A few years ago now. Sorry. I'm not saying I know how you feel–'

'But you know what it's like. How far gone were you?'

'I was eight weeks. It's awful. Some people, well, the things they say.'

'Like what? I haven't seen many people–'

'It doesn't matter.'

'Tell me. I'll be prepared.'

'Lee's Mum. She said, 'at least it was early'.'

Lowri cringed.

'Exactly. A miscarriage means a lost child, no matter when it occurs,' said Heather.

'It must have hurt.'

'People are just trying to help. It just comes out wrong. That's all.'

'I feel nothing, numb,' said Lowri. 'It's like all my plans have been torn up, and I don't know what to do next. I think I will just hide away and do my work.'

'I had the café. I had to go out, but it was awful.'

'How was Lee?'

'Very upset. He would love to have had children. He's so good with Poppy. I wanted him to have a child that was his, but it was not to be.'

'You sound quite philosophical about it all.'

'I didn't feel it, but you know how it is. You put on a smile and really people don't want to talk about it.'

'I can see that. So, how are things at the café?'

'Really busy. Dave is putting on some craft classes. People are already starting to build up to Christmas. Of course, with some of the pottery he does, they make it, fire it and then decorate, and it takes time. Come December it'll be more people just decorating ready made pots and plates. Anyway, it's all very popular, and it knocks on to the café.'

'That's good.'

'It is, and we have some good news. A woman in the village called Gita is coming to work, part time you know. It will be such a help.'

'That's great.'

'You know, if you fancied some work, just say.'

Lowri stood up and went to find the biscuit tin. She was completely thrown by the suggestion. She put the tin down, took off the lid, took a bourbon biscuit and then pushed the tin towards Heather, who was sitting forward eagerly. Lowri realised she was being serious.

'I know you have your work. Maybe you are too busy. I thought it might be a way of coming out and meeting people.'

'I don't think so. Really Heather, I can't bake, or anything like that. Really, I'm not being modest. I'm hopeless.'

'Carina and I can do all that. In any case, I don't suppose you have the qualifications for food handling and preparation.'

'No, nothing like that.'

'That's OK. What I need is someone on the till, to serve people.'

Lowri bit her lip. 'Look, Heather, I know you are being kind, but people are not going to want to be served by someone who looks like me.'

'What do you mean?'

'My face, Heather. Look at me. I'm enough to put anyone off their food.'

'Don't be silly.'

'I'm not. I've seen the looks, heard the comments.'

Heather sat back in the chair. 'You know, Gita was worried about coming in her sari and now you're concerned about your scar. You mustn't worry. Let's face it, not many people look perfect. Look at me: they might think 'better not have too many scones or I will end up like her.'

Lowri smiled. 'You know that doesn't happen.'

'You never know what people are thinking. I've learned that much.'

'You're right. Seriously, thanks for the offer. I'll see how things go.'

'I'll give you my number. Ring me when you feel like popping in.'

Lowri added Heather to her phone.

'Good. Now send me a message so I've got yours – Thanks. Right, I'd better get off.'

Lowri saw her to the door. The village was in darkness, but she could see light rain shining in the beams of the street lights. She stroked Cassie's head.

'I think we will just go in the garden tonight.'

Cassie charged around the garden. Lowri looked over at Jack's studio. She went back into the house, took down the large key from the hook and went back out. Suddenly, she really needed to see what was in there. Following the beam from her torch, she made her way over, went straight to the door, and tried to put the key in the lock. She shone her torch: the previous lock had been replaced by an enormous, brand new shiny one.

Chapter Nineteen

The next day it was raining. Lowri looked out of her window. As she dressed she realised it was time to go and finally get some decent walking clothes, not 'climbing the Alps' type clothes, but boots that didn't leak over trousers, as hideous as they were, and a proper waterproof coat. For these things she guessed she would have to drive into Newport. First she let Fizzy in and Cassie out. 'I'll be back Cassie and we can go for a proper walk.'

Getting in the car Lowri felt the memories of the crash coming back: she hadn't driven a car for weeks. As she drove out of the village, she was aware she was driving more slowly than others, and could sense local drivers creeping up behind. The route was straightforward.

Newport High Street had the same generic shops as most places but seemed very small. There wasn't an indoor shopping centre with posh lifts and eating places, nowhere was even pedestrianised, but the shops she needed were there. For the first time in her life she went into camping shops. Inside she found there were a lot more clothes than she expected and a lot seemed to be reduced. A young boy who looked like he should be in school came over and proved very helpful; he seemed excited to find someone who actually wanted help.

When she returned home, she realised how easily tired she became lately. 'Sorry, Cassie. I'm worn out. I need to rest first.'

Later, she took Cassie up on to the downs. There was nobody about. It was as if she had the whole place to herself. She breathed in the calm. Out here, life made sense. Autumn was sliding into winter, which would give way to spring. There was a cycle: meaning. Cassie went charging off. There was something very secure about being here on an island. Lowri hadn't expected to feel like this but, as she stood looking around, she knew, amid all the uncertainty in her life, this was the place she wanted to be.

Feeling calmer, she returned home, logged on and went back to work. There was something quite comforting about the translation she did: it was not difficult for her but interesting enough to stop her thinking about everything else.

The next few days she took Cassie further afield. Using a local guide book she went each day to a new place. They visited Parkhurst Woods although, of course, they saw no squirrels; they walked around Carisbrooke Castle and watched the buzzards circling and quarrelling with crows. One day they went even further to visit Quarr Abbey. Lowri turned off a busy road to Ryde, along track surrounded by woodland. She took Cassie down past small pens of pigs and sheep. Some parts of the abbey were in ruins, some lived in by Benedictine monks. Lowri saw signposts to an art exhibition, but guessed they wouldn't want Cassie in there. There were families around, some of the children incongruously wearing masks, and then she remembered that this was Saturday the thirty-first: it was Halloween tonight. Leaving them behind, she went off in to the woodland, looking over at the sea in the distance. Both worn out, she took Cassie back to the café. It was dry even though it was cold and she was able to sit out side with cake and coffee. She was surprised to see Peter, the vicar from Elmstone.

'Oh, Lowri. Sorry, I didn't see you there.' He leant down and stroked Cassie.

Lowri thought how much more relaxed he seemed. He sat on the edge of the seat opposite, while Cassie moved closer, enjoying the attention.

'I come over here when I can. It's very refreshing.'

'Do you go to the services?'

'Sometimes. I've stayed the odd night, followed the monks routine: early start before five, strict routine of services, and there is always work. It's a hard day but enormously satisfying.'

'Would you like to be a monk?'

He grinned. 'Frequently. No PCC meetings and fund raising for leaking roofs, no quarrels over organ restoration. I have that tripled with three churches.'

'And, of course, there is your work preaching and visiting.'

'Now, that I don't mind. I enjoy the one to one work. It's the rest I struggle with. Still, sacrifice and service: that's what it should be about, shouldn't it?'

'I guess.'

His face broke into a smile. 'Listen to me! There are doctors and social workers out there who would love to have my life. How are you, then, Lowri? I was so sorry to hear about the loss of your baby.'

Lowri looked up, relieved that someone had mentioned her baby, not just 'a miscarriage.' 'It has been so hard. Coming to a place like this is healing. It's peaceful here.'

'I'm glad it's helping you. Sometimes we need something other than words.'

'Nicola has been a great support.'

He beamed. 'I'm sure. Nicola is an exceptionally kind person, easily overlooked and undervalued. But then the ability to show kindness is often underestimated.'

'Yes. I can see that. I mean, stand her next to someone like Carina and who would notice her?'

Peter nodded. 'Mind you, if I had to choose, I would rather be Nicola. She has an inner stability and assurance that Carina does not.' He stood up. 'Right, I'd better get back to what they call the real world, or at least a different

183

one. I have no doubt I shall see you around. Take care now.'

After he had left, Lowri noticed a couple arrive at the table next to her. They had a small dachshund and the woman was heavily pregnant.

'You sit down, love. Now, what do you fancy. Tea? peppermint? Great. So peppermint tea, and what to eat? a scone or sponge?'

He stood waiting for her to make up her mind, watching earnestly.

'I think some flapjack if they've got it.'

'Wonderful.' The man glowed at his partner as if she had just answered the winning question on Mastermind. The woman sat back and closed her eyes. She must have been at least six months pregnant. She rested her hands on her stomach. The man returned and carefully placed the drinks and cake in front of her. Suddenly, the woman clasped her stomach. 'She kicked. Our baby kicked.'

The man laid his hand tenderly on her stomach, enthralled.

Lowri thought about her own pregnancy. No-one had looked at her like that. No-one had shared her joy. Jack had tried. At least his first words had been 'that's wonderful', but the father of her baby, his look had been one of horror. She realised he didn't even know that she had lost the baby. Would he care? Maybe he would be relieved? It was a terrible thought. Tears welled up. There was a baby inside that woman, and there wasn't one inside her; she had never felt a kick. Maybe she never would. All the healing of the past days seemed to disappear. The wound was as raw and open as before.

Quickly she picked up Cassie's lead and walked to the car: she needed to get home. The house was empty. Lowri tried to work but all the time she kept seeing that couple.

Eventually she turned on the TV. She was watching mindlessly when the door bell rang.

For some reason she expected to see Heather. However, instead, she opened the door to a find a group of young children dressed up, trick or treating. A mother stood behind the children dressed as ghosts and fairies.

Lowri smiled at them 'Hang on let me see what I have.'

Lowri ran into the kitchen. She grabbed the packet of mini Mars bars she had bought earlier, and went back to the front door. She started to hand them out to the children.

'What are you dressed as?' She asked one of the children but the girl stared at her. Lowri put her hand to her face. She had forgotten.

The mother stepped forward. 'I'm sorry. That's rude, Stacey.'

Lowri looked down at Stacey, who looked mystified.

'I was in an accident. This isn't pretend,' she said.

'Does it hurt?' Stacey asked.

'Not too much. Stiff. Uncomfortable, but I have cream for it.'

'Good.'

Lowri smiled at the little girl, who smiled back.

'Thank you,' said the woman.

Lowri went back into the house feeling good: the child had accepted what she said, and it had seemed nothing but the truth.

It was much later. Lowri was thinking of going up to bed when the door bell rang again. Casually, she went to answer the door, but what greeted her was deeply shocking. It was a group of teenagers. One boy had used specialist make-up to create incredibly realistic scars as if he had been slashed seven or eight times on his face. On his neck, it was if a chunk of skin had been bitten off, and blood ran down. It was horrific. Next to him, another boy also had made-up scars and a gouged out eye. She felt sick. Why dress like that? It was so personal. Her scars were not some kind of joke, or scare tactic. Why did people think scars were scary anyway? Why did the bad guy always have a scar? Is that why people looked at her like they did? Were they scared of her? The wind was howling; the only light was the street light. One of the boys stepped towards her threateningly, and held out a bucket.

'No. Go away,' she said, her voice shaking.

'Hey, want another scar to match that one, freak?' said the second boy.

Suddenly she cracked.

'Don't you call me a freak! Where do you get off, dressing up like that? It's disgusting, ignorant, and cruel.'

One of the boys laughed. 'God, the freak is getting all worked up.'

'If you call me a freak again I shall–'

'You'll what?'

It was like the world turned blood red. Lowri grabbed the small stone statue from the table by the door.

'See this? This perfect, bloody statue. One more word and I shall smash it over your thick, stupid, ignorant head.'

One boy grabbed the arm of the boy who was laughing.

'Come on. Leave the mad cow.'

'I'm not mad. I'm not a monster. I am a person with a bloody scar: that is all. No-one is perfect. Get that: no-one.'

The boys walked away quickly, and Lowri slammed the door. Taking the statue, she threw it on to the stone floor. It shattered in pieces. Lowri fell to the floor, head in her hands, and wept. What had she become? She had never shouted at anyone like that before. What on earth was happening to her? Cassie came running up to her, frightened by all the noise.

186

'It's alright. Sorry. Mummy has been stupid. Be careful, I need to get these bits up before you hurt your paws.' She picked up the pieces and took them into the kitchen.

For weeks following this, Lowri kept very much to herself. She felt like a tortoise going into hibernation, working and adding to her Facebook page. University broke early. Jack spent his days working in the manor. When they were together, they were kind, polite, and gentle with each other. Sometimes they even ate meals together, chatted about their day, and watched TV. For the first time for what felt like a very long time, Lowri felt a stillness descend on her life.

Then one evening, she was sitting alone watching TV, curled up with Fizzy one side of her, Cassie the other, drinking hot chocolate. Suddenly, she felt a sharp pain in her stomach; she put down her mug and rushed to the toilet. To her horror, she realised she was bleeding. She panicked: what was happening? That terrible, sick, dread that she felt the day of her fall came back. At first, she sat waiting for the pain, but slowly realised that it was not going to happen. Relieved, she understood that this must be her first normal period since losing the baby. She hadn't expected to go back to normal so soon. When she realised what was happening an unexpected deep sadness wrapped itself around her like a blanket. Of course, she had known she wasn't pregnant anymore, but this was like the final seal in her mind. It was as if her baby had never been. She went to her bedroom and reached into her drawer, took out the fossil, and found comfort. The stone was still there: it hadn't gone away. Her baby would always be a part of her. Clasping the fossil, she started to cry, sob, deep hard sobs.

Still crying she changed into her nightie and curled up tight under her duvet until she finally fell asleep.

Chapter Twenty

Late one evening in early December, Heather was in her living room working on her laptop. She was exhausted. Thank God they had Gita working in the café now: it had been manic. Earlier she had been checking the accounts. The takings had been very good but, despite that, only Heather knew just how deeply in debt they were. The demands for money just kept rolling in, as well as Poppy constantly sending her bills and receipts. She tried always to reimburse Poppy quickly. She didn't want her to know how bad things were, but others were getting impatient.

Maybe tonight things would go her way? She was completely engrossed when her husband Lee returned from work.

'Oh, gosh,' she said, quickly shutting the laptop. Lee looked exhausted.

'Sorry love, I didn't mean to startle you. You still up working? It's gone midnight.'

'I lose track of time when I'm writing.'

'I don't know how you have the energy after work. Were you busy in the café again today?'

'Yes. We had a couple of coaches in.'

'Did you use the new mincemeat I made for you?'

'I did. A customer asked me for the recipe for our pies, but I said it was my husband's secret.'

Lee went into the kitchen and poured himself a glass of water. She could hear him gulping it down. It had been a long, hard, day.

'How were things at the hotel?'

Two bloody office parties at lunchtime, three this evening. You know, leaving dos and birthdays. Oh, and a hen party. That was fun.' He came back and slumped into a chair. 'Honestly, Heather, when it's large groups they all get so pissed I might as well serve them fish fingers instead of Ventnor Lobster.'

'You could never do that. Anyway, people always get drunk. You know that.'

'It's so depressing. I hate Christmas. We have so many bookings.'

'That's because of your reputation. Never mind. One day, maybe you'll have your own place and you'll be serving your own taster menu to discerning customers.'

'We just have to keep saving.'

He didn't see her cringe.

'I've managed to get some time off tomorrow, by the way,' he said. 'I'm going surfing.'

'It's freezing.'

'I know, but the surf's pumping. Did you order that bread maker for Mum?'

'It's nearly two hundred quid, Lee. We can get her something much cheaper than that. She only wants to make the odd loaf.'

'I don't like to scrimp on her Christmas present.'

'I know. Leave it with me.'

'And did you ring the jewellers about your eternity ring? They've had it for ages.'

'Still not in. Don't worry. There's no rush.'

'OK. Now, you need to keep Poppy's feet on the ground with this wedding. That sister of Alistair's is feeding her with all sorts of ideas. Poppy was telling me about them in the car. It's madness, and not even what Poppy wants, half the time.'

'It matters to her what Alistair's family think of us, love. It's only natural. I don't want them to think we've skimped on the wedding.'

'Don't let them bankrupt us.'

'We're fine. Look, it's Poppy's big day. I want her to have her dream wedding.'

'But you're not a fairy godmother, and we don't have an endless supply of money. We had a simple do: you got your dress in the sale in Newport. Mum did the food, but it was a great day, wasn't it?'

'It was. It was perfect, but it's not what Poppy wants.'

'I guess not.' He stood up slowly. 'I'll go on up. Why don't you join me?'

'Soon. Just a bit more writing to do–'

Heather listened to him going up the stairs. She was breathing fast. She slowly re- opened her laptop.

It was Jack who brought up the subject of Christmas.

'So, what shall we do on Christmas Day? My parents are off on their cruise. It's me and you. Shall I see if I can find a place for us to eat out?'

'I don't think so. Let's just stay in. I could get the ready-made stuff from the supermarket. How about that?'

'That's fine. I'll go to church in the morning if you fancy coming.'

'I'll leave it, thanks.'

'What are we going to do about Carina's party?' Jack asked.

Lowri was surprised he even mentioned it.

'We're not going to that, are we?'

'I was thinking maybe we could.'

'Really?'

'We need to do some things together, and this is the biggest social event over here.'

'But it's dressing up. I hate that.'

Jack laughed. 'Don't let Carina hear you call it dressing up. It's a very sophisticated event, and most people hire something.'

'Good grief. You really want to go?'

'Yes. I think it would be good for us.'

'So, I have to hire something?'

'That's it. Sort of medieval.'

'Not a sexy devil, then? Nicola teased Carina about vicars and tarts.'

'Really? She would have been so cross.'

'She was a bit. OK. Will you sort yourself out?'

'Of course. It's easy. I have a costume I've used for various events at uni.'

Lowri sighed and turned to start searching costumes for a smart masquerade ball. After she had ordered some clothes she made coffee, looked out, and saw that it was a crisp sunny morning. On the spur of the moment she decided that she would take Cassie down to the beach. Surely one of the luxuries of living by the sea was that you didn't only save it for days out on hot sunny holidays, but you could go for shorter visits in any weather, any time? She wore plenty of layers, and drove down to the Compton Bay.

The sky looked sharp light blue. The car park was nearly empty. However, there were a few vans, with surfers walking around holding their boards. Lowri took Cassie on the lead to the top of a steep flight of steps leading down to the beach. Cassie was pulling hard on the lead and Lowri, frightened of being pulled down the steps, let her off. Cassie charged down ahead of her. Lowri looked along at the miles of contrasting golden and dark sands, with rolling waves, tumbling multi-coloured sandstone cliffs, and the white chalk cliffs in the distance. The winter sun seemed to highlight everything.

She started to walk along the beach. The cliffs were amazing shapes and colours. Walking along the tide line, she saw a man with his dog. Cassie dashed down the beach to greet the dog. Lowri started to walk towards them, calling Cassie, who took no notice. As the man came towards her, she recognised him. Oh no, she thought, it's that man Dave from the Longstone. She kept calling Cassie, but she was running in and out of the waves with the other dog.

'Hi again,' shouted Dave. 'She's still not coming back, is she?'

Lowri scowled: why was Cassie being so difficult?

Dave came closer. 'Great to have the place to ourselves, isn't it? Fabulous morning.'

Lowri looked around at empty stretches of sand: he was right. They were the only ones there apart from the black dots of surfers in the sea.

'I come down looking for bits and pieces. Found some shells, and some nice shaped stones.'

As Lowri watched Cassie playing, she realised she had no option but to chat.

'I was on the beach further along from here with Nicola. You know, the hospital chaplain?'

'Yes I know her. She tried to get me to go to church, but it's not my thing. Still, I like her. Sort of person you can talk to.'

'You're right. She has been very kind to me. She's very good at finding fossils.'

'I know. I ask her to tell me what I've found sometimes.'

Lowri looked out at the sea. 'Nicola is going to come down swimming with me sometime. Do you like to go in the water?'

'I've got to love it. I've never lived anywhere where you can just go for a swim when you feel like it. Down here I like to belly board; the waves are fantastic.'

'What's that, then?'

'Don't you know?'

'No, sorry,' she mumbled.

'No reason you should, I guess. You have a small board and lie on it. Go in on the waves. I expect the guys who are into real surfing think it's for wimps, but it's good fun. You ought to try it.'

'Do you need lessons?'

'God, no.'

'I'm not at all sporty. I can't swim. That's why Nicola said she'd come with me. Though, to be honest, I haven't even got a swimming costume.'

'Get one, then, and have some lessons. Everyone should be able to swim.'

'Mm. Yes, maybe I should. I wouldn't know where to go. I'd have to go to a beginner's class. That would be embarrassing: swimming with a load of toddlers.'

Dave laughed. 'Don't look so worried. It was only a suggestion.'

'Why did you sound so cross, then?' was what she wanted to say, but she daren't. She still found him rather frightening.

'Nicola said something about some dinosaur footprints down here?'

'Oh yes. Have you seen them?'

'Not yet.'

'Come on...I'll show you.'

Without waiting for her, Dave started walking quickly away. Lowri followed. 'I was looking up at the cliffs. They're beautiful,' she said, breathlessly.

'The purple, blue and pink sediments were deposited about a hundred and twenty six million years ago, incredible. Here we are: one of the footprints.'

'And that really is a fossilised dinosaur footprint?'

194

'Yup. It's of an Iguanodon's foot. Left about a hundred and twenty five million years ago. Hard to get your head around, isn't it?'

As they were looking, Lowri heard Cassie barking. Along the water's edge she saw someone riding a large black horse.

'That's Carina's husband, isn't it? He said he came down here.'

'Comes to escape the mistress of the manor. I hear your husband is getting on well with the fresco down there. I'd like to see that when it's finished.'

'It'll take a long time. He's a perfectionist with his work.'

'The thing I like about pottery is that, at least in the early stages, you can start again when you make mistakes.'

'I can understand that, although I guess the aim must be not to make mistakes in the first place.'

Dave laughed. 'Nothing wrong with mistakes. The only way to avoid mistakes is to do nothing.'

Lowri found herself smiling. 'That's the first time I've heard a positive spin on it.'

'My speciality.'

They walked along together, the dogs chasing each other.

'Heather told me about, you know, you being ill,' Dave said awkwardly.

'Losing my baby, do you mean?'

'Yes, sorry. I don't know how to put it.'

'It's alright.'

'Nicola actually gave me a fossil.' Lowri took the ammonite from her pocket. 'She said my baby would never be forgotten.' As she stared down at the fossil, her shoulders started to shake, and as hard as she tried she couldn't stop. She pressed her eyes together tightly, but the tears squeezed though. She roughly wiped them away, but still more came. It was so embarrassing to cry in front of this man she hardly knew. Then she felt Dave touch her very gently on the shoulder. Without looking up, she turned and was enveloped by him. It was like being in the shelter of a huge rock.

'Shush. Cariad,' he whispered,

She looked up, shocked. 'That's Welsh.'

He smiled self-consciously. 'My gran was Welsh.'

Quickly, Lowri wiped her face. 'Sorry. I don't know what happened.'

'It's OK.'

'I think I'm over it, but then something happens, makes me remember Aniolku.'

'Who?'

'Oh, sorry. It's the name I gave to my baby. It's Polish for angel. It's the name I chose.'

'That's beautiful.'

'I was in a café a while back, Quarr Abbey, it was. I saw this couple. She was pregnant and he was looking at her like–' she looked at a heap of pebbles on the beach. 'Like she was diamond among those stones.'

'She's a lucky woman, and he's a lucky man to feel that way.'

'I think so.'

Dave smiled. 'Well, you have Jack. I'm sure he appreciates you.'

Lowri looked around. A few surfers were appearing and disappearing in the waves. Cassie and Ceba were running on the sand, free.

He smiled. 'Having a good time, aren't they? Sensible animals, dogs. Live in the present.'

'Heather told me you come from London? She said you were very successful up there?'

196

'Moderately so.'

'Why did you leave?'

'I've not exactly left. I have part ownership of a gallery up there, and my flat. I came here for a kind of break, get some new ideas, inspiration. I saw the job in the pottery and thought it would be an interesting place to work for a while.'

'It sounds a bit mundane for you.'

'My friends in London think I'm mad and it was a risk, but I like having space to think. I even enjoy working with the kids. I love their enthusiasm; it reminds me why I went into pottery in the first place. Also I have come to love the island, I didn't expect that, I thought it would drive me crazy being so small and away from the action of London.'

'But you've grown to love it?'

'I have, I don't go back to London nearly as often as I should. So, what do you do?'

'I work for an agency. They send me stuff to translate. Either English to Polish or the other way around. It's interesting. It can be work for Polish businesses setting up, and wanting work edited and checked, or sometimes Polish people want things translated. I've also done some work for educational publishers. It's all sorts really.'

'You must be very good at Polish.'

'It was my degree subject. I love it.'

'That's impressive.'

'Not really.'

'Yes, it is. You're funny. You're brighter than you let on. I'm used to the opposite up in London. So many people seems desperate to be thought of as smart, put on an act. They come and look at the ceramics at the studio, talk about them loudly using all the jargon, but I can spot someone churning out Wikipedia; it was so annoying.'

'They just didn't want to look stupid. I can understand that.'

'I suppose so. I think you must be a much nicer person than me. After all, I never even got an A level, let alone a degree. I expect I'm just bitter and twisted.'

They walked down to the waters edge. Dave picked up stones, and threw them into the sea. Lowri's heart leapt as she watched Cassie run in after them with Ceba. However, both dogs soon returned and were barking at Dave to throw some more.

'How did you learn to do pottery? Surely you needed to go to college?' she asked, shouting over the dogs.

'I left school after GCSEs and worked in a pottery outside London. I would travel on tubes and buses every day. I'd been put in touch with this woman by my art teacher from school. Anyway, I learned a lot from her, did courses. I was lucky. I got breaks. Then I teamed up with another artist. She had all the drive. You see, I've been very lucky. That's all. Still, I think to be able to speak languages like you do must be amazing.'

Lowri shrugged. 'I love languages. I'm lucky I can do it. That's all. I have some pottery actually. It's from Poland. Do you like Polish pottery? I bought it when I was out there.'

'Ah, Boleslawiec pottery. Yes, a lot of skill. I love the creamy white and blues. It's becoming quite popular. Very high quality clay. I worked with some once: beautiful stuff. You can fire it at really high temperatures. After it's been glazed, it's virtually waterproof.'

'I don't know the technical stuff but it is lovely. You can buy it in some of the shops in London.'

They walked towards the steps.

'Right. I need to get my head together now. I've got a big group of school kids coming in later,' said Dave.

'What are you doing with them?'

'They're very little. They will make some simple pots this week and then next time they can decorate them. The problem is they only come with one teacher and there are a few children with like special needs. They get frustrated.'

'Can't the teacher sort them out?'

'It's a class of thirty. It's difficult, and they are so excited coming into the pottery.'

'I think that's great, a really good thing to do.'

'Of course, I don't want to squash their enthusiasm, but it's difficult.'

'You need to be firm to begin with, I guess.'

'You mean shout at them more?'

'No. My friend who is a teacher said you must speak in a quiet, low, firm voice so they have to listen.'

'I should go on a course I suppose. So, have you worked with kids much?'

'No. I helped out on trips with Jack.'

'Did you need checks for that?'

She frowned. 'Actually, I did get registered on the DBS. What with the Polish groups I did as well. I pay into a scheme that automatically updates my certificate, covers me for my voluntary work as well.'

They climbed up the steps and put their dogs on leads.

'You up to much this morning?' asked Dave.

'Usual work. I've been hiding away lately.' Lowri's hand went automatically to her scars. She realised that she hadn't thought about them at all when she had been with Dave, although he must have noticed them.

Dave put his head to one side. 'I don't suppose you fancy coming to help me this morning?'

'You must be joking. I'm not arty at all.'

'I don't need someone arty. I need someone to sit with the kids who need help.'

'What does it entail?'

'Just encouraging them.'

'I'm not creative.'

'It's only pinch pots. I'll be there anyway if you need help.'

Lowri thought of another day in the empty house on her own. 'Well, alright. If it's OK with Heather?'

'She'll be pleased I've got help.'

'What time are they coming?'

'About eleven.'

'Shall I come about half ten, then?'

'See: you're a natural.'

She laughed. 'I'll see you later.'

As she drove back to the house Lowri started to worry about the work. What had she let herself in for? What if the children were really naughty for her? What if she showed them the wrong way to do things? Maybe she shouldn't go, but then how would she let Dave know? Still fretting, she went back into the house wondering what to do.

Chapter Twenty One

After a lot of worrying, Lowri decided she should go to the pottery. She only had to go once, and then never again. From her wardrobe, she found her oldest trousers, and put another layer of make-up on. As she left the house, she felt very sick and nervous.

When she arrived, Heather was serving a customer. She looked up and gave a welcoming smile.

'Lowri – Dave told me you are coming to help him.'

'Is it alright? I don't know how much help I will be–'

'I'm sure you'll be fine.'

'I brought my DBS check.'

'Well done. Thank you. Want a coffee?'

Carina came in from the kitchen. and looked surprised to see Lowri.

'She's helping Dave,' explained Heather.

'Good luck with that. You'll be alright, won't you?' Carina spoke quietly in her warm, sympathetic voice.

'What do you mean?' asked Lowri.

'Children can be cruel, you know,' Carina glanced at her scars.

Lowri felt herself blushing. 'I put on as much make-up as I could–'

'Don't be ridiculous, Carina,' said Heather, shooting a look of annoyance at her. 'Lowri will be fine. Let's get you coffee. Can you take one through to Dave as well?'

Lowri took the mugs through. The studio was bigger than she expected. Dave was setting out a number of long wooden tables. He looked up.

'Ah, coffee. Brilliant,' he shouted.

Lowri walked over to him and handed him his mug. Looking down at her own, she said, 'By the way, if any of the children find it difficult, you know, with my face, tell me. I won't be offended in the least. I can go–'

'What on earth are you talking about?'

'It's just–'

'Come on. Stop talking rubbish. Now, we have work to do.'

Lowri blinked, feeling a bit stupid for bringing it up. Dave, however, had moved on.

'There will be thirty kids. They'll all need a slate to work on, ball of clay, small water dish, and one of these utensils.'

'I can do that.'

'I'd grab an apron. Gets pretty messy in here.'

Lowri started to arrange the places with Dave. They were only just ready when they heard a rising grumble of noise coming towards them like a wave about to break.

'They're here,' said Dave. He went quickly to meet them. Lowri followed. They found places for coats and bags. The children were very excited. They huddled like lively puppies around the front table, where Dave demonstrated the pinch pots they were going to make that day. He spoke well to them. He spoke gently, but the children listened and most seemed enthusiastic and confident. They started putting on aprons. Dave was talking to the teacher, who then came over to Lowri.

'Dave said you'd be able to help a few of the children who might need a bit of extra support?'

'That's right.'

'Great. I've put the three of them together. Polly will just need encouragement. John can get easily frustrated, and Philip has problems with fine motor skills. I've put Ruby next to Polly. They are great friends, so they should be OK.'

Feeling full of trepidation, Lowri went over to the small group. As the teacher had said, Ruby was already tuned into helping Polly. John was busy bashing his clay, and seemed to be occupied, so she sat with Philip. She found that if she held the clay for him he was able to work quite well. Suddenly, John slammed down his clay.

'It's rubbish. I can't do it.'

She looked at his pot. 'Remember, Dave said not to push your thumb through the bottom.'

'I have. It's ruined.'

'No. The good thing about clay is that you can start again. See. Look, no hole. Now, try again. A bit more gently this time.'

Lowri spent her time working between the two boys. She didn't have time to look up, or think about anything else. At one point, John said, 'So what happened to your face? Were you glassed in a pub?'

Shocked, she said, 'No, it was a car accident actually.'

'Does it hurt?' Polly asked.

'No, it's alright.'

'My Mum lost all her hair,' said Philip. 'She's got cancer.'

'I'm really sorry,' Lowri said, thinking how hard it must be for him and his mother.

'She's got a wig. She likes it, said she always wanted curly hair.'

'My Dad got glassed,' said John.

'Was he hurt badly?'

'Not as bad as the other one.'

'Oh, right. Well, shall we get back to the pots?'

Dave raised his voice. 'Mrs Brown and I are going to come round with a piece of paper and put your name and class on it to put with your pots. When you come next week your pot will be ready to decorate'.

The session had gone quickly. When the children finally left, a hush fell over the studio. Carefully, they moved the children's work and started to clear up. It took nearly an hour to have a completely clear space again.

'It's a lot of work,' said Lowri.

'It's great having you to help. You did so well with the kids.'

'They just needed one to one.'

'That's right.'

'So, what will you do for the rest of the day?'

'Some of my own work. I make mugs and some bespoke pieces for sale in the café.'

'You use the wheel for that?'

'Sometimes, yes. I'd love the children to have a go, but it's too difficult to organise,'

'You could do adult classes.'

'I guess so. Have you ever tried?'

'No, never.'

'Jack's the artist then?'

'Of course. What are you working on at the moment?'

She followed him over to the wheel.

'This is my latest pot.'

Dave held up a stunning bronze coloured pot, decorated with fish.

'That's beautiful.'

Lowri glanced at Dave. He was such a big man, tall: broad, arms with the muscles of a boxer, his shaved head making him look formidable. He was the sort of man who, if she saw him out, words like threatening, fighter, scary, trouble, would spring to mind. And yet he had produced this stunning piece of work.

'I have never seen anyone use a wheel.'

'Want to have a go?'

'I'd be useless.'

'Come on. Give it a go. I'll give you some of the more expensive clay. It's a bit harder to handle, but it'll have a nice finish for you to decorate. Before we start, we have to wedge the clay, get rid of all the air pockets. Hang on, you could be doing this.' He handed her the piece of clay. 'Use the heel of your hand. Push it about fifty times.'

Lowri began using her fingertip.

'No, the heel. And really push it around. Go for it.'

'I'm sorry.'

'It's OK. It's not hard. You'll learn quickly: you see.'

She began again. The clay felt cold and smooth.

'Good. Now, just slap it between your hands.'

'Like this?'

'That's fine. Great. Come over to the wheel. Now, you have to decide how to sit.'

Lowri sat down. Dave laughed.

'What have I done wrong?'

'Nothing. You're so tiny. That's all. Hang on, I'll find a higher seat.'

Lowri was fascinated. 'This is so different to watching Jack work. He's very remote from his work: uses long brushes, sits back a lot. He is very neat and calculating.'

'All artists are different. I always was a very messy person.'

'Now, we need to centre it on the wheel.'

Lowri took her clay and, with Dave's help, she got it as close to the centre as she could.

'And we'll start the wheel. Don't panic. It'll be alright. Put your elbows on your knees, and add a bit of water. Now, put both hands on the clay. We want to centre the clay by placing one hand on the side and the other on top of the clay cone.'

Dave sat close by helping her all the time, but still Lowri found she was holding her breath; there was so much to think about.

Eventually, he said, 'Now, use both thumbs. Press into the centre of the clay. Raise the walls. Hey, that's great. Use a finger on the inside and your heel on the outside.'

Everything seemed to happen at once: the clay went faster and faster out of control. Lowri grabbed at it, and it collapsed in a heap.

Dave stopped the wheel.

'I'm so sorry. What a waste of clay. I should never have done it.'

Lowri started to get off the seat.

'Hey. Don't give up. Come on. We can just start again. It's not the end of the world.'

'There's no point.'

'Yes, there is. Come on, try again.'

Lowri scowled at him but sat back down. They started the whole process again. This time she managed to keep things under better control.

'Good. Don't panic now,' said Dave.

The pot started to take shape. Eventually Dave slowed the wheel down.

The pot was far from perfect. Using a wire, Dave removed it from the wheel.

As he reached to help her down from the seat Lowri noticed a tattoo on the inside of his wrist. It was a blue rectangle with a smaller yellow rectangle inside, split through with blue. Underneath there was written a date, 01.03.13. She glanced up at him, saw a flash of pain in his eyes.

'There you are: your first pot,' he said.

'The rim isn't right. Look, I missed some bits on the outside–'

'It's fine.'

'It's not perfect.'

'If we wanted perfection, we could use moulds. But this is your work: you created it.'

'It's not very good.'

'Are you always so hard on yourself?'

'Just honest.'

'It was your first time.'

'Sorry. I enjoyed it.'

'Good.'

'I'll fire this. You can decorate it.'

'Don't bother. It's rubbish. I bet that's what you think. I can't take it home to Jack. He'd laugh.'

He looked serious, almost angry. 'Stop being obsessed with what other people think. You'll never try anything new if you do that. Remember, sometimes we have to find out what we're not to find out who we are. To do that you have to take risks, try new things.'

'I like to play safe. That's all.'

'There is nothing wrong with mistakes, with things being not quite perfect. You know in Japanese pottery there is something called Kinstukuroi. It is the art of repairing broken pottery with lacquer, dusted or mixed with powdered gold, silver, or platinum. The idea is that we don't have to be ashamed of breaks and scars: they are part of us, our history. Actually, they make us more beautiful.'

Lowri smiled at him, watched him speaking with intensity and passion. She had seen him as rather brusque: this was a different Dave, the one who had held her on the beach. Again, the tattoos and the shaved brown bristly head faded and she saw gentle, dark brown eyes, deep pools of kindness.

'Thank you,' she said quietly. Lowri looked down at her dirty hands. 'Good job I don't have expensive manicures. Still, I can see why the kids were really into it. Would you like me to come back next week, and help supervise the children painting their pots? It would be a shame if John threw his on the floor in temper.'

'That would be great, thanks.'

For the rest of December, Lowri found herself gravitating more and more to the pottery. She recognised quickly that she had no great aptitude for the creative side, but she loved the atmosphere in there. There were always new skills to learn and jobs to be done. Slowly, she felt she became of real use to Dave. Then, one evening, she had a call from him asking her to go in early next day to set up for him. When she arrived, she found Heather on her own.

'Dave rang me last night. He had to dash to the dentist: an abscess or something. He's been trying to ignore it for weeks and now he is in agony.'

'That sounds typical. Good of you to help out. We ought to sort out payment for you.'

'I am earning with translation work at the moment, so don't worry.'

'That's very good of you, Coffee?'

'Yes, please. No Carina yet?'

'She'll be in soon.'

'I see Ken some mornings riding on his own. Carina doesn't like it, then?'

'Not her thing at all. Ken's first wife loved it.'

'Was his wife young when she died?'

'Not very young, but it was sudden. They went away on holiday and she died while they were away.'

'Oh no.'

'Ken was in bits when he came back.'

'How awful.'

'Yes. It was I suppose a year later he went on holiday to Italy. That's when he met Carina. To be honest, I don't think he knew what hit him when he met her, but before he left Italy, after six weeks, he was married.'

'That's amazing. And then they had Lizzy?'

'That's right. She was pregnant within a month or two of coming here. It was all very exciting. I think Ken was pretty shocked. Anyway, she adores him which is wonderful.'

At that moment Carina arrived.

'You two having a nice chat?'

'We are.' Heather looked out of the window. 'I'd better go and let the world know we're open,' she said and went out through the front door.

Lowri went into the pottery. She was starting to take out the trays ready to set out the tables when Carina came in.

'I was wondering if you and Jack are coming to the ball.'

'Sorry. I haven't had chance to answer. Yes, we'd love to come.'

'Good, everybody comes.'

'Jack said–'

'I thought you would like that: you know, it being a masked ball.'

Lowri frowned, and then noticed Carina looking at her scars.

'Sorry,' said Carina quickly.

'You mean because of my scars.'

'No matter.'

'You think people still notice–'

'Maybe.'

'What do you mean?'

'It's just I heard Heather and Dave talking.'

Lowri froze. 'What were they saying?'

Chapter Twenty Two

Lowri stood in the pottery looking intently at Carina.

'Please, you have to tell me.'

'It is nothing.'

'I need someone who is prepared to tell me the truth, Carina. Please, no-one else will.'

'Dave was asking Heather what he should do. There had been some complaint from a school. It's was from the parent of a child coming in today.'

'A complaint about me?'

'You are not to worry. I shouldn't have said anything, and maybe I misunderstood them.'

'I don't think so. Why didn't Heather or Dave say something, tell me what it was about?'

'This boy's father had been in an accident. Seeing you and your scars, well it reminded him. He's been screaming, having nightmares.'

Lowri shrank back, horrified. 'That's terrible.'

'The school rang Dave and he was asking Heather what to do. She said to ignore it. She didn't want to upset you.'

'I wish they'd said something. I could have stayed away.'

Lowri noticed Carina's grimace.

'What is it?'

'It's hard. You see, it's not the first time it's happened.'

'Good grief. I never realised.' Lowri, close to tears, grabbed Carina's arm. 'It would be better if I didn't come anymore, wouldn't it? It would save the embarrassment.'

'Of course it's your decision.'

'I hate the thought of upsetting this child, but I promised Dave I would set up. I'll do that quickly and then leave a note for Dave. He'll understand.'

'Look, why don't you just go? Tell me what to do. I've nothing else to do for the next half an hour. I can explain to Dave.'

'Oh, no.'

'It might be best. He might come early, and then you know how he is. He'll try to make you stay. This way I can explain it all for you, Now, you tell me what I need to do.'

Lowri tried to steady herself, it was hard to think. 'Um, these are the trays. There are thirty children. They need a set each. There's eight to a table. Over there, the clay is all balled up ready, so you give each a ball. Oh, and aprons are in the cupboard over there.'

'That's all straightforward. I can do that.'

'Are you sure Heather won't mind?'

'Of course not. You go. Oh, one more thing—'

'What?'

'If I were you, I'd think seriously about moving back to Southampton. You'll feel more at home there. Over here, well, this is Jack's home, isn't it?'

'But I'm starting to love the Island, and people have been very friendly.'

'You never can tell though what they are thinking, can you? Now, off you go: quickly, now.'

'Thank you so much, Carina. I know it's not easy to tell people these things.'

'I could let you out of the exit here, save you bumping into Heather. Don't worry, now. I will explain what happened. They will all understand.

'Oh, thank you.'

Lowri slipped out of the side door and walked quickly home.

Heather was sorting out the till when she saw Carina coming in from the pottery.

'Everything OK?'

'I was just asking Lowri if she and Jack are coming to the ball.'

'I hope so.'

'So do I. I also told her she is very lucky. You have been a good friend to her.'

'I try.'

'That's what I tried to explain: you were just being kind when you took the cakes to her.'

Heather looked up from the till. 'What do you mean? Did she have a problem with me going to see her?'

'Oh no. Not at all. Who would?'

'Why did you have to explain my visit then?'

'Lowri is a funny girl. I thought, you know, that she was a very sweet girl. I felt sorry for her, but now I am not so sure.'

'Why? What did she say?'

'I don't like to hurt your feelings.'

'What was it?'

'She said you smother her. She says you are always asking questions, nosy, being like a fussy mother. She says she is an adult. She can look after herself.'

'Goodness.'

'I told her you are being kind but she is, you know, I think she prefers the men to look after her.'

'Oh now. She's happily married.'

Heather saw Carina raise one eyebrow in that cynical way she had.

'You think so?'

'Of course.'

'Why then does she chase someone like my Ken?'

213

'Oh no.'

'She made him walk her home after the Halloween party.'

'That was a long time ago, and he was just being kind.'

'You think?'

'Look, you've nothing to worry about. Ken clearly adores you, and Lowri is married to Jack.'

Carina came closer to her. She spoke in a loud whisper. 'You know they do not share a bed?'

'How do you know that?'

Carina touched the side of her nose. 'When I visited her, she said Jack sleeps in the other room while she is ill but–'

Heather remembered her own visit. Lowri was in her own room then. She shook her head. This was nonsense.

'Look, I am sure they are very happy. Now stop feeling insecure. If you do, heaven help the rest of us.'

Carina smiled and put her arm around Heather. 'You are so kind. I don't know what I would do without you.'

Heather smiled. 'And I don't know what I'd do without you. Honestly, apart from Lee and Poppy, I don't know anyone else I trust any more.' She glanced around the room. 'We have that big group coming in for morning coffee soon, don't we?'

'Of course. I'm sorry. I didn't have time to make the cupcakes. I'll get on with them now.'

'Gosh, thanks. I'll finish sorting things out here.'

Heather started putting out scones, hiding her upset over what Lowri had said. Honestly, sometimes she gave up on people: she would give Lowri a wide berth for a bit if that's how she felt.

The group that were arriving were from a local woman's reading group. There were about twenty of them, which was great for business on a usually quiet Monday

214

morning. It was while Heather was taking orders that she saw Dave come in.

'Sorry, I had to go to the dentist. He's given me antibiotics. Couldn't do anything today.'

Heather looked through the window.

'Your class is arriving.'

'Thank goodness Lowri came in early.'

He rushed into the pottery, but immediately returned. Heather had never seen him in a panic before.

'Where's Lowri? Nothing has been done.'

Heather shook her head. 'I've no idea. I saw her go in. Let me asked Carina.

She went into the kitchen. 'Do you know where Lowri is?'

'No, why?'

'She's disappeared. She hasn't set up for Dave.' Heather looked around, but Dave had gone.

'Shall I ring her?' asked Carina. 'Maybe she's unwell.'

'No. I'll do it,' said Heather. She was angry. Lowri hadn't seemed unwell this morning. Why hadn't she set up for Dave? Lowri answered quickly.

'Where are you? Are you ill?'

'No. Um, I thought it was best to leave.'

'But nothing is ready for Dave.'

'Carina said she would do it.'

'She has her own work. She had a load of cup cakes to make.'

'She said she didn't have anything to do.'

'It was your job. You said you'd help.'

'But Carina said–'

Heather was too frustrated to listen to any more excuses. 'Look, I need to go and help Dave. The class is here. It's very embarrassing for him. If you don't want to work here it is better that you say, then we all know where we stand.'

'I won't come any more. Please tell Dave I am sorry to have messed him about.'

Heather put down her phone; how could she have got Lowri so wrong?

Carina came over to her. 'I have the cakes in the oven. You go and help Dave. I can cope here.'

'Thanks,' said Heather. 'I know I say it all the time, but I really don't know what I would do without you.'

Back at home Lowri sat crying. She was so shocked by what Carina said. She really thought everyone had got used to her, but they were just hiding their feelings. Maybe Carina was right and she should go back to Southampton, but not yet. No: she would stay here and hide away.

She picked up the invite to the ball, the masked ball. She threw it down. People didn't need to buy masks. They already had them: Heather, Dave, all smiling at her, pretending to accept her. Only Carina had the courage to tell her the truth.

Chapter Twenty Three

A few days before Christmas Lowri decided to put up some decorations. She bought a small tree from one of the farms, and decorated it with baubles she had bought in the local newsagent's. There was a little angel in a white dress. This she placed on the top of the tree, thinking of Aniolku, her angel at Christmas. Before Aniolku, she had known in her head that one day soon she would want children. Discovering that she was pregnant had brought home the reality of this, and it had been wonderful. Now, despite all the heartache of losing her baby, she knew that she wanted to try again, but she had a lot of questions in her head. Whatever Jack said, she was unsure of him. He had secrets, and she didn't know if one day he would suddenly go and leave her again. Would she want to bring up a child on her own? She had always said 'no', but now she wasn't so sure. She longed to have a baby growing inside her, but she and Jack never slept together. One day she needed to talk to him properly about it.

She stood all their Christmas cards on the book shelves; it was surprising how many they had. One was from her aunt, June, back in Merthyr Tydfil. There was an interesting note with scrawled writing inside: 'We are very excited. On the last weekend of January your Uncle Gareth is coming over from America. It will be the first time he has come back in forty years. If you would like to come and stay, I am sure he would love to meet his niece for the first time. I think it would be good for you to talk. Drop me a note if you can come. You are very welcome to stay with me if you would like to. Love from June.' Lowri looked at it thoughtfully. It was a long time since she had been to Merthyr Tydfil, it would be interesting to meet her mother's brother. They had only ever swapped Christmas cards: yes, she would try to go.

On Christmas Day, Jack went down to the manor to carry on painting, saying Carina had told him she didn't mind. After lunch they each gave the other a book they had asked for and in the evening they watched TV.

On Facebook, Lowri created a wonderful day. It had started with Jack waking her up to a breakfast of Bucks Fizz and Eggs Benedict. The present had been diamond earrings and a weekend spa retreat. She wrote about going to church, and then going out for a magical Christmas lunch with friends. In the afternoon, they had gone for a walk along the beach and in the evening they had drunk fine port and played games. Friends, envious, wrote about chaotic early mornings, the day spent in the kitchen, and tired, over-wrought children. As she read their comments, Lowri felt a pang of guilt mixed with fear. Had she gone too far this time? What if someone she wasn't friends with on Facebook was to stalk her, expose the truth?

Lowri put on her coat and went for her walk on her own with Cassie. She was becoming increasingly interested in the world she was finding, and she began to concentrate on keeping a nature diary on her Facebook page. She listened to bird song, went home and tried to identify each bird with the help of the internet. It was far more confusing than she expected, but she kept trying.

She realised, though, that the day of the ball was fast approaching.

'I can't go,' she suddenly said to Jack one day. 'It's no good. I can't face everyone.'

'What's the matter with you? You were looking so much better, going down the pottery, meeting people, and then it all stopped. I don't understand.'

'I just didn't want to go any more. I do have my own work, you know.'

'Heather has been funny with me. It's not like her at all. Have you had a row or something?'

'No, nothing. I just wish people were more honest, that's all.'

'Heather is one of the most honest people I know.'

'Is she? People are always pretending, Jack. When we came here, I felt guilty about you and me pretending to be a couple, but I'm starting to realise that everyone tells lies. They say one thing to your face and another behind your back.'

Jack frowned. 'Hey, this isn't like you. You are so, well, trusting. You always give people the benefit of the doubt.'

'I did. Maybe I have been taken for a mug.'

'Look, I don't know what the matter with you is, but we are going to this ball.'

'No.'

'Yes, we have to. You can't stay here locked up, getting all messed up. Come on. We had a delivery. Was it your costume?'

'Well, yes.'

'Please, do it for me. I don't want to go on my own. It's not far. I did think we'd walk so that we could both drink. Carina will be really pleased we are going. She keeps asking me what's happened to you.'

'You know, she suggested I move back to Southampton.'

'Did she? Why was that?'

'I think she thought I'd find it easier over there.'

'I can't think why. Anyway, she was saying to me how much she hopes we will both be at the ball.'

Lowri felt herself starting to weaken. 'Really? I suppose I could come home if I don't like it?'

'Of course.'

She sighed. 'Well, OK then. With any luck people won't even know who I am. What will you wear?'

'I shall go as Raphael.'

'Again?'

He laughed. 'Why not?'

'What about the mask?'

'I have a plain black half mask. You know, that you wear on your eyes. That should be fine. What are you wearing?'

'You will have to wait and see.'

On the night of the ball Lowri went to her room and started to assemble her costume. She heard a knock on her bedroom door, and Jack came in.

'Time to–' He started, then stopped, and stared at Lowri.

'What do you think?'

He stood staring. He had gone quite pale. 'My God, Lowri.'

Lowri had taken the jumper off her mirror. She glanced at her reflection. Her face was covered in very pale foundation, almost white, her eyes made up with white mascara, and her lips with the palest of pinks. Over this she placed the white mask. This partially covered her hair, then her forehead, her nose and much of her cheeks, fanning into her lips, so that her scar could not be seen. The mask was decorated with silver and crystal. Her hair framed her face, and she wore a silver spiky crown. Her dress was long, light blue and white, and around her shoulders she wore a white fake fur cape.

'I'm Jadis, the White Witch from Narnia. What do you think?'

'I don't know. It's amazing, but scary: really frightening.'

'She isn't a comfortable character, is she?' Lowri looked at herself and realised why she had chosen this costume, why it fitted so well. This was who she was: inside she felt cold, numb, and she was glad. She was tired of tears and hurt. This was who she could be now. Maybe Jack saw that. Maybe that was why he looked so upset. Trying to lighten the mood, she said, 'You need to behave tonight, or I will turn you to stone.'

Jack tried to laugh, but failed.

'We'd better get going,' she said. 'I need to wear a coat and wellies. I'll take my silver shoes and cape to change into.'

Lowri felt at one with the cold and frost. Once out of the village, they crossed the road. Jack switched on his torch. It was eerie walking through the trees. They hung over them, their bare fingers reaching down. Then they went up over the downs, climbing the hill, the sea in the distance invisible. They reached the Longstone, tonight making a frightening outline, looking far bigger than it did in daylight.

Lowri glanced down at Dave's house, saw the lights on, and wondered if he would be going to the party. She dreaded seeing him after leaving him in the lurch that day, but on the other hand he possessed a kind of sanity she found comforting.

Looking up at the Longstone, she said, 'Of course, I represent evil tonight.'

Jack looked puzzled.

'Jadis, she brought evil into Narnia,' she explained.

221

'That was a story. But then I believe that beauty will always defeat evil.'

'So you think beauty equates to goodness, ugliness to evil?

'I don't know. I guess I have always thought that.'

'I think a lot of people do. I'm not so sure.'

Lowri walked carefully through the woods, shining her torch at her feet. The roots from the trees reached out across the path. It was easy to trip over or slip on the hard icy mud. She was relieved when they arrived at a gate into the garden at the back of the manor.

The paths had been lit with fairy lights: here was order. There were lanterns hanging in the trees. 'Wow. Carina has done well,' said Jack.

'She did all this, you think?'

'Of course. Though, she'll have had caterers and people to help.'

'Not Ken, though.'

'He'll have been hiding in the stables for days I expect.'

'Wonder if he'll be in costume?'

'She'll have ordered at least a mask for him. He'll have no option.'

'He's much older than her, isn't he?'

'Gosh, yes. I think it shows more lately. Carina is very tactful, of course; very loyal, but just occasionally she says things.'

'Like what?'

'Well, like on Lizzy's birthday. She was saying how she'd love to have more children, that she fell pregnant easily with Lizzy, but Ken just said no more and refuses to even talk about it.'

'That seems a bit tough.'

'You'd think he'd do anything for a woman like that. She doesn't say much, but she's mentioned things like him forgetting their anniversary, her birthday, things like that. I know she gets upset.'

Lowri looked up at him in the darkness. 'She confides in you a lot, doesn't she?'

'Not really. We just get talking when I'm painting.'

They reached the area of the weeping willow and the pond. There were lights around the edge of the pond, which was covered in a thin sheet of ice.

'This is where you set the painting of Carina, isn't it?'

'Yes. It was perfect. We did some painting here and some up at the studio.'

'What did Holly think of you spending weeks painting this beautiful young woman?'

He stopped abruptly, and snapped at her. 'She understood at first, but then she started to nag a bit. It was silly. I kept telling her how much the painting meant to me, but I don't think she ever really understood.'

'Like your fresco at the moment: it's taken over your life, hasn't it?'

'Of course. This is something I have always longed to do. I'm learning so much as I work. I am taking photographs, keeping notes. I just wish I could do something like this full-time.'

'Really? You'd like to give up lecturing?'

'Yes. If this paid the bills, I'd jump at it. However, I can't see Ken paying for any more work. This has cost him a lot and it's not like it's something he's particularly interested in.'

Jack sighed, then said, 'Gosh, it's cold. Come on, let's get inside.'

Lowri looked down at the house: music, laughter, and voices escaped and crept into the air outside. Through the windows she could see lights and people in fine clothes.

Suddenly, Lowri wanted to turn and run. The game had become a reality, and it wasn't fun anymore. Before she could think, Jack grabbed her arm and her towards the house. The front door was open.

'Hang on. Let me change my shoes and coat. I'll leave my bag here.'

'I'll put my torch in your bag.'

Ken was close to the entrance wearing as close to normal clothes as he could: a black dinner jacket. The only difference was the small black mask around his eyes. He seemed determined to act as if it wasn't there.

'Hi. Glad you could come,' he said clutching his glass of whisky as if it was a lifebelt saving him from drowning.

Lowri, looking past him, saw that the house was heaving with people. All were dressed extravagantly. The strains of medieval music were much louder now. There was a large Christmas tree, tastefully decorated with discreet lights. Holly and pine garlands filled the air with their scent.

'Very impressive,' said Ken looking her up and down, 'if not a bit scary. I would never have known it was you.'

'That's the idea,' she replied.

'There's lots to drink. Let me get you champagne.'

Lowri followed Jack in and they pushed their way through the guests. Carina came over to them.

'Ah, Carmine,' said Jack, his face lit up. Lowri thought at first he had mispronounced her name, but then she remembered the painting Carina had based her costume on; it was indeed Carmine from a painting by Raphael. The dress was off the shoulder, low cut, in rusty red and gold. It clung tightly to her chest then flowed down to the floor.

224

Her blonde hair was curled away from her face. She carried a stick mask of palest gold, embellished with fine red and pearl beads, the essence of virginal beauty and innocence. Everyone else looked cheap and tacky, despite their fine Tudor dresses and elaborate masks covered in feathers and gems that twinkled. Tonight belonged to Carina. Everyone and everything else here was simply the painted scenery of the play in which she was the star.

'I knew you would recognise it,' she said to Jack.

'It's perfect, every detail.'

'And you are my Raphael,' she said, threading her arm through his.

Lowri looked at them. They fitted perfectly. Suddenly, it all made sense. So it was Carina he loved. She was so obviously in love with Ken. Jack must know she would never leave him but, yes, that was it. Why on earth hadn't she realised it sooner? No wonder he spent all his time at the manor. The truth of what she saw hurt more deeply than she expected. After all, she didn't love him any more, did she? However, she was sure that if only it hadn't been someone quite so beautiful it might have been easier. Jack had actually said that he didn't feel attracted to her any more. Well, now she knew why. The Carina's of this world would always win.

'Lowri, how lovely to see you. How are you? You look extraordinary. I feel quite underdressed,' Carina was saying.

Lowri suddenly felt ridiculous. Why had she dressed in such a stupid costume?

'You don't mind if I pinch Jack a minute,' Carina continued, 'I just need to show him something upstairs.'

Lowri watched as the two of them walked elegantly towards the stairs. Carina unhooked a red cord, and led Jack up the oak staircase.

Not sure what to do next, Lowri went into a large room and started to watch the group of players. She recognised the lute, harpsichord and pipes, but not much else. The music was haunting. She looked around and caught sight of Heather. Heather was wearing a long red dress and simple mask that covered her eyes. Lowri watched as she gulped her glass of champagne. When she moved her glass, Lowri saw her lips pointing downwards. They trembled, and the mask on her eyes did nothing to hide how miserable she was feeling. Then she looked over. Lowri's eye's met hers, but there was no smile. Lowri understood that. Heather was very angry with her over the misunderstanding at the café. Lowri turned to walk away. However, Heather came over to her.

'Hi, Lowri. How are you?'

'OK. You?'

The smile appeared. 'Of course.'

Lowri could see the dark rings under Heather's eyes: she looked exhausted.

'You've been busy?'

'We've been rushed off our feet.' Lowri didn't understand the accusation in Heather's voice.

'I'm sorry. '

'Dave needs someone in there. There is so much to do. I hope he finds someone soon.'

A waitress walked past with canapés. Lowri took one, and started to nibble on a mini quiche. Heather pursed her lips, and frowned. She flushed. Lowri wondered what the matter was. She had never seen Heather cross.

'Heather, I'm sorry if I upset you somehow, but you should have told me.'

'Told you what?'

'About that boy. I didn't want to upset him–'

'What boy?'

Lowri explained what Carina had told her.

'Carina's got her wires crossed there. We never had a complaint. Dave has never said anything to me.'

'Stop trying to protect me.'

'I'm not. Honestly, there has been nothing.'

'Oh, that's odd. It's why I left. Carina said it was best to go. She said she would set up for me.'

Heather looked sceptical. 'Are you making this up?'

'No. Of course not. I liked working in the pottery. I miss it now, to be honest, and it gets lonely all the time on my own.'

'I suppose it's better than being smothered.'

Again Lowri heard that hardness which didn't fit with Heather's voice.

'Smothered?'

'Carina told me you thought I was interfering too much.'

Lowri shook her head. 'No. No way. You have been so kind. Maybe Carina gets in a muddle with her English. Honestly, ask Jack. I had often told him how grateful I was that you had been so friendly. Especially as I'm married to your sister's former husband. I've never had anyone bring me cakes before. It's wonderful.'

Heather grabbed another canapé. 'Gosh, these things are small. I could do with a pasty or a meat pie.'

Lowri laughed, and then Heather said, 'I don't really see how Carina got things so wrong, but anyway let's try again. Please, I'd like you to come back.'

'But would Dave want me to?'

'Of course. He was hurt. He thought he'd done something to upset you.'

'Not at all.'

'Good, actually the pottery will be closed for two months, Dave needs some time off.'

227

'But he's coming back?'

'I hope so.'

Lowri looked around the room. 'Is Lee here? I'd like to meet him.'

'No. Busy night at the hotel. He'll be there all night. Oh, look. There's Gita and her husband. She's the one I told you who is helping out. She's great.' Heather waved to them. Gita smiled back, shyly. She was wearing a sky blue, heavily decorated sari, holding a beautiful mask on a stick.

'I must catch her later. You know, she's done all her food hygiene certificates. She can do everything now. Anyway, what about Jack? Where's he got to?'

'Carina took him off to show him something. Has Dave come tonight?'

'God, no. This isn't his type of thing. Oh, by the way, my sister Rosemary has come over with her husband. I must introduce you to them. Heaven knows where they've got to, though. There are many people here who will want to catch up with Rosemary. She was always popular with everyone.'

Lowri felt the room swirl around. She grabbed Heather's arm.

'Hey, are you OK?'

'Yes, fine. Just a bit dizzy. I'm not sure how long I will hang on here.'

Heather grabbed a glass of water from a passing waiter.

'Have this. You ought to try and make it to midnight. It's great. We sing, people take their masks off, and finally we get decent food.'

'What's the time now?'

'It's ten. Only two more hours.'

'I don't know.' Lowri was now frantic to leave. If she could get away from Heather and see Jack she should be able to get away from this place without meeting Simon.

'I just need to find Jack,' she said.

'OK, and don't forget, now. Think about coming back.'

'Thanks. I'm glad we saw each other.'

'So am I.'

Lowri drank her water, but still felt giddy with the heat and the noise. She had to get outside. She headed to the patio doors and went out into the garden. Outside there were a few people smoking. She glanced at the steps, and walked around to the front of the house. In front of the closed stable doors she could see Ken, standing alone, holding a bottle of whisky.

Chapter Twenty Four

'Hi, Ken.'

Slowly, he turned to look at Lowri. The smile that was always on his face had melted away, leaving an older, more vulnerable man behind.

'What's the matter?' Lowri asked gently.

'I was just remembering.'

She waited.

From his pocket, Ken took a photograph, and handed it to Lowri. She held it under the beam of the security light. It was of a couple: Ken and a woman. They were standing in front of the stables. The woman was wearing jodhpurs, a hacking jacket, and a riding hat. Red curls and a pale freckled face shone out of the picture. Ken looked so different. Of course, he was younger, but his face was relaxed; no anxious crinkles around his eyes, his lips not tight and clenched.

'Is this your first wife?'

'Yes, Jane. She was wonderful, Lowri.'

She handed the photograph back to him. He stared at the photo, seemed to want to get into it, to be there, not here. Lowri reached for the ribbons behind her mask, and removed it. It was a relief. She hadn't realised how tight it had been.

'I should never have married again.'

'Heather told me how much Carina helped you getting over your loss.'

'She swept me away. She was so exciting, young, full of life, and then, of course, she got pregnant.'

'And of course you have Lizzy–'

His face softened. 'She is the one good thing to come from our marriage.'

Lowri glanced down at the half empty bottle: he was very drunk. There was a stone seat that looked out over the fields.

'Let's sit down,' she said quietly. They sat next to each other. Ken put the bottle and glass next to him.

'The party is going well. A lot of people have come. Do you do this every year?'

'Ever since we got married...I hate it.'

'It's just one night. It means a lot to Carina–'

He took another swig. 'I don't love her.'

'Hey, that's the drink talking.'

'No. The drink lets me speak the truth. You don't know what she's really like.'

She lies, uses people, you know she never seems to understand anyone else's feelings, not even Lizzy's. Everything is always about her. These are awful things to say about my own wife but they are true.'

'Don't you think you might be exaggerating? She is bound to have been used to getting a lot of attention, getting her own way, but she loves you, you know that.'

Ken shook his head 'It's all an act; it's not me she wants.' He looked hard at Lowri. 'She is obsessed with getting what she really wants. Nothing will stop her. I started to hate her, but I began to realise that she's ill: she needs help. I spoke to our doctor, but he said he can't do anything unless Carina goes to see him.'

'What do you mean, she's ill?'

'Mentally, not physically. Most people think she is wonderful. They may think she's a bit vain or selfish, but they're always telling me what a lucky chap I am. If only they knew. God, I would leave her if I could.'

'You can't mean that.'

'I do. You know what my dream is?'

'What?'

231

'My dream would be to take Lizzy to Ireland, build us a new home with stables. She would love it, and it would get her away from Carina. Lizzy could be happy and free out there.'

'Carina is her mother. You couldn't take her away.'

'Carina wouldn't care: Lizzy's not why she makes us stay.'

Lowri shook her head. Ken had to be wrong about this. She looked at the bottle in his hand. 'Ken, you've been drinking a lot. It will all seem better in the morning.'

'No, it'll be worse.'

Lowri turned towards him. 'Whatever you say, Carina loves you. She's always saying it.'

'It's a façade, an act. She despises me.'

'You're the one with the money. You could leave at any time.'

Ken shook his head. 'You don't understand. She has this hold over me. She's blackmailing me. She won't let me and Lizzy go until she is ready. It would be too humiliating to be divorced by me. No, she will only release us from this prison when she's ready. You must know she has plans. I mean, it involves you.'

'Lowri shook her head. 'I don't know what you are talking about. In any case, how on earth can she be blackmailing you?'

Ken put away the photograph of Jane. 'When I first met Carina I told her things. I thought she understood. Now I know I was handing her a knife to hold to my throat.' He stumbled over the words and took another long swig from the bottle.

'We should go in,' said Lowri quickly. The intensity and hate in Ken's words frightened her. 'It's very cold. I'd better put my mask back on. At least I have an excuse to hide my scar.'

232

Ken looked at her, and touched her scar. 'Don't be like that. What is it they say? Scars show you have survived.'

'Maybe. Come on, let's go in.'

They went in together and Ken left her, she guessed in search of more drink.

Lowri turned, and saw Nicola. 'Hi. I didn't know you were here.'

'Good to see you.'

'It's a huge event, isn't it? I'm sure Carina is loving it: belle of the ball and all that.'

Lowri looked at her curiously, and then said, 'I'm sorry for how things ended when you stayed. I'm not sure what happened.'

'Jack can tell you some time.'

'When we were on the beach you said you know who it is that Jack was in love with. Well, I think I know who it is.'

Nicola looked shocked. 'Really? Did Jack tell you?'

'No, but I've worked it out. I know it is Carina.'

Lowri saw Nicola grimace. 'You think that?'

'Of course. I am right, aren't I?'

Nicola was about to speak, but then said, 'You must talk to Jack, please. Now tell me how you are?'

Frustrated, but realising Nicola wasn't going to say any more, Lowri said, 'Doing OK. I still have my fossil.'

'Good.'

'I like your dress, by the way.'

Nicola laughed. 'I borrowed it from an amateur dramatic company.' Then she looked over at Ken. 'Is he alright?'

'Very drunk.'

'This isn't his sort of thing.'

'I don't think so. Actually, I'm looking for Jack. Have you seen him?'

Suddenly, she heard Heather behind her. 'There you are, Lowri. This is my sister, Rosemary.'

Lowri turned around and found herself facing a tall woman with cropped brown hair, grinning at her. She wore little make-up, and her dress was a simple long black velvet empire-style. It looked elegant. She had stuffed her mask under her arm.

Instantly, Lowri put on her fixed smile. Rosemary looked far more together than Lowri expected. Although much slimmer than Heather, Lowri could see they shared the same soft features and easy smile.

'Lowri, how lovely to meet you. I hear you and Jack are back together again. Heather keeps me up to date with all the gossip. I know all about you: you translate Polish and have a cocker spaniel.'

Rosemary was being so natural and affable that Lowri started to relax. 'I have a cat as well,' she said. 'A little tortie. Nothing posh like your Maine Coons.'

Rosemary's eyebrows shot up. 'How on earth did you know that? Or has Heather been filling you in on me?'

Lowri laughed nervously.

'I didn't tell you, Lowri,' said Heather, frowning.

'Lucky guess,' was all she could think to say.

'Heather told me about your accident,' Rosemary said.

Under her pale make-up, Lowri could feel herself blushing.

'I'm a lot better now.'

'It was strange. I think my husband, Simon, must have been in France about the same time.'

Lowri looked at her carefully, trying to sense if she was hinting that she knew about them, but she was pretty sure she didn't.

'Heather was telling me you have been through a rough time since. I am so sorry.'

To her horror, Lowri realised she was referring to the miscarriage.

'Um, thank you.' She felt sick. She had to get away. However, Rosemary carried on chatting.

'I haven't seen Jack yet.'

'I haven't seen him for a while either.'

'I hope you settle here. It's a lovely place. We ought to get over more often. You know, we are really looking forward to coming over for Poppy's wedding. It will be great to have the family back together on the Island.'

'Carina was telling me you were planning to go to Italy before that,' interrupted Heather.

'Eh? We haven't any plans to go.'

'Oh, that's what she said. Are you sure? You can tell me, you know.'

'Of course. Why wouldn't I?'

'I know you and Simon are better off than me and Lee. It doesn't bother me.'

'I never thought it did,' said Rosemary.

Lowri could see the look of confusion on Rosemary's face.

'How is Lee, by the way?' Rosemary asked.

'Working tonight.'

'Poor chap. He never stops. He'll have his own place one day, just you wait and see. The Isle of Wight is getting some really good eating places, quite the reputation. I have friends come over from the mainland for gastro evenings. You'll see, Lee's turn will come.'

Lowri could see a clear way to the front door, and was about to make excuses and slip away when Rosemary said, 'I love your costume. I've been taking photos, just on my phone. I'll send them to Carina and Ken.'

'That's great. Now, I just need to go and get a bit of fresh air.' Lowri was just about to walk away when she saw Rosemary look over some heads and beckon someone.

'There's Simon. You must say hello before we lose each other.'

'No, I can't,' said Lowri in horror. Rosemary didn't hear her, but Heather asked, 'What's the matter, Lowri? You look really upset.'

'Nothing,' she said, but she was watching Simon coming towards her. He appeared calm and in control. 'How lovely to meet you. Lowri, isn't it?'

She was stunned by how convincing his performance was. It flashed through her mind that she had imagined their relationship. Then he held her gaze with such intensity she knew it was real: nothing had changed.

Lowri couldn't speak, but she kept staring at Simon. He was wearing a black suit, white shirt and bow tie. His mask was black, but embellished with tiny diamonds and his blue eyes sparkled through the slits.

'I was telling Lowri about how you must have been in France at about the time of her accident,' said Rosemary.

'Yes. Coincidence, isn't it?'

Then from the top of the stairs Carina banged a small golden gong.

'Can I have your attention?'

The hubbub slowly died down as people shushed each other. Lowri could see Carina clearly loved all eyes being on her but surely that was natural. She was used to being admired, Ken must have been exaggerating.

'Thank you. First, Ken and I would like to thank you all very much for coming. You all look wonderful. We've a long night ahead so we have something special laid on for you to give you a break. What I need is for everyone to clear this hallway. You can stand around the edge or come up here to watch over the balcony. We are very lucky to have a group of four dancers who are going to perform a programme of medieval masked dances for us. So, if we could clear them an area here, they will be accompanied by our group through there in the living room.'

The first group to move blocked the front door, and then all the exits out of the hallway. Lowri realised there was no way she could leave at the moment.

'Come on. Let's go upstairs. We'll get a good view from there,' said Heather. Rosemary and Simon seemed to be walking to the edge of the room. Lowri followed Heather up the stairs.

Slowly a space was cleared, and the dancers moved into place. Each dance was announced. They ranged from slow and stately to fast and lively. Lowri watched the dancers at first, trying to calm herself down. She allowed herself to look at the guests standing at the edge of the room. She still could not see Jack, but she saw Nicola close to Ken. The other side of her was Peter. Eventually, her eyes fell on Simon. He was staring in a fixed way at the dancers. The dancers occasionally rested, and then the group would play. All the time people were offered champagne and canapés.

When they finished, Carina stepped forward.

'It's nearly twelve o clock, the unmasking. So, can we all form circles here. Come on down from the balcony. We must make as many circles as we need. Lowri followed Heather down the stairs. At that moment, she spotted Jack, who came over to her.

Some people held hands, but most were holding glasses or food. There were circles within circles. Lowri found herself part of the inner circle. Carina started the countdown to midnight, and then at twelve o'clock streamers were fired from the balcony above, the group played, and they all sang. After this, everyone cheered and most people removed their masks. Lowri kept hers on. People started kissing and hugging, Jack hugged Lowri.

'Happy New Year,' he said, and she smiled up at him.

'Happy New Year,' she replied.

While all this had been happening, the buffet had been laid out in two of the rooms.

'Thank God, food,' said Heather. 'Come on. This is worth going to.' Before she could escape Heather propelled Lowri into a side room. The table groaned with an array of joints of meat, including a goose, all being carved by the chefs. There were also whole cheeses, tarts and pies, all kinds of plaited loaves, baked potatoes and huge pats of butter. Caterers served people and Lowri soon had a plate of food. She and Heather found seats.

'There is an art to eating on your lap,' Heather said. 'Still, it's jolly good. There will be puddings next. I told you it was worth hanging around for. So, what did you make of my sister and her husband?'

Lowri put down her knife and fork. 'Your sister is very friendly.'

'She's great. We've always been close, not quite so much lately, but still she's lovely.'

'She seems very together.'

'Of course.'

'She's never ill with nerves or anything?'

'Goodness, no. Why would you think that?'

'Just wondered.'

'No. Simon, now, she has to keep an eye on him.'

'Why's that?'

'I'm not sure. She doesn't say much, but sometimes she puts off meeting up. She tends to stay quite close to him at things like this.'

Heather looked over. 'Good: puddings are coming out. What do you fancy?'

'I'm not that hungry.'

'Rubbish.'

A woman Lowri didn't recognise came over and greeted Heather warmly.

'Coming for pudding, Heather?'

'You bet.'

Lowri smiled. 'You go. I'll stay here.'

'Can I get you something?' Heather asked Lowri.

'I'm fine. You go on.'

Laughing and chatting, Heather left her.

Lowri needed to get away. She could see a queue forming at the downstairs bathroom. There was a cord across the stairs. She unhooked it quickly, and made her way to the stairs. Walking along the landing, she felt alone. The banisters had garlands of pine and ivy decorating them. No-one could see her. She could see down, though, and it was odd to look down on everyone. A cloud of noise separated her from them. She walked slowly, pushing on the doors. Most were locked. But one led to a beautiful bathroom. It was cool and quiet in there. She wanted to stay there. She looked at her face in the mirror: she looked so pale, and it wasn't simply the make-up. Her eyes were red; she was exhausted. Nothing was going to stop her leaving now. Resolutely, she left the bathroom and started to walk back to the stairs. From one of the rooms, however, she heard someone call her name.

'Lowri, come here. Now. Quick.'

Chapter Twenty Five

Lowri turned and saw him sitting on the edge of a bed.

'Come in,' Simon repeated.

In a daze, she walked into the room.

He walked over, and took her in his arms. 'God, I've missed you.'

Lowri rested against him, took in the feel, the smell of him, and wanted to stay there. Then she remembered being left lying on her own in the hospital, and standing alone on the downs, and pulled away.

'You chose to leave me, Simon. You can't just come in here and expect to act like nothing has happened.'

'Listen – I need to explain.'

'It's too late for that. You lied to me, abandoned me. I don't want to talk to you.'

He reached out to her, held on to her arms.

'Don't go, please.'

Defiantly, she shook him off, and then, raising her hands, she undid her mask, and threw it on the bed. His eyes focused on her scars. 'Oh Lowri, I'm so sorry.

He leant forward and touched her face. Then he kissed her scar and smiled.

'You are still so beautiful, stunning.' She looked deep into his eyes, drinking in the words.

Lowri shook her head. 'Even if I was passable before, I'm not now.'

'That's rubbish. You are gorgeous.' His voice was husky.

'I don't feel it.'

He held her hand. 'I am so sorry about the baby. Heather told Rosemary.'

'It was devastating.' She pulled away, the reality of the situation dawning on her.

'How is Jack?'

'Very upset.'

'It must have been awful for you both.'

She stared at him in disbelief. 'Simon, the baby was yours.'

He blushed. 'I know. I'm sorry. I've been trying not to think about it.'

'When you heard I'd lost it, didn't you feel anything?'

He shrugged helplessly. 'I don't know what I felt. It was difficult being so far away from you.'

Lowri couldn't understand him. Every day she woke she felt something was missing, but he didn't seem to feel anything.

'How are things with Jack?'

'We are still together.'

'I treated you badly, didn't I?'

'You did.' She saw his eyebrows rise: he hadn't expected that. Lowri continued. 'You lied to me, told me you'd left Rosemary, when you had no intention of leaving her.'

'I wanted to, but I was so worried about her.'

'Heather says there is nothing wrong with Rosemary. She said you are the needy one.'

'Rosemary hides things well from the family.'

'Really?'

'Don't you believe me?'

'I don't know. Maybe not.'

'I would have stayed with you in the hospital if I could.'

She shook her head. 'You have no idea what I've been through: the accident, the scars, and then to lose my baby. You haven't been with me through any of it.'

He went to hold her. She pushed him away.

'Don't, Simon. You have no right.'

241

'You've changed.'

'Grown up a bit, I think.'

'Look, I still want to leave Rosemary when the time is right. She's not well at the moment: that's all.'

'Rosemary seems fine to me. I don't think you actually want to leave her.'

Simon walked over to the window, and stared out into the blackness.

'OK. I'll tell you the truth. Rosemary had a drink problem.'

'What?'

'She had, still has, a drink problem. I have to watch her. Not long before you and I went to France she went on a bender. We rowed, and she promised that was the last time.'

When he turned around, Lowri saw that he was very pale. His hands were clenching and unclenching.

'You should have told me. I would have understood.'

'It felt disloyal. That's all. And, anyway, now you know.'

They both went back and sat on the edge of the bed, close but not touching. They could hear the music from the party coming from downstairs.

'So, how are you finding it here on the island?'

'I love the place. I've been down to the beach and up on the downs. Cassie loves it as well.'

'It's a good place to live.'

'I've helped out in the pottery a bit. There was a bit of confusion. Carina told me some of the children were getting upset by my scars.'

'Gosh. Honestly?'

'Heather tells me its fine. I think Carina got it wrong somehow.'

242

Simon gave an indulgent smile. 'Ah, the beautiful Carina. She's rather gorgeous, isn't she?'

Lowri felt irritated. 'It's not what her husband said to me earlier.'

'Really? Good old reliable Ken. I always thought he did rather well. His first wife was nothing to look at. Carina seems pretty devoted to him. Lucky man.'

'Maybe he was just drunk. He doesn't like parties like this.'

'No. Not like Carina. Still she's very devoted to him.'

'I can see that.'

Simon moved and sat closer to her. 'Funny story about that. It was years ago. Jack was still with Holly. In fact it was not long before they split up. We all went out for Holly's birthday and, of course, we were giving presents. Then Holly told us about the present Jack had given her earlier that day, a black mare called Midnight. Ken had apparently tracked it down for Jack. Holly was over the moon, went over and gave Ken a big kiss.'

'Oh, Ken has a painting of the horse in the dining room. He said it died.'

'Apparently.' Simon dismissed this fact. 'Anyway, you should have seen Carina's face. I think she was very upset at Holly kissing Ken.'

'Really?'

'She started laughing but it was a hard laugh. She said in a loud voice to Jack that she hoped Jack was holding on to his wife, she seemed to be after Ken now and we all knew what she'd been like when she was younger. Well, Jack looked really puzzled and asked Carina what she was talking about. Holly had gone very red.'

'And what was it?'

'Carina sort of lowered her voice, but the other people in the pub could hear. Carina pretended to brush it off, said

243

that no-one worried about the past. It was years ago. Everyone was allowed a dalliance in their teens. It was just a shame it was a married man. Of course, she left everyone wondering what had been going on.'

Lowri saw Simon smiling, loving the story.

'Rosemary told me later what had happened. It had been when Holly was seventeen and it had been with her driving instructor. She'd gone out for drinks, nothing more, but it had got round the village. Carina had made it sound so much worse.'

'How on earth did Carina know? It must have been years before she arrived.'

'Holly had confessed it to her over a few glasses of wine. They'd got on well, you see.'

'Why did Carina mention it that night?'

'It was just her way of saying 'hands off my man'. Lucky Ken to have a woman like that to fight for him. Anyway, enough of all that. 'Simon reached and touched Lowri's hair. 'I've missed talking to you. You and I get each other, don't we? Those meals were some of the best times in my life.'

Lowri shrugged. 'A lot has happened since then.'

'I know that, and I know that you aren't happy.'

'I'm coping.'

'Life has to be about more than coping, Lowri. There should be music and dancing, meals where the touch of fingers makes you shiver.'

She swallowed a hard stone of sadness.

'I know I've made mistakes,' Simon continued, 'but I love you. Jack doesn't love you, does he?'

'He looks after me.'

'You need more than that.'

She looked up at him. 'You have Rosemary.'

'Not forever. It's just a matter of time. Look, I'm over here every Monday. Why don't we meet? I've seen a nice looking hotel not far from the hospital. We can meet there, have a meal and, well, you know, it will be like old times. We can plan our future: the gite in France, the sunshine.'

As he spoke, Lowri could feel the sunshine on her face. She realised how long it had been since she had felt warmth. From his pocket, Simon took out a piece of paper with a phone number on it. 'Look, I've got a new phone. You can text me on this number any time. I've told Rosemary it's for confidential business. She'll never look at it, and it's very discreet.'

Suddenly, the word 'discreet' took Lowri back to the airport, back to being the other woman.

'No, Simon. I can't do that.'

'Come on. It's not hurting anyone, and it could be a lifeline for both of us. Let's face it: you haven't got many options, have you?'

The harsh words slapped her face and Lowri started to shake. 'My life may not look much to you, but I won't be your mistress, your bit on the side. I'm worth more than that.'

Simon smiled, put his arms on her shoulders, and looked deep into her eyes. 'You and I need each other. Phone me.'

Suddenly, there was a flash. Lowri turned, and saw Carina in the doorway.

'You two are missing all the fun, or are you having your own party in here?'

Lowri jumped up, and grabbed her mask. 'I was just, um, talking. I need to go and find Jack.' She pushed past Carina, ran along the hallway and down the stairs.

Chapter Twenty Six

Lowri forced her way through the crowd and headed for the front door. In the porch she found her bag and ran out into the garden. Once away from the house she changed her shoes, put on her coat, threw her mask and heeled shoes in the bag and walked quickly through the garden.

The other side of the gate was dark woodland. She turned on her torch and made her way along the icy path. She heard rustling, but kept walking until she came to the clearing at the top, and found herself at the Longstone. Breathless, she sat on the shorter stone.

'Had a good party?'

Lowri's heart leapt, it was pitch black.

'It's me, Dave.' He approached with his torch.

Lowri could hear Dave's dog Ceba running around, in and out of the bushes.

'Been to the ball?'

She scowled. 'No. I always dress like this. Why didn't you come?'

'Got visitors. Anyway, it's not my kind of thing. Did you enjoy it?'

'Not really.'

'Why are you on your own?'

'I escaped.'

Dave sat down next to her. 'You've not been into the pottery in a while.'

'Carina told me there had been complaints from the teachers about children getting upset by my scars, so I kept away. Actually Heather has just told me it didn't happen but now I don't know who to believe.'

'Heather is right, no-one complained. I don't know what Carina was on about.'

'So it's not true? I wasn't sure if Heather was just being kind.'

'No. Sounds to me like Carina is stirring up trouble.'

'I am sure she doesn't like me.'

'Strange woman. Anyway, think about coming back although we're closing the pottery for two months.'

'Heather told me.'

'Things are usually very quiet in January and February. I shall go back up to London for a while. I should at least show my face and not leave everything to Millie.'

'Millie?'

'The woman I share the business with.'

'I suppose she's expecting you to go back for good some time?'

'Of course, it's hard though, I keep putting it off.' He shone his torch down at the house, 'That has to be one of the best places to live. My landlord wants to sell, he's moving to Spain and wants shot of it. He told me what it was valued at, you know it's less than my two bedroom flat in London, it's crazy.'

'So why don't you leave London, come and live here?'

He laughed nervously 'It's too big a risk. Up there I have contacts, there is always work. Here people will pay a lot less for pottery. I could make a living but that's all.'

'Well, I'm sorry you're going away.'

'Really?'

'Yes.' As she said it, she knew she meant it. 'You are, I don't know, normal.'

He laughed. 'You didn't think that when you first saw me.'

'Oh no–'

'Come on: you were scared shitless. I saw your face.'

'I suppose you do look a bit different to most people I know. The tattoos and that.'

'Still, sometimes men who look the part in their posh suits and tidy hair cuts aren't so nice inside, are they?'

Lowri looked out into the blackness. 'It's been a horrible night, you know.'

'Fancy a hot chocolate?'

The suggestion seemed to come from nowhere. Lowri looked up to see if he was joking, but he said, 'Seriously, do you?'

'You have visitors–'

'It's only Jacob. Come on.'

Lowri followed him down to the house, closely followed by Ceba.

As Dave opened the front door he shouted out, 'Hi, Jay. Just brought someone in for a drink.'

Lowri followed him into a hectic but cosy living room. Piles of books and newspapers lay everywhere. The room was quite dark, with a log fire blazing.

'Sit down. I'll get the drinks.'

She took off her boots and curled up on the soft linen sofa. Idly, she picked up the nearest book: it was on fossils, with pages of photographs.

Dave came in with a tray. The mugs she recognised as his own, and there was a plate of chocolate biscuits.

'This is all so homely.'

Dave laughed. 'That means messy.'

A man of similar height but more slender build came in.

'Hi, I'm Jacob,' he said, and held out his hand.

She shook it formally. 'Lowri,' she said. As she shook his hand, she noticed small, thin scars on his wrist and arm.

'Lowri has been to a fancy dress party,' said Dave

'A masquerade ball, actually,' she corrected him.

248

'Same thing, adults playing at dressing up.'

'You sound like you disapprove.'

'He does,' interrupted Jacob. 'He is very dull. Look at us: stuck out in the back of beyond drinking hot chocolate like an old married couple.'

Lowri shot a look between them: suddenly she understood.

'Seems a very sensible way to spend the evening,' she said.

'Exactly, too sensible.'

Jacob picked up his drink, then sat back, and closed his eyes. 'Who am I kidding? This is bliss.'

They all laughed. The clock chimed.

'I think I'll go on up,' said Jacob. 'Good to meet you, Lowri.'

Dave and Lowri sat on the sofa in front of the fire sipping their drinks.

'How long have you been together?' she asked.

Dave looked confused. 'What do you mean?'

'You and Jacob. How long have you been a couple?'

He threw back his head and guffawed. 'Jacob is my brother. I'm not gay. Whatever gave you that idea?'

'Oh, sorry. I thought he said you were a couple.'

Dave shook his head. 'Jacob is gay, though. He came out years ago. It was a terrible time for him – you might have noticed his arms?'

'I did.'

'He self-harmed. He was so unhappy. I had this tattoo done to support him.' Dave showed Lowri the rectangle with the date on it.

'That's really lovely. I'm sorry–'

'It's OK. So, tell me. Why have you left the party all on your own?'

She sighed. 'It was all so complicated.'

'Where's Jack?'

'Still there. I couldn't find him.'

'I bet it's a very posh affair.'

'It is. Hang on, I'll show you my mask: see if you can tell who I am.'

Lowri took out her mask and lifted it to her face.

'Ah, I thought so.'

'You know?'

'Jadis, wicked witch of Narnia?'

'That's right.'

He looked puzzled. 'Why did you want to become someone evil: a cold, cruel woman? Why dress up as that?'

'I don't know. It seemed to be how I felt.'

'But you aren't a cold person. I know that. Don't pretend to be that. It's sad. Just look at you: the ice queen. That's not you, Lowri. You're warm, vibrant, loving–'

He looked very upset.

'Hey, it's only a costume, only a mask.'

'Well, don't become it. It's possible to play a part for so long you forget who you are deep down.'

'Maybe I'd rather forget who I am. I'm not a very nice person, you know.'

'I find that hard to believe. Oh, I've just remembered: I have your pot.'

'I made that ages ago. You kept it?'

'Yes. I've glazed it. I brought it back here because I wanted to make something to go with it.'

He went over to a cupboard, took it out, and handed it to her. Lowri held the pot and gasped. Dave had transformed it into something beautiful. It was a pale blue glaze, with a white angel, and the name Aniolku.

'Wow. You've made something pretty terrible really special. Thank you.'

'I have spelt the name right, haven't I? I looked it up.'

'Oh yes, perfect.'

'And I made this for you. You don't have to use it.' He handed her a small structure sculpted from pieces of driftwood. 'It's a little stand for your pot: there are small claws to hold it steady.'

'It's perfect. You made this?'

'Mmm.'

'Why have you taken so much trouble over this?'

'I don't know' he looked away, blushing slightly, 'I just wanted to do something, it is awful what you went through.'

Lowri blinked hard.

'What's the matter?' he asked.

'I was talking to someone earlier about losing my baby. They should have cared and they didn't, but you did all this, for me.'

'People don't know what to say sometimes. I am sure Jack is devastated as well but maybe it's harder for him to show it.'

Lowri wiped her face. 'You don't understand. It's not like that.'

'What is it like, then?'

She stared into the flames, which were slowly consuming a log.

'It's all fake: my life. Nothing is what it seems. If you knew me you wouldn't like me.'

'Why on earth do you say that?'

'Because you are real: you don't pretend. Me and Jack: it's not real. We care for each other, but he doesn't love me and I don't love him.'

'I'm sure that's not true.'

'It is. I can't explain, but it's the way it is. We have settled. The baby, you see, the baby wasn't his.'

Dave put down his mug and looked at Lowri intensely. She hugged her mug more closely as she said, 'see: it's all lies.'

'He was going to bring the baby up, though.'

'Yes. He's very kind, you know, but he loves someone else, someone who for some reason can't love him back. He's settling for me, you see. We don't sleep together or anything. Oh God, please don't tell anyone I told you that.'

'What about the father of the baby?'

'He didn't want to know. He had someone else as well. I thought he was free, but he wasn't.'

Dave took her mug from her hand and placed it on a small table, then put his arms around her.

'You don't deserve to be settled for. You are worth so much more than that.'

Lowri rested into his arms. She felt safe and warm.

'No. No, I'm not.'

Dave lifted her face gently and kissed her on the lips. Lowri found herself kissing him back, hungry to be loved. The kisses became deeper and more intense. Then he stopped, held her back.

'What's the matter?' Lowri asked.

'It's not the right time, is it? You've been drinking and–'

She interrupted him. 'You don't need to make excuses.'

'Hey, don't be like that. If things were different–'

'Look, I'm fed up with people lying. If you find me ugly, unattractive, just tell me. At least Jack is honest enough to say that.'

'He said you were ugly?'

'Well, not in so many words. But it's alright. That's up to him, isn't it?'

Dave frowned. 'You live in a funny old world, Lowri. Don't run yourself down. Just remember, you are lovely and deserve the best.'

'It's easy to say all that.'

'But I mean it. Don't settle, Lowri. Please, don't settle for being second best. You are worth so much more.'

She looked away.

Dave stood up. 'Come on. I'll walk you home. Someone should be looking after you tonight.'

The clock chimed three. Lowri put on her boots and coat, carefully put her pot and its stand in her bag, and they left the house.

The sky was still very dark. Dave put his arm around Lowri's shoulder and they used his torch to guide them down through the fields. When they arrived back at the house he kissed her lightly on the forehead.

'Night, then,' he said. 'Have a lie-in in the morning, if Cassie lets you. I'll see you in the spring.'

'That sounds a long time away.'

'Not really. I saw my first snowdrop this morning.'

'Thank you for my pot, the chocolate and walking me home.'

Dave grinned. 'My pleasure.' Then the smile left his face. 'I'll miss you.'

'I'll miss you as well.' Lowri tried to smile, and then turned away. She fumbled for her key. Dave waited until she opened the door.

'See ya,' he said, and walked away.

Lowri let herself in. In a few hours it would be daylight. The house was very quiet. She didn't go into the kitchen to disturb Cassie, but went straight up to bed. Glancing at Jack's room, she saw the door was open: he hadn't returned yet. She changed quickly, removed the make-up. So much of the evening seemed a blur. From her bag, she took Simon's phone number, put it in her drawer, and then on her bedside table she placed her pot on its stand.

She lay down and gazed at it. 'Perfect,' she whispered, and closed her eyes.

Chapter Twenty Seven

When Lowri woke the next morning, it wasn't the rich costumes, the music of the ball, even her conversation with Simon that sprang to mind. Rather, it was the memory of sitting with Dave that lingered, like the coals still glowing with warmth from the night before. She touched the pot, the one she knew he had spent so much time on: it was beautiful. Last night, Dave had made her feel cared for, cherished.

Jack proved elusive over the next few days. There was one message from Dave saying he had left and asking how she was. Her reply was fairly mundane but she found herself smiling as she typed it.

Lowri forced herself to work hard on her online translation for a few days and added bits to her Facebook page. She realised that she hadn't taken any pictures at the ball, so she copied some from the internet and posted them instead. People were impressed, but the general demand seemed to be for a photograph of her. She found a photo of a woman in a blue silk dress and silver mask. It drew a lot of likes and compliments, and it was easy.

Lowri settled into a routine of taking Cassie out each morning and then getting on with her work. January brought ice rather than snow. As she walked up on the downs she crunched through the frozen white grass and mud. The birds that were around were easily spotted. Blackbirds, robins, great tits, all scrabbled around for food; the rooks were black spots in a white sky._She took a picture of the cottage, its roof covered in frost, and sent it to Dave. He replied with a picture of the heavy traffic gridlocked outside the gallery.

One morning, she had returned from her walk and was taking her boots off when Jack came rushing into the kitchen.

'It's a disaster,' he said, looking very pale and in a huge panic.

'What on earth has happened?'

'They're coming. My parents are on their way here: now, today.'

'But they are on a cruise–'

'They're back, and now they are coming here. Apparently, Mum has new medication and is feeling a lot better. They thought they'd come while she felt up to it.'

'Goodness. They're lucky we weren't away or anything.'

'Dad knew we had nothing on. He's not stupid.'

'What time ferry are they on?'

'Dad said they expect to be here at half seven. Also, he said they would be hungry!'

'When was he last here with your Mum?'

'Years ago, when I was still with Holly. God, what a nightmare.'

Lowri touched his arm. 'It doesn't have to be.'

'But they will be staying here.'

She knew what he was thinking. 'We'll need to sort out the beds.'

'Yes. They can go in the guest room.'

'I need to make the bed; that's all.'

'Yes, but, I need to come in with you. Is that alright?'

Suddenly she remembered New Year's Day.

'Jack, stop a minute. I need to tell you something.'

'Mm. What?' She could see he wasn't really paying attention.

'Jack, it's important. At new year, I left the ball early.'

'So?.'

256

'The thing is,' she felt herself blushing. 'Something happened that night, after the party. I think I have feelings for someone else.'

Jack's eyebrows shot up. She had his attention now. 'Who's that then?'

She swallowed hard. 'Dave from the pottery.'

Jack grimaced. 'He doesn't seem your type. Is it serious? Have you slept with him?'

Lowri looked away. 'We're just friends. He's away for two months at the moment.'

'That doesn't sound too heavy then.'

'I'm not sure. I don't know–'

'We'll worry about it when he comes back then.' Lowri was amazed at how easily Jack dismissed it. It didn't seem to bother him at all.

'Now my parents,' said Jack, and as quickly as that he magicked her disclosure away. 'As I say, we'll have to share a room.' He looked at her seriously. 'That OK?'

Although not quite sure what he meant, she replied, 'Fine.'

'They're going back Sunday afternoon.'

'So, only two nights.'

'Yes. We can do that, can't we? I'll get the vacuum out. We need to clean the place up. Have we got any decent wine in? Food?'

'Nothing at all. I'd planned pizza for myself this evening. I'd better go to the supermarket. Anything I should avoid?'

'Not really. Mum eats small amounts of whatever is put in front of her. Dad likes lots of meat.'

'I'll get some steak, and lamb for a casserole. They're not expecting anything fancy, are they?'

'Don't worry–'

'Weren't we invited to Carina's for lunch on Sunday?'

257

'I'll ring and cancel.'

'I'd better get going. I'll leave you to do the cleaning. Can you put the bedding in the wash?'

'OK. See you later.'

It was while she was buying the steaks that her phone rang. 'Don't bother with a joint for Sunday. Carina insists we go there.'

'Oh.'

'I really don't want to take my parents there, but there's no way out. This is a complete nightmare.' Jack rang off.

When Lowri got back to the house she was shocked at how neat and tidy everything was.

'You've worked hard.'

'Thanks.'

It was then that Lowri saw the car arriving. It was huge, black, glistening. Taking a deep breath, she went out to meet Jack's parents.

Jack's father, Charles, was tall like Jack, and wore what she guessed was his country gentleman outfit of tweed jacket and smart trousers. Jack's mother, Daphne, walked slowly, bent over a walking stick and looked frailer than when Lowri had last seen her.

'Welcome.'

'Very nice to see you again, Lowri,' said Charles and, turning to Jack, said 'Good views. I remember, air you can breathe.'

Jack nodded, but looked solicitously at his mother, took her arm, and helped her into the house. 'Alright, Mum? I can't believe you were able to make this journey.'

'Nor me Jack. I'm a bit stiff.'

'The ferry was heaving,' said Charles. 'They shouldn't take on that number if they haven't enough seats. We had to go up to the area where people go with their dogs. Honestly, the racket.'

As if on cue, Cassie came charging to greet them. Lowri moved to grab her collar. Charles looked down at her. 'Lively dog.'

'It's a lovely house,' said Daphne. 'You keep it nice and warm. Oh, Jack. Is that one of your paintings?' She was looking up at the painting of Carina as Venus.

'It is.'

'Isn't he talented?' she said to Lowri. 'We are so proud of him.'

Lowri smiled to herself. It seemed to her that in his parents' minds Jack was about twenty, not fifty.

'I'm sure you are.'

They went through to the living room.

'Are you hungry?'

Charles rubbed his hands together. 'I'll say.'

'I'll go and put the steaks on. The rest of the meal is ready and laid up. How do you like your steak?'

'Rare for me, like to see the blood. Well done for Daphne.'

Lowri left them with Jack, who walked nervously around the room. Lowri had prepared the dining table. She and Jack hadn't used it together yet, but she didn't see that she could let Jack's parents eat in the kitchen. She had scrabbled around for the matching crockery and cutlery, and even lit a candle. As she stood cooking, she heard Jack taking them into the room, his voice louder, more nervous, than usual.

Jack opened a bottle of claret, and poured his father a glass. His father sipped it. 'That's very acceptable, Jack.'

'Hope your steaks are alright?'

'I hear you were in an accident: nasty gash to your face,' said Charles.

'It was painful, but it's healing.'

'Still, it got you two back together. I can't tell you how pleased we are. We don't want another divorce in the family.'

'So, Lowri,' interrupted Jack's mother, 'how are you finding living over here?'

'I like it, thanks.'

'Did you read my latest column, then, in the Herald?' asked Charles.

'Not sure, Dad.'

'It's alright. I know you didn't. I think you'd approve of it, actually. I was writing about the state of our universities.'

'Really?'

'I was saying they should bring back the grants.'

'I'm impressed, Dad.'

'I know you think I am all right wing, but I don't believe in having a generation starting their lives in debt. I've never believed in loans. If you can't afford it, you don't buy it. Never even had a credit card.'

'I agree about the grants, anyway, Dad. There are students I know whose parents get put off coming and it's a shame. I go into a sixth form over in Southampton. There are talented kids, but there is no way their parents would let them take a loan to do an art degree. It's got to have a job at the end, or they think there's no point. It's sad.'

'Are you still doing your translation work?' Daphne asked Lowri.

'Yes.'

'Good that you've come over here,' said Charles. 'You two should sell that house over in Southampton now, settle down and start a family.'

Daphne coughed, and Charles looked at her. He looked flustered. 'Oh sorry, but at least you know now you can have them.'

Jack's eyes were wide in horror. Lowri took a very long swig of wine and refilled her glass.

'How is your painting down at that manor going, Jack?' Daphne asked.

Lowri realised Daphne had spent a long time perfecting the art of changing the subject.

'Still a lot to do, but I love it.'

'Must be setting them back a bit,' said Charles.

'It is, but luckily for me it's what they want and they can afford to pay for it.'

'How do you have time for all this?'

'Holidays, weekends, evenings—'

'You lecturers have too much time off, if you ask me.'

'The idea is we do research, and this painting is part of that.'

'Jack goes away giving all those talks as well,' said Daphne.

'Of course. Wonderful to think of you over there teaching the Italians about their own heritage,' agreed Charles.

Lowri started to clear away the plates, and brought in a large chocolate cake.

'Ah, you've been baking?' said Daphne.

'Actually I bought it,' she confessed.

'I don't blame you,' said Daphne, smiling.

After the meal Daphne went upstairs to bed. Jack and his father took Cassie out for a walk. Before they left Lowri finished clearing up, then made her excuses for an early night.

It was strange to get into bed knowing that soon Jack would be joining her. She heard him shout good night to his father. It felt like a stranger coming into her room. Jack looked around awkwardly. He was holding a book as if it was a weapon. She didn't look up, but was aware of him quickly getting himself undressed. He flicked through his book, started to read.

'Your mother must have found it a difficult journey.'

'She's on stronger pills now, but she's not really any better. Dad was saying that she really needs a heart operation but they're worried she may be too weak for it. We could lose her at any time.'

'I didn't realise—'

Lowri saw the pain in Jack's eyes. 'She's a wonderful Mum. I don't know what me and Dad would do without her.'

'I'm really sorry; we must look after her.'

'He said that the news about us expecting the baby gave her a new lease of life.'

'Oh.' Lowri tried to stop him wrapping a cloak of guilt around her. It wasn't fair: she didn't deserve this. However hard she tried to shake it off though, the guilt clung to her. 'Did your Dad enjoy the walk?'

'He likes it here. I had to watch him. He's not getting any younger. Made sure he used his torch, but he likes being out in the countryside at night.'

'Your mother is so proud of you.'

'She is.'

Suddenly, Jack slammed his book shut.

Chapter Twenty Eight

Lowri held her breath as she watched Jack put his book on the table. Her heart was beating fast but a voice in her head said, 'Lowri, stop. He doesn't love you. You're worth more than this,' and so she said, 'Think I'll go to sleep now.'

Jack smiled. 'Good. Right. I thought we'd take my parents out tomorrow. You know, Osborne House, then the castle–'

'Fine. As long as it's not too much for your mother–'

'We'll just do the house at Osborne. It'll keep Dad busy, and we'll find her places to sit. 'Night then.'

The next morning Lowri woke to find Jack was already up. It was early. Looking out the window, Lowri was relieved that it was dry.

Jack's father was an early riser as well. She went down to find him eating toast.

'Jack showed me where everything is. He's had a run and is taking Cassie out now. He doesn't stay still for long, does he?'

'Not really. I'll let Fizzy in.'

'You like having all these animals around then?'

'It's company.'

'Jack out a lot?'

'He stays over in the Southampton house sometimes and, of course, he's down the manor painting. Did you and Daphne sleep well?' she asked, pouring cereal into a bowl.

'Daphne finds it difficult to get comfortable. Sometimes I get up, make her a cup of tea.'

'That's kind.'

'Done it for years. Start looking for a cuppa myself now.'

Lowri poured milk on her granola and sat at the table.

'You're quite a bit younger than Jack, aren't you?'

'Only ten years'

'Holly was younger too. Not as much as that, though.'

'I never met her, of course–'

'She was a nice enough girl. Never understood her going off like that. I mean, he was a good husband to her. I don't believe in divorce at the drop of a hat. People need to work at it. I admire you two giving it another shot.'

Lowri cringed. 'Some marriages just don't work.'

'If a man is hitting the wife or something, then fair enough, but Jack would never do anything like that'.

'Of course not.'

'A man needs a wife and family. Everything is so confusing nowadays. I think a child needs a proper married Mum and Dad. That's the bedrock of a society.'

Lowri bit her lip and said, 'I think what matters is that a child feels wanted and loved. I don't think it matters if the parent is single, a gay, transsexual, lesbian, whatever. What matters is that a child knows they are loved unconditionally.'

She saw his face darken, but all he said was, 'I think that this is a subject unsuitable for the breakfast table.'

He went back to munching hard on his toast. Lowri took a deep breath and knew she had to change the subject.

'We've been making some plans for today. Jack was thinking of heading off to Osborne House. How do you fancy that?'

Charles coughed. 'I'd like to do that, yes.'

'I'll go up and change. Do you need the shower?'

'No. You carry on'

It took some time to get everyone ready. Jack drove. His mother looked around the house with them and then, after a drink in the café, they drove to Carisbrooke Castle. Lowri

264

found Jack's parents enthusiastic and easy to take around. As Jack had said, his father was happiest when active.

Jack and his father went up on the ramparts, while Lowri walked slowly around the chapel and the museum with Daphne.

While they were stood looking at the chapel, Daphne said quietly, 'We were so sorry, you know, about the baby. Charles isn't very tactful. It must have been very distressing for you.'

'It was.'

'It's not talked about, is it?'

'People just don't know what to say.'

'Charles never does.' Lowri heard the teasing in her voice, and realised that Daphne maybe wasn't quite as downtrodden as she appeared. 'We both long so much for a grandchild, you know.'

'I understand–'

'I hope you don't mind me asking, but you and Jack, you are happy, aren't you?'

'Of course.'

'Good. We are so pleased you two are back together. You're good for him, Lowri. I'm sure together you will make a very happy home for some lucky child.'

At that moment, Jack and his father returned and they all drove back to the house. Daphne looked exhausted and went to rest while Lowri prepared the evening meal. She put a casserole in the oven, then watched Jack and his father in the garden. She saw his father walk towards the studio, but Jack manoeuvred him away and into the house.

They came into the kitchen. 'Dad and I will take Cassie out before it gets dark. She's had a long day inside.'

Jack smiled at Lowri and she watched them leave through the back gate. Is this how normal couples are? She wondered. It seemed easy and natural when Jack's parents were here. Jack smiled at her, talked to her, and was around. She liked it, enjoyed playing the part.

They ate supper: casserole and baked potatoes seemed pretty safe. For pudding she produced profiteroles, and was relieved when no-one asked her if she had made them. They drank a lot of wine that evening, Lowri found herself laughing and even flirting with Jack. It reminded her that they had only been married for five years, and when they met, that attraction had been there: she hadn't imagined it. She saw the good-looking, charming man she had fallen in love with. As their eyes met, she thought he understood. The fear of looking at each other had gone. Instead, they were laughing at each other's jokes, and gently teasing one another. She thought about the baby she so wanted. This would be a good situation for a child: a safe place to be loved and cared for.

Everyone was tired after such an energetic day. Jack and Lowri walked up the stairs together. They got into bed. Neither read. They turned the light off. Jack was very close to her.

'I was thinking, Lowri. Mum and Dad, they are so desperate for a grandchild, and you and I, we want a child, don't we?'

'Well, yes.'

'Surrogates and things are very complicated. Do you think you and I could, well, try–'

Lowri lay in the darkness. She put her hands on her stomach and knew deep down she was ready to have a baby growing inside her again. Was it right, though, to conceive a baby with a man she didn't love? One hand reached up to her face, felt the scars, heard Simon's words, 'How many options do you have?'

Lowri leant over and kissed Jack on the cheek: it felt cold. She could feel his body tense. Nether of them spoke, but they parted. Lowri turned over. She couldn't make a baby this way, not with a man who was holding his breath, wishing he wasn't there. She waited for Jack to say something, reach out, ask her what was wrong, but he did nothing. Lowri curled up, wondering how it was possible to feel more alone in her bed with someone lying next to her than when she was on her own.

The next morning Lowri woke to find Jack gone. She went downstairs to find he had gone out for a walk with Cassie. She was drinking coffee and nibbling toast when Charles came into the kitchen. She asked Charles if he and Daphne would be coming to church.

'I don't think so. We don't usually, and those pews would be so uncomfortable for Daphne. We'll stay here and keep house. You and Jack go off. Jack said he'd come and get us to take us to this manor place for lunch.'

'To be honest, I could do with catching up on some work. We'll let Jack go on his own.'

The morning passed quietly. Daphne read and Charles took Cassie out again. Lowri hid in her work and wished they were staying home for lunch. However, Jack came back and soon they were all driving to the manor. As she got out the car, Lowri avoided looking at the steps where she had fallen. Carina was in a particularly hospitable mood and came floating out, her fair hair loose.

'Welcome, Charles and Daphne. It is so wonderful for Ken and I to welcome you to the manor.'

Charles smiled expansively. 'Thank you for inviting us. This is an extraordinary house.'

'Oh, thank you, Charles. That is so kind. Now, Daphne, I must take you to see how Jack's fresco is coming on. I'm sure you are dying to see it.' She linked arms with Daphne and took her into the house. 'Jack and I are passionate about the Renaissance.'

'I am sure your husband is very proud of what you're doing.'

'Of course. I'm very lucky to have such a wonderful husband. I'm sorry my daughter, Lizzy isn't here today. She's gone to a friend's.'

Lowri let them go ahead, and stayed alone in the hallway. She saw Jack, his Dad and Ken going into the living room and went to join them. Ken served them drinks.

'This is all very comfortable,' said Charles contentedly. 'You have a lovely set up here, Ken.'

'Thank you, Charles.'

'But it's the stables where your heart is?'

'Of course.' Ken turned to Lowri. 'When are you going to come and have a ride? You know Nicola would be very happy for you to ride Biscuit. He would be a lovely gentle ride for you.'

'I'll have a think about that. Thank you, Ken.'

Carina appeared in the doorway with Daphne. 'You all look cosy. Not long now. You sit here, Daphne. I must go and check on my, as you call them, Yorkshires. I have been working hard to learn how to make a good English roast dinner.'

'Well, that's smashing,' said Charles. 'So many woman nowadays don't have time for these things.'

Daphne sat next to Lowri. 'I wouldn't want to do the dusting here,' she joked. Carina called them to the table. It looked splendid, with the best linen napkins on the old oak table, crystal glasses that shone, and tall candle sticks.

'Goodness, this is wonderful,' said Daphne.

'I've opened a white to go with the starter and we'll have good full bodied red for the main,' announced Ken.

'What a shame,' said Charles. 'I'm driving later, so I'll have to leave it for now.'

'Well, I made a very good punch for you. I always think it's hard on the driver just to be given water or lemonade.'

'That's very kind.'

'Now I have a choice of starters,' continued Carina. 'I went down to Ventnor yesterday, got some lovely fresh crab and dressed it, but I know seafood isn't for everyone, so there are some little cheese soufflés if you'd prefer.'

'That sounds just right,' said Daphne.

'I thought it might. Jack told me you like a lighter meal.'

After the starter came a magnificent roast beef joint and the fluffiest Yorkshires Lowri had ever seen.

'Now those are impressive,' said Charles.

'You must tell me your secret,' said Daphne. 'Charles loves his Yorkshires.'

'I thought we might be having pasta or something, you being Italian,' said Charles.

'Oh no. I like to make Ken a proper English roast. Do have some horseradish. I make it myself.'

Lowri gritted her teeth. Carina was holding court, and Lowri was desperately trying not to hate her for it.

Later, of course, came the puddings. Lowri watched resigned as homemade chocolate cake, and profiteroles were displayed.

'You have a real gift for this,' said Daphne.

'I help out in my friend's café, bake for her. I have been introducing Italian pastries there.'

'It's good that Jack has such friendly neighbours,' said Charles 'I'm sure you all enjoy doing things together. Carina, you must teach Lowri about cooking.'

'So how do you find living here after Italy?' asked Daphne.

'It's a shame about the weather, but here I have Ken and Lizzy. What more could I want?'

'How lovely, a proper family,' said Charles.

The table fell quiet.

'Let's take our coffee into the living room,' said Carina. 'Ken, go and put some logs on the fire: cheer us up on a grey old day.'

They sat drinking coffee and feeling very lazy until it was time to go.

'We're booked on the ferry,' said Charles. 'I have to thank you so much for your hospitality. It's been the highlight of our weekend.'

As they drove back to the house, Lowri sat in the back with Daphne.

'Carina is a lovely girl, isn't she? Her husband Ken is a very nice man but a lot older than her.'

'Mmm.'

'A real home maker that girl. When we were on our own she was saying how much she would like to have more children, she said she's like her mother and if Ken was willing she was sure she could have a proper family. It's a shame though he doesn't want any more isn't it'

'She mentioned that to Jack.'

'I love the work he is doing down there. He is lucky to have found someone who understands his passion for his work. Holly never did you know. I expect Jack is down at the manor a lot, do you mind?'

'No, he loves what he is doing.'

'I have to say he looks very at home there.'

Lowri was glad when they arrived back at their house. Fortunately it was time for Jack's parents to leave. Daphne was profuse in her thanks, and Charles said, 'It's been a wonderful stay. Thank you. Now, we have brought you some very late Christmas presents. Where are they, Daphne?'

From a carrier bag, Daphne produced a large wrapped present.

'We thought now that you two are together again we should get you something for your home,' said Charles.

'I think you should open it,' said Jack to Lowri.

Lowri undid the carefully wrapped box. Inside were two gifts. The first was a large framed picture with a key in the middle: 'the key to happiness, your forever home together'.

Jack laughed nervously. 'Anyone would think we were just getting married.'

'Somehow this feels like your first proper home,' said Daphne.

'Your turn,' said Lowri to Jack handing him a large white envelope.

Jack opened it and his eyes widened. 'Gosh. Mum, Dad.'

'What is it?' asked Lowri.

He handed it to her. 'It's lifetime family membership to the National Trust.'

Charles was radiant. 'It covers you two and how ever many children you have for life.'

'It must have been very expensive,' said Jack.

'Worth every penny;' said Charles. 'Now, we must be off. Thank you again for a lovely stay.' He picked up the bags and they all went out. Jack and Lowri watched as they drove away.

As soon as they were back in the house, Jack picked up his coat.

'I'll go down to the manor, then. I'll be gone for a while. Don't wait up.'

As suddenly as their life as a couple had started, it ended. Lowri looked down at the picture... our forever home together.

Chapter Twenty Nine

During the week Lowri was looking at her phone when she realised that the following weekend was the one she had been invited to go to Merthyr. One evening she managed to catch Jack and talk to him about it. He seemed pleased that she was going. She guessed that he too was finding things difficult since his parents had stayed.

'That's fine. I'll take care of Cassie and Fizzy, and I can run you to the Red Jet.'

And so on the Saturday morning Lowri packed up her small bag. She picked up a photograph from her bedside table: should she take it? What would he think? Eventually, she decided to pack it; if it didn't feel right, she didn't have to show it.

As they drove to the ferry Lowri could see a few buds on the trees; there were even a few daffodils out.

'They're too early, aren't they?' she said to Jack.

'Those always come early. Must be sheltered, I guess. So, what time is your train?'

'Ten past, then a connection from Cardiff. I'll get a taxi at the other end to Aunty June's.'

'Is your aunt like your Mum was?'

'Not really. A lot chattier and more confident. She'll be so excited to see her brother.'

'Why on earth hasn't he been over before, or she gone over to see him?'

'My mother didn't have the money and June never seemed bothered. And Uncle Gareth, well, he never made it back. They write letters and that.'

The ferry was a bit bumpy and the weather was grey. At Southampton Lowri caught the free bus to the station, grabbed a coffee and boarded her train. She pushed her holdall into the gap between the seats and found a table.

She was squashed against the window, her coffee in front of her, and the young man opposite seemed determined to colonise the table with his laptop, phone, drink and paper. To her left a large woman placed her elbow firmly on the joint arm rest; her husband opposite opened his paper.

Lowri managed to reach for her phone, relieved that no-one so far had seemed aware of her. The young man opposite did occasionally glance at her coffee. She assumed he was worried it might spill on his things but she was pretty sure that if he had been asked to describe her he would have struggled to say anything beyond saying she was an older woman with coffee. She sent a long text to Dave telling him about her journey. He replied quickly, 'Give my love to Wales. How have you been?' Lowri started to tell him about Jack's parents' visit, but kept it light, telling Dave about the places they had taken them. 'Sounds good. Better get back to work,' came the reply. She was a bit hurt he didn't ask any more questions but guessed he was busy.

The only interruption on the journey was the guard asking for tickets. The woman next to her asked him numerous questions about her journey most of which she seemed to already know the answers to.

Eventually, Lowri saw they were coming into Newport, last stop before Cardiff. There was a splatter of rain on the window. Jack said it always rained when they came to Wales. He was often proved right.

Cardiff station felt noisy and dark. Lowri held on to the oak handrail that led her down a steep flight of steps, not easy for old people, she thought. She looked at the departure board, found the platform for Merthyr and began her ascent up the steps. Standing on the platform, she listened to the valleys voices: the harsh consonants, and long soft vowels.

'What you been buying then?' said one girl.

'Oh, been to Primark. You know, for thirty quid I got three skirts and two tops. Lush eh?'

'You going to that band in The Red House tonight?'

'Guess so. You?'

'Yea.'

Lowri smiled, already feeling at home.

The train was old. She watched out of the window as the city fell away and they passed through small scruffy stations with the magnificent backdrops of hills.

At Merthyr terminus she got off the train and walked to the taxi rank.

'You come far, then?'

'Isle of Wight.'

'Good God. When did you leave?'

'This morning.'

'Really? I'd have thought it would take a long time. Never been there.'

'It's a beautiful place.'

'It's like part of Britain, isn't it? Same money and that?'

'Yes, all the same,' replied Lowri, grinning.

'So, you got family here?'

'I'm going to meet my uncle for the first time. He's coming from the States, but I grew up here.'

'What the name of your Mam then?'

'Susan Johnson, lived in Clarence Street.'

'No, I don't think I know her.' He seemed disappointed.

Lowri looked around, 'this place doesn't change, does it?'

'No money. They've done up the hospital. You know, they were going to take away our A and E. If I'd had a heart attack my wife would've had to drive me all the way down to the Heath in Cardiff. Well, I'd never have made it, would I?'

Lowri paid, got out, and looked up and down the street of terraced houses. A lot of the small front gardens had gone and were growing cars instead of flowers. Most had new windows and generally looked smarter. Her old house was at the other end of the street. She would wander down and have a look at it later.

She stopped at the little metal gate that led into her aunt's house, suddenly she felt a bit nervous. Was it going to be odd meeting this uncle? She walked up the driveway of June's neat house: she had gravel and tidy potted plants. There were new crisp white nets hanging up; the brass letter box shone. She knocked on the door and June, short with freshly permed hair, welcomed her.

'Lowri, it's so exciting. Come in.' Then she stopped. Lowri noticed her looking at Lowri's face.

'I'm sorry, Aunty June. I should have told you I was in an accident.'

'Oh dear. I'm sorry. You must tell me all about it later. I've just made a cup of tea. Your uncle is in the living room and he's dying to meet you.'

Lowri followed her down a narrow hallway, which was decorated with china plates, and photos of grandchildren.

'She's here, Gareth,' her aunt was calling.

Lowri tucked her bag out of the way, hung her coat up, and went into the living room. She was shocked when she saw her uncle. She had expected him to be quite large but had pictured someone younger. As she looked at him she could see the likeness to her mother: the same dimple in his chin and ears. She could see him inspecting her in the same way.

'Lowri had an accident,' her aunt explained, misinterpreting his gaze, 'but she's fine now.'

'I wasn't looking at the scars,' he said quickly. 'You remind me of your mother. You've her eyes and her hair.'

Lowri smiled; his American accent seemed glamorous here. 'I was thinking the same, that you had her chin.'

'For real? It's great meeting family, isn't it. So you had an accident? I'm sorry to hear that.'

Lowri's hand automatically went to her scars. 'It's a while back now.'

June brought in a small trolley with tea and plates of small cakes. They sat sharing news, then June said she needed to go and check on the steak and kidney pie in the oven. Lowri realised that she was going to be expected to eat again soon.

'I was thinking of going for a little walk along the street. Just to have a look at my old house. Would that be OK?' she asked.

'Of course.'

'I'd love to walk with you, Lowri, if that's OK with you,' said her uncle.

'Good,' said June. 'It will give me time to get myself sorted out.'

'June tells me you live on an island, Lowri.'

'I do. It's lovely. There are lots of beaches and walks up on the downs.'

'I remember going up to Brecon as a lad.'

'Oh, the Isle of Wight doesn't have the mountains of Wales. It's much gentler. What's it like where you live?'

'Real nice. I had my garage for years, only wound it up recently and decided that I ought to come over here before it was too late. I'm sorry I didn't make your mother's funeral, but my wife was sick at the time.'

'That's a shame. How is she now?'

'Much better thanks.'

They arrived at Lowri's old home. It had been painted white, and a smart car was parked where she remembered her mother had neat borders of pansies. It looked so small.

'Funny how places always look so much smaller when you get older,' she said to her uncle.

'This road looks just like the one me and your Mum were brought up in. It was only a few streets away from here. She didn't move far, your Mum.'

'She went to Bristol for a while, but then she came back.'

'I'd gone to America by then so I missed all that. Missed seeing you as a baby.'

'What made you go? I mean, your sisters haven't gone far, have they?'

'My Dad had a cousin out there. I went to work in his garage to start with before I got my own. I don't know. I just wanted to get out of Merthyr, and it was a chance to do that. It doesn't suit everyone. Some people like to stay in one place.'

Lowri looked around, 'I remember playing out here, even on the colder evenings. We played skipping and chalk hopscotch games. I suppose the children are all watching TV and on computers now.' Looking over the road she said, 'I ought to go and buy a bottle of wine for this evening, then get back to see if I can help.'

'I'll carry on walking if you don't mind.'

'No, of course not. See you later.'

The shop that she remembered being owned by a couple called Mr and Mrs Haywood was now a franchise; the packets were mostly own brand. There was a whole wall devoted to alcohol. Lowri guessed it must be where the money was. She chose a light red and went to pay. As she held out the bottle, she noticed the woman assistant was staring at her. They both looked at each other carefully, trying to work out why the other looked familiar, then Lowri realised it was Ceri, from school, and now from Facebook.

'It is Ceri, isn't it?' she asked, hesitantly. 'I'm Lowri.'

'My God, Lowri! What happened to you?'

Lowri panicked. For a moment she had forgotten about her scars.

'I had an accident.'

'But you never said, you know, on Facebook–'

Lowri looked down. 'No, I didn't know how to tell people.'

'You should have said. We all talk about you, say how lucky you are, and what a wonderful life you have–' She saw Ceri purse her lips.

'Sorry. It's a bit awkward.'

'Why? You had an accident. Not your fault.'

'No, but the scar – I'm embarrassed.'

'It's nasty, but worse things happen. I wish you'd said Lowri. We are your friends.'

'I'm sorry.'

They stood in silence as Ceri took the bottle and swiped the bar code.

'I'm sorry,' Lowri said again. She took a deep breath. 'You know, it wasn't easy at school. I was teased about my height, weight, being nerdy–'

'That was just a bit of fun,' said Ceri. 'You always laughed.'

'I was hurt, though. Didn't you ever think you'd gone too far?'

Ceri grimaced. 'I suppose if I'm honest, maybe we went a bit over the top.'

'I used to cry, you know, and so with the Facebook thing I wanted you all to see I'd made something of myself. Really, I just wanted you to like me.'

'Well you never seemed like it. To be honest, Lowri, we all assumed that you thought you were better than us. You looked superior, like.'

'Well, I didn't feel it. Anyway, it was a long time ago, and I shouldn't have lied like that.'

Ceri smiled. 'Look, it's alright. Loads of people write stuff on Facebook. You know, my friend she went to Skegness on holiday with the kids. It rained and her partner got pissed the whole time. She said she'd been having too much fun to take photos but that it had been the best time ever. So, see, we all do it.'

'So, are you alright? You've got three children?'

'That's true at least. Lovely they are, when they're not murdering each other. And I've got a good chap. Looks after us all.'

'I'm really glad for you.'

'Thanks. You haven't got kids?'

'No, not yet. I'm here to see my Aunty June. I'd better get back. She's cooking us a huge tea.'

'Right. It was nice to see you.'

'And you.'

Lowri left the shop. She didn't breathe until she was outside. She felt so stupid, but then, however petty it might sound, she was glad to have talked to Ceri. When she got back, though, she would have to sort out her Facebook page. She had no doubt that Ceri at that moment was busy texting everyone in Merthyr about what had happened.

Lowri arrived back at the same time as her uncle. They all enjoyed the pie and the wine. Her uncle opened a bottle of port. As her aunt and uncle sat reminiscing Lowri was preoccupied, thinking about the photo in her bag. Should she show it to them? What would her uncle think? Then, she realised this might be her only opportunity: she had to be brave. Quietly she left the room, took the photograph from her bag and went back into the room.

She smiled nervously at her uncle. 'I think there's something I want to show you.'

Chapter Thirty

It was very late but Heather was still at the café. Now every one was back at work after the Christmas break, the bills had started to come in again and she had no idea how on earth she was going to pay them. She had managed to keep off her laptop since the night before the ball, but now it seemed to be the only solution.

As she waited for the programme to load she remembered the first time she had gone on the site: it was last summer at a friend's hen do. They had been out drinking and gone back to her house. Her friend suggested they all play online, apparently the site called it Sparkly Princess Friday, and everyone wanted to play. When filling in her details Heather had used a bank account and card she had been winding down, so that Lee wouldn't know. She put down ten pounds and was given 'start up' money on the site. They had a great time, and had all broken even. It had been fun.

A few nights later after a long day in the café she thought of going back on. It was a warm, welcoming world: they remembered her. 'Welcome back, Heather. Great to see you.'

Soon, it become her treat after a day at work. She always played the slots, and she started to place more bets. The first 'real' bet had been two hundred, on an incredible night when she had won over five thousand pounds. She put the money into her wedding fund and immediately paid off the wedding dress. The designer had been impressed: she usually got paid in full at the end, but Heather wanted to have it paid off; one less thing to worry about. It felt good and she thought how great it would be to pay off other bills as well. She started to put down bigger and bigger bets: when she won it was the best feeling ever. She had a few bad losses. Somehow it seemed logical to start using their savings. A few good wins and it would easily be worth it. She went on so frequently that the site made her an elite member. She had been sent a wonderful hamper, (a grateful supplier, she told Lee). It always seemed easier to remember the wins and not the losses. Soon she was using other parts of their savings, determined to win it back. The losses somehow always seemed to out run the wins, and the night before Carina's party, Heather played all the money they had left. She lost. She couldn't believe it: she had lost again, but that must mean a win was on the way

Heather found a lender which asked few questions, put the money straight into her account. The interest, of course, was high, but one good win and she would be clear.

She sat waiting for the music and the greeting. 'Hi Heather. Great to see you. We have some new bonus games for you today. Have fun.' She moved closer to the screen, slowly becoming immersed in her world.

Slots there were so much more exciting than the machine in the pub or on the ferry. Here there were twenty five play lines. The ways to win were numerous. She placed a hundred coins on every spin, and she would bet on every play line. She never went to auto play: pressing each time gave her a feeling of control. She took a deep breath. Her hand hovered over the play button. This was her favourite bit: the anticipation.

Then she pressed it. Music kicked in. Reels spun. Pay lines presented themselves as she won, 'wilds' animated in front of her eyes, and 'scatters' rewarded her with different bonuses. She was on a winning streak; life was good. She imagined paying back all the money: no more worries. Time as always, drifted away. Heather was in her own world: no-one, nothing else, mattered. She didn't hear the door open, the footsteps behind her.

'So this is what you're writing–'

Shocked, Heather turned around.

'Carina. What the hell–' She slammed down the lid of her laptop.

'I saw a light on: came to see what was going on.'

'What are you doing out at this time?'

Carina sat down next to her.

'I went to your house. No-one was there, so I thought you must be here.'

Heather blushed, looked down at her closed laptop. 'Don't tell anyone: it's only a bit of fun.'

'Is it?'

'Of course. I never put down much.'

Carina shook her head. 'I don't believe you Heather. I know exactly what you've been doing.'

'You can't.'

'You leave your laptop around. Your passwords are pathetic, by the way.'

Heather saw an unpleasant sneer on Carina's face which she had never seen before.

'You shouldn't go on my laptop. It's nothing to do with you.'

'But it is, Heather. I always think the best way to know a person is to know their weakness. I know yours.'

'I don't do it for myself.'

'Of course you don't. On the surface, people might think you are just another middle-aged woman addicted to online gambling.'

'I am not an addict. How dare you!'

Carina laughed. 'Not an addict. You can give up any time, can you?'

'Of course.'

'I don't believe you. Just try next time you think of going on. Anyway, gambling isn't your main addiction.

284

No, your main addiction needs people to like you. Every day you live your life to please people, begging them to like you. You gamble, not to get things for yourself, but so you can buy things for other people, so they will love you. You are weak: you don't just want to be liked. You need it like the air you breathe.'

'I do it because I love people. I want to make them happy.'

'Not really. It's all about you, Heather. You think if you make people happy, if you wave your magic wand and make their dreams come true, then they will like you.'

'That's horrible.'

'It's the truth, but you prefer lies. You pretend to be some genie who can make all their wishes come true. You say you do it because you love them, but you do it because you fear that, if you don't give them what they want, they will leave you, give up on you.'

If there hadn't been a grain of truth in them, the words would not have hurt so much.

Heather stood up. 'I think you'd better go. I don't know why you are being so nasty to me when all I have ever done is show you kindness.'

Carina shrugged. 'We both use each other. I used you for company, someone to notice me, praise me: see, I know my weaknesses as well. You used me to keep this place going, cheap labour. It worked. Now, however, we can take our relationship to a whole new level.'

'How's that? Do you want a raise? I can't do that—'

Carina gave a cynical smile. 'I wouldn't ask you for money. I've seen your bank accounts. You need money, and I need – well, something. See, we can help each other.'

'I don't understand.'

'Look, Heather. I have some pretty high cards: I can ruin your business, your marriage—'

'You wouldn't–'

'Oh, yes. What would Lee make of all the cheating? The lying? And then there's Poppy's wedding–'

'What about it?' Heather felt sick, it was as if Carina had transformed into some kind of demon.

'Well, I could take away the manor and, if all those people waiting for bills to be paid: the cake, the cars, the flowers– If any of them knew there was no chance of getting paid – I wonder what they would do?'

'You wouldn't do that to Poppy–'

'Look: none of that needs to happen. I am very happy to put money into your account: you could sort out the books, pay all the bills. I could be your genie, you see: all your problems gone.'

'You'd do that?'

'I could. It would be a loan, of course, but no interest, no embarrassment. You just pay it off as you can. But it would only be fair if you were to do something for me. We all have dreams, you see, and you have it in your power to make mine come true.'

'What is it? Tell me, what do I have to do?'

Carina's eyes were bright with excitement. 'I need you to do something for me. It's Lowri. She won't listen to me, but she likes you.'

'We're friends. I can't do anything to her if that is what you're thinking. She has been through so much.'

Carina stood up and went into the kitchen. She found two glasses and an opened bottle of wine in the fridge. She brought them back to the table.

'You need a drink,' she said to Heather. 'Now, listen to me. Lowri is not the angel you think she is. The night of the ball I overheard her talking to Simon upstairs in a bedroom.'

Heather looked confused. 'She doesn't know him.'

'That's what you think. Back in Southampton they had been having an affair.'

'What? No. They only met at the ball.'

Carina took her phone out of her bag, and showed Heather a photo. She looked at the image of Lowri and Simon sitting very close together, talking intently on the bed.

'You're right,' she said. 'Oh no, I never thought Lowri was like that.'

'Oh, there's more.'

'What?' asked Heather faintly, her mind still putting the pieces together: the mention of the Maine Coon cats, the look on Lowri's face when she saw Simon.

Carina got up and went over to the wood burner which was nearly out now. She wandered about, then returned to her seat.

'What?' repeated Heather.

'They were together in France. When Lowri had her accident, she had been with Simon. He left her in the hospital. I heard her say it, and there's worse: She was pregnant with Simon's baby.'

'No?'

'Yes, I heard her.'

'But Jack–'

'Exactly: She doesn't love Jack. She's just been stringing him along. I heard her say that she'd told Jack the baby was his.'

Heather shivered, and went over to the wood burner. 'This is awful. Poor Rosemary. Do you think we should tell her?'

'I think it's best left. They seem to have finished the affair now. Why put Rosemary through all that hurt? The only reason I'm telling you is for you to know the sort of person she is, and so you should have no qualms in doing what I ask.'

'And that is?'

Carina grabbed Heather's hand; her nails dug in.

'I need you to make Lowri leave the island, go back to Southampton. That's all; it's not a lot, is it?'

Carina pressed her lips together: they were white under the lipstick.

'I can't make Lowri leave.'

Carina let go of her hand roughly. 'You have to.'

Heather almost expected her to stamp on her foot.

'What would I say?'

'To start with, you tell her that you know about Simon; you hate her and everyone else here will too: she has to leave. Her life will be miserable.'

Heather grimaced. 'That seems a bit heavy.'

'It has to be. It will be doing Jack a favour.'

'Why can't you do this?'

'She knows I don't like her. Coming from you it will really hurt. But you are going to need to be strong.'

'What do you mean?'

'That scar on her face: she hates it, doesn't she?'

'Of course.'

'Think how much worse it would be if she was to get badly scarred, her whole face a mess.'

'What on earth are you saying?'

Carina laughed. 'It's alright. We won't actually do anything, but what we need her to think is that something could happen. Fear: that's the key. She can imagine far worse things than we could ever do.'

'That's terrible, sadistic, and cruel.'

'But we're not doing anything.'

'We would be: we'd be messing with her mind.'

'She can cope: we just need her to go. That's all.'

'I couldn't even start to threaten anything like that.'

'Listen: this is what you say. It's easy. Say it's a close village: if someone here gets hurt they sort it out without bothering the police. People have been attacked. No-one reports it, that kind of thing. You can say you are concerned for her, don't want anything else to happen to her face–'

'I don't know–'

'Come on. Poppy and Lee need you. Lowri will be fine: you don't owe her anything. But Lee and Poppy, this café: they are your world; they depend on you; they have to come first. As soon as you tell me you've spoken to her, I will put the money in your account. Everything will be perfect.'

'But why do you want to do this? Why do you want me to get rid of Lowri?'

'I don't think you need to know that now, do you?' Carina walked to the door. 'Good night, Heather. I will not be in for a few days.'

Heather sat alone: had that really happened? She glanced over at the picture of her mother and family on the wall. 'Please don't judge me, Mum. I just don't know what to do.'

Chapter Thirty One

Lowri travelled back the following afternoon. She lay back in her seat, her eyes closed. It had been a short but emotional trip.

She had shown the photograph to her uncle who had, understandably, looked very confused. 'I remember sending that photo to your Mum. I was showing her how much weight I'd put on. How on earth did it end up in a frame with 'Dad' written on it?'

'I don't know how much you know about Mum and the time when I was born? About her marriage to my father?' she added nervously.

She spotted the glance between her aunt and uncle. Her aunt sat forward. 'We know your mother was never married.'

'Oh, so you know the truth?'

June nodded. 'Susan told me and she wrote to Gareth. Of course no-one else around here knew. She told you when you were older, didn't she? '

'She did. I was about twelve. It was such a shock.' Lowri looked over at her uncle.

'When I was very young, Mum gave me this photo in the frame. I had never met you. She had hidden any photos of you, so I believed her when she told me this was a photo of my Dad.'

'So you believed that for years?'

'Oh yes. I would tell my friends this is my Dad, and then the story Mum had told me. That she'd met this wonderful man when she'd gone to work in Bristol. They got married and then he'd tragically died when she was pregnant with me. He'd been a wonderful man. He'd had no family so she'd come back to bring me up in Merthyr.'

'I was never easy with your Mum saying all this to you,' said June, 'but it's what she and your Gran wanted. They said it made you and your Mum respectable.'

Gareth put some more coal on the fire. 'I can see why it was such a shock when your Mum told you the truth. What made her do that, do you think? I guess the story was pretty well accepted by then.'

Lowri watched as the flames curled around the coals. 'I'd started seeing some boy at school: Martin, his name was. I remember Mum coming and talking to me in my bedroom. She said that she needed to tell me something now while I was young, before I made the mistakes she had.'

'You were only twelve,' said Gareth.

'I know. She was so nervous, but she said no-one had prepared her for life and she didn't want the same to happen to me.'

June took a sip of port. 'We had a very sheltered upbringing. Chapel was our life outside school and Gran was very strict about what we read or saw on TV. All we knew about sex was that you didn't do it outside of marriage. Susan went off to Bristol without any idea how the world worked.'

Lowri nodded. 'That's what Mum said. I think she was worried I'd hate her for what she did.'

'It's not an easy thing to tell your child.'

'No. I'd had this picture of my Dad,' she looked at her uncle. 'I don't just mean the photograph, I mean in my head. He was kind and generous, a hero. It's what I told my friends.'

'And then you learnt the truth.' June winced, feeling Lowri's pain.

'Yes, that he was a man my mother met in a bar who bought her drinks, who took her back to his hotel and who she slept with. He told her he travelled around working and would be back the following week, but he never returned. She couldn't even be sure of his name.'

June shook her head. 'It was so unlike her to do such a thing,'

'I don't understand it,' said Lowri. 'She was so strict. She told me she wasn't drunk. He didn't make her do anything she didn't want to do. She never made any excuses for herself.'

June sighed. 'No, Susan wouldn't do that. I do know, though, that she was very lonely. That was the first night she'd gone out with the people from her office.'

'So what was the photo business?' asked Gareth.

'It was like the ring, I suppose. It was Mum's way of adding credence to the story.'

'But you still have the photo in that frame, even now, when you know it's a lie.'

'I know. Mum told me to keep it with me. She still wanted me to appear respectable when I went off to university, even when I got married.'

'But you must have told people the truth? Your generation don't care about these things,' said Gareth.

'I never have. It would've felt like I was letting Mum down. I still wear her ring as well.'

'But you brought the photo to show me.'

'I thought I should. I feel guilty, and think you should know what I've been doing.'

Her uncle sat back, looking thoughtful. 'It's a bit odd, to be honest, but then Susan thought she was doing the right thing, I guess.'

Lowri took the photograph and turned it over. The hinges on the back were stiff but she pushed them back and took out the photograph.

'I think it's time it came out of there,' she said, 'but I'd like to keep it, put it in a new plain frame if that's alright. I mean, you have always been with me.'

'I think that's really nice,' said Gareth, looking pleased.

June leant forward and patted Lowri on the knee. 'Try not to feel too badly about your Mum. She meant it for the best.'

'I know,' said Lowri, 'but there's one thing that still worries me.'

'What's that?'

'When I went to university, Mum told me it was what she'd have loved to have done, and I saw it in her face how much it meant to her. It worried me that all those years she'd been frustrated, that in fact,' Lowri licked her lips, the truth can be so difficult to speak, 'since the day she told me the truth, I have been scared that she saw me as the greatest mistake of her life.'

June put her glass down with such force that Lowri thought she would break it. 'Now, listen to me, Lowri. Your mother never ever saw you as a mistake. She always said you were the best thing that happened to her. I had this feeling you might think that, and that is why I asked Gareth to bring something to show you.' She looked over at her brother. 'Go on. Show the letter to Lowri.'

Gareth took a letter out of his pocket.

It was then that Lowri realised that this had all been set up by her aunt. Lowri had come, thinking that she was in control and that she was going to sort a few things out, when actually June had planned it all. Her uncle handed her the letter.

Dear Gareth,

I hope you are well. I have some very exciting news. Lowri has been offered a place at university. Can you believe it? I am so proud of her. She is such a quiet thing; but she is lovely with people. I hope this gives her confidence to know just how special she is. I never wanted her to feel less than what she was. Maybe it's why it took me so long to tell her the truth about her father. Obviously, I made a few mistakes in my time! But Lowri, I am sure, was meant to be. I am sorry if I am sounding boastful but I can never believe I produced such a wonderful child, beautiful inside and out.

Sorry, that is enough about me. How are you?

Lowri glanced at her uncle; he looked thoughtful. 'You must have known this is how your Mum felt about you?'

Lowri sighed. 'I'm sorry. I don't mean to sound ungrateful. Of course, I knew Mum loved me. She was always there for me, took care of me. I have a lot of lovely memories of her sitting on my bed, reading me stories, and when I was older she would sit with me while I did my homework. I miss her every day.'

'But—' said June.

'I don't mean to be disloyal to her, but she was a very private, understated kind of person. There was a lot she didn't talk about, and I guess as a child you fill in the gaps yourself. We only talked that once about her meeting my father and I think I picked up that word, 'mistake'.'

'Why didn't you ask your mother about it?' said Gareth.

June interrupted. 'I can understand that. You didn't actually see Susan after she'd been in Bristol. She changed. She lost her confidence. She became a lot more reserved.'

Her uncle turned to Lowri. 'You must keep that letter.'

'Oh no. I couldn't.'

294

'Yes. It sounds like she told me things she should have told you. You keep it.'

'Thank you. It's a lovely letter. What do you want me to do about the photo?'

He put his head to one side. 'You do what you like. It doesn't bother me.'

Lowri nodded. 'Thank you. I think I will put it in a new plain frame. I don't need the old one now, do I? But I would like to keep your photo with me. After all, you've travelled around with me all of my life.'

'Now that's a nice thought, Lowri. Thank you.'

June stood up with the air of a woman who had successfully completed a mission. 'Good. Right. Time for a refill.'

As Lowri sat on the train she felt glad she'd been back. It had been good to get away, to clear her head a bit. When she got back to the island she would make some changes. The first thing, of course, was to sort out the Facebook page. As fun as it had been, it would be good to be free of that. The other would be to sort out her work. She didn't want to hide behind her computer all the time now. Being in the pottery had shown her that she could cope with the world, but that wasn't the right place for her. Maybe she would go back to her Polish group: there was no reason not to go over on Mondays, not to lead the group, but to see the members as friends. Maybe she could find some tuition or college work using her languages as well as carrying on her translation work. Her mother was proud of her accomplishments: now she would be proud of them as well.

It was early evening. Heather had rushed home from the café. Lee was working. She had the house to herself. She was excited, worked out the solution to all her problems. Last night, after talking with Carina, she lay in bed knowing in her heart that whatever she said to Carina and however angry she was with Lowri, threatening and blackmailing were just not her. If only she wasn't reliant on Carina for money she wouldn't have to do it. If she had another way of getting the money she could sort out the account, pay for the wedding. Then, even if Carina was to say anything to Lee, she could say it had been a mistake but that she had sorted it all out. If she made enough they could afford to hold the wedding somewhere else, not be reliant on Carina for the manor. She wanted to talk to Lowri about Simon, but in her own way: this would give her the freedom to do that. Carina wouldn't like it, of course. Well, that was her problem and if she could sort out her money, she wouldn't have to have any more to do with Carina's scheme.

Her mind, of course, went to her gambling site. That money from the loan was sitting there: if there was a way she could get a decent win on that she could put everything right. When she got into work that morning she had found an email that seemed to confirm this was the right thing to do. It was from the gambling site saying that because they valued her so much they were offering her some special bonus games that day. They were suggesting big wins, but the offer was only until midnight tonight. This was it: this was the answer. The buzz at the thought of the games had been with her all day. In fact she had sneaked off a few times to try but each time she had been called back. It had been very frustrating, and she had counted the minutes until she could leave and get home.

Excited, she signed in. The familiar music came up and a message: 'Welcome back Heather.' She felt like she could finally relax. Part of her knew that it was an automatic message, but it still felt personal and caring. Her hands, which had been shaking, started to steady. Then she remembered her father. He had been a smoker. All day he would be saying how he was longing to get out of the kitchen and have a smoke, but her mother would only allow him so many breaks. His favourite smoke was at the end of the day. Heather could picture him: sat back in the courtyard. As a child she watched his hands shaking less as he took the first drags. Of course, he had been addicted; she knew that. But she wasn't: she could stop. She could shut this down right now if she wanted to.

Carina's voice taunted her. 'Of course, you're an addict. Just try stopping next time you're on.' Heather stared at the page: she could stop anytime she wanted. She wouldn't close down but she would just watch it: it didn't matter whether she played or not.

Heather crossed her arms tightly, breathing fast. She clenched her fists. Her fingers seemed to be trying to escape the fist, wanting to press the keyboard. The screen seemed to be shouting at her to play. Her head hurt, but if she just played one game it would all stop. She knew she didn't want to do this, but it was shouting at her to play.

Heather watched the pink shining pictures of cute animals and fairies dancing around: her warm, cosy little world. As she looked, however, the faces of the fairies slowly seemed to change: their big blue eyes became cold; the mouths that smiled transformed into snarling grins. All the faces started to laugh at her. 'Leave me alone,' she screamed at the screen. Tears ran down her face: she could stop this pain if only she pressed the play button – one touch.

Chapter Thirty Two

Heather reached out to the screen. Her hand hovered over the keyboard: just this once. 'Hi, love. You busy writing again? Lee said. 'I'm expecting a trilogy at least.' Heather froze, startled by his sudden appearance.

'Heather are you OK? Is it bad news?'

He came over to her and looked down at her screen before she could close it.

'What are you doing?'

'Nothing.'

'You shouldn't mess with those sites. I know they start as a bit of fun, but this bloke at work got in a terrible mess with one. He was on it all the time on his phone at work.'

'I know,' she said.

Lee picked up an apple from the fruit bowl, and bit into it hungrily. 'How has your day been?'

Heather watched him. Carina said he would leave her if he knew. It made sense: she'd spent all their savings. Why would he want to stay with her?

'Are you going down with something? You look terrible. By the way, Poppy rang me. She didn't want to worry you, but the florist wants the next part of the deposit. I think you arranged to pay some of the deposits in instalments. Is that right?'

Heather nodded, then bit her lip hard. 'Lee, I'm in a bit of a muddle. I can't pay the deposit quite yet.'

'Oh, why's that?'

'Money is tight–'

'I know the wedding is becoming expensive. Maybe we need to cut back on a few things.'

Heather shook her head. 'No, you don't understand. We have no money. We are in debt.'

'Look, if all the money in our wedding account has gone, then you can dip into our other savings. I may have to wait a bit longer until I have my own place, but Poppy should have her day.'

Heather burst into tears. She couldn't bear him being so kind. 'It's all gone, Lee: everything.'

Lee looked confused. 'You're joking, aren't you?'

'No, really. Everything: all our money. Every penny has gone.'

He sat and stared, unable to speak. Eventually he asked. 'But how?'

Heather glanced down at the laptop, feeling ashamed. 'This wasn't a one off today. I've been gambling for a while.'

'I don't believe it. You're not the sort.'

'All the time I've been telling you I was writing a book, I've been gambling. I thought it would help with the wedding, and it's all gone wrong. Oh God. It's a nightmare.'

Lee put his arm around her. 'We can sort it out. You need to stop it, of course

'I don't think I can. Honestly, Lee. I'm frightened.'

'You mean you think you've got a real problem?'

'I do. Oh, God. I've got us into such a mess.'

'Have you lost a lot?'

'Everything and more. I used money lenders. We're in debt.' She daren't look at him.

Lee grabbed the table edge. 'Heather, how could you?'

Heather felt the shame, like a blanket engulfing her. 'The cost of the wedding mounted up. I kept thinking one more win and it would all be alright.'

'Why ever didn't you tell me?'

'I thought you'd be angry.'

Heather started to cry.

'I kept going, and kept losing. The night before the ball, I lost everything again.'

Lee stared at the table. 'What are we going to do, Heather?'

Heather took a deep breath. 'Last night Carina said she'd give us all we needed. We could pay it all off.'

'Did she? We'd still have to pay her back, though.'

'When we can, yes. There are a few more strings attached, though.'

'What?'

'She wants me to force Lowri to leave the island.'

Lee grimaced. 'That's weird. That doesn't make any sense. Was she drunk or something?'

'No. You don't understand. She knows things Lowri has done. She's not what she seems.'

Heather told him about Simon, about the threats Carina wanted Heather to make. His face darkened.

'You have to blacken her name around the village and threaten to hurt her?'

'Well, yes.'

'You didn't agree to this?'

'I had to. She said she would tell you about my gambling, ruin the wedding, tell the people we couldn't pay.'

'I never realised she could be so hateful. We don't want anything to do with her or her money, Heather. She's mad. I can't imagine how you could even think of doing such things.'

Heather sobbed. 'I know. I know. I don't know who I am anymore.'

'You need to get help.'

Heather took a deep breath. 'How can I tell anyone what has happened? What will people think of me? Carina could ruin me. And Poppy: what on earth am I going to do

300

about her wedding? She's coming round tomorrow evening. What are we going to do? Do you hate me? I'm so sorry. I'll do anything. I could sell the café–'

'You'd do that?'

'Of course.'

Lee stood up. 'I need to go out, think. I'm so confused.'

Heather heard the front door slam.

Lowri arrived back on the island. It felt like she was coming home. She remembered Nicola talking about people who became part of the island, and she knew it had happened to her. Jack was waiting for her with Cassie at Cowes. When she saw him, he nodded an acknowledgment, but there was no smile.

'It's good to be home,' she said, cuddling Cassie.

'You've only been away one night.'

'It feels longer.'

They walked to the car in silence. Jack started the engine. Then he said, 'I've been down to the manor, been looking at the work. I really need to crack on. Carina will be opening the manor in March. The thing is, obviously I still have uni work, but I was thinking, I might sleep at the manor for a while. I just have so much to do.'

'Has Carina asked you to stay?'

'She did suggest it. They have loads of room, obviously. I can work late, get up early.'

Lowri didn't reply. Jack turned on the radio.

When they got to the house, Jack was about to get out of the car. Lowri took a deep breath, and said, 'Jack, if you're having an affair with Carina, I would rather you tell me.'

'What do you mean? Of course I'm not.'

'Come on: I've seen you together. Just be honest, Jack.'

He turned to her. He was breathing fast; his eyes were screwed up in anger.

'I have a right to ask,' she said, defensively.

'That's not what's upset me. I wasn't going to bring it up but, really, I don't know how you have the nerve to talk about being honest.'

'What are you talking about?'

'Carina told me about you and Simon. How could you have an affair with him? Poor Rosemary. To think he was the father of your baby and you never told me. I'm shocked, Lowri. I never thought you'd do something like that.'

Lowri glared at him. 'Hang on. You said you didn't want to know who it was. Let's keep some things private, you said. Also, I told you that he'd lied to me. He told me he'd left Rosemary.'

Jack shook his head. 'I don't believe you could have been that naive. You're a bright woman.'

'Thanks for making it sound like an insult.'

'Really, Lowri. It was Holly's sister you were hurting.'

'I didn't think I was. How come Carina is telling you all this anyway?'

'She overheard you talking with Simon at the ball. She didn't want to tell me.'

'Oh no; she just happened to mention it?'

'Don't be like that.'

Lowri shook her head. 'For God's sake, wake up Jack. You believe everything she says, don't you? You don't see what's happening. She's after you: That's why she has you working down the manor all the time.'

Jack opened the car door. 'I've had enough. You're as bad as Holly. Next there'll be the ultimatum: it's your work

302

or me. Well, I'll tell you this: I choose bloody work every time.'

He slammed the car door so hard the car shook. Lowri sat very still. This was the first time she had ever known Jack shout at her.

Lowri got out of the car with Cassie and by the time she reached the house Jack was running out with a holdall. He didn't speak. He just ran to the car and screeched off.

Lowri knelt down and held Cassie close. 'Well, Cassie, it's me, you and Fizzy now, let's go in.'

Lowri made coffee and turned on her computer. She was angry at Jack. She could hear a whole script in her head that she wished she had said to him, but she knew it was getting her nowhere. Instead, she needed to channel this anger and try at least to control the parts of her life she still could. She went to her Facebook page. She started to compose her post.

"*These pictures are of me. Last September I was in a car accident. I was ashamed of my scar, but now I own it. I am very sorry I lied to you all, put up old photos, and pretended all was well. I do now live on the Isle of Wight. Nothing is easy at the moment. I have made some bad decisions. I'm not proud of some of the things I've done. I'll try to be more honest now. If any of you want to un-friend me that's fine. I quite understand.*
Lowri x"

She started to re-read what she had written, then stopped herself, knowing how close she was to deleting the text. Quickly, she pressed post.

Next she sent an email to the Polish group asking about joining them occasionally when they meet up. She started to look at jobs. She was surprised that immediately she found agencies looking for Polish tutors. She filled in the application forms and sent her CV off. Then she found Cassie.

'Come on. Let's get out.'

Lee lost track of time as he walked. It was dark now. As he came back into the village he saw lights on in the church. At the side was the small churchyard. It was a place where he liked to go and think.

He was about to walk around the side of the church when he noticed the lights being turned off. Nicola came out and started locking the door. She looked surprised to see him.

'Cold evening to be out walking?'

Lee tried to smile, but couldn't.

'Are you alright?'

He sighed: why pretend? 'Not really. In fact, I feel like my life has just fallen apart.'

'What's the matter?'

'It's family. Private business.'

'Of course.'

'You're a vicar, aren't you?'

'That's right. I'm a chaplain. I work at the hospital.'

'So people tell you their problems?'

'They do.'

'Do you sign like that Hippocratic oath? Like doctors. You know, not to tell people's secrets?'

Nicola smiled. 'I am very discreet. My job is to listen. It's surprising how often, when people talk something through, they themselves know the answer. It dawns on them as they talk.'

'I wish that could happen, because, honestly, if I've got any answers they're pretty well hidden.'

'You can tell me if you want. I don't gossip around the village.'

He nodded, and believed her. 'It's Heather.'

'Is she ill?'

'No. Well, maybe–' Slowly, he told her what had happened.

'How do you feel?'

'Upset. You know, angry that she spent all the money, but more that she has been lying to me, hiding it all away. Of course, the money matters but, you know, she has helped me a lot. When we met I had nothing. She kept me for ages. I thought getting my own business, I'd finally be able to support her.'

'Are you both in a lot of debt now?'

'I haven't seen the figures. I think we've hit rock bottom. Heather is so quick. I trusted her and, to be honest, I couldn't be bothered. It's my fault. I should have kept an eye on things.'

'You mustn't blame yourself. Do you think Heather realises she has a problem?'

'I think so, yes.'

'That's a start then. There's a group, a support group, for people with gambling problems here on the island.'

'Really? It's common then?'

'It's a growing problem. The online sites make it so easy.'

'There's this guy at work. He's doing it on his phone all the time.'

'That's it. I've signed various petitions over time, but there are adverts all the time on TV. It's hard to get away from it.'

'I think Heather would find it very humiliating to go to a group: she has the café. People look up to her.'

She will need help, and so will you. That is, if you think your marriage can survive this. What do you want to do?'

'I love Heather. I know there are people who would think I was weak, but I don't want to leave her. It's hard though to think about forgiving her.'

'Forgiveness is a journey. It's not about letting somebody off the hook. It's as much about helping you heal as Heather.'

'You think we could get help then?'

'I do. You'll need to make changes. You probably need her to agree to let you take charge of all the money, everything. So she can't start up again. She needs to get off the sites. Block them. I have a card for someone–'

Nicola pulled out a small wallet full of business cards.

'A card for every problem?'

'It feels a bit like that. Seriously, this person is very good, very practical. She'll help you with the finances as well. She's very well qualified, takes on people voluntarily–'

Lee took the card. 'Thanks, and thank you for listening. I guess you pray a lot?'

'Every day.'

'Well, say one for us.'

He left Nicola and started back towards the house. However, when he arrived home, he didn't go in. Instead, he got into his car. He headed purposefully towards the manor.

Lee drove around the main road and straight down the drive. Slamming on the brakes, he leapt out of the car, and banged on the front door.

Carina answered. She smiled sweetly at him but didn't invite him in.

'Good evening, Lee. How lovely to see you. Everyone is here tonight: Jack is painting, medieval music on his iPod, and Ken is in the kitchen–'

'It's not Jack or Ken I want: it's you.'

306

'Really?'

'It's about Heather. She's told me everything.' He stepped towards her, but she met him, pulling the door behind her.

'What's the matter?'

'You know.'

'I know Heather has got in a mess and, as I told her, I am happy to help.'

'Don't pretend you're helping us. Heather told me what you asked her to do. I came to tell you she won't be talking to Lowri. We don't want your money.'

Carina crossed her arms. 'So, Heather is prepared to sacrifice her daughter's happiness for the sake of a few words with the local whore?'

'We don't go round blackmailing people. We'd rather go without.'

'Rather go without the manor? What will you do? Have Poppy get married in a barn? Have sandwiches and crisps from bowls? How quaint.'

Lee started to understand. 'Hang on. Go without the manor?'

Carina laughed. 'You don't think I'll let you use the manor now, do you?'

'You can't take the manor away from us.'

'I just did. Actually, I don't think I need you any more, so you can tell Heather she's missed her chance. I'm managing very well without her.'

Lee clenched his fists and then said. 'Have it your way. Keep the bloody manor. We'll do this wedding without you.'

He turned away. It was terrible to have lost the manor. He had no idea how he was going to tell Heather and Poppy. On the other hand, after talking to Carina, he was relieved that she had no hold over them. In any case, he knew for sure now that he didn't want Poppy getting married there. Carina had infected the place: it was not a fairytale castle now. It was a sinister, unhappy place. No, he was glad the decision had been taken out of their hands. Slowly, he drove home, and went into the house.

Chapter Thirty Three

The next morning Lowri went out with Cassie up to the downs. It was a beautiful morning and walking slowly calmed the storm of the day before. As she looked around she was reminded of the nature books and sites she read while researching her Facebook page. It was exciting to have a better understanding of the things happening around her. She would have recognised the long maroon and yellow catkins, but she wouldn't have known it was a large queen bee she saw and that it was looking for somewhere to nest. As she climbed the side of the downs she heard the sad sound of a buzzard wheeling above her searching, and knew now that it was setting out its territory. There was more birdsong but, as always, she wasn't sure which bird she was listening to: maybe this spring she should aim to try and learn a few.

At the Longstone she stopped walking, pleased to realise that she was less out of breath than she used to be, her body slowly healing from the accident. She glanced down at Dave's house: it looked empty and abandoned. This was just the sort of day she would have liked to have met him and Ceba, tell him about her time away; he would want to know about that. She walked down to his cottage and opened the gate. In front of his house were snowflakes and crocuses. She knelt down, took a photo of them and sent it to Dave. He replied with another photo of the traffic outside his gallery and said 'Missing the downs. How are you?'

She replied that it was beautiful up here, that Ceba should be here, and that Cassie missed her very much.

When she got home she was about to start work when she heard a knock at the door and was surprised to find Ken.

'I'm sorry. Are you busy?' He looked red and flustered.

'No, of course not. Come through to the kitchen.'

'Is everything alright?' asked Lowri.

Ken coughed, tapped his fingers on the table. 'It's very awkward. I don't know how to say this.'

'What? It's alright Ken, you can talk to me.'

'It's about Carina and Jack.'

'I think I know what you are about to tell me.'

'Do you?'

'Is it about Jack being in love with Carina?'

Ken let out a heart rending sigh and shook his head in despair. 'It's so much more complicated than that. To start with, Carina loves Jack.'

'Carina loves Jack.' She repeated the statement, let it sink in. Then she shook her head. 'But Carina loves you?'

'No. I don't think she ever has. I knew as soon as we came here she'd married me for money. Then, of course, she met Jack. He was married to Holly, but she fell for him and has never stopped loving him. I know it because she told me.'

'But she always says she loves you–'

'I told you: she lies. She wants Jack and the manor. That's all she has ever wanted. Of course, at first Jack was married to Holly, but then Holly left. I said then that she could have the manor.'

'But it must be worth a fortune–'

Ken shook his head. 'I don't say it often, but I'm pretty wealthy. I have land and enough money to make a new life for me and Lizzy in Ireland.'

'Lizzy would have only been a baby when Holly left. Carina would never have let you take her.'

'Oh, she said she had no trouble with that. I told you, she's not well. She felt very little for Lizzy. I did everything for her.'

'I can't imagine that. She told Jack and his mother that she wanted a large family, that you wouldn't let her.'

Ken laughed, but the sound was sharp and hard. 'I wanted more children. She refused. Anyway, we had it all agreed between us, but then she found there was one thing she could not control.'

'That was?'

'Jack. Once he'd finished the painting of Carina he only came over on weekends.'

'Why did you hang on? Why ever didn't you just go?'

'Carina didn't want to be left alone in the manor: it was too humiliating. She didn't want me to go until she had Jack. I tried to persuade her to let me go, but she wouldn't. She said if I went she'd fight me for Lizzy, and I could never have abandoned her. Also, she knew something about me that no-one else here knew. For ten years she has threatened to use it if I ever tried to leave her.'

'What was it? What ever have you done?'

Ken stood up and walked over to the window. He couldn't look back at Lowri.

'Yesterday, I went to the police station and confessed.'

Lowri was suddenly very afraid and felt very alone. She glanced at the open door behind her. She mentally tried to work out her escape route.

'I confessed to travelling with Jane to Switzerland and taking her to the clinic where she died.'

Lowri watched Ken's back: his body seemed to shrink, as if he wanted to disappear. Slowly, he turned around.

'Jane had been diagnosed with motor neuron disease. She didn't want anyone to know. We had been members of the Dignitas Association for a few years. I always thought

311

I'd be the first one to get anything really bad. I didn't want her to have the burden of looking after me if something happened. When she was diagnosed she was given two years to live. I never mentioned Dignitas, but she told me one day that she had been in touch. It was where she wanted to go.'

Ken sat down, his hands claw-like on his face, as if he would tear off the pain. 'She didn't want me to go. She was worried I'd get into trouble, but there was no way I'd let her go alone. She made me promise not to tell anyone. I agreed. When I came back without her, people accepted that she'd had a heart attack on holiday. No-one questioned it.'

'Your doctor would have known–'

'I never talked to him about it. He never mentioned it.'

Lowri gently took his hands, and pulled them away from his eyes. 'I'm very sorry, Ken.'

'I felt guilty for a long time, like I should have stopped her. It was also horrible lying to people here who really loved her. I'd told Carina when we first met in Italy. When we were back here, she threatened to go to the police with the information if I ever went against her. I thought I was unlikely to go to prison, but I was too frightened, for Lizzy's sake, to take the risk.'

'Didn't you think she might be bluffing?'

'It crossed my mind, but then she told me she had been the reason Holly's horse died. She told me she'd done it to make Holly take her seriously. She was laughing when she told me. It was then that I realised she was ill, and dangerous.'

'You really believe she killed Midnight?'

'The vet had been adamant it was an aneurysm, but I started to doubt it. Why would anyone pretend to do such an evil thing? No, I decided that somehow she was responsible.'

There was a clunk of the cat flap, and Fizzy came in. To Lowri's surprise she jumped up on to Ken's lap and settled down.

'Goodness. She never does that with people she doesn't know,' said Lowri, distracted.

Ken stroked Fizzy gently. 'She's very sweet.'

'Sorry. I haven't asked if you want a drink. Would you like a coffee or tea or something?'

'Nothing. I'm fine. You have something, though.'

Lowri stood up and wandered to the kettle, trying to assimilate everything Ken had told her. 'So, Jack was divorcing Holly. You and Carina had Lizzy. What do you really think Jack felt about all this?'

'I don't think he loved Carina then. He was devastated when Holly left him, but he didn't turn to Carina. Of course, the person he turned to was you.'

'Surely she should have given up then?'

'You'd have thought so but, no, she read up on the renaissance thing. She knew quite a lot already. When she suggested the fresco, Jack leapt at it. When she heard that you two had separated, she thought she had him. I'm sorry to tell you, but I was relieved. I just wanted to get me and Lizzy away. Still he didn't make a move.'

'Surely she must have tried to seduce him? I mean, look at her: not many men could resist her, could they?'

'Jack is very single-minded. He loves his work. Carina has pride. She wouldn't throw herself at him, but she tried. I heard her tell him I'd forgotten her birthday and things: all lies, but he believed it. Of course, then you had the accident, and you were back together. I really don't think she could believe it.'

Lowri shivered. 'Blimey; she must really hate me.'

'Oh, I'm sure she does. The thing is, she will always blame someone else for her not getting Jack. The one thing she would never allow for is that he does not love her. She really believes she can have any man she wants. Actually, I said to her that I thought she was starting to succeed with him. She's not sure, though. She threatened me again. This time she said she would tell Lizzy that I murdered my first wife. Well, something snapped. I had to put an end to it, and that is why I went to the police. They have everything now, and Carina knows.'

Lowri's eyes widened. 'What did she say?'

'She was completely thrown. She knows now Lizzy would ask to come with me. It would be a battle, but she can't be sure she'd win. The trouble is, Lowri, I think now she is cornered and that frightens me. I have a nasty feeling that in her mind the only thing between her and Jack now is you.'

'But Jack and I had a huge row. I'm sure she knows about it. I'm not a threat.'

'As long as you are here on the island, married to Jack, you are.'

Lowri suddenly felt sick. She had never had to face the unreasonableness of obsession, and it was very scary.

Ken gently picked up Fizzy and put her in her bed. He stayed standing up.

'Have you spoken to Jack?' Lowri asked.

'I tried. He insists Carina loves me, and he thinks I'm the jealous husband. Carina has filled his head with a load of rubbish about how jealous I get and how she always has to prove to me how much she loves me. See: she's clever'

Lowri turned, her eyes burning. 'I don't see why I should be driven out. This is my home now.'

'She's dangerous.'

'I shall stand up to her.'

Ken shook his head, walked to the front door. 'Talk to Jack, and then get the hell out of here.'

Chapter Thirty Four

When Heather woke earlier that morning she found she was on the sofa. She realised she had fallen asleep waiting for Lee to return. Aching all over, she pulled herself up and went into the kitchen to make coffee. Lee must have heard her, because he appeared.

'I left you asleep,' he said.

'You were gone a long time.'

'I needed time to think: that's all.'

'Have you been planning how to leave me? I heard the car go. Have you been to see your parents? They must be so angry with me.'

'I've not been to them. This is between me and you, no-one else, and it is up to you and me to sort it out.'

Heather stared. 'You mean you're not leaving me?'

'No, of course not–'

She burst into tears. 'But–'

He held her. 'Look, I hate that you lied to me, but we'll sort things. Actually, I met Nicola when I was out.'

'Oh no. Does she know?'

'She does. She's not going to tell anyone. But we can't hide this, Heather. We need help.'

Heather cringed. She hated to admit it, but her major fear was what people would think. Everyone in the village respected her, told her she was the spitting image of her mother. She dreaded the gossip and the snide looks.

'What did Nicola say?'

'Before we go into that, I need toast and coffee. You go and sit down.'

Heather went back into the living room. Lee came in soon after.

'What shift are you on today?' she asked, looking at the clock.

'No work for me today. I sent a text: first time I've had a sick day. They can cope. You had better close the café for the day as well. We have a lot to sort out.'

Heather's eyes widened: it was like they had swapped roles. She was the one who did all the organising.

'I think that's a good idea, actually. Obviously, Carina isn't going to work with me. I'll text Gita. Maybe she'll put a notice on the door.'

'Good. Now, about Nicola–'

'What did she say, then?'

'She gave us details of these people we can talk to.'

Heather nibbled her toast. 'I meant it, you know, about selling the café. Maybe we'd be better off leaving here, starting again somewhere else.'

'Why should we do that? This is our home. I don't know about the café; we need to see someone and look at all the options. Nicola was really helpful. We can go and talk to her any time.' He looked around the tiny sitting room. 'Good job we paid off the mortgage. At least we have a roof over our heads. Remember I wanted to move somewhere bigger? You were the one who said stay.'

She looked down. 'I had some sense, then.'

'When we met I had nothing. Now, I have a home; you and Poppy. We look after each other through it all, don't we?'

Heather looked down, too embarrassed to answer.

'You're going to have to let me look after you for a bit,' Lee said. 'You're not going to find that easy. I was thinking I should take over the money for a bit. I know that's awful, but until you're better I think it would be best.'

'And what about the wedding?'

'This evening we will have to talk to Poppy together. Before that, though, I think I should go and talk to her and Alistair.'

'Not without me.'

'Yes. I need it to be calm when I tell her. Honestly, it's the best way.'

'She'll hate me, Lee. I've let her down. And what will people here think if I don't give Poppy a proper wedding?'

'The village can go hang,' said Lee. 'What matters is Poppy.'

'I don't know what we'll do. The only thing we've actually paid for is her dress. All the rest are half-paid deposits. It's awful. I'm meant to be her mother and I've ruined the most important day of her life. All we have are a dress and a manor.'

'Ah.' Lee fidgeted awkwardly. 'About the manor–'

He told her about his meeting with Carina.

'She took that away? Oh, Lee. How could she?'

'She's just plain nasty. I don't envy Ken or Jack, or any bloke to be honest. Even with all her looks, they're welcome to her.'

'I think you could be right, but still. How on earth are we going to tell Poppy?'

'I don't know, but before we see her, we're going to try and sort a few things out so we know exactly how we stand financially.'

Much later that day, Heather was sitting waiting for Poppy and Lee to arrive. It had been a long day and she was exhausted. They had managed to talk to people in the bank, and someone at the Citizens Advice Bureau. At the meeting they had worked out a few initial budgets. As things stood, she could keep the café, but she and Lee had agreed that they would cut their losses with everyone

318

connected to the wedding, losing all their deposits. They then went back to speak with Nicola. Heather had even made her first tentative steps to contacting a group for people with problems with gambling addiction.

Of all the things they had done, though, this was by far the most stressful. The longer time went on, the more convinced she was that Poppy would not be coming to talk with her, maybe would never speak to her again.

Although they could keep the café, they would need a back loan. At the end of the day, Poppy would either have to postpone the wedding or Alistair's family would have to help. It was horribly embarrassing. Heather felt dreadful, but there was nothing else that she could do.

She heard the front door. She sat up, breathing fast. Lee came in first. He gave her a weak smile. He was followed by Poppy, deathly pale, and red-eyed.

Heather stared at the table. 'I'm so sorry, love.'

'Dad told me everything. I understand.'

'You have every right to be angry with me, you know. We've even lost the manor.'

'I know.' Poppy burst into tears. 'I know it's not your fault, Mum, but it's the worst thing ever. I can't believe it. It's my worst nightmare.'

'I know.'

'I don't understand, Mum. You of all people–'

'Now, Poppy–' Lee interrupted.

'Leave her, Lee' said Heather, standing up. 'She has every right to hate me.'

'I don't hate you,' said Poppy, sniffing. 'I don't understand. You've always been so careful. You don't do stupid things. What happened?'

'It started off as fun and then, well, now I have a problem. I shall get help but it won't solve the problem of how to pay for the wedding.'

'I don't understand about Carina? Why isn't she helping? They're so well off.'

'I told you,' said Lee. 'She was trying to blackmail Mum into doing something.'

'I don't believe she's being like that. I've always liked her. She's so pretty and nice. She seemed so excited about having the wedding there.'

'People are not always what they appear,' said Lee.

'Where is Alistair?' Heather asked.

Poppy sniffed. 'He's talking to his parents on the phone. It's so embarrassing. Georgia will be so angry.'

'It's not really anything to do with his sister, is it?' said Lee, firmly.

'I suppose not, but I wanted to impress her.'

At that moment Poppy's phone rang. 'It's Alistair,' she mouthed, and left the room.

Heather slumped into her chair. She looked up at Lee. 'This is worse than I imagined. Listen. I just thought, if we sold the café–'

Lee frowned. 'That's ridiculous. Anyway, it would take months, and we can't do that to pay for a wedding.'

Poppy came back in. She walked slowly, as if she'd been give some terrible news. Heather's heart sank Had Alistair called it all off? Had he left her?

'Alistair said his parents will pay for everything. They know we can't have the manor, but they suggested a marquee somewhere down Cowes, at one of the yacht clubs. His Dad has contacts down there. He can get it at short notice.'

Heather blinked. It hurt on so many levels, but she had to think of Poppy and, of course, this was the way for her to have her dream wedding. 'It's very good of them to offer. Of course you must accept it. When things are better maybe we'll be able to give them some money towards the cost.'

'I don't know, Mum.'

Heather frowned. She assumed Poppy was just embarrassed about the offer. 'Listen. This is a very kind offer. We should take it. It's going to take me and Dad a long time to get clear. Even if you postpone the wedding it might be a couple of years before we could pay for one. Alistair's parents are very well off: you can have the day you want. Me and your Dad, well, we'll be more like guests.' The words were agony to say and yet somehow Heather was keeping a smile on her face: she had to think of Poppy.

Lee came over to them. 'Your Mum's right. It's an old fashioned idea anyway that the bride's family pay for everything.'

Poppy nodded. 'I suppose so, and this way you wouldn't have the worry, would you?'

Heather reached out her hand to Poppy. 'That's not the point. But think: this way you can have everything, maybe even a second wedding dress—'

Poppy tried to smile, but her lips quivered.

Heather continued, 'I know it's not the manor, but it's lovely down there, very smart.'

She watched as Poppy bit her lip. She knew how hard she was trying not to cry.

'You're not to worry about me and Dad. We'll be fine.'

Poppy was clenching her hands together, her knuckles white. Suddenly, the words burst out as if they'd been held behind a dam. 'But it's not the wedding I want. It will be their wedding, not mine. It's been bad enough up until now: Alistair's sister always telling me what to do, basically telling me I have no taste. This might as well be her wedding.' She burst into tears.

321

Heather put her head in her hands. 'I'm sorry. There's nothing I can do to make this go away.'

Poppy suddenly stopped crying and stood up. 'I need to talk to Alistair.'

Heather was worried now. 'Don't do anything stupid. You love Alistair. At the end of the day, what matters is that you get married.'

Poppy didn't answer, but went into the kitchen and shut the door.

Heather looked over at Lee. 'What do you think she's doing?'

'I've no idea.'

They could hear Poppy talking fast but couldn't make out the words. Finally she came back into the room. She looked different, older somehow. To Heather it was suddenly like looking in a mirror. She had never thought Poppy was like her, but there was a determination in her eyes she recognised.

'I've spoken to Alistair. We both agree about this. We don't want his parents to arrange and pay for the wedding. Alistair has been getting as fed up as me, said he feels left out of his own wedding.'

'But what will you do? Will you go to a registry office or something?'

'Now, Mum, you're not to take this the wrong way.'

'What do you mean?'

'A while back me and Alistair were messing around, talking about ideas for a different kind of wedding. Well, now we can do it.'

'And what is that?'

Poppy's eyes lit up. 'We would both love to get married on the beach.'

'Goodness. I don't think anywhere around here is licensed for that.'

'It doesn't matter. What I thought was that Alistair and I could get the legal bit done in the registry office and then we could have a ceremony on the beach, at Compton. We can do it to fit in with the tides, and after than that we could go to the café. What do you think? Mum, it wouldn't have to cost too much. You and Dad could do the food. Aunty Rosemary could do the Photos. It could be wonderful. We have friends who would play in the evening. We could have dancing. I have the dress. Everything else we can do ourselves.'

Lee burst out laughing. 'After all we've been through, this is what you want?'

'I know, Dad, but we didn't realise.'

Heather frowned. 'Are you just being kind?'

No, Mum, really. Me and Alistair have some money. We can get some flowers and things.'

'I don't know. What will Alistair's family think?'

'We'll soon know. Alistair is talking to them now.'

Heather hugged her daughter. 'You are being so wonderful.'

Poppy looked at her seriously. 'Mum, you have always been there for me. My turn now.'

Lee's eyes were shining now. 'I can get us decent drink through wholesalers. The food will be the best: I promise. What about the cake?'

'What about it, Dad?' said Poppy, grinning. She looked more serious again. 'And you are not to worry about cost. We will pay for anything that's needed. OK? Everything's out in the open now.'

Heather nodded. 'I don't know what I did to deserve you two as my family. but thank you.'

Chapter Thirty Five

Lowri sent a text to Jack asking him to come and see her. He took all day to reply but said he would be there in the next few days: he was at a really important point in his painting and time was tight. Lowri decided to wait because, as unnerving as she found Ken's words, there was a part of her that wondered if he might not be over-dramatising things. As the days passed and nothing out of the ordinary happened she managed to persuade herself that Ken had been over-reacting and that somewhere there was a logical explanation for everything he had said.

She soon received a reply from the tutoring site. With her range of languages they said she could get as much work as she wanted, so she put her details up and waited for replies.

The month of February passed quietly. The meeting with Jack didn't happen. Lowri worked and walked Cassie. Part of her knew she was waiting for Dave to come back. Each evening as she walked she would look down at his cottage waiting for lights to come back on. She saw little of Jack, who was either lecturing or down at the manor.

One evening Heather came to see her. Lowri was shocked at how pale she looked; her hands were shaking.

'Are you alright Heather?'

'Not really. A lot has happened. The thing is, I need to talk to you.'

'Come and sit in the living room. I have the fire lit in there. It's nippy today.'

'There's no easy way to say this.' She hesitated. 'I know you've been having an affair with Simon.'

Lowri sighed. 'Did Carina say something?'

Heather nodded.

Lowri clenched her fists: when would she be rid of this? 'I'm sorry. He told me he'd left Rosemary.'

'When was it?' Heather's voice was hard.

'Last year, when I was living in Southampton. We met in a restaurant. It was a pure coincidence that he was married to a relation of Jack's ex. We realised it, and that's how we got talking.'

'So you knew he was happily married to my sister?'

'No. Of course not. When we first chatted he said things were not going well, but we just met for meals. We were both lonely. Jack had left me, and, as I said, Simon said his marriage was failing.'

'So that made it OK? You don't know what my sister has been through for him.'

'No. He was the one looking after her.'

Heather looked puzzled. 'What do you mean?'

'Simon told me about Rosemary's drink problem.'

Heather's eyes widened. 'I can't believe he said that! It was him: he was the one with the problem. When he was a junior doctor he was drinking to keep himself going. It has been Rosemary who has stood by him. If it wasn't for Rosemary he would have lost his job. It was years ago now, but she never relaxes, always keeping an eye on him. Without her he'd be lost.'

Lowri stared. 'Are you sure?'

'Of course. I was around when it all happened.'

'But why did Simon say that then?'

Heather fiddled with some coasters on the table.

'You're not the first person he's had a fling with.'

'Really?'

'No. I get so angry. He messes her about but she always takes him back. I've told her to leave him, but she won't.'

Lowri blinked very fast. Simon had been lying to her all that time?

'He seemed such a good man: warm, caring. I met him when I was so unhappy.'

Heather cringed. 'He looks for people who are needy. But he fathered a child with you? That's a first. Well, as far as I know, anyway.'

'He didn't want to know. When Jack found me in the hospital in France, Simon had just left me. He said it would destroy Rosemary.'

'It would be the final straw, he was thinking,' said Heather bitterly. 'What a bastard.'

'I've been such a fool. I wish Jack knew some of what you've been telling me. Carina told him about Simon.'

'He never knew who you'd been seeing?'

'No. Carina told him. He's so angry with me. What a mess. Heather, why can't I be normal like you? Settled with your café, and a lovely husband and your daughter getting married.'

Heather sat back. She started picking her lip. 'You've got it all wrong. I've done something terrible. I've jeopardised everything.'

'I can't imagine that.'

'I have.'

Heather told Lowri about the gambling and all the money she had lost.

'But you've always looked so together–'

'I know. I've never wanted to ask for help, but now I have to. I never want to get in this mess again. I guess I have to admit that I have an addiction. I would be even more of a fool if I thought I could cope with this on my own.'

'How will you pay for the wedding?'

Hannah seemed to relax as she told her about Poppy's plans. 'I really think she is happy about them. She's been dashing around organising things; it's certainly going to be a different kind of wedding.'

Lowri put another log on the fire, watched it send sparks up the chimney.

'Ken came to see me. He was warning me.'

'How is he? He looks so stressed whenever I see him.'

'He's going through a lot.'

Heather looked down. 'I've seen a different side to Carina recently. She's not the person I thought she was.'

'You know she is in love with Jack?'

Heather looked away. 'Oh, is that why she wanted me to force you to leave?'

'When did she do that?'

'Oh, nothing,' said Heather, but she was very red. 'She wanted me to say some things, but I wouldn't. She has been awful, to be honest, said we can't have the manor for the wedding.'

'Because you wouldn't say these things to me?'

'Yes.'

Lowri's face softened. 'Thank you for standing by me.'

Heather grimaced. 'I'm not a saint. Let's leave it that I didn't do anything and I'm glad of that.' She looked at Lowri more seriously. 'You said that Ken was warning you?'

'He thought she might hurt me somehow, but I think things have settled down. Maybe his imagination was running away with him.'

'I don't know. You be careful. It was obvious to me she wants you off the island.'

'I will just have to be careful. Look, I meant to tell you: I am starting a new job, tutoring.'

'Good for you.'

'It's time I think. When Dave comes back I'll have to tell him that I won't be able to help in the pottery.'

'To be honest, I don't know what is happening in there now. He rang me up. He's thinking of staying up in London. I was sorry, hoped we'd have him a bit longer.'

Lowri stared into the fire, stunned.

'He's not coming back?'

'No. I think it's this girl Millie. I think they might be getting together or something.'

Lowri forced a smile. 'What will you do?'

'I'm not sure. We could advertise. I think we might get someone from the college to take the work on.' Heather stood up. 'Thank you for being so understanding. It's been an awful time. It's quite a relief to have it all out in the open.'

'Thanks for coming round.'

'And you be careful now–'

When Heather had gone, Lowri sat down. It was difficult to believe Dave was not coming back. She had been planning things to tell him, looking forward to her first swim in the sea, and now it had all been snatched away from her. Cassie jumped up next to her. Lowri found herself shaking, then she sobbed hard, painful tears until, exhausted, she went to bed.

The next morning Lowri felt hung over with sadness; everything seemed an effort. She got dressed and was about to take Cassie out when her phone rang. It was tempting to leave it, but she picked it up, and started to read the message. Her hands started to shake. 'My God' she shouted. Cassie came running to her, wagging her tail. 'He's come back,' she told Cassie. 'Look. He's back. He wants to see me.'

Her lips trembled and she wiped away tears as she answered Dave's text: 'Yes, free today–'

Dave called for her soon after. It took a minute for Lowri to adjust to his appearance. She had forgotten how tough he looked. Then he smiled. 'Did you miss me?'

They drove down to Compton Bay. They were wrapped up. The wind was strong, but there were miles of empty beach. The dogs rushed down the steps ahead of them.

'Heather told me you might be staying in London permanently. You never said anything about it to me.'

Dave picked up a stone, seemed to inspect it, then threw it into the sea. 'I thought I should let Heather know what I'm thinking.' He was picking his words carefully.

'You've had enough of it here?'

He looked around. 'I'll never have enough of this. No.'

'Why are you going then?'

'I'd forgotten how much I get from working with other artists.'

'People like Millie?'

Dave gave her a sideways smile. 'Heather has been talking, hasn't she?'

'So you are back with her?'

Dave started to walk towards the sea. 'We've been out a few times. Now, tell me. How are things with you?'

'Jack is out a lot. He's sleeping down the manor now, trying to get the fresco finished.'

Dave turned his head quickly. 'Are you alright?'

She smiled. 'Getting a lot done. I'm starting some tutoring.'

'Well done. You'll be good at that.'

'Some other stuff has happened though.'

'What's that?'

Lowri found herself telling him about Ken's visit.

'Wow. I always knew Carina was strange, but she needs help. Where do you think Jack fits into all this?'

'I don't know. He's really obsessed with his work. It's possible he really doesn't realise how much Carina wants him.'

'And how do you feel about it all, about Jack?'

Lowri remembered the time Jack's parents came.

'Something happened with Jack, while his parents were here.'

'What?'

'It's embarrassing.'

'Go on. Tell me.'

'We were, well, Jack and I shared a room when his parents were with us.' Lowri stumbled over the words. 'We talked about trying to have a baby, but then he made it quite clear that the thought of it was really stressful for him. Not very flattering, but then I realised I didn't want to make a baby like that. Maybe it's what you said about not settling, but I'm not sure now about things with Jack. In fact, we had this huge row. He found out about Simon. I've never known him so angry with me.'

Dave kicked the sand. 'What will you do?'

'I don't know, but I'll survive. That's what I'll do.'

Dave walked towards the waters edge and started to throw stones for the dogs.

'It's March the first on Tuesday. I go for my first body board. Do you fancy coming?'

'It'll be freezing.'

'Come on. Borrow a wetsuit from someone. It's great fun.'

'Maybe.'

'And will you have time to help in the pottery? I mean, can you fit it in with all your new ventures?'

'Oh. So are you staying for a bit?'

330

'I can't just land Heather in it, not with Easter coming up. I have to give her time to find someone else. I think there may be students from the college who might be interested.'

'I think she mentioned that. OK then, I'll help.'

'Good, nine-thirty tomorrow?'

Dave dropped her and Cassie off. Lowri decided to ignore Cassie's sandy feet, put a jacket potato in the microwave, grated some cheese on top, and settled to a night of TV.

Next morning Lowri was excited as she took Cassie for her early morning walk, looking forward to going to work. She tried very hard to push to the back of her mind that Dave might be leaving soon and determined to try and enjoy what time they had left. She was about to have breakfast when she heard the front door open.

'Hi, anyone at home?'

Lowri recognised Jack's voice and stepped into the hallway. Cassie ran to greet him.

'Happy Saint David's Day!'

'You remembered. Come on through.'

'I came to say sorry, actually. I am hardly one to be lecturing you, am I?'

'Thanks for coming round. You're up early?'

'I caught an early Red Jet. I thought I'd pop in before I start work.'

She poured some granola in a bowl. 'Want some?'

'Yes, thanks.'

'So how is everything going?'

'The fresco is starting to take shape. So much to do. I tell you, those renaissance chaps didn't have a day job to worry about. Everything takes so long. Still, I love it. And on that front, I actually have some exciting news.'

331

'Really? What's that then?'

'Carina has suggested they commission me to go and work at the manor for a year. Ken is happy with that. I've talked to the university. They are willing for me to have a sabbatical, unpaid of course, but they'll benefit. I keep notes. It's a very interesting piece of research. I've already been contacted by a few journalists and specialists interested in what we're doing. Carina is hopeful we might even get some funding.'

'A whole year painting at the manor?'

'Yes. It's wonderful, isn't it? We were thinking of more rooms, although I'd love to have a go at a ceiling.'

He was walking around the kitchen with his bowl in his hand, slopping milk on the floor, which Cassie was licking up

'Jack–' Lowri spoke sharply.

He looked up, rather like a child who finds themselves unexpectedly about to be told off.

'What's the matter?'

'Jack, Ken came to see me. You need to listen to this.'

Reluctantly, he sat down on the edge of the seat, ready to get up again.

Lowri told him what Ken had said about Carina's obsession with him.

Jack shook his head. 'It's not true, none of it. Carina has never made a pass at me. I've never slept with her.'

'Jack, do you love Carina?'

'No. No way. It's not like that.'

'You need to take this seriously. It's not just Ken. She's been trying to get Heather to make me leave. Ever since she came here all she has wanted is the manor –and you.'

Jack gave a condescending smile. 'It's not true. I'd know.'

'Listen to this.' Lowri told Jack about Ken's first wife and Carina blackmailing him over her death.

'No. It's alright,' he said eagerly. 'Carina told me about Ken and Jane. She said she felt desperately sorry for him and would always support him.'

Lowri frowned. 'When did she tell you this?'

'Yesterday. She told me Ken had gone to the police. She'd tried to stop him because she was frightened of losing him.'

'Oh, Jack!' said Lowri in frustration. 'I don't know what to say to make you believe me. I'm frightened of her.'

'Well, you don't need to be. Carina wouldn't hurt anyone. She's not like that. Now, to happier things, I hear Dave is back?'

'Yes, I saw him yesterday.'

'How was it?'

'I don't exactly know, but I have been thinking, Jack. I don't think you and I are really working now. I want to be on my own.'

'To be with Dave?'

'No. Well, I don't know, but I think we need to split up properly now, don't you?'

'What do you think we should do?'

He always looked to her for plans. 'I'd like to stay on the island, but I expect you'd like the house back. We'll need to think about a divorce, won't we? And then sort out the money.'

Lowri saw him squirm; he really did hate everyday life.

'We need to Jack, and this place must be worth a lot. I can rent a flat somewhere for now.'

Jack sat back on his chair, and bit his lip in concentration. 'Look, for now, why don't you stay here?'

'I can't.'

'I don't see why not. I'm living down the manor. I could live there for the year I'm working there I guess: I'll talk to Carina about it. We could think of selling the house over in Southampton. When and if I go back I can find something smaller. I don't want to be there that much.'

Lowri looked around. 'OK. Thank you. We could do that for now.'

'Good.' Jack stood up. Watching him, Lowri was surprised at how unemotional he was; it was odd. 'Back to work then,' he said, his mind already there.

As Lowri left the house, she saw the name board saying 'Holly's House' swinging in the sunshine. She went to take it down, but she couldn't. This house, as much as she loved it, wasn't hers.

The walk down to the pottery was lovely. She remembered the Saint David's days of her childhood. At school they had the Eisteddfod in the morning. Lowri had always entered the competitions for the less extrovert children. It wasn't for her, sitting on the stage playing and singing. She wrote essays, entered projects. The best part of the whole thing was a half day off school.

Lowri went in through the café. Heather looked up at her smiling.

'Dave said you were coming in. Like old times.' Lowri thought Heather looked very tired: her smile was less broad, but she was there and had the determined look of a survivor. Gita was busy in the kitchen. 'Nice to see you again Lowri.'

Heather looked back at her gratefully 'Best thing I ever did was asking Gita to work here. You know, her daughter and son are helping on the weekends.'

Lowri moved closer to her. 'I should tell you that Jack and I have separated again.'

'Oh no. Are you leaving?'

'No. He's moving into the manor for now.'

Heather's face tightened. 'He shouldn't do that.'

'I told him everything. It's his choice. Carina is giving him even more work to do there.'

'She could snare him in the end, couldn't she?'

'Maybe. I don't know. I hope not. How is everything with the wedding?'

'It's going remarkably well. I thought Poppy might start regretting the changes. I've been waiting for her to ask Alistair's parents to help out, but she's stubborn and actually seems very happy. Alistair does as well. Reading between the lines, I think he's had a lifetime of his sister dominating his life. He seems to be relishing doing something without her interfering. Lee is busy on the cake. It's going to be incredible, and I have started cooking and freezing. I don't know how people manage without industrial sized freezers. I must give you your invitation. The date is May seventh. Make sure you save it.'

'I'm really looking forward to it. Right, Dave is waiting for me.'

Heather gave her a knowing smile. 'Yes, he certainly is. I'm relying on you to persuade him to stay, you know.'

Lowri laughed and headed for the pottery.

As Lowri entered, she took in the familiar smell. Dave looked up. His smile filled the room. 'We have a few days to sort things out. A group is in on Friday. This is great, isn't it? Back to normal.'

They had a busy morning. At lunch time Lowri went home to let Cassie out. In the afternoon Dave went back to his own pottery while she cleared up. When they had finished he said, 'You coming body boarding, then?'

She laughed. 'I haven't seen Nicola, and I have nothing to wear.'

'Oh no. You need to get sorted out.'

'Tell you what, if I can pick up Cassie, I'll come down. At least I can paddle and watch you.'

'OK. I'll go home and fetch Ceba, and come and get you.'

At the beach Dave put on his wetsuit and they walked down the steps.

'We need to walk quite a way along the beach to get away from the rocks.'

They seemed to walk quite a distance until Dave was satisfied. He went straight in. Lowri took off her shoes and rolled up her trousers, the sea was freezing. As she watched Dave, she knew today was the time to tell him.

Lowri strolled up the beach and sat on the towel. She pictured herself down here with her toddler, making sandcastles. Dave emerged from the sea and was walking up the beach. Lowri felt that shiver of excitement she always did now when she saw him.

'That was great,' he said as droplets of cold water sprayed on her. 'I'll miss this.'

He removed his wetsuit, wrapped the towel around his shoulders, and sat down next to her.

'Jack came to see me this morning.'

'How did that go?'

'We've decided to separate. It's permanent this time.'

Dave raised both eyebrows. 'Really?' The scepticism in his voice annoyed her.

'I can make decisions and stick to them, you know. But it's complicated.'

'In what way?'

'I'm sure Carina is in love with Jack.'

'Why do you think that?'

336

Lowri told him everything that had happened in his absence.

'What a mess. Carina has played everyone along, hasn't she? Jack should keep well away.'

'That's what I said, but he said he wanted to do the painting. Who knows? Maybe, deep down he is in love with her.'

'He's mad if he stays around her. Poor Ken. I've always liked him. Anyway, my concern is you. Do you seriously think Carina would hurt you? If she scares you, I shall have a word. She won't play games with me.'

'I think it's best left now. Don't stir things up.'

'I'll leave it for now, but you tell me if anything happens. OK?'

'OK.'

'I tried to warn Jack but he's excited because Carina is giving him more to do. Maybe she'll be happy now.'

The dogs came rushing over to them, both shaking sand and water. Dave stood up and pulled Lowri up to her feet.

'Let's start back. It's getting cold.'

They began the trek back to the steps.

'So, if you and Jack have separated, are you thinking of going back to Southampton?'

Lowri shook her head. 'No, definitely not. Jack said to stay in the house for now. I shall get my own place eventually. I shan't leave.'

'Right. Good.'

Dave drove to Lowri's house.

'Have you heard from Millie?' Lowri asked.

Dave switched off the engine. 'You've been very honest with me. I think I should be with you.'

Lowri wanted to stop him. She didn't want to hear about his feelings for Millie. However, she crossed her arms tightly and said, 'Go on then.'

'While I was in London, Millie and I saw a lot of each other. She made it clear she wanted to get back together, but we talked and, well, there were reasons we couldn't.'

'Why was that then?' Lowri's voice was shaking.

'You must know.' Dave sounded as if he was in agony.

'Tell me.'

He surrendered with a smile. 'Because I love you, Lowri. It's killing me, but if you don't feel the same, I have to leave. I can't watch you and Jack get back together or you with anyone else. You're the reason I will go back, or you will be the reason I stay.'

'But you said about other artists, you know, working with them? And there's the money: you said you won't make enough here.'

He shrugged. 'Priorities change. I can happily live without the London crowd. As for money, I could sell the flat and I'd have half the business. I wouldn't be rich, but it's manageable. Maybe I'd have to organise a website or something.' He stopped. 'And, if I'm being really honest, you remember when I said about being useless at school and how I got to art school?'

'Yes.'

'Well, I've always wanted to prove to the rich kids there, the ones who had connections from their posh schools and whose parents set them up in galleries, I wanted to prove to them that I could make it big, that I was better than them.'

Lowri smiled. 'I never realised you cared about what people thought of you.'

'I'm only human. Anyway, I don't care about them now. So, Lowri, do I stay or do I go?'

Chapter Thirty Six

Lowri clenched her teeth: it seemed so much responsibility. Dave was placing his future in her hands. She took a deep breath. 'This is all very scary, you know. I know how I feel right now. I know what I want.'

'And that is?'

'I think I love you, Dave. You are the real reason I knew I couldn't live with Jack anymore. I don't want you to go away.'

His face broke into a smile that made his eyes shine. 'That's all I need to hear.'

'But,' she added quickly, 'What if it all goes wrong? I might drive you mad. You might drive me crazy. We don't know each other that well. I'd hate you to sell up, come here, and for it all to go wrong.'

Dave leant over and kissed her. 'It's OK. This is my decision.'

Lowri kissed him back, but then the dogs started to whine.

'Let's get them out of the car,' said Lowri. She looked at Dave. 'Fancy coffee?'

They washed the dogs. Then Lowri, still smiling shyly, took Dave's hand. 'Come and see my Polish pottery.' Dave followed her upstairs and they went into her room. He walked over to the pottery but then looked back.

'That can wait.

Lowri walked into his arms. He stroked her hair, her cheek. H kissed her. Slowly, they undressed, and held each other very close. Lowri lay with Dave, lost in a tender dance. After making love, they stayed very close, their faces touching, Lowri wanted to stay there forever.

Lowri and Dave settled into a dream-like pattern of working, going to the beach, spending nights together at her house, Ceba easily fitting into the different routine.

Lowri bought herself a swimming costume and for the first time went in the sea. It was cold, but far more exhilarating than she expected.

One evening they were walking by the Longstone when Dave said, 'I heard from Millie this morning. I started to tell her what I want to do.'

'Was she very upset?'

'Not too bad. She has had an offer to go in with someone in a gallery in St Ives, so I think she'll go for that now, but I do need to go and sort things out properly. There's a lot to do and I need to put the flat on the market, but it shouldn't take long.'

'What about the house here?'

'I've spoken to the landlord. He's open to offers. I think it should work out.'

Lowri looked away, 'So when are you going?'

'Next week, I think. I spoke to Heather. There are no groups. She's so delighted I'm staying she's happy for me to go and sort things out.'

Lowri sighed. 'I know you need to go, but I'll miss you.'

'It's the last time, Lowri. When I come back it's for good. One more thing–'

'What's that?'

'Can Ceba come to stay?'

Lowri laughed. 'I shall hold her as hostage to make sure you come back.'

Dave went to London on the Sunday evening. Lowri wandered around the house wondering what to do with herself. Cassie and Ceba had taken to sharing the bed in the

340

kitchen and seemed very content. She found her laptop and started to sort out who she was going to tutor. School-aged children needed early evening appointments, but that work would start in earnest in September. There was one adult who was pretty flexible but wanted an intensive course, and they arranged by email to start one morning a week. The lady only lived in Newport: it was ideal.

Dave and Lowri sent each other regular texts and phoned; the week passed slowly. She had been coping well until Wednesday evening. She rang Dave, but instead of him a rather drunken voice answered, 'Hi, this is the gorgeous Millie. How can I help you?'

'Oh. Er, can I speak to Dave, please?'

'I'm afraid he's not available. He has some very important business to attend to.' She burst into laughter and ended the call.

Lowri threw down the phone. What was going on? Her pride wouldn't let her ring back. Dave had better explain soon. Then her phone rang again: it was a text; good. However, when she picked up her phone, fortunately undamaged, to her horror the text was from Simon.

'I miss you so much. We have to talk this evening. I'll meet you at the Longstone up on the downs, seven o'clock. See you then. xx'

Lowri's first reaction was to simply say 'no'. She didn't need to complicate her life. However, she was curious to know what was so important. In the end she sent a text back: 'OK. See you there.'

Lowri checked her watch. It was an hour until she had to meet Simon. She took Cassie out into the garden, and while she was there she looked over at Jack's studio. Why had Jack been so mysterious about her looking in there? Why shouldn't she go and look inside?

341

The padlock was on. Jack, she guessed, had the key. In films she had seen people hacking off padlocks with one blow from an axe, but she couldn't see that working for her in real life. She looked at it, and realised it had a combination lock: she only needed to work out the numbers. Lowri started to try out obvious number combinations: his birthday, her birthday, and the years of their birth, to no avail. Then she thought of Jack. What did he care about? Renaissance, Michelangelo: when was he born? She had sat through enough boring lectures: picture the power point. Fourteen seventy something? What was it Jack said to the students? Add the one and the four to something to make the five at the end. She moved the cogs, 1475. The lock slid open.

Cassie and Ceba were next to her, wagging their tails.

'Dare we go in?'

She opened the door. It was dark inside, but Lowri felt for the light switch. There were heaps of sketches ready for the fresco. At one end there was a huge sheet covering some cases. She opened one. It was full of clothes, various ornaments, and there were also some letters and photographs. She picked them up, then realised who all this must belong to. One of the photos was a wedding: it was Jack and Holly. There were many more: Holly in various places on the island, but also on holiday, In a lot of them Jack had his arms around Holly. In some they were kissing or Jack was looking at Holly, completely enraptured. Then she found the one which really took her breath away. It was a large photo of Holly. On the picture Jack had written, 'Holly, the love of my life'. Lowri blinked back tears. Jack had never said that of her, never looked at her like that. All the time he'd been with her he'd still been in love with Holly. All the time she'd been devoted to him, he'd been thinking of Holly. She had thought when she married Jack that he was the love of her life, but looking at all this she knew now he'd never felt like that about her. Never. How had she got it so wrong? She thought of Millie laughing down the phone. Was that going to happen with Dave? He hadn't phoned back. What was he doing?

Lowri didn't bother shutting the shed: let him know she'd been in there. She shut Cassie and Ceba safely in the house, left the garden and walked up on to the downs.

It was not completely dark: the moon shone brightly. As she walked, Lowri realised she was wearing new comfortable jeans, trainers, and she had no makeup on. She hadn't even noticed the gradual change in herself. It was coming to meet Simon that made her self-conscious. She wouldn't have dreamed of coming to meet him like this before. He was waiting, and held out his arms. She walked towards him, but not into his embrace.

'Why?' she demanded.

'I miss you. I had to see you. How are you? I have news.'

'What?'

'I've left Rosemary.'

'You said she was ill,' she said, testing him.

'I know–'

'She's not, is she? You lied to me. You are the one who was ill. I wasn't your first affair, either. There have been others.'

Simon sat on the stone. Lowri sat next to him, but kept her distance. 'I thought you loved me. Why lie?'

'Because I thought you'd despise me if you knew about my problems.'

'You thought I was that shallow?'

'I was scared I'd lose you.'

'What about the others?'

343

'They were nothing. It was you I wanted. I still do. Listen, I've left Rosemary. I can't live without you. Let's get away.'

Lowri shook her head. 'No, Simon.'

'Why not? It would be wonderful.'

'No. We've finished and, anyway, there's someone else now.' She spoke with more conviction than she felt.

He bent down and picked up a round smooth pebble. He started to roll it in his fingers. 'So you are getting married again?'

'It's very new.'

He dropped the stone, then grabbed her arms. 'Then this is our chance: me and you. We could go to France together, have a family. Don't you see? It could be perfect. I can take up the job in the hospital. You wouldn't have to work, just stay at home with the children.'

Lowri stepped into the dream. It nearly consumed her: an easy life, no worries about money. What if Dave was back with Millie? At least with Simon she knew what she was getting.

Simon leant forward to kiss her, but she pulled away.

'What's the matter?'

She looked down the hill. 'I don't love you and I deserve better than you.'

He grabbed her again. 'We've been through so much, me and you. We're suited. We need each other.'

She shook her head. 'I won't settle.' Lowri looked back at Simon. He looked vulnerable and needy. Lowri realised that he needed her more than she needed him. Is this how it had been with Rosemary?

'How is Rosemary?' she asked. 'She must be devastated that you are leaving her. She's stuck by you, hasn't she?'

'She will be OK. She has her work and the kids.'

344

'But she must love you. She stayed with you through a lot. She must be heartbroken.'

'I don't think so. The thing is, Carina rang her last week. I think it was Thursday. She told her about us and the pregnancy.'

Lowri felt a wave of guilt crashing over her, 'Oh no. That's awful. Why did Carina do that?'

'Spite, I think. I told you: she's messed up, that girl.'

'What a horrible way for Rosemary to find out.'

'It was. She was distraught. She packed her bags. She's at my daughter's at the moment.'

Lowri turned her head sharply towards him. 'So she actually left you?'

'Not exactly.'

'Yes, she did.'

'Well, in a way, yes. Carina did ring me to apologise. She was the one who suggested I come and see you.'

'Really?' Lowri stopped. 'Hang on. I know the real reason she told Rosemary.'

'What are you talking about?'

'She still wants me off the Island. She'll have heard about me being with someone. I bet she's worried I'll settle down here. She won't be sure of Jack until I've gone. She thought she'd get me to go away with you. God, she's clever. Messed up, but clever.'

'Look, I don't know what you're talking about with Carina, but at the end of the day me and you work. We can look after each other.'

'No. This is the end, Simon.'

'What's the matter with you, Lowri? This isn't you.'

'But it is, Simon. This is me.'

'You are my number one now. I promise. We are together now. You and I can go to France. We can have our happy ever after.'

Lowri shook her head. 'No, this isn't a fairy story. I don't need a handsome prince to come to save me, not that you are doing too well in that role anyway. You are a cheat and a liar. I don't want you to be part of my life anymore.'

Simon grabbed her shoulders. 'I can't live on my own. I need someone to look after me.'

She pushed him off. 'It won't be me. Just leave. Don't ever contact me again.'

He stepped back. Apparently resigned, he walked away, but not down the hill. He took the path down behind the Longstone to the manor.

Lowri went straight home and upstairs. From her drawer, she took the large envelope, her life with Simon. Downstairs a fire was made up, ready for the next chilly evening. She lit it first. She added the envelope to the flames and stood watching them consume it.

Exhausted, she had a shower, settled Cassie down, and went to bed. She placed her phone on the bedside table, waiting for Dave to ring, but she found a book and tried to get lost in someone else's world. Her eyes closed without her noticing, even the book falling off the bed, didn't wake her up.

It was much later that a loud banging on the front door reached into her subconscious, and stirred her from the deep sleep. She opened her eyes. Her light was still on. It was five in the morning. The banging continued. She heard Cassie barking. Lowri grabbed her dressing gown, went downstairs, and opened the door.

She was shocked to find Carina, standing in a long white dress and, rather oddly, wearing woollen gloves. However what Lowri focused on was the large carving knife she was holding in front of her.

'Go inside. I need to talk to you,' Carina said.

346

Lowri backed away. Carina was slurring her words. She wondered if she was drunk.

'Simon told me you'd turned him down. Why won't you go away with him?' Carina stepped towards her, the knife pointing at her.

Lowri swallowed hard. 'I don't love him,' she said. Her mind was racing: sound reasonable, she thought: defuse the situation.

'You have to go. Leave Jack and me alone.'

'Listen. Jack has left me. You've got him at the manor now.'

Carina shook her head. As she moved, the blade of the knife shone.

'He won't be mine until you go.'

'We are not together any more. I'm not a threat to you.'

Carina looked up at her portrait and smiled. 'He kept that here because he loves me. She knew that.'

'Do you mean Holly?'

Lowri's eyes were darting around. She needed to grab something or get away. She could hear Cassie scratching at the kitchen door, and was frightened she would get out. She didn't want her anywhere near Carina.

'I made her go. She knew I was serious. I heard her asking him to stop painting me, to leave me alone but, of course, he had to finish it. She went then. You see, I made her leave, and you have to go as well.'

Lowri shook her head. She couldn't lie. 'No. I can't do that. I'm sorry.'

Carina seemed to sway slightly on her feet. Lowri thought she was going to faint. 'If you don't leave, I'll have to kill you.' Carina's voice was quiet and reasonable.

'But everyone will know it was you. You will go to prison. You will lose Jack and the manor,' said Lowri, trying to keep her voice calm.

'No-one knows I am here.' Carina held the knife up and smiled. 'Once I've killed you, I'll take a few things from your room. They'll think it was burglars.'

Carina stepped forward. She was very close to Lowri now, but Lowri held her breath. She was too scared to move. Carina lifted the knife, and ran the point of it close to Lowri's right cheek.

I could scar the other one. He'd never want you then. No-one would. Look at you: you're a freak'

Suddenly, the front door, which was ajar, swung open, a voice shouted out, 'Carina, stop.'

Lowri saw Jack standing in the doorway. Behind him, the night sky was starting to give way to day. Carina saw the flash of hope in Lowri's eyes and glanced over her shoulder 'What are you doing here?' she shouted at Jack.

'I was working. I heard you talking to Simon earlier. I've been blind. Everything they said about you was true. When I saw you driving away, I had a horrible feeling where you might be going. This has to stop.' Jack walked towards Carina. 'Give me the knife, and we can talk.'

Carina shook her head. 'If I get rid of her, we can get married.'

'I can't talk to you while you're holding that.'

'Tell me you love me and I will give it to you.'

Lowri stood very still, her heart thumping.

Jack shook his head. 'I don't love you. There is only one person I have ever loved.'

'Her?'

Carina waved the knife at Lowri.

'No. The person I always loved was Holly.'

'That's a lie. She left you. I told her you loved me. Why else would you have kept painting? You know, I told her how you cried because she was barren. She had to leave you to someone who could love you, give you a family.'

Jack went white. 'You said that?'

'Oh yes. I told her how upset you were with her and, of course, there was Midnight.'

'What about her?' Jack's voice shook.

'I told her Midnight was a sign: the universe wanted her to go.'

'Did you hurt Midnight?' he asked, his voice little more than a whisper.

'Holly thinks so.'

'My God, Carina. All these lies. What about Ken?'

'Ken is a fool. I never loved him. How could someone like me love an ugly old man like that?'

Jack stepped towards Carina. 'Give me that knife. You are not going to hurt anyone any more. Give it to me.'

He reached out and moved to grab her wrist. Suddenly, Carina thrust the knife into his arm. Blood flowed from the wound. Jack screamed with pain. Carina stared at him, then ran out the door. Lowri started to follow her.

'Leave her,' shouted Jack. 'She'll kill you.'

'Your arm,' said Lowri. There was blood everywhere. Jack fainted. Lowri ran back upstairs, grabbed her phone and, her hands shaking, called for an ambulance. Once it was dispatched the operator told her what to do, what to check, where to apply pressure on Jack's arm. From then on she gave a stream of reassurance, while Lowri sat shaking, staying close to Jack, frantically worried about what Carina was doing.

An ambulance arrived quickly. Lowri stood back, relived that professionals were taking over. Jack was now conscious. The paramedics assured her he was stable. Lowri ran upstairs to get dressed, then rang Ken, who soon arrived to the house.

'Lowri, I am so sorry. Nicola's gone round to look after Lizzy. I've no idea where Carina is. She hasn't come home.'

He turned to Jack. 'I'm so sorry.'

Jack was frighteningly pale, his lips white, as he whispered, 'I didn't believe any of you.'

Lowri went to him. He looked at her. 'I was a fool. She could have killed you.'

'But she didn't. We're alright.'

'I have to go and find her,' said Ken.

As Lowri got into the ambulance with Jack she saw Ken disappear on foot out of the village.

Ken walked quickly across the road and into the fields. There was a low mist. As he climbed the downs, the shades of sunrise spread across the sky. Birdsong was filling the trees. Robins and blackbirds greeted a new day. In the distance, the Longstone stood alone, still silhouetted against the sky. Then he knew. He ran towards the stone. From a distance, she looked dramatic, beautiful even, draped across the smaller Longstone, the mellow, yellow-red morning light softening the image. However, closer to, he saw her face, traces of tears on her cheeks. For the first time, he saw the woman behind the smile.

Chapter Thirty Seven

Lowri was sitting in the garden the next day when she heard banging on the front door. Wearily, she got up and answered it.

'I'm sorry,' said Dave. 'She took my phone.'

Lowri fell into his arms. 'It's been awful.'

'What's happened? You look like a ghost. Millie was just being stupid.'

'Not the phone. So much has happened here.'

They went into the garden. Lowri had moved the seat into a patch of sunshine and Fizzy was next to it curled up asleep. Slowly Lowri went through the events of the past few days. Dave listened aghast until she came to the end. 'So Jack is still in the hospital?'

'He'll be out in a day or two. He lost a lot of blood. I offered for him to come here, but apparently he'd rather go to the manor. He wants to finish the fresco. Nicola has moved in and is looking after Ken and Lizzy.'

'Thank God for Nicola, and how are you?'

'Shattered.'

'The business with Millie was so stupid. I was in my flat. She came round, really drunk. Anyway, she ran off with my phone.'

'That's very childish.'

'She's just awful when she's pissed. Anyway, I got it back this morning and tried texting, but the battery was flat. She'd even nicked my charger, I had to buy a new one, I'm so sorry.'

'It's alright. You're here now.'

'And I'm not leaving you alone ever again. I could have lost you. So do they know how Carina died?'

'Obviously there will be a post-mortem. It will be a while until there is a funeral. Ken knows she was buying all kinds of stuff from rogue websites: drugs for her looks, to keep her thin, to make her sleep; all sorts.'

'She didn't need any of that rubbish. It could be really dangerous.'

'The doctor told Ken that these sites sell unapproved drugs which contain all kinds of stuff. They're going to analyse everything she was taking. The doctor is pretty sure it was one or a combination of them that killed her.'

'It's terrible she thought she needed to do that.'

'It is. To think that underneath all that confidence and bravado, she was very insecure. Ken told me that when she was little her father left her. She adored him. He'd called her his princess. I guess that's what she was trying to be.'

'That's tragic. I have to be honest. I didn't like her, but for all that, I wouldn't wish this on her. What will Ken do now?'

'I don't know. He's planning to take Lizzy over to Ireland for a while. I don't know what he'll do after that.'

'And Jack?'

'He'll finish his damn fresco whatever happens. I don't know after that. I expect the university will let him go back, or he could afford to go off to Italy for a bit.'

That night and for the rest of the week Lowri suffered terrible nightmares. She was sitting up shaking early one morning when Dave sat up next to her.

'I went up to my house yesterday. The police tape round the Longstone has been taken down. Do you think you could face going up there?'

'I don't know. The dreams I have are awful.'

'I know, but maybe facing it will help.'

Before they left Lowri picked some light pink tulips. Together they walked up through the fields to the Longstone. It was very quiet. No other dog walkers were up there. Dave held her hand, and they walked over to the stone. The stone that had been covered in blood in Lowri's dreams was clean. Lowri laid her tulips on it, and they stood quietly together. Dave gently let go of her hand and slowly walked away. Lowri knelt down and whispered, 'I forgive you. I set you free.' The weight of anger seemed to lift. She felt she could breathe deeply again.

'Thank you,' she said to Dave. 'I feel I have made peace.'

March drifted quietly into April. Lowri began her work with her student. She fitted in the pottery with her translation work. She even made it back to her Polish group in Southampton on a Monday.

She and Dave went walking in woods carpeted with bluebells. One day they went early to Parkhurst forest and saw the red squirrels, some babies or kittens, lithe and nimble, jumping between needle-thin branches. Birdsong was extraordinary. She pointed out the chiffchaffs, swallows and house martins returning for the summer.

Lowri woke early on May Day. She had told Dave she would be going up to the downs early. It was something she wanted to do alone: this would have been the due date for her baby, Aniolku.

It was a glorious morning, very peaceful, although the birdsong was riotous. She heard her first cuckoo over in the woods, but the rest merged into one wonderful anthem. As she arrived at the Longstone, she was surprised to see a group of people, who she realised must be druids. She sat apart from them on a small wooden bench, Cassie beside her. She saw Nicola approaching.

'You're up very early,' said Nicola.

'I didn't realise this happened–'

'I come up every Beltane.'

'Every what?'

'At Beltane the druids honour the fertility of all living things, the returning warmth of the Sun, the greening of the Earth.'

'You don't believe in that, though, do you?

'I think it's good to connect more closely to nature. I see beyond it to a creator, but we forget nature too often. It's good to honour it, to honour life.'

They sat quietly together watching the ritual.

'This is the day I chose to remember Aniolku. I think of my baby most days, but the thoughts float in and out of my head. I needed a particular day to think of him or her.'

Nicola nodded and said, 'Would you rather I left you?'

'No. You were with me when it happened. I'm glad you're here now. You really helped me, you know. That day was cold and dark.'

'It was awful.'

'Sometimes now, I feel warm, and then I feel guilty, like I've got over things too soon. But I haven't forgotten. I think about Aniolku every day. It's just I don't cry every time now.'

'There is no shame in letting go. You will never forget. It will always be a part of you. There is a time for all things: to grieve, to dance, to cry, to sing.'

Just then, Lowri looked down at her feet and saw a broken egg shell, dropped from a nest, still some remnants of the start of a baby bird.

'It happens everywhere, doesn't it?'

'What does?'

'Things dying before their time. Out here in nature, it's the way of things.' Lowri put her hand to her face. 'My scar here is changing, but it will always be part of me,'

'Exactly. You've been through a lot. You're allowed to have some moments to laugh and enjoy life.'

Lowri looked at the Longstone. 'Have you heard from Ken?'

'He emailed me. He's doing alright. He'll be coming back to sort out the manor, but I think eventually he and Lizzy will make a new life over in Ireland.'

'He told me about going to the police.'

'I'm sure they won't prosecute. No, he will be able to put that behind him now. I haven't seen anything of Jack. Is he at the manor?'

'Of course. Painting when he can. His arm is much better.'

'I do send him texts but he always seems busy,' Lowri said.

'I hear that you and Dave are an item now?'

'Yes.' Lowri smiled.

'Heather is very pleased because it means he's staying at the pottery.'

The druids came to the end of their ritual. Lowri and Nicola walked back down the path.

When Lowri returned, she decided to make breakfast for Dave and herself. Scrambled eggs for a change. However, as she poured the cooked eggs on to the toast, she felt dreadfully sick and rushed upstairs. It had been an upsetting morning.

When it had happened three days in a row, though, even Dave started to notice.

'This sickness – I was thinking. We haven't always taken precautions, have we?'

Lowri cringed. 'No, I guess not. There have been a few times–'

'It's just I was wondering– do you think you could be pregnant?'

355

Lowri blinked. This was crazy. She should be thinking this, not Dave.

'I suppose so. Oh dear–'

Dave frowned. 'Don't say that. I can't think of anything more exciting. Can you? Shall I go out and get one of those tests?'

'OK. I suppose we should find out.'

'I'll go before work. I can drive to the little Tesco. That will be open.'

Dave rushed off. Lowri took the dogs into the garden. Fizzy came over yawning. 'Don't tell me what you've been up to,' Lowri said to her. 'I think we have a very different way of enjoying the birds in the spring.'

Dave soon returned. 'Got two. You know, just in case.'

They went inside. Lowri's fingers fumbled over the packaging. She read the instructions, looked around the room, and found an old plastic cup.

'Out you go, you're not watching me pee.'

'Well, call me when you're doing the test.'

When Dave returned, she dipped the stick for fifteen seconds, then lay it down. Dave picked up his phone, set the alarm for five minutes, and they waited. They stared at the display. Never had five minutes seemed so long. As the seconds ticked by Lowri realised that with all her heart she wanted it to be true. The wait became unbearable; a small egg timer flashed in the corner of the screen. Then she heard the alarm on Dave's phone. They both looked. The word shone out: pregnant. She picked it up and stroked the word: she was pregnant.

'That's brilliant,' said Dave.

Lowri burst into tears.

'What the matter?'

'I'm frightened. It's too perfect: you, the baby; it could all go wrong.'

'I'm not leaving you.'

'But the baby–'

Dave held her close, just like he had done that time on the beach. 'Shush, Cariad.' He stroked her hair. 'Whatever happens, I'm here with you now. We'll get down to the doctor's, make sure they keep a good eye on you. OK?'

She looked up and smiled. 'Thank you. I so want this baby.'

'So do I. Look, let's go for a walk. There's something I want to ask you.'

They called the dogs and went out, up on to the downs and to the Longstone. Dave started to walk towards the nearby house. He stopped at the gate.

'I was thinking,' he said, 'Why don't we live here? We stay mainly at your house, but this will be mine soon. This could be our home.'

Lowri was trying to think why she found the idea so disconcerting. It was a lovely house, the setting idyllic, and she and Dave were always together. She never even thought of the old school house as hers. She stopped. It might not be hers, but it was more hers than this one. What if Dave was to leave her? What then? She'd have nowhere. As it was, she thought Jack may even one day be thinking of letting her have the school house as part of a settlement.

'Are you worried about leaving the other place?'

'I think I am.'

'I do understand, but we have to take a chance. Selling the flat, coming here, is a big risk for me. We have to trust each other.'

'I know.'

'The thing is, we could get married if you'd like.'

Lowri burst out laughing. 'That must be the most unromantic proposal ever.'

'Sorry, but I mean it. I'd like to get married one day.'

357

She nodded. 'So would I. Not yet though.'

'We could put the house in joint names. Would that help?'

Lowri stood thinking. 'That's very generous. I will have money. After the divorce.'

'That's OK. I know I can trust you!''

'Thank you, and yes, yes. I can't think of anything I would love more.'

Lowri sent a text to Jack, asking if they could talk sometime. She told him about the house, but not about being pregnant. He replied that he was very busy, it all sounded fine; he'd be in touch.

There wasn't a lot to move, but Lowri did want to leave everything clean. It was while she was feeling very grubby after scrubbing out the cooker that she heard a knock at the door. Quickly wiping her hands, she answered it.

'Hi,' said a woman. 'I'm Holly.'

Chapter Thirty Eight

Lowri pushed back her hair. 'Goodness. Hello. Sorry. I'm cleaning out the kitchen. Come in.'

Holly was shorter than she expected. She had brown eyes that blinked repeatedly behind large black frames. Her slim hands were busy: either tucking her hair behind her ears or lightly scratching her cheek. Lowri had built up a picture of a large assertive woman but, although she must be about five years older than Lowri, she seemed younger.

'I hope you don't mind me calling. I've come a few days early for the wedding.'

'Of course not. Come in.' The words came out in a fast stream.

Holly followed Lowri in, warily, her eyes darting around the room.

'Are you staying with Heather?'

'Yes. I'm escaping her. If you stay still for two minutes she finds you a job, and then half the time she does it again. Heather doesn't change.'

Lowri wondered how much Holly knew about what Heather had been through.

'I saw my name still hanging outside.'

'I've never wanted to take it down.'

Holly walked around the hallway, drinking it in, but her nervous smile disappeared when she saw the portrait of Carina.

'I never saw it finished.'

'It's very good.'

'Oh, yes. Even I knew it would be one of his best works. It was a big thing asking him to abandon it.'

Cassie came running in from the garden and charged up to Holly. 'Oh, she's lively,' she said, her hands held high.

Lowri grabbed Cassie. 'Let's go in the garden. She'll find plenty out there to distract her.'

Outside Holly looked over at the studio.

'Have you come for your things?' asked Lowri.

'Maybe. This woman, Nicola, in the village, heard I had come to stay with Heather. She came round to tell me she had put some of my things in the studio. Apparently, before you came here, Jack had never cleared anything out.'

'I only found them recently. I hadn't realised until then that you were the person he was in love with. The night we separated I'd heard him on the phone. I heard him say I was a mistake, but he never told me who he was talking to.'

Holly looked at Lowri, her eyebrows knitted in concern. 'That's my fault. I thought it would be worse for you to think he was still wanting his ex-wife. It seemed worse than another woman. Maybe I was wrong.'

Lowri picked a leaf from the bush behind her and started to tear it into tiny pieces. 'I don't think it would have made it worse or better. Once he'd said the other person was the love of his life, there was no going back.'

'It must have been heartbreaking.'

Lowri looked up, tried to remember how she had felt. 'I was terribly upset, but I'd known things weren't right. We'd never had what you'd call a passionate relationship, more like good friends, but the loss of that can be just as devastating.'

'I can see that. I'm sorry. He seemed so convinced that we should try again. After you separated we talked a lot on the phone, but we didn't get anywhere'

'Had you married again or anything?'

'No. I never got over Jack, you see.'

'So why didn't you two get back together? When Jack came to me after my accident he had given up, said it would never work. We were both low, it's why we settled for each other. If you love each other, why haven't you got back together?'

Holly threw her tiny hands up in exasperation. 'Love: one word to cover too many things. When we talked we kept going round in circles. He couldn't see what he'd done to upset me, said I always looked OK, that me leaving had come out of the blue. I guess I wasn't very good at telling him how I felt.'

'But that's no excuse; he should have seen it. You know, Jack has never told me much about why you broke up–'

'I don't suppose he would. To be honest, I don't think he's too sure even now. If he starts to think too much he goes and paints, escapes from it.'

Lowri saw a song thrush singing high in the tree: his song filled the garden.

'I'll tell you. You have a right to know.' Holly's voice softened.

Lowri felt as if she was being read a story.

'When Carina arrived on the island with Ken, I think we all fell in love with her. She was so exotic, beautiful. She flirted with me. She flirted with Jack. Jack of course was entranced: his Venus had arrived, and he couldn't wait to start painting her. He raved about her beauty, her perfection, oblivious of the effect his words had on me or Carina. She was obviously flattered. He spent hours with her, but I don't think he had any idea she was falling for him. She, of course, was newly married. She talked about how much she loved Ken. I was the first one to doubt her, but if I tried to say anything I just sounded like the jealous wife, so I put on a brave face.'

'It must have been very hard.'

'The trouble was that, before she arrived, Jack and I had been sinking into a bad place in our marriage. We both wanted children. His parents were obsessed with having grandchildren. His Dad would go on about his mother not having long to live and she needed a grandchild to keep her going. It was really difficult because as hard as we tried nothing happened. I kept trying to be positive, but it was awful.'

'I can understand that,' said Lowri. 'His parents' first conversation with me was about their longing for grandchildren. Like you, we kept trying–'

'I had tests. They didn't find any problem with me,' said Holly.

She gave Lowri a quick glance. She seemed to be gauging what she knew but, getting no response, she continued, 'I think the first time I realised how serious Carina was about Jack was the night of my birthday.'

'Was that when you were telling them about Jack giving you Midnight?'

'That's it. I saw her face. She was furious. She dug up some stupid story I'd told her when I was drunk about some bloke in the village. It was spiteful. I hadn't expected her to be like that. Of course, poor Midnight died soon after. I was devastated. You see, it was like Jack trying to reach out to me and save our marriage. He'd never done anything like that before. Midnight was a stunning mare. Ken had helped find her, and she was to be stabled at the manor. A few days after Midnight died Carina came to see me.'

Holly suddenly got up and walked over to the studio, knelt down by the little cross. 'This is where I put Midnight's ashes.' She sat down on the grass. 'I was

362

obviously still very upset, but Carina seemed triumphant. She told me that Midnight's death was a sign.'

'Of what?'

'That Jack and I weren't meant to be together. All this anger and hate came out of her. She was like a different person, spitting poison. She said that she and Jack loved each other and I that had to leave.'

'You must have been so shocked. To come out with that.' Lowri bit her lip and asked hesitatingly, 'Do you think she killed Midnight? I think Ken does.'

To her surprise, Holly said, 'Oh, no. I talked to the vet. He was sure it was an aortic aneurysm. They can kill a horse instantly, and may occur after a lot of exercise. He even pointed out a small amount of blood on Midnight's nostrils. Poor Ken. Carina played games with us all. I don't think he knew what to believe with her.'

Fizzy came into the garden and lay in the sunshine.

Holly looked over at Fizzy. 'Carina reminded me of a cat killing a mouse. You know, how they play with them, throwing them up in the air to break their back? She played with us like that. She'd picked up on how I hated my looks. I'd had anorexia. She'd go on to me about how Jack embarrassed her by going on about how beautiful she was. She twisted Midnight's death, but the cruellest digs were about Jack and I wanting children.'

'What did that have to do with her?'

'Nothing, but when she fell pregnant with Lizzy, Jack told her that I couldn't have children and that he was desperate for them.'

Lowri grimaced. 'He shouldn't have done that. The hospital hadn't confirmed that, had they?'

'No. But he'd already said it to his parents and I'd let it go because I knew what his Dad was like. It was easier to tell him it was my fault.'

'That's not fair.'

'I know, but I pretended I didn't mind. But then for him to repeat it to Carina of all people. Her face when she came to see me: I would never have believed a smile could be so cruel. She said that as I was barren–'

Lowri gasped.

'Yes. She used that word. She said I should leave Jack to be with the person he loved, to be with someone who could give him and his parents children.'

'That's terrible. You must have told Jack about it.'

'I tried to, but he brushed it off. I knew there was anger inside me, but he seemed so reasonable. You know, even when he told me he'd offered to decorate the nursery for her, bloody cherubs or something, I didn't think I could object. I just sort of smiled and said, 'how lovely'.'

'Oh no.'

'I didn't know what to do, but inside, the whole thing nearly broke me.'

'Didn't Jack realise? Holly, I know he loved you. Why did he let all this happen?'

'Although he'd never admit it, I think he felt it was a reflection on him not having children, particularly with the way his parents carried on. He was very anxious to protect his pride, particularly in front of this beautiful young woman.'

'I thought he was better than that. What did you do?'

'The next move may have not been my best, but I was desperate.'

'What was that?

Holly stood up. 'Come inside.' Lowri followed her in as if the house now belonged to Holly, not her.

Holly climbed the stairs. She stood in front of the painting. Carina looked down on them both, laughing.

'I asked him to stop the painting,' said Holly. 'I said if he loved me he would stop. He said if I loved him I would never ask him to do such a thing.'

'Goodness. Stalemate then.'

'Exactly. Neither of us are very confrontational, so we left it just hanging. The final straw came a few days after, when I found a letter from the hospital that he'd received months before. It was hidden in his study. I hardly ever went in there but I wanted some of his nice writing paper. The letter was hidden under a pile of it.'

Lowri frowned. 'What was the letter about?'

'It said that he had a very low sperm count, and that conceiving a child would be very difficult.'

Lowri stared. She started to breathe heavily. 'He's never told me that. I never knew. We were trying. I was going to have tests, and he never told me.'

'Nor me. He had never told me.'

'What did you do when you found out?'

'I was so upset. He'd told his parents, everyone, that the so-called 'problem' was mine. The fact he'd told this lie to Carina made it even worse.'

'Why on earth did he do it? '

'Shame. Apparently a lot of men do it. He actually said he'd spoken to doctors. No-one had said that he was actually infertile but he must have known with those odds how hard it would be. Maybe I should have stayed and carried on fighting, but I'd lost heart. Carina seemed so much stronger. It was impossible not to believe she'd get him in the end.'

'Lowri looked up at the painting. 'I felt like that. You see, I thought he loved her. She convinced herself, and then me, in the end. Jack seems to have been deliberately blind to what she was doing.'

'She acted a part and I think it suited him to believe her.'

'Did you talk to Carina about leaving?'

'I didn't tell her about Jack, but I said I was going. She changed again, like a chameleon. She became pretend-nice Carina. She said she was so sorry, but it was the right thing to do, that she and Jack were meant to be, but that she was going to take time to break it gently to Ken. He was the last person, she said, she wanted to hurt.'

'And so you went?'

'I did. We sorted everything out through solicitors. I didn't want anything, certainly not this house. I'd read about a community and decided to go there. It has been a very loving and healing place. I was very frightened to leave it. Coming here now was a big risk.'

'Have you spoken to him since you've arrived?'

'Not yet. He knows I'm here. He seems to be avoiding me. He's doing some painting. He said to go down there, but I think he should come and find me.'

'He does get lost in his work.'

Suddenly Lowri saw a cloud of fury descend on Holly. For the first time, Lowri heard anger in her voice.

'I think maybe you and I have made too many excuses for Jack. If he doesn't think I'm not worth leaving his painting for, then I'm better off without him.'

Holly flicked her hand dismissively towards the painting and turned away. She took hold of Lowri's arm as they walked down the stairs. 'Heather tells me you're pregnant. I'm so pleased for you: you've been through so much.'

Lowri put her hand to her cheek, and took it away again. 'It's been hard. I think my self-esteem was at rock bottom after the accident. It made me settle for people who didn't love me like they should, but I've ended up living here, learning to be myself a bit more and, of course, now I've met Dave, who seems to like me as I am.'

Holly grinned. 'That's special. Hold on to that.' They reached the front door.

'Do you want your stuff?' Lowri asked.

'If you don't mind, I'll leave the past in there.'

'It'll be for Jack to sort out.'

'Good.'

'I hope it works out for you.' Holly opened the front door. 'I'm glad we met.'

'It's been nice to meet you, Holly. I hope Jack talks to you.'

Lowri went back into the garden, where Cassie was busy digging.

'I wonder what will happen there, eh?'

Chapter Thirty Nine

Lowri ran downstairs in her new dress, Dave was standing looking a little uncomfortable in his suit. 'I'm ready to go.'

He looked over at her. 'You look great. I like the new hair.'

Lowri ran her fingers through the new short cut self-consciously. 'It feels weird. I've never had hair this short.'

'It suits you. I can see your face now.'

'The girl in the hairdressers' was so nice. I was worried my scars would upset her, but when I told her what had happened she took me on as a sort of mission.'

'She did a good job. Glad the weather has held up, it's taking a big chance having a wedding outside.'

'I was thinking that, but Poppy was so excited to get this place. I shall take a shawl: it could be chilly with the wind coming up off the sea.'

The venue was a short drive away, along the military road.

'Wow! This is quite something,' said Lowri, looking around the huge lawn.

The chairs were set out facing the sea, and at the front was a gazebo covered in white roses.

Dave gestured towards Jack. 'He's on his own. Let's go and sit by him.' Lowri noticed that Jack, despite wearing a suit, looked dishevelled. She guessed he had come straight from the manor.

Lowri sat between Jack and Dave. It felt rather odd, but neither man seemed too bothered.

'How are you?' she asked Jack.

'It's finished.'

'Great. Are you pleased with it?'

'It's such a relief. It was a lot harder than I expected. It's been strange working down there on my own.'

'I shall come and see it soon.'

'I phoned Ken. I think he'll sell the manor. There'll be no more frescos.'

Lowri glanced down the front towards Holly. 'Holly came to see me.'

'Oh no. Have you been swapping notes on me?'

'Kind of. Have you spoken to her yet?'

'No. I've had so much to do.'

Lowri scowled at him. 'For goodness sake, Jack. It was very hard for her to come here. You have to talk to her properly. She deserves it.'

'I've been busy.'

'No. You've been hiding.'

He sighed. 'I suppose so, but I do get a bit caught up in what I'm doing.'

Lowri raised her eyebrows, and screwed her eyes up. 'It's no excuse. Holly told me about the letter from the hospital.'

Jack looked around nervously.

Lowri lowered her voice. 'I know you were embarrassed, but you should have told Holly, and me for that matter. It wasn't fair.'

'Ah. She told you. I'm sorry.'

'You should have been honest with her and me, and you should have told your parents.'

Jack's face creased in despair. 'How on earth do I do that? My Mum will be devastated.'

'It's the truth. I think they would handle it better than the lies.'

He gave her a half smile. 'So you say I need to talk to Holly and my parents. Is that all?'

Lowri grinned. 'It's a start.'

Jack looked down at her and frowned. 'You look sort of blooming. You're not–'

She blushed. 'Yes. Dave and I are expecting.'

'Gosh. That was quick.'

'It was. I'm sorry. You know–'

'No. It's OK. I'm pleased for you.'

'I'm very nervous after last time, though. We have a scan on Monday.'

'I really hope it works out for you. Dave is a good chap and you deserve some luck. How is it living up by the Longstone? A bit remote, isn't it?'

'I like it. The thing is, Dave hasn't made it his, if you know what I mean. I don't feel like I'm living in someone else's home: this is ours.'

A young man started to play the guitar, gently picking out the notes. Poppy walked down the aisle between the chairs with Lee one side and Heather the other: they looked very proud.

Heather was shaking. She wasn't used to people looking at her like this, but Poppy wanted her to walk down the aisle with her and Lee. She was relieved to hand her over to Alistair and to be able to sit down.

In the distance the deep blue sea sparkled, and the sun shone: it was a perfect day. Heather saw Poppy glance back at her, her smile warmer than the sun.

Heather felt Lee's hand rest on hers: it could have all been so different. When she thought how easy it had been to become immersed in the world of online gambling, how it nearly destroyed everything, it frightened her. A few clicks and she had become part of their world. They had her bank details and, from then on, they claimed her. It had seemed so cosy until she tried to get away. Coming out of it had been like extracting herself from the clutches of an octopus. Blocking herself from her own site had been hard enough, but even when she had managed to do that other sites reached out by email, on TV or phone. Although she had been reluctant to join a support group, by the time she had gone it had been a relief to meet others who understood what she was going through. As she heard the stories of other members she realised how fortunate she had been. She had met people who had lost not just all their money but their partners, family, and homes. Some had turned to drink and drugs. Most members of the group looked like the sort of people who came into her café every day. It was an invisible addiction, people hiding the agony of fighting it every day.

One thing she had learned, though, was that you never really knew people or what they were going through. She had got Carina so wrong, and had been completely unaware of Ken's suffering.

Heather felt Lee squeeze her hand: the service was about to begin.

Rosemary sat next to her, with Simon. Heather couldn't believe she had taken him back yet again but guessed that she always would. Further along sat Holly, legs and arms crossed, as self-contained as ever, but still, it was wonderful to see her. Jack was sat further back. Heather wondered whether they would speak.

Later, she would try to get a photo of the three sisters together; her mother would have liked that. Although it wasn't what they'd first planned she was glad now that the reception would be at the café, a place where Heather always felt the presence of her mother. She would quietly raise a glass to her mother there.

Afterwards, the party went on into the early hours. Exhausted, Lowri and Dave started to walk home. As they left, Lowri saw Jack and Holly talking together intensely, and wondered what they were saying. Lowri and Dave

371

reached the Longstone, but as they walked to their home Lowri could still hear the strains of music from the party below.

On Monday morning, Lowri crept out of the house with Cassie. She saw Fizzy creeping through the hedge: she loved it up here. Lowri had been worried she would try to make her way back to the village, but she had more than enough to hunt up here.

Lowri's appointment wasn't until the afternoon. She needed time to think, time on her own. The sun was rising as she walked over to the Longstone. The birds were greeting the day. She heard her first cuckoo over in the woods. She still couldn't believe that she was living up here: she was waiting to 'go home'.

She walked down through the fields. Crossing the road, she entered Elmstone village. So much had happened since she had first arrived here. Cassie went running on ahead and stood at the gate of the school house.

'We don't live here now,' Lowri said to her but then, looking up at the house, she was surprised to see Jack open the front door.

'Hi,' he shouted.

'You've moved back.'

'Come and see.' Lowri couldn't remember the last time she had seen him looking so happy.

Opening the gate, she walked along the path with Cassie.

'What's happened?'

'I did what you said: I talked to Holly.'

'Good.'

'Come in.'

She went inside.

'Look.'

Lowri looked up the stairs and saw the empty wall: the painting was gone.

'I took it down to the manor. I'm going to send it to Carina's family in Italy.'

'You're going to part with it?'

'He is.' Lowri turned, to see Holly in her dressing gown.

'We've been making plans,' said Jack. 'I am going to go back to the university full-time.'

'Of course, you said no more frescos. Do you mind?'

Jack shook his head. 'No. I loved doing it, but it was exhausting. Anyway, I need to be free of the manor now. I'm lucky the university want me back.'

'Jack is going to spend some time with me in Scotland this summer,' said Holly.

'How exciting.'

'And then,' said Jack, 'maybe Holly might come back here, live in this house with me. There's plenty of work for a good solicitor over here.'

Holly smiled. 'We'll see, but, yes, it would be good to be back here and be close to my family. I'd forgotten how much this place is part of me.'

Lowri nodded. 'I understand that. I'm really pleased.' She walked out of the house. 'I hope to see you again soon.'

Looking back, she thought that the house looked at peace. It belonged to Holly and Jack: she hoped Holly would come back here to live.

The appointment for her scan was at two o'clock. Lowri and Dave drove to the hospital. Neither dared to speak. Dave held her hand tightly as they walked along the corridors of the hospital and didn't let go even while they waited for the nurse to call them.

Lowri was shifting on her seat.

'Are you ok?'

'They told me to drink lots of water, but now I want to pee.'

At that moment, her name was called.

'Lowri, isn't it?' said the nurse, who seemed very relaxed.

Lowri lay on the bed, and felt the familiar cold gel on her stomach. Dave was very close. They waited.

'Ah. There we are,' said the nurse, 'Lovely. A nice strong heart beat.'

Lowri could have cried. 'Our baby is alright?'

'Oh yes. Spot on, I'd say'

Lowri smiled at Dave, who squeezed her hand.

'It all looks really good.' The nurse said, looking at her now. 'You don't need to look so anxious.'

'I lost a baby last year.'

'I'm very sorry, but, believe me, everything looks very good at the moment. We will be doing extra scans just to make sure. Try not to worry.'

'I'll try.'

'Good. Well, I'll just print you off a photo.'

Lowri took the picture and stared at it in wonder. Their baby lay sucking its thumb, looking very content and safe. They both left the hospital in a dream.

Back home, they stood in their garden looking out at the downs.

Dave lifted up her chin. 'It's lovely to see you so happy.'

'It's great to feel it. You know, I feel full of smile.' Lowri pointed to her face. 'You know, behind this one is another, and then another, and another.'

Dave kissed her lips and then her scar. 'I love you for your scars. I love you for your smile. I love you for what is

374

behind your smile. I love you for you.'

I hope you have enjoyed reading "Behind the Smile". If so, please take the time to post a short review on Amazon or Goodreads. It really makes a difference in encouraging others to take a look at it. Thanks.